Gallows Rock

Also by Yrsa Sigurdardóttir

The Thóra Gudmundsdóttir novels

Last Rituals
My Soul to Take
Ashes to Dust
The Day is Dark
Someone to Watch Over Me
The Silence of the Sea

Standalones

I Remember You
The Undesired
Why Did You Lie?

The Freyja and Huldar Series

The Legacy
The Reckoning
The Absolution
Gallows Rock

About the Author

Yrsa Sigurdardóttir works as a civil engineer in Reykjavík. She made her crime fiction debut in 2005 with *Last Rituals*, the first instalment in the Thóra Gudmundsdóttir series, and has been translated into more than thirty languages. *The Silence of the Sea* won the Petrona Award in 2015. *Gallows Rock* is her thirteenth adult novel and the fourth in the Freyja and Huldar Series.

About the Translator

Victoria Cribb studied and worked in Iceland for many years. She has translated some thirty books by Icelandic authors including Arnaldur Indriðason, Ragnar Jónasson and Sjón. In 2017 she received the Orðstír honorary translation award for her services to Icelandic literature.

Gallows Rock

Yrsa Sigurdardóttir

Translated from the Icelandic by Victoria Cribb

HODDER &
STOUGHTON

First published with the title *Gatið* in 2017 by Veröld Publishing, Reykjavík

First published in Great Britain in 2020 by Hodder & Stoughton
An Hachette UK company

1

Hardback ISBN 9781473693395
Trade Paperback ISBN 9781473693401
eBook ISBN 9781473693418

Typeset in Sabon MT by Palimpsest Book Production Limited, Falkirk, Stirlingshire

Printed and bound in Great Britain by Clays Ltd, Elcograf S.p.A.

Hodder & Stoughton policy is to use papers that are natural, renewable
and recyclable products and made from wood grown in sustainable forests.
The logging and manufacturing processes are expected to conform to the
environmental regulations of the country of origin.

Hodder & Stoughton Ltd
Carmelite House
50 Victoria Embankment
London EC4Y 0DZ

www.hodder.co.uk

This book is dedicated to the Traplord$

– Yrsa

Pronunciation guide
for character names

Baldur – BAL-door
Didrik – DITH-rik
Einar – AY-narr
Erla – ED-la
Fanney – FANN-ay
Freyja – FRAY-a
Geir – GYAYRR
Gudlaugur – GVOOTH-lohgur
Gunnar – GOONN-arr
Hallbera – HADL-baira
Heidrún – HAYTH-roon
Helgi – HELL-ghee
Huldar – HOOL-dar
Jóel – YOH-el
Leifur – LAY-voorr
Lína – LEE-na
Maren – MAAR-en
Margeir – MAR-gyair
Sigrún – SIK-roon
Sigurlaug Lára – SIG-oor-loyg LOW-ra
Thórdur – THOHR-thoor
Thormar – THOR-marr
Tómas – TOH-mas
Ugla – OOG-la

Chapter 1

Sunday

There was a crunching of tyres on gravel. Then a sudden jerk as the vehicle came to a halt and Helgi was flung along the back seat, his cheek grating over rough, smelly fabric. This couldn't be his car. Slowly opening one eye, he registered that it was dark. Then the driver flicked on the ceiling light and Helgi took in the rubbish on the floor: crumpled drink cans, a scrunched-up crisp packet, used paper napkins, two broken cigarettes, a hot-dog wrapper. Taxis really were disgusting these days. But maybe it wasn't a taxi. Could he have hitched a lift? Jumped into some random car in the city centre? It wouldn't be the first time Helgi had done something drunk that he'd never have dreamt of sober.

It hurt to think. Pain shot through his head, his stomach clenched ominously in sympathy and the next minute he was retching. Sitting up was beyond him, so he would just have to throw up on the seat. Judging by the smell, that would be nothing new. Christ, what *had* he been drinking? He usually steered clear of the sort of piss that left you feeling like this. But booze must be to blame for the state he was in. He was all too familiar with the sense of lethargy, the befuddled brain, though it was years since he'd been this wasted.

When the spasm arrived, Helgi managed by some miracle

to shift his head to the edge of the seat, hurling the acid contents of his stomach onto the floor. The resulting mess on top of the rubbish was so revolting that he closed his eyes. There was an exclamation from the front seat, followed by an outbreak of loud cursing. Even in his bleary state Helgi could tell what that was about. No one wanted vomit in their car.

The driver's door opened with a metallic screech, then slammed shut, cutting off the cursing and plunging the car into darkness as the ceiling light went off. There was the noise of gravel underfoot. Then the door by Helgi's head was wrenched open and cold fresh air streamed inside. His nausea receded a little and with it the headache. The relief was indescribable, but he wasn't allowed to enjoy it for long. Somebody grabbed him roughly by the shoulder and heaved. Helgi wanted to protest that no one pushed him around like that, but the words wouldn't come out. It was as if the nerves connecting his brain to his tongue had been severed.

An angry voice penetrated his confusion, ordering him out of the car. The driver must want to get rid of him because he'd thrown up. To his own astonishment, Helgi found himself obeying. He hadn't intended to sit up but his limbs and muscles seemed to act of their own accord. A concerted effort and he was on his feet outside the car. He filled his lungs. The fresh air tasted even better out here. There was a full moon, the sky was clear and there wasn't a breath of wind, as if the world had been frozen into perfect stillness. Leaning his head back to admire the night sky, he lost his balance and was caught by the same rough hand. Helgi was grateful for its support: the gravel at his feet looked sharp.

Once he had stopped rocking and was standing more or

less upright, he was given a shove and ordered to start walking. Again, Helgi's body obeyed without any input from his brain. He was vaguely surprised that the man hadn't given him an earful about chucking up in his car. It was all very strange, but he couldn't martial his thoughts enough to work out what was going on. Perhaps he was in the middle of one of those dreams where you wake up with a gasp just as you're about to fall off a cliff.

The gravel underfoot gave way to a series of grassy sheep paths, winding through the unmistakeably jagged terrain of an old lava-field. Helgi peered at the ground in front of him; at the frosty grass, pale in the moonlight. It was all he could do to keep his footing. He staggered along in front, the man following close on his heels. Every time Helgi started to veer off course or paused to recover his balance, the hand propelled him forwards. He wanted to tell the man that he wasn't being deliberately difficult, but his tongue felt too thick and unwieldy to form the words.

The path led briefly uphill, then down again, through a series of grassy hollows which opened out between the lava walls; ideal picnic spots in summer but bleak and uninviting now. Thinking he recognised his surroundings, Helgi raised his head groggily to get his bearings. Not far off, the lava-field ended and the sea began: it was black in the darkness except where the moonlight glittered on the ripples. The sight brought back a childhood memory of walking with his grandfather along a shore not unlike this one – maybe even the same one. They had accidentally flushed out two eider ducks, which had flown away in alarm. His grandfather had gone over to the spot where the birds had been sitting and found two big, bluish eggs lying in a soft brown nest. Crouching beside it, Helgi had touched the down with his finger and it had felt as insubstantial as air. When he straightened up, his grandfather had drawn his attention to the gulls that had formed a wide circle around them. They were far enough away that the siege wasn't immediately obvious, but they appeared to be closing in. When his grandfather told him what they were doing, Helgi had wanted to throw stones at them.

It was a horrible dilemma and, sadly, he had been just old enough to understand. If they stayed where they were, the gulls wouldn't dare approach, but neither would the parent birds. The eggs would grow cold and the embryos inside them would die. If, on the other hand, he and his grandfather moved away, the eider ducks would eventually come back but by then there was a risk that the gulls would have raided the unprotected nest. In the end, Helgi's grandfather had decided that they should continue on their way, and they had left, walking almost backwards, watching in the hope that the ducks would come swooping in to save their eggs. But there had been no sign of them; at least, not before they lost sight of the nest. Helgi never found out what had happened afterwards.

Now, though, it was winter and there were no eggs. No eiderdown either. It had all been collected, cleaned, stuffed into duvets and sold off to wealthy foreigners.

Another hard shove from behind alerted Helgi to the fact that he had stopped moving and he slowly set off again, following the winding path up a slope. Shortly afterwards, he was ordered to stop.

Raising his eyes, he stared in dull surprise at a tall black rock formation, split into two halves that reared up like something out of *The Lord of the Rings*. A heavy plank, like a footbridge, had been laid between them. Had his dream led him to Mordor? Before his sluggish brain could come to any conclusion, he was pushed forwards again, this time towards one of the rocks. It was covered in last summer's dry grass, which made it fairly easy to scramble up. Following the man's orders, Helgi stopped near the top, then climbed onto a narrow ledge that jutted out into the cleft between the two lava outcrops. There he stood, gazing out over the moonlit sea that looked deceptively innocent and gentle in the still weather.

Swaying dangerously, Helgi realised that sooner or later he was going to fall. But, oddly enough, the thought didn't alarm him. It wasn't so terribly far to the ground, after all, and besides he was dreaming, wasn't he? The abysses in his dreams tended to be bottomless, though: he couldn't usually see down into a dry grassy hollow surrounded by jumbled lava.

The hand now swivelled Helgi round to face its owner, who had climbed up behind him. The lower half of the man's face was obscured by a scarf. All that could be seen were his eyes, which were narrowed with an expression of such loathing that Helgi flinched and dropped his gaze. His attention was caught by some sort of tool, black and a paler colour – yellow, perhaps – in the man's right hand. With his left hand, the man seized Helgi's coat and dragged him closer, then started undoing his top buttons. Next, he pulled a white sheet of paper from his pocket and held it against Helgi's chest. Helgi strained his eyes, trying to read the few lines written on the paper, but the letters were upside down. The moon was so bright that if his brain had been less fuzzy he might have been able to decipher it. The effort dispersed the fog in his head a little and in that brief window of lucidity he recalled being handed a piece of paper and forced to sign it. But there had been more writing on that one . . . He had been able to read it all right and the contents had been pretty earth-shattering. But in a good or a bad way? The fog closed in again and he couldn't remember.

The tool appeared before his eyes, pressed against the paper on his chest. Helgi frowned, puzzled, and waited. He felt no fear, only curiosity. The tool wasn't one he recognised – not that he owned any tools himself. What could it be for?

Helgi watched the man's fingers tighten on the handle, then a loud snap echoed in the hush. He felt an agonising stab in his chest that left him momentarily winded. He was about to topple backwards off the ledge when the hand grabbed him again. In spite of the searing pain, he was relieved. If the man had saved him from falling, he couldn't mean him to come to any real harm.

Something was slipped over his head and, looking down again, he saw a thick rope lying above his throbbing chest like a clumsy necklace. Perhaps his companion was belatedly concerned for his safety: after all, he couldn't fall off if he was tied to the rock. But when the rope tightened around his neck, Helgi wanted to point out that this couldn't be a good idea – it would make more sense to tie it round his waist. But his tongue still felt too thick to shape the words, and the agony in his chest was making it hard to breathe.

It didn't matter. This was a dream. It had to be. If he fell, he would fly. Any minute now he would wake up and the pain would disappear, along with the sense of unreality.

While his companion cursed, Helgi gazed out to sea, noticing that waves were beginning to ruffle the calm surface.

On the other side of the bay, he could see familiar white buildings with darker roofs: the presidential residence at Bessastadir. He was definitely dreaming. His befuddled brain recalled something connected to this very shore and he recoiled from the thought, afraid of throwing up again. Returning to the present, he became aware once more of the beauty of his surroundings and the jarring stream of abuse issuing from the man behind him.

Helgi didn't really take it in. The view was so soothing that even the pain in his chest seemed to fade. His gaze moved from the president's residence to the bay itself. All his attention was focused on the waves glittering on the black surface of the sea. Far out on the horizon a bank of cloud hung like a thick black band across the sky. He felt himself nodding off, which was strange given that he was already asleep.

He was roused by a shove, this time in the small of his back. It was to be the last. Helgi tumbled forwards off the ledge and floated through the air for a few brief seconds until his fall was arrested by the violent jerk of the rope. But he couldn't have flown anyway. This was no dream.

Chapter 2

The body stirred in the wind, turning a slow half-circle first one way, then back again. Huldar averted his eyes as the blue face reappeared, with its horribly black, protruding tongue. The man's head lolled on his chest as if he were staring down at his feet, surprised that he'd lost a shoe. The shoe in question was now sealed in a plastic bag in the Forensics van, waiting to be taken for analysis, though no one expected it to shed any light on the reasons behind this sad suicide. Nevertheless, the police had observed standard procedure when it came to gathering material, though this time the treatment of the shoe was almost the only thing that had been done by the book.

Huldar looked away from the dead man, taking in the rough terrain of Gálgahraun. The lava-flow had formed thousands of years ago, long before any human had set foot in Iceland, when the Arctic fox ruled supreme. Huldar had taken part in a police training exercise in the area several years before, during which they had been given a potted history of the lava-field. Its unusually irregular, rugged appearance had been caused when the glowing lava rolled over a marshy area close to the seashore, causing the marsh to boil and the half-solidified sheets of lava to explode. There were fissures, craters, spires of rock and endless jumbled lumps and bumps in every direction. Even the carpet of moss that had covered the lava-flow over the centuries couldn't soften its harshness. It was a bleak, restless landscape.

'Strange spot to hang yourself in, don't you think?' Huldar remarked, glancing at his colleague Gudlaugur.

'No stranger than anywhere else.' Gudlaugur was still staring up at the man dangling from the noose. 'At least this way he made sure none of his loved ones would find him. I'm guessing that explains the location.'

'Maybe.' Huldar was unconvinced. The whole operation would have required an extraordinary amount of effort. For one thing, the spot was quite a distance from the road, and, judged with his carpenter's eye, the plank that served as a gallows probably weighed a ton. There were any number of things Huldar would rather spend the last minutes of his life doing than lugging a heavy plank across a lava-field. But he didn't share this thought with Gudlaugur. The young man was looking conspicuously hungover on this Sunday morning: red-eyed, his hair uncombed, sucking a constant succession of Ópal liquorice lozenges. He was in no state to be disagreed with on the rare occasions he opened his mouth.

Huldar turned back to the two rocks rearing out of the lava-field, the fissure like a gash between them, and watched his colleagues scratching their heads over the best way to get the man down. The rope was tied round the plank and it was clear that any attempt to cut it would send the body plummeting to the ground, with the additional risk that it would be bashed against the sharp rocks on the way. It went without saying that they would rather get the man down in one piece. Erla was standing directly below the suspended figure, gesturing upwards as she called out to the officers who had scaled the rock formations on either side. They were making valiant attempts to follow her orders but it was one thing to issue commands when you were standing on level ground, another to put them into action while clinging precariously to a ledge. Any minute now, Erla's patience would run out and she would start climbing up there herself to show them how to do it. After which pointless exercise she would no doubt be even more exasperated than she was already.

The plank creaked and groaned alarmingly as an officer began to worm along it on his stomach. It wasn't clear what he meant to achieve: it would have required superhuman strength to haul the body up, then crawl back to safety, dragging it behind him. But the protests from the plank soon changed his mind and he beat a hasty retreat. Erla, unable to hide her frustration, sighed explosively. It must have been her suggestion.

'Wouldn't it be better to borrow a net from the fire brigade? You know, the kind they use to catch people when they jump out of burning buildings? If we spread it out underneath, that should stop the body getting damaged.'

Huldar had to suppress a smile before turning his head. The voice belonged to Lína, the young woman on work experience from the University of Akureyri. She was the first of the crop of students taking the new degree in policing to do an internship in CID, and although no one said so aloud, the team were mostly sceptical. Their prejudice stemmed in part from an unspoken fear about what would happen when every other new recruit arrived brandishing a degree certificate. Would the rest of them be put back in uniform, relegated to pounding the streets among the tourist hordes, answering callouts to deal with rowdy parties or issuing fines for petty offences?

Huldar couldn't care less. If he suffered another demotion at work, he had his carpentry to fall back on. Besides, the intern was a constant source of entertainment, especially when it came to her talent for rubbing people up the wrong way.

She was forever pointing out that they weren't doing things by the book, or correcting their terminology or quoting the contents of textbooks and academic studies at them. Every time this happened near Erla, you could practically see the smoke coming out of her ears. Huldar could barely contain his glee on these occasions, or when he saw Gudlaugur's nose put out of joint by one of her tactless remarks.

'There's no time to borrow a net now, Lína. Good idea, though.' Huldar watched her smile in response to his praise. She was small, reaching no higher than his chest, with red hair and a complexion of such ivory whiteness that you could barely make out the brief gleam of her teeth against her skin. Then, her face serious again, she turned her attention back to the proceedings.

Huldar suspected Erla of having base motives for bringing Lína along. Officially, it was to teach her about crime-scene procedure, but no doubt Erla had been secretly hoping to shock the young woman into losing her breakfast. Lína was made of sterner stuff, though. She had elbowed her way to the front and stood there, studying the dangling body with no more emotion than if it had been a light-fitting. When she had finally lowered her eyes, she had frowned and wondered aloud why Erla hadn't given orders to cordon off the area. Erla's gruff retort that there was no time for that now had done nothing to shut Lína up, and in the end Huldar had pulled her aside and explained that this was the exception that must surely have been mentioned in her textbooks: a situation in which standard procedure had to be abandoned in favour of speed. He had been rewarded with a grimace: Lína clearly didn't regard the present circumstances as sufficiently urgent to warrant a deviation from the rules.

She was alone in that opinion. The rest of the team were well aware of the need for a quick turnaround. It wasn't every day that they got a call from the Icelandic president's staff at Bessastadir to report a dead body. Normally, two officers would have been sent to deal with the incident, accompanied by a forensic technician, but on this occasion the place was crawling with police. In the panic following the notification, almost every available officer had been ordered to the scene and several more had had their weekend leave cancelled. No doubt the logic had been that this would speed up the process of removing the body, but in practice it was having the opposite effect. Most of the officers were just milling around with nothing to do, getting underfoot.

Erla's phone rang and Huldar watched her answer it. She closed her eyes and rubbed her forehead as she listened to what appeared to be a scolding from on high. It was hardly surprising if the top brass were seriously rattled. They wouldn't want to be exposed as incompetent in front of the security team of a foreign superpower. Huldar smiled at the thought, but his grin faded when Erla shot a glance in his direction, ended the call and shoved the phone back in her pocket.

'Time's up! Cut the rope!' she bellowed at the men on the rocks. 'The motorcade has set off and is due at Bessastadir in half an hour. We need to be out of here by then. The body will just have to get a bit knocked about. I don't suppose the dead man will care either way.'

Huldar saw Lína open her mouth, her disapproval all too plain. Presumably the section in her textbook about gathering material at the scene had omitted anything about visits by foreign dignitaries. Laying a hand on her shoulder, he whispered into the delicate white ear: 'I wouldn't say a word if I were you. It won't do any good.'

Lína clamped her lips in a tight line. Although inexperienced, she was no fool. She knew the background, having heard Erla's briefing before they set off. She looked across the bay to Bessastadir, a dissatisfied frown on her face. Huldar would bet that the president wouldn't get her vote next time, though he'd had nothing to do with the incident. His only sin had been to arrange a reception to mark the start of the official visit by the Chinese foreign minister. Personnel from the minister's security team, who had turned up in advance to carry out a safety check, had spotted the corpse hanging from the rocks on the other side of Lambhúsatjörn Bay. Its presence had been completely overlooked by the Bessastadir staff, since earlier that morning the area had been obscured by a thick blanket of fog.

Unsurprisingly, the discovery of the body had created pandemonium at the Foreign Ministry, where staff had the unenviable task of trying to dissuade the Chinese embassy and security team from turning the minister's plane around. In the end, they had managed to convince the visitors that it wasn't a protest staged by Falun Gong, merely an incredibly unfortunate coincidence. As a result, the day's programme was to go ahead as planned – on condition, naturally, that the dead man was spirited away before the minister's arrival.

But the staff of the Foreign Ministry had underestimated how long it would take the police to deal with the situation.

By the time the Police Commissioner's office had handed the matter over to Erla, the Chinese minister's plane was already preparing to land at Keflavík. Erla's orders were that all signs of the dead man and the police presence were to be gone from Álftanes by the time the motorcade drove past, even though the site wasn't actually visible from the road. The point was that it could be seen from the residence at Bessastadir. On no account must the president be put in the embarrassing position of having to explain what the crowd of police officers were up to on the other side of the bay. After this fiasco it was doubtful that Iceland would ever be offered the loan of a giant panda, but there was still hope that the visit might result in enhanced trade links.

Huldar and Lína watched the activities of their colleagues with interest. The men had split into two groups, one on each steep rock, and were now struggling to extend a pair of clippers far enough across the gap to cut the rope. It was an impossible feat, as it turned out. Erla checked the time on her phone, then called out to them to dislodge the plank, noose, body and all.

Through a concerted effort at either end, the men succeeded in heaving up the plank, then letting the whole lot fall.

While this was going on, Huldar nudged the pale, silent Gudlaugur and they went to fetch the stretcher lying beside the sheep path leading to the rocks. They got back just as the dead man hit the ground, and went over to the body, which was now lying in a heap with the massive plank on top. Their colleagues, having scrambled down from the rocks, helped them to cut the rope and shift the heavy wood. Then Gudlaugur turned over the body, assisted by another man, and more officers lined up on either side, ready to lift it onto the stretcher. Huldar discreetly withdrew at this point. He had no desire to see the man's grotesque death mask up close.

'Stop!' Lína's voice rang out with a note of authority, like someone used to being obeyed. Which was a joke, considering how young and inexperienced she was. Huldar had cast an eye over her CV when they heard she was joining the department, so he knew that she had done the usual selection of summer jobs: in the Akureyri parks department, on the till at a supermarket, in a fish factory and at a cinema. It was hard to guess which of these jobs could have lent her such an air of command. Perhaps she had developed it while haranguing cinemagoers to switch off their phones before the film.

'You don't give the orders round here.' Erla's face was black with fury at this interference. Waving her arms at the group standing around the body, she snapped at them to get on with loading it onto the stretcher.

'But—' Lína was undeterred.

'But fucking what? Don't you understand a fucking order?' Erla was seriously stressed and, as usual, this was reflected in her language.

Huldar shot Lína a warning look. Ignoring him, she persisted: 'Can't you see? There, on his chest.' She pointed at the body.

Although it was guaranteed to bring down Erla's wrath on their heads, few of the officers could resist the impulse to follow Lína's pointing finger. One by one they lowered their eyes to the dead man's chest, where a tiny metal plate could be seen poking out. Their faces puzzled, they moved closer. But Huldar knew exactly what he was looking at: the head of a nail. A four-inch one, probably. Under it was a torn scrap of paper, as if it had been used to pin a note to the man's chest.

Erla had clearly grasped the situation. She emitted a heart-felt groan.

This could hardly be a suicide. Few people would have the determination to drive a socking great nail into their own flesh like that. This was almost certainly a murder scene, and the police had approached it like a bunch of amateurs. In all the panic, it hadn't even occurred to anyone to call out the pathologist.

For the first time since she had begun her work experience, Lína's expression of disapproval was entirely justified.

'Stand back.' Erla sounded calm, though she was surely anything but. 'Cover him up so he can't be seen from Bessastadir. Not even with binoculars. Camouflage him under some grass or something – anything that'll help him blend in.' She closed her eyes and rubbed them irritably. 'Then let's get the hell out of here and wait until their bloody snobfest's over.'

Chapter 3

Baldur sat down at the table again, reeking of smoke. He'd nipped out for a cigarette, though they'd only just got here. Not that Freyja was surprised. He'd recently been released from prison and was still getting used to having the freedom to do as he liked – within limits. For the moment he was staying at Vernd, the halfway house, and apart from having to spend the night on the premises and fulfil his work requirement, his time was his own. So it was hardly any wonder he grew as fidgety as a little boy every time there was a quiet moment.

He ruffled the hair of his daughter Saga, who was sitting in a high chair between them. Ignoring him, the little girl went on chewing the rasher of bacon he'd given her after she'd turned her nose up at the slices of fruit. Father and daughter got on well, despite being so different. He was the happy, outgoing type, but Saga was the most serious child Freyja had ever met. Where he was fair and never stopped talking, Saga was dark and withdrawn, her face set in a perma-scowl. He liked nice clothes, whereas Freyja could hardly persuade Saga into anything but boots, leggings and a top, though Fanney, her mother, somehow succeeded in forcing her into girly dresses and cutesy shoes. Once in a blue moon Fanney even managed to put a slide in her daughter's hair, but only when Saga was wearing mittens. The moment she got them off, the slide would be sent flying.

Baldur winked at his daughter and she blinked back, still too young to close one eye at a time. Then he turned back to Freyja, his face alight with pleasure: 'Have you ever seen a cuter kid?'

Freyja squeezed out an answering smile. She had stood in for her brother, taking care of his parental duties while he was behind bars. But however much she loved her niece, *cute* was not the word she'd have chosen to describe her. Still, Freyja couldn't help but be pleased at her brother's delight in his daughter, especially as he'd had so little contact with her up to now. That didn't seem to affect their ability to bond, though. It had just happened, with no particular effort. Perhaps it helped that they were both a bit eccentric, each in their own way.

'Hey! I forgot the big news.' Baldur pushed his food away almost untouched and pulled over his coffee cup. 'I meant to tell you in the car.'

'What?' Freyja wasn't expecting any news. Baldur was keeping his nose clean at the moment, so as not to jeopardise the prospect of his imminent release on probation.

'I've sorted out a flat for you.' Baldur passed Saga another rasher of bacon. The first fell unheeded to the floor as she reached for the next. Out popped her little pink tongue and she started licking the bacon like a lolly.

Freyja dropped her fork on her plate and the scrambled egg she had just loaded on it tumbled off. 'What?' She really hoped her brother wasn't pulling her leg. He knew how much sleep she'd been losing over the problem of finding somewhere to live. For now, she was still in his flat, but that arrangement couldn't last much longer. There was no way she was sharing it with him once he got out of the halfway house. She had no intention of sleeping on the battered sofa in the living room while he and that week's girlfriend got down to business in the bedroom next door. And the thought of sharing the sofa with a boyfriend while Baldur was in the flat was no more appealing. To date, though, all her attempts to find a flat had failed. Those on the market were either too expensive or their owners were looking for a different kind of tenant. She'd seriously begun to consider moving to the countryside or even abroad. 'Please don't tease me.'

'Tease you? I'm not.' Baldur picked up Saga's glass and held it to her lips in the hope of persuading her to take a sip of orange juice, but she twisted stubbornly away until he gave up.

'How could you find me a flat? I've been trying for over a year without any luck.' This was typical of Baldur. People bent over backwards for him. If he went to view a property, you could bet your life the landlord would rustle up a contract on the spot. But Baldur could hardly have been looking at flats: he'd only just got out of jail.

'You know Tobbi?'

'Tobbi?' The name sounded familiar but Freyja couldn't put a face to it.

'Yeah. My mate Tobbi. Don't you remember him?'

'Vaguely.' Baldur had so many friends, each more disreputable than the last. It didn't help that he made no distinction between friends and acquaintances. Everyone he knew fell into one of two groups: friends or wankers. The first group was much larger, as Baldur was oblivious to the fact that not everyone who laughed at his jokes was his friend. Wankers were those who, one way or another, got in the way of his enjoying life to the full. As his closest family member – an honour she now shared with Saga – Freyja belonged to neither category.

'Well, anyway, Tobbi's got a flat he's willing to rent you.' Baldur wiped the crumbs fastidiously off the table before resting his arm on it. His hair had just been cut and his new outfit couldn't have been cheap. Where the money had come from was a mystery to Freyja, but she didn't dare ask. It was better not to know.

'Me? Why me?' Her initial excitement at the news was rapidly fading. The offer bore all the signs of being trouble, since when it came to trouble, Baldur was a past master.

'Because I told him you needed somewhere to live. He was just complaining that he couldn't find a good tenant, and as soon as I mentioned you he jumped at the idea.'

Freyja frowned and noticed that Saga immediately copied her. 'Baldur, no one has trouble finding a good tenant in Reykjavík. All you have to do is stick a sign the size of a postage stamp with "To let" on it in your window and before you know it people will be queuing round the block. The flat's not miles out of town, is it?'

'No. It's in Reykjavík. More or less.'

'More or less? What does that mean?'

Baldur rolled his eyes. 'It's on Seltjarnarnes, all right? In a classy modern block.'

Freyja sighed. She'd known there had to be a catch: Seltjarnarnes was the upmarket suburb on the peninsula at the westernmost tip of Reykjavík. 'I can't afford a high rent, Baldur. You know that.'

'The rent's not high. It's very reasonable.' The figure he mentioned sounded as if it was for a garage rather than a flat.

'How big is it? You're not talking about a garden shed, are you?'

'No. God, you're being negative. I thought you'd be pleased.' Baldur had stopped smiling and his mood was in imminent danger of tipping over into a sulk.

Freyja laid her hand on his. The two of them stuck together – through thick and thin. If he was offering her some deeply flawed flat, it was because he meant well. It would be out of a genuine desire to help. 'Sorry,' she said. 'I've just been burnt before. That rent is ridiculously low. There has to be a catch.' This Tobbi character must owe Baldur money or a favour of some sort. If so, she would bet her life that there was nothing kosher about it.

Baldur bent and put his hands over Saga's ears. 'Tobbi's on his way to jail,' he whispered. 'He got a year and a half.' Baldur lowered his hands again before Freyja could point out that Saga didn't even know what 'jail' meant. 'He doesn't want to rent his place to a stranger because he's leaving all his furniture and stuff behind. But he'll trust anybody I recommend. I told him you've been looking after my place, so he knows you've got house-sitting experience. It's a win-win situation.'

It would never have occurred to Freyja to describe her time in Baldur's flat as 'house-sitting experience', but if Tobbi thought she had the necessary qualifications, that was great. In fact, the offer didn't sound bad at all.

Her phone started ringing in the pocket of her coat, which was hanging over the back of her chair. She checked the screen. 'Damn.' She looked at Baldur. 'I've got to go. Work.' As she got up, she added: 'But I'm willing to talk to your friend. Could we go and see the place together – as soon as possible?'

Baldur nodded. He opened his mouth as if to add something, but seemed to think better of it and just said goodbye, promising to call that evening.

Freyja kissed him on the cheek and Saga on the top of her head. Then she paid the bill and hurried off, walking on air at the thought that a flat might finally be within her grasp – if it worked out. Where Baldur was concerned, it didn't pay to count your chickens.

Freyja pressed the bell again, harder this time and for longer. She could hear it chiming inside the flat, but the moment she lifted her finger, there was silence again. The only sounds they had heard inside since they had arrived were the jangling of the doorbell and the ringing of a phone that went unanswered.

'Shall I try again?' Freyja looked at her companion, a tall, thin young man with a Viking beard, a gold ring through the middle of his nose, and tired eyes. Although they must be around the same age, as a full-time employee of Reykjavík's Child Protection Agency he had far more experience of these types of cases. She only put in the odd evening and weekend, having started taking shifts on top of her day job at the Children's House to save for her rent once Baldur got out of prison. If his friend Tobbi turned out not to be a complete idiot and his flat passed muster, she might be able to give up the overtime. But for now, here she was, attending a callout on a Sunday, standing in the incongruously wide corridor of one of Reykjavík's new luxury apartment blocks. Even if she worked twenty-four seven, she'd never be able to afford anywhere this swanky.

'Give it one more go. The child may be asleep. Or too frightened to come to the door.'

Freyja rang the bell again, pressing it for a long time. Nothing happened. 'No one could sleep through a racket like that.'

'Maybe not. You never know.' The social worker, whose name was Didrik, stepped up to the door and hammered on it so loudly that his knuckles looked red afterwards. Then again, the lurid tattoos emerging from his coat sleeves and covering the backs of his hands made it hard to tell their actual colour.

At this point the door of a flat down the corridor opened and a middle-aged woman stuck her head through the gap. She seemed a little disconcerted when she saw Didrik, no doubt taking him for a debt collector or other type of lowlife – certainly not an employee of the Child Protection Agency. Freyja, by contrast, looked highly presentable, dressed up for the brunch she'd been forced to leave halfway through. When it became apparent that the woman wasn't going to speak first, Freyja said: 'I'm sorry about the noise. We're from the council. We received a report that there was a child in this flat, alone and possibly at risk. Was it by any chance you who rang?'

The caller had contacted emergency services because the council didn't man the phones at the weekend. In cases like this, the police were normally sent to the scene first, but today there hadn't been a single officer available, so the job had been passed all round the system before eventually landing on Didrik's desk. By then, any details about the caller had gone astray.

The woman made a face as if Freyja were accusing her of something, and shook her head. 'No. I've only just got home, actually. And I haven't noticed a thing.' Her carefully made-up eyes strayed to a large tub containing an exotic plant that stood in the corridor between them. From the way she was looking at it, you'd have thought it demarcated an invisible line beyond which nothing bad could pass. The woman folded her arms. 'Are you sure you've got the right address?'

Freyja hesitated, wondering for a moment if they could have made a mistake. Perhaps the poor child they were supposed to be helping was in the next-door building, or even in the next street. It wasn't often that social services were called out to properties like this, not because the residents were wealthy – mistreatment could occur in any social group – but because they were mostly well past childbearing age.

Didrik answered before Freyja could, sounding sure of himself: 'Yes, this is definitely the right address.'

The woman frowned. 'That's strange. There are no children living in that flat – unless they've just moved in. The man who lives there is single. You must have got the wrong place. As far as I know, there are no children in the whole building. Families can't afford these flats, especially not the one you're trying to get into. That's the most exclusive apartment in the block.'

'It's possible the child's visiting or is being babysat here.' Freyja thought of telling the woman that children had a tendency to wander off, but she didn't want it to sound like a rebuke. Out of the corner of her eye, she saw Didrik pressing his ear to the door as if he'd heard something. Next moment she thought she caught a faint sound herself, like the brrring of an alarm clock, though it could be coming from the woman's flat.

The woman didn't look round, however, so presumably it wasn't her alarm. 'My neighbour's not the babysitting type.'

'No, maybe not. But we still have to take all tip-offs seriously.' Freyja forced her mouth into an insincere smile and
the woman responded with an equally chilly twitch of the
lips.

Didrik removed his ear from the door. It was unusually
tall, reaching almost to the ceiling, as if the architect had
wanted to leave the possibility open for the residents to keep
a pet giraffe. 'There's someone in there.'

Freyja turned away from the woman, who appeared
distinctly put out. It was always galling to be proved wrong.
The faint ringing Freyja thought she'd heard had now stopped.

Didrik pressed the bell and pounded on the door again as
hard as he could. Then, as they watched, the handle slowly
began to move and finally the door opened a crack. 'Hello,'
he said through the opening. 'My name's Didrik and I'm from
the council. We got a message about a child in trouble at this
address. Could we have a quick word?'

There was no answer from inside. Didrik cleared his throat
and repeated his request but was met by silence. Glancing at
Freyja, he raised his eyebrows, then stepped aside, gesturing
at her to give it a try.

'Hello,' she said in a gentle voice. 'My name's Freyja. Could
you open the door for us? We just need to make sure
everything's all right. Then we'll go away again, if you like.'

'I want to go home.' A high little voice, unmistakeably that
of a small child. It was impossible to tell if the owner was a
girl or a boy, or their exact age. Freyja guessed at anywhere
between three and six.

'We can help you go home. But first you need to open the
door so we can see you.'

Slowly the gap widened and a fair head appeared. A pair

of wide eyes stared fearfully up at Freyja from under a blond fringe. It was a little boy, maybe four years old. He had a padded green anorak on, though there was no reason to think it was cold inside the flat, and a pair of bulky snow-boots fastened with Velcro, as if he had just come in or was on his way out. 'I want to go home,' he repeated in a plaintive voice.

'Of course. We'll take you home.' Careful to make no sudden movements, Freyja crouched down until her face was on a level with the child's. 'What's your name?'

'Siggi.'

'Hello, Siggi. Is there a grown-up in there who we can talk to?'

'No. I'm all on my own and I want to go home. This isn't my house.'

Freyja reacted matter-of-factly, as if there was nothing remotely unusual about finding a little boy alone in a flat that wasn't his home. 'Where do you live, then?'

'In Iceland.'

Freyja smiled. 'Me too. But where in Iceland?'

'In Reykjavík. It's a city. It's got a mayor.'

'That's nice.' Freyja pointed at her companion. 'This is Didrik. He works for the mayor. Could you open the door properly so we can talk to you inside? Didrik's got a picture of an eagle on his arm. He can show it to you, if you like.' Freyja had been on a callout with Didrik before, when he had persuaded a little boy to come out from under a bed by rolling up his sleeve to show him his tattoos. The boy had been especially taken with the eagle, soaring with outstretched wings among the other colourful designs.

The blond child in the green anorak was thinking. Chewing his lip, he stared at what he could see of Didrik's highly

decorated arm, then warily opened the door. Freyja straightened up, peering into the smart apartment. 'Who lives here?
Is it your daddy?' The boy shook his head. 'Your mummy's
friend, then?' Another shake. 'Your uncle, maybe?'

'I don't know.'

'It doesn't matter. You can't know everything.'

Freyja and Didrik went inside, without another word to
the woman who was still standing forgotten in the corridor.
She wasn't their problem.

It was evident from the interior of the flat that whoever
lived there had money to burn. The hall opened out into an
impressive living area, minimally furnished with designer
pieces, the chrome gleaming as if newly polished. One wall
was dominated by a huge gas hearth, the other by a single
abstract painting. No doubt the differently coloured brush-
strokes were charged with meaning about the fragility of
man's existence or some other similarly profound message,
but, if so, it went straight over Freyja's head. Some of the
furniture looked more like artworks than practical objects.
She had never set foot in such an exclusive apartment.

The wall of windows at the far end of the room shone as
if they'd just been cleaned, despite being on the eleventh floor.
The adjoining wall turned out to be a set of French windows,
opening onto a large terrace with a view over Faxaflói Bay.
Freyja walked over and looked out. The terrace was tastefully
furnished with an outdoor table and chairs. Presumably it
was only used in summer – if then. In countries by the sea,
a good view was all too often accompanied by a howling
gale.

Wherever she looked she was struck by the same thing:
the place appeared unlived in. There were none of the usual

signs of habitation: no post piled up on the chest by the front door, and certainly no half-empty glasses on the tables, open newspapers or books lying on the sofa, or socks littering the floor.

While Freyja was surveying the living room, Didrik took off his jacket, crouched down beside the little boy and began to tell him about the designs on his arm. She signalled to him that she was going to check there really was nobody else home. Didrik nodded and encouraged the curious child to touch his tattoos with a tentative finger.

Freyja commenced her search in the open-plan kitchen at one end of the living area. It was the same story here: no signs of life, apart from a single brightly coloured parcel on the kitchen table. Freyja went over and peered at the label. 'To Hallbera – from Helgi'. The writing was feminine. She turned in a slow circle, examining the rest of the kitchen.

All the surfaces looked as if they had just been wiped clean, the empty stainless-steel sink was shiny and unmarked by scratches, and the few objects on display all appeared to be in the correct place. One wall boasted three ovens, none of which appeared ever to have been used, and a built-in coffee machine that looked as if it was fresh out of its box. Whoever lived here must employ a whole team of cleaners, while people like her could only dream of getting a woman to come in for a couple of hours a week. Freyja stopped short of opening the fridge or cupboards. No one could be hiding in any of them and she was supposed to be checking whether there was anyone else in the flat, not giving in to her curiosity.

Next, she went into the corridor, which led to a master bedroom with a walk-in wardrobe, a bathroom and an office space. There was another bedroom as well, with a small en-suite. Every door she opened revealed another spotlessly clean, tidy room. Freyja was particularly interested in the wardrobe, since it established beyond a doubt that a single man lived here – presumably the Helgi who had bought the gift for Hallbera. Whoever Hallbera was, she evidently didn't live here, since there wasn't a single feminine garment to be seen. On one side of the space were rows of identical designer suits, stiffly pressed shirts for every imaginable occasion, and countless smart leather brogues in shades of brown. The other side was devoted to casualwear: piles of jeans, T-shirts and jumpers were neatly folded on the shelves, with pairs of running shoes and moccasins below them. She couldn't resist sneaking a peek inside the massive unit in the middle of the wardrobe, which served as both table and chest of drawers. It was no surprise to discover that the drawers contained an assortment of rolled-up silk ties, leather belts, colourful socks, and other accessories. She'd seen enough films featuring rich bachelors to know what to expect. The only difference between this room and the ones in the movies was that there was no secret compartment concealed behind the clothes, containing a stash of forged passports, bundles of dollar bills and a wall hung with firearms.

Despite the surface gloss everywhere you looked, the flat struck Freyja as depressingly soulless and impersonal. Even the desk in the home office was bare apart from a monitor planted in the middle, a cordless keyboard and a mouse. There wasn't a speck of dust to be seen here either. The only signs of occupation were in the master bedroom. The bed had been made but on the side nearest the door there was a dent left by a small body, presumably that of the little boy. Beside it was a large, old-fashioned alarm clock and, on the bedside table, a half-empty bottle of orange juice. Next to the bottle were two used crayons, one red, the other green.

Freyja returned to the hall and shook her head at Didrik. She couldn't tell from his reaction what he made of the news that there was nobody else in the flat. He merely turned back to the little boy, who appeared totally out of place in his cheap anorak and clumpy snow-boots. 'Have you been here all on your own for a long time?'

'I don't know.'

'Do you remember who brought you here? Was it your mummy or your daddy?'

'No.'

'Who was it, then?'

'A man.'

'A man you know?'

'No.'

'Does the man live here?'

'I don't know.'

'Is his name Helgi?'

'I don't know.'

'Do you know a woman or a girl called Hallbera?'

Siggi shook his head, so Freyja changed tack:

'Did you come here this morning or yesterday?'

'I don't know.'

Didrik stood up. 'How about we get out of here and go and buy you a hot dog or an ice-cream? Are you hungry?'

'Yes.'

'After that we can go to my office and look for your mummy.'

The boy opened his eyes wide, instantly brightening up. 'Is she there? Is she hiding?'

'No.' Didrik smiled as he pulled his jacket on again. 'But

we can make some calls from my phone and use my computer to find her. You can find out anything with my computer. About you *and* your mummy. We'll soon have you back with her.'

Freyja held out a hand to take Siggi's, but just as the small fingers were placed trustingly in hers, the doorbell rang. The boy snatched back his hand, staring at the door in alarm. Freyja and Didrik were also startled by the loud, unexpected sound and didn't immediately react, each expecting the other to take charge. But when the bell shrilled again, Freyja went to open the door.

Outside stood a diminutive redhead in police uniform.

And behind her was none other than Huldar.

Chapter 4

Out of the corner of his eye, Huldar watched Freyja take the wrapper off a straw and poke it into a carton of chocolate milk, before handing it to the little boy. The child was sitting on Huldar's office chair, swinging his short legs. The chocolate milk seemed to hit the spot, since he gulped it down until the carton was sucked together in the middle. Apparently he had been promised a hot dog too but there were none available at the police station and no one had had a moment to run out and buy one. Instead, the boy had been given a biscuit, a cheese sandwich and chocolate milk from the canteen. He hadn't so much as looked at the biscuit or sandwich.

Despite his rather meagre snack, the boy seemed perfectly happy. His eyes grew round every time a uniform appeared, and he craned his head as far as his short neck would allow in order to watch it go by. In fact, the child seemed so contented that Huldar was half afraid he would never get his workstation back. On returning from the canteen, Huldar had found the hipster from the city council pinning a drawing to the wall above his desk. It showed three stick figures, with lines for mouths and wonky circles for eyes. One of the figures was much smaller, and one of the big figures was drawn considerably larger than the other. Perhaps it was just as well that the boy felt at home at the police station, since it was fairly obvious he had no future as an artist.

Strictly speaking, Huldar should have taken the drawing down immediately, as personal items were not permitted, but the boy had seemed so proud to see it hanging there. And then Freyja had come back just as Huldar was giving the child his snack, and after that there had been no question of coming across as a miserable spoilsport. Especially when he noticed that she'd reapplied her lipstick in the ladies', possibly in his honour.

'Run that by me again.' Erla was close to losing her rag. The day that had begun badly was rapidly deteriorating and she was feeling the pressure from all sides. The head honchos at the Police Commissioner's office, desperate not to lose face in front of the other state institutions, were breathing down her neck. They had already torn a strip off her when she informed them that she'd had to leave the body behind in the lava-field. Huldar hadn't envied her as he listened to her trying in vain to get in a word of explanation between the storms of invective at the other end.

No one in CID was in any doubt that Erla had reacted appropriately. No one apart from Lína, that is. She would have preferred it if the investigation had continued in defiance of the state visit. Erla's bosses, on the other hand, would rather the body had been whisked away, regardless of whether or not it was murder. Erla's reaction had been a compromise: she had put the investigation on hold while the visit lasted and made do with camouflaging the body. But, as so often when you try to please everybody, she had ended up satisfying no one. At least the Chinese delegation had finished their visit to Bessastadir, and the body had been taken to the mortuary while Huldar was at Helgi's flat.

'When we knocked on the door, they were already inside,'

Huldar repeated. 'Freyja, the little boy, and the guy from Reykjavík City Council – that hipster over there.' He jerked his chin towards the young man who was tending to the boy at Freyja's side. To be fair, the guy had done nothing to earn Huldar's dislike, apart from apparently making a good impression on Freyja. Perhaps, after all, the lipstick had been for the hipster, not him. Huldar's mood darkened at the thought, though he had almost given up hope of winning her over. Still, a man could dream, and a hipster like that had no place in his fantasies, especially not when he put his hand on Freyja's shoulder and whispered in her ear. Huldar quickly turned his attention back to Erla. 'They'd been called to the address after receiving a tip-off about a child in trouble. The boy opened the door but I gather he doesn't have a clue what's going on. Doesn't know the man who owned the flat and can't explain what he was doing there.'

Erla made a face. She had a piece of heather caught in her hair, which Huldar was trying not to stare at. No one else had had the courage to point it out to her, and she wouldn't be amused when she discovered later that she'd been walking around with it, looking like an idiot, ever since they'd covered the body in grass. 'Why not get in touch with his mother or father, then?' she asked impatiently. 'They must know what their son was doing there.'

'All he can tell us is that his father's called Sibbi and his mother's called Systa. Which isn't exactly helpful. He doesn't know his patronymic or when his birthday is, only that he's four years old. Lína's searching the National Register for all the four-year-olds called Sigurdur. With a name that common there are bound to be loads, so it's going to take a while to track the parents down.'

'And what are we supposed to do in the meantime? Turn the office into a kindergarten? Maybe I should order a Lego table, like the ones they have at the bank?' Erla snorted derisively. 'In case you haven't noticed, we've got more than enough on our plate right now. Can't she . . . what's her name . . . take the boy to the Children's House and sort it out there?' Erla was perfectly aware of Freyja's name. 'It's too early to interview possible witnesses, especially witnesses who can barely talk yet. If he doesn't even know his own name, what are the chances that he'll be able to point us to the murderer? In fact, I can't understand what the hell you thought you were doing, bringing him into the office at a time like this. Don't you ever fucking think?'

Huldar reminded himself that Erla needed a safety valve, that this wasn't really about him. Ignoring her outburst, he explained patiently: 'I brought them here because I couldn't decide what else to do. And I thought the boy might be able to shed some light on the case. Are you seriously telling me you don't find it a strange coincidence that an abandoned child should turn up at the murder victim's flat?'

'Sure, I find it bloody strange. But not as strange as a man being hanged on the Gallows Rock. I mean, it's a tourist attraction. It hasn't been used to execute anyone for centuries.' The desk phone rang and Erla snatched up the receiver. Almost in the same instant, Lína appeared in the doorway holding a sheet of paper. Without waiting for Erla to finish her phone call, she announced to Huldar: 'There are a total of four thousand five hundred Sigurdurs in Iceland, most of them first names. But there are only a hundred and three who were born between three and five years ago. I widened my search a bit in case the boy got his age wrong.'

'Over a hundred is a lot of kids, Lína.'

'It's not quite so many if we assume he's right about living in Reykjavík. Thirty-eight boys are registered in the city.'

'That's not quite so bad, but can't we narrow it down further? Use his dad's nickname to rule some of them out?'

Lína smiled, looking pleased with herself. 'I've already done that. I checked which men's names are most likely to be shortened to Sibbi, but unfortunately it's rather a lot. Sighvatur, Sigurbjörn, Snæbjörn, Sindri, Steingrímur and Sigurdur were the ones that cropped up most often. I also found examples of a Thorsteinn and an Ingibergur who were nicknamed Sibbi. There doesn't seem to be any logic to it, except that most of the names begin with an S. If we work on that basis, we're down to fifteen boys with the right sort of patronymic. Plus three who are named after their mother, rather than their father. But one of those is only just three and the other is five, going on six. I don't think our boy's that young or that old.'

'OK, so we're talking fifteen or sixteen boys?'

Lína nodded.

That would make the task more doable, though the list didn't cover those Siggis who lived in Reykjavík but were legally domiciled elsewhere. Or those with fathers whose names didn't begin with an S, but were still nicknamed Sibbi. Let alone boys who were known as Siggi though their full name wasn't Sigurdur. 'Does Siggi exist as a name in its own right?'

'Yes, actually. There are two Icelanders christened Siggi, but in both cases it's a middle name and they're the wrong age.'

Erla ended her phone call and got to her feet. 'That was

the pathology department. They're ready to examine the body.'

Huldar sucked in his breath as if that would make him more inconspicuous, and prayed that she wouldn't ask him to go with her. He had a better idea: if he took on the little boy's case, that would give him an excuse to spend some time with Freyja. Besides, he had an ingrained horror of corpses. But it was no good. Erla announced that Gudlaugur could take care of the Siggi business, and ordered Huldar and Lína to accompany her to the National Hospital. Evidently, she hadn't given up hope of rattling Lína's composure.

The dead man lay fully dressed on the pathologist's steel table, arms at his sides, legs straight out, one foot wearing a shoe, the other only a sock. There were bits of moss and dried grass caught on his clothes following the hasty attempt to camouflage him, and two of the fingers on one hand appeared to be dislocated or broken. They could have been fine before the man had been dropped unceremoniously to the ground. Fortunately for Huldar's delicate stomach, he could only glimpse these injuries through the 'dead man's gloves', transparent plastic bags tied over the hands to preserve any potential biological traces under the victim's nails.

It was a grim, unsettling sight but, no doubt contrary to Erla's hopes, Lína appeared unmoved. She bent so close to examine the corpse's contorted features that for a moment Huldar thought she was going to kiss it on the forehead. Even the pathologist was disconcerted and asked her to step back.

'The post-mortem won't happen until tomorrow.' The pathologist, noticing that Erla was about to protest, forestalled her: 'It can't be helped, I'm afraid. We're closed at weekends and I've only come in to carry out the preliminary examination as a special favour. You'll have to be content with that for now.'

Huldar hid his relief and made a mental note to avoid being anywhere near Erla the following day, to avoid being dragged along. Lína, he felt sure, would take it in her stride.

The pathologist finished doing up his white overalls, donned a paper mask, then pulled on his latex gloves with practised ease, snapping them over his wrists. His assistant followed suit and the atmosphere lightened a little once the man's sour expression was concealed behind a mask. He seemed even more resentful than the pathologist about being called out on a Sunday.

'Any theories about why that particular site was chosen?' It was the pathologist who had spoken, though they couldn't see his lips moving. 'It's a bit off the beaten track.'

'Maybe that had something to do with it. You wouldn't expect to bump into anyone in the middle of the night in a lava-field. No chance of being disturbed. No one around to hear any screams. Yet still close to Reykjavík.' Erla shrugged. 'Then there's the name, Gálgaklettur – the Gallows Rock. Maybe that had something to do with it. It certainly fits the crime.'

'Is it an old execution site?' The pathologist trained a large lamp on the corpse.

'Apparently,' Erla said. 'They've found bones thought to be the remains of criminals buried on the spot. I suppose it saved the bother of lugging their corpses to an official burial ground. But we haven't come across anything like that so far and I hope to God it stays that way. We've got enough to contend with. A bunch of archaeologists grubbing around on the site wouldn't make my life any easier.'

The pathologist's eyes narrowed above his white mask and he retorted testily: 'Speaking of which, your treatment of the body hasn't exactly made my life easier either.'

After a bit more grumbling about the state of the corpse, the two men began going through the victim's coat pockets and extracted three credit-card receipts. 'I'll have these scanned in and sent over to you. They might shed some light on his final hours.' The pathologist dropped the receipts into the open evidence bag held out by his assistant, then continued his search. The resulting meagre haul consisted of an open packet of chewing gum, a book of matches and an expensive cigar, still in its wrapping. That was it.

As soon as the police had got the all-clear and returned to the scene, they had removed the man's wallet and discovered his name and address. Their initial research had provided little information: the man, who was listed in the telephone directory as an investor, apparently lived alone and didn't have a social media presence. A trawl of the news archive resulted in no hits either, though these days you'd expect a self-styled investor to make plenty of appearances. Especially when, on the evidence of his luxury apartment, the man must have been doing very nicely indeed.

As the pathologist and his assistant dealt methodically with the material they had taken from the victim's pockets, Huldar caught the gleam of satisfaction in Lína's eyes. No doubt she was smiling under her mask. He could read her mind: finally, here was something being done by the book. They removed the bags from the dead man's hands, scraped under his nails and placed the results in small evidence bags. Next, they took off his coat and examined it carefully both inside and out to make absolutely sure that there was nothing else to be found. Inspection completed, they crammed it into a much larger plastic bag. The pathologist watched as his assistant placed this on the bottom shelf of the trolley beside them. 'Cashmere,' he remarked. 'Must have cost a bloody fortune. He clearly wasn't short of money.' Using a small set of tweezers, he lifted the victim's left shirt cuff. 'Bloody expensive watch, too.' He dropped the cuff again before Huldar, Erla or Lína could get a proper look at it. Not that it made any difference, since none of them were particularly clued up about luxury items.

'Whereas the nail in his chest looks like the kind of thing you could pick up in any DIY store.' The pathologist bent over the body to examine the head of the nail, then straightened up and made way for his assistant, who was armed with the inevitable camera.

'Which do you think killed him, the nail or being hanged?' It was impossible to tell from Erla's expression which cause of death she'd prefer.

'Being hanged,' a female voice piped up. 'That's obvious. You can see from the distorted face and protruding dark tongue. The typical appearance of a strangulation.' Lína turned pink above her mask as the pathologist looked at her with raised eyebrows, unaccustomed to being interrupted. Erla, meanwhile, was scarlet with rage at the tactless intervention, which had made her look ignorant.

'And you are?' The pathologist sounded more surprised than annoyed.

'She's here on work experience,' Erla said grimly. 'I promise you she won't open her mouth again. Please, carry on with what you were saying.' Erla directed a murderous look at Lína, who dropped her eyes to her feet, turning even pinker.

'May I point out that we've found no phone or keys in the deceased's possession, which is unusual, to say the least.' The pathologist glanced at Lína, as if waiting for her to contradict him. When she kept her eyes meekly lowered, he asked: 'Were these removed at the scene, like the wallet?'

'No, that's all we took.' Erla stared thoughtfully at the dead man's face. 'There was no sign of a phone or keys, though we haven't actually finished combing the area yet. We've tracked down his mobile number but the phone's switched off. We'll just have to hope it turns up.'

The pathologist didn't comment on this, and remained silent until his assistant had finished taking pictures and stepped back, leaving the way clear for him to resume his examination. 'I can't quite work out what the nail's doing there – what purpose it could have served, other than to inflict pain. Is the victim known to have owed money to drug dealers or had debt collectors after him?'

Erla answered hastily, as if doubting Lína's ability to obey orders and keep her mouth shut: 'We know next to nothing about him yet. The investigation's only just getting off the ground. But I understand from those who've seen his apartment that he must have been seriously loaded. Even if it turns out that he was a user, it's unlikely he'd have had any problem paying up. When we spotted the nail originally, there was a scrap of paper under the head, but it seems to have become detached in all the commotion. I'm guessing the nail was there to fasten a piece of paper – presumably a message of some sort – to his chest. But it must have been torn away by the wind before we got there.'

Huldar bent down to take a closer look. The pattern on the head looked familiar. 'I'm guessing it's a three- or four-inch nail fired from a nail gun,' he said, adding: 'I trained as a carpenter.'

'Three to four inches.' The pathologist was silent for a moment. 'That's not very precise.'

'Aren't you going to pull it out?' Like everyone else, Erla was staring, transfixed, at the nail.

'No. We'll do that during the post-mortem. All I'm going to do now is remove his clothes, bag up his belongings and record them, take a blood sample and measure his body temperature. The rest can wait until tomorrow.'

Huldar stepped back smartly. He'd always managed to avoid seeing the thermometer plunged into the corpse's liver at the scene and he had no intention of watching now, or of seeing the blood sample taken. When his phone rang, he seized on the excuse it offered to withdraw into a corner. Gudlaugur's name flashed up on screen and Huldar prayed his colleague would be characteristically slow to get to the point.

But for once Gudlaugur didn't beat about the bush. 'We're having no luck finding the boy's parents. I tried calling Erla but her phone's switched off. Freyja and the social worker are getting restless. He can't see why the kid should have to hang around at the station while we're trying to identify him. He's insisting on taking him away and getting him a proper meal and stuff.'

'Why can't he go out and buy something for him? We'll be back in half an hour, an hour at most. It's not like he has to stick around. Freyja can wait with the kid. That bloke's not helping at all, as far as I can see. Seems like a waste of space.'

'You're wrong about that. He's a good guy.'

Huldar bit back a mischievous comment about Gudlaugur not being able to see past Didrik's good looks. That kind of teasing wouldn't go down well, especially since their friendship still hadn't recovered its former warmth. That was Huldar's fault. Ever since Gudlaugur had told him he was gay, Huldar had found it hard to behave naturally around him. It wasn't because he objected to Gudlaugur's sexuality – far from it – he just found himself permanently walking on eggshells. He was terrified of saying or doing something that could be misconstrued, which only made his behaviour seem even more forced and unnatural. 'Try and keep them there until we get back,' he said instead. 'I'll pick something up for the kid on the way. A hamburger or a pizza, or both.'

'OK, I'll try, but I'm not promising anything. It's not like they're under arrest. They're free to leave whenever they like.'

'All right, thanks.' Once he'd rung off, Huldar was forced to turn back and face the body on the table. He tried to distract himself from what was going on by plotting how best to talk Erla into letting him handle the boy's case with Freyja. He would have to word his request very carefully, in case she got the idea that he had ulterior motives. Which was, of course, partly true.

Chapter 5

Brief though the video was, its contents were so bizarre that Thormar had to play it twice to work out what it was showing. It didn't help that a noisy children's party was going on in the background and by the time he'd given in to the impulse to check his phone, the mayhem had reached its height. Tanked up on sugar, the knee-high guests were tearing around the flat to a cacophony of screeches, squeals and wails. Although most were no more than three years old, they had been quick to grasp the layout of the rooms and establish a circuit. Now they were racing from kitchen to dining room to sitting room to hall, then back into the kitchen to start a new lap.

Thormar pressed 'Replay', pretending not to notice the glare his wife Sigrún was directing at him. He'd promised to help with the party. Promised to stay away from his phone and computer for the duration. He was allowed to turn on the TV, but only to put the film on for the kids. But when his phone had bleeped to alert him to a message on the forum, his wife's orders were temporarily forgotten. At first he'd taken the precaution of turning his back to her, but after he'd worked out what the video was showing he was so shaken he forgot to hide what he was doing. Sigrún was glowering at him but right now that didn't seem to matter.

Just then, a little girl with two pigtails tied with pink ribbons and a smudge of icing on her upper lip came charging into the room, mouth open wide, squealing at the top of her voice, and collided violently with Thormar's legs. He yelped, almost dropping his phone, and only just managed to stop himself grabbing the girl and giving her an earful. Venting like that might provide temporary relief but it would be extremely unwise. Sigrún wouldn't like it and the girl's mother would be even less impressed. There was no point asking why the mother was doing nothing to restrain her overexcited daughter, since the woman's indifference seemed to be par for the course. Once the mothers had made themselves comfortable in the sitting room with cups of coffee and plates of cake, they seemed to have put their offspring completely out of their minds. When a child hurt itself and came running to its mother's arms, the woman would look momentarily bemused before, after a second or two, recalling that this grubby, squawling brat was hers. After a perfunctory 'There, there,' the child would be returned to the fray.

The only woman not sitting down was Sigrún. Instead, she was busy rushing around after the children, trying to stop them swallowing house keys, throwing glasses at each other, knocking things over and fighting over the most coveted toys. She'd spent half an hour making herself presentable before the guests arrived but now looked as if she'd been hit by a tornado. This was doing nothing to improve her mood.

Thormar had helped out as best he could, wondering all the while why she didn't just get her teenage son, Fannar, to lend a hand. The kid was glued to the computer in his room as usual, but it wouldn't kill him to help. Thormar knew better than to say anything, though. He was only the boy's stepfather and they weren't that close. It was hard to have any sort of relationship with someone who spent most of his time shut away in his room.

Thormar glanced furtively at Sigrún. Seeing that she was bending down to untangle a lollipop from a little girl's hair, he grabbed his chance. He had to watch the video again. Perhaps this time he'd be able to spot something to confirm that it was a hoax. It couldn't possibly be real. He tilted his phone to avoid the glare from the ceiling light.

The recording was dark, as if it had been filmed at night. Even so, Thormar could tell that the man was his friend Helgi. He was wearing the coat from last night's pub crawl, but now there appeared to be a white napkin on his chest that Thormar didn't remember seeing. They'd lost track of Helgi during the evening, so he must have got it after they'd separated. The rope around his neck certainly hadn't been there before.

But it wasn't the rope or the napkin – if that's what it was – that had shocked and disturbed him. It was what happened next. Thormar held the phone as close to his face as he could without losing focus.

A gloved hand appeared in the frame and pushed at Helgi. His eyes and mouth formed wide Os of astonishment as he fell over backwards and disappeared. The camera panned out to show the dark shape of a man dangling in mid-air. His legs were kicking in the void, his hands scrabbling frantically at the noose around his neck. The flailing of his limbs grew ever more spasmodic until finally they stopped moving altogether. His arms dropped limply to his sides, his legs hung straight down. The man spun gently one way, then the other. Then the recording ended.

Thormar exhaled a long breath. The comments his friends had posted underneath mirrored his own thoughts exactly.

Is this supposed to be funny? Which one of you posted it?

I thought this forum was for a different kind of movie, heh heh heh. Not sure this really does it for me.

Thormar considered adding a comment himself but couldn't think of anything else to say. Besides, if he started tapping on his phone there was a real risk that Sigrún would tear it from his hands and hurl it out of the window. No, it could wait.

'Thormar!'

He looked up, closing his phone smartly as he met his wife's incensed gaze. She was holding a lollipop covered in hairs.

'Take the girls more coffee, will you?'

It took him a moment to realise she was referring to the mothers rather than the swarm of children, though the women had little right to be called girls any more. Slipping his phone into his pocket, he obeyed.

He fetched the jug of freshly made coffee and absent-mindedly refilled the cups as they were held out. The women barely even registered him but carried on gassing away as if he were a waiter rather than one of their hosts.

Once he'd completed this task, Sigrún ordered him to wash the hands of a little girl who had smeared chocolate icing from the birthday cake all over the newly decorated wall in the entrance hall. He took the wet cloth his wife handed him without protest, tracked down the child and wiped her short, sticky fingers. Then he nipped into the loo, aware that Sigrún would grow suspicious if he spent too long in there. Taking out his phone, he selected Helgi's number. He wanted to hear what the hell he'd meant by that sick joke. But all he got was the standard recorded message:

The phone is switched off or cannot be reached at the moment. Please try again later.

Chapter 6

Siggi was sitting at a table in the Children's House, eating a hot dog. It was all he could do to get his small hands round the bun, let alone his mouth. In the end he gave up and started nibbling at bread and sausage in turn. After eating two thirds, he put it down on the plate Freyja had given him and said loudly and clearly: 'Thank you.'

'You're welcome.' This further evidence of the boy's good manners proved that he had been well brought up, which made it all the harder to understand why no one seemed to have noticed his absence. The police insisted that no one had called to report him missing, and emergency services told the same story. Freyja wondered if the phone call from his distraught parents could have got lost in the system. But she was assured that this was impossible.

'Where's Mummy?' Siggi looked around the small coffee room, as if expecting to see her hiding there.

'She's not here. We're looking for her.'

'Is she lost?'

'No, I don't think so. Sometimes we look for people who aren't lost.'

Siggi made a puzzled face. 'Why?'

Freyja smiled at him. 'Well, that's the thing. Sometimes you just think people are lost because you can't get hold of them. But I'm sure *she* knows where she is.'

'My mummy isn't lost.'

Freyja said nothing; she wasn't at all confident that he was right. His mother might not be lost according to a child's understanding – standing at a crossroads somewhere, scratching her head – but the risk was all too real that something bad had happened to her. It didn't bode well that Siggi had been found in the flat of a man who had died in suspicious circumstances. Neither Freyja nor Didrik had been entrusted with any details of the case, merely told that the owner of the flat was dead and the death was being treated as murder.

Huldar put down the cup of weak coffee that Freyja had given him. She'd had to make do with a glass of water herself as there hadn't been enough coffee for a full pot. Judging by the faint grimaces on the men's faces as they sipped it, the scrapings at the bottom of the tin hadn't been enough to stretch to two cups either.

'Right. The question is, should we start . . . you know . . . ?' Huldar caught Freyja's eye. She knew what he meant. The moment Erla had got back to the police station with Huldar and the young redhead in tow, she had ordered Freyja and Didrik to take Siggi away, adding that Huldar should go with them and make sure they got some information out of the boy. Huldar hadn't seemed too displeased, until it became clear that Didrik would be accompanying them. But his objections had been over-ruled on the grounds that Siggi was officially the responsibility of Reykjavík children's services until his legal guardian could be found. As Freyja was only a casual employee of the Child Protection Agency, Didrik's presence was required, and that was that.

Up to now, Huldar had at least managed to be civil to

Didrik but Freyja knew him well enough to see that it was an effort. She awarded him brownie points for his self-control, although this mainly consisted of behaving as if Didrik wasn't there, and never addressing a word to him unless spoken to first.

Despite the urgency of the interview, Freyja had insisted on feeding Siggi first. Huldar had made the mistake of buying him a pizza with mushrooms on it, to which Siggi had reacted by wrinkling his nose, shaking his head and clamping his mouth shut. Most four-year-olds would have to starve for a lot longer before they'd eat something as disgusting as a mushroom. So they'd stopped off at a kiosk to buy a hot dog on the way to the Children's House. Although this had created another delay, Freyja knew she'd have better luck getting information from the child if he had a full stomach. If he was hungry, he'd only fidget and have difficulty concentrating on what she was saying. The interview would be tricky enough anyway. Children his age were too young to fully grasp the situation they were in, let alone work out how they had ended up there. To them, life simply flowed along, carrying them with it. There was no point memorising the things they encountered along the way, unless they happened to be of particular interest, like cats, dogs or ice-cream parlours.

'How would you like to come and sit with me, Siggi?' Freyja smiled at the boy. He had ketchup at the corners of his mouth, and sticky fingers. 'It would be really great if you could talk to me for a bit.'

'What about?'

'Oh, this and that. It might help us find your mummy.'

The boy thought for a minute, then nodded. Freyja led

him into the small interview room where she parked him on the squashy sofa and handed him the cuddly teddy with the missing eye. It held an unaccountable fascination for children, especially when they were distressed, and Siggi proved no exception. While he was inspecting the toy, Freyja showed Didrik and Huldar into the room next door, where they could observe the conversation via a two-way mirror and speakers. At least in this instance, she thought, there was no danger of the two men chatting and disturbing her concentration.

She switched on the sound system, donned the microphone, then went back in to join Siggi. Under normal circumstances she would have put in an earpiece too, so she could relay questions from the police, lawyers or judge observing in the next room. In those cases she had to use her expertise to couch the questions in simple enough terms for a child to understand and answer honestly. She had to be careful not to put words into their mouths or pose leading questions. Kids had a tendency to tailor their responses to please adults. But this time she would be the one asking the questions. The boy was still such an enigma that any details she could elicit would count as fresh information.

So far, the only facts they'd established were that his name was Sigurdur and that he was called Siggi for short; his mother was known as Systa and his father as Sibbi. Less helpful nicknames would be hard to imagine. Siggi had told them he lived in Reykjavík but couldn't be more precise about the street or the area. They were hoping he would turn out to know more, but at the police station he'd been so distracted by the exciting surroundings that it had been impossible to get him to concentrate. There was always a chance that information would come pouring out once they'd got him into a less stimulating environment.

'So, Siggi, do you like the teddy?' Freyja took a seat next to him, her gaze on the mirror facing the sofa. She assumed Huldar was watching her.

'Where's his eye?'

'It fell off. But it doesn't matter because he can see perfectly well with the other one. Did you know, spiders have eight eyes, so they probably wonder how we manage with only two.'

'Eight?' Siggi sounded impressed.

Freyja nodded and began to edge the conversation round to the point. 'Have you got a teddy bear at home, Siggi?'

'I've got a rabbit. But she's only got two eyes. Not eight.' Siggi stared at the bear for a bit longer, then put it down in his lap.

Freyja didn't pursue the subject of the rabbit. One advantage with children this young was that they didn't notice non-sequiturs. 'What's your mummy's name, Siggi?'

'I told you. She's called Systa. But I always call her Mummy.'

'Do you know what a nickname is?' When the boy shook his head, Freyja explained. He seemed to follow what she was saying, so she continued: 'I think Systa's a nickname. Have you heard people call your mummy a different name?' She was itching to suggest some but stopped herself. The woman could be called pretty much anything – 'Systa' only meant she was someone's big or little 'sis' – and there was a risk the boy would simply jump on one of her suggestions at random.

'No. She's called Systa. Systa's a nice name.'

'Very nice.' Freyja hid her disappointment. 'What about your daddy? Has he got another name as well as Sibbi?'

'No. He's just called Sibbi.'

Again, Freyja resisted the impulse to supply him with some men's names. 'Have you got a granny and granddad, Siggi?'

'Yes.' The boy sat up, suddenly enthusiastic. 'I've got two grannies and one granddad. I've got a dead granddad too. He's not alive any more because he got very old and died.' No hint of sadness, so presumably the loss hadn't been recent.

'What are your granddads called?' Freyja asked. Perhaps the police could use their names to track down the parents.

'I don't know. Granddad. My dead granddad hasn't got a name. He's just dead.' Siggi frowned. 'Don't you want to know what my grannies are called?'

Freyja smiled and said yes she did.

The boy sat up again, proud at having influenced the course of the conversation. 'One of my grannies is called Sísí and the other one is called Granny.'

Freyja could feel her smile becoming increasingly strained. 'I see.' Names were obviously a dead end. Sísí could be short for anything. 'Tell me a bit about where you live, Siggi. I know it's in Reykjavík but can you tell me *where* in Reykjavík?'

'In Reykjavík.' Siggi seemed hurt that Freyja wasn't satisfied with this.

'All right. Then tell me something else. Do you know what your street is called?' Siggi shook his head; his dismay at being found wanting was obvious. Freyja quickly asked something she was fairly sure he would be able to answer. 'Where do you go to nursery?' Children of Siggi's age didn't necessarily know their own address but they all knew the name of their childminder or nursery school.

54

'I don't go to nursery. Mummy says I can go in the summer.'

Freyja could imagine Huldar groaning out loud at this answer. Didrik too, no doubt. This wasn't going to be straight-forward. If they failed to track down the boy's family, it would be Didrik's job to arrange an emergency placement, with all the hassle that involved. Freyja decided to digress a little and ask the boy some general questions that he would be able to answer easily. By the end, she had established that his favourite food was spaghetti, he could cycle with stabilisers, he'd been to the zoo loads and loads and loads of times, and could count up to fifteen, though once he'd managed to get all the way up to twenty. Having answered all these questions without once having to stop and think, the little boy had cheered up considerably, and Freyja was able to direct the conversation back to his family. 'What does your daddy do for a job, Siggi?'

'Daddy's a *lectrishan*.'

'Wow, an electrician! That's cool. Do you know where he works?' Freyja hadn't been expecting him to, so she wasn't surprised when he shook his head. 'And what does your mummy do?'

'She's a teacher.'

'Gosh.' Freyja opened her eyes wide to please the boy. 'Do you know the name of the school where she teaches?'

'No. She doesn't go to school. But she's going to teach at school when I go to nursery.'

So his mother wasn't currently employed. It seemed they'd hit a brick wall with his parents. Freyja moved on. 'What can you see when you stand outside your house, Siggi? It might help if you close your eyes and imagine you're standing there and looking around.'

Siggi squeezed his eyes shut. Evidently feeling that this

wasn't enough, he raised his hands from his lap and put them over his face. 'I can see cars.'

'What else? Can you see Hallgrímskirkja – the big church with the tall, pointy tower?'

'No.'

'Can you see the sea?'

Siggi thought about this, then shook his head. 'No. Just cars.' Then he brightened up, took his hands from his eyes and opened them again. 'And houses!' he exclaimed happily.

'Do you live in a house, Siggi, or in a block of flats?'

The boy closed his eyes again before answering. 'A house. A big house.'

Freyja wasn't sure he'd understood the question. 'Do other people live in the house too? Not just you and your mummy and daddy?'

'Yes, lots. It's a big house.'

'A big house like that is called a block of flats, Siggi. Are the other houses you can see blocks of flats too?'

'Ummmm . . . yes.'

'Can you see mountains as well?'

'Ummmm . . . a little bit.'

There were a number of districts that would fit the boy's description. Too many. Perhaps she could find out if the boy lived in one of the new suburbs. 'Are there any building sites near your block, Siggi?'

'I don't know.'

'Are there any cranes? Any big yellow machines or workmen? Any concrete mixers? Or houses that nobody lives in yet because they haven't got any windows?'

'No. They've all got windows.'

Freyja went on asking about any landmarks that the boy

might recognise. About the zoo, burger stands, cinemas, kiosks, ice-cream parlours and playgrounds. He didn't think any of these could be seen from his house. She also asked about local sports clubs but Siggi didn't know any by name. At this point, having run out of ideas, she gave up asking about the area and hoped that the information Siggi had already provided would prove sufficient. She told the boy he could open his eyes.

'Do your mummy and daddy have a car, Siggi?'

'Yes.'

'Do you know what kind of car it is?'

'A white one.'

Freyja smiled. 'Do you know what make it is?'

Siggi beamed, pleased that he had an answer. 'A Yaris. It comes from Japan.'

Of course his parents would have the most popular make of car in Iceland. Freyja had learnt this fact during the countless hours she'd spent searching online for a vehicle of her own, now that her brother would be needing his old rustbucket back. But at the moment saving up for a flat was a more urgent priority. Work more, spend less. Not a very inspiring mantra. Which made it all the more vital that Baldur's friend's flat should turn out to be the answer to her prayers.

Realising that her mind was wandering, Freyja brought her attention back to the little boy. 'Now, I'm going to ask you about the place where we found you, Siggi. You remember, don't you? It was only a little while ago.'

'At the man's house.'

'That's right. At the man's house. Had you been there before?' Siggi shook his head. 'Do you know the man who lives there? His name's Helgi.' Again he shook his head. 'Does he know your mummy or daddy?'

'I don't know.'

'Has Helgi, the man who lives there, ever come round to your house or met you somewhere else with your mummy or daddy?' The question was too long and Siggi looked confused. When Freyja broke it up into two shorter ones, he answered no to both.

'Then tell me, how did you get into his flat? Who brought you there? Was it your mummy or daddy?'

'No. It was the man.'

'You mean Helgi? The man who lives there?' Siggi shrugged expansively, so Freyja took out a photo of the murder victim that Huldar had given her. It was a typical business profile picture, showing only his head and shoulders. Apparently this was the best the police could come up with at present. The man in the photo was in his early thirties, and wore a jacket and shirt – presumably one of the ones she'd seen hanging in his wardrobe. He was average-looking, neither handsome nor ugly, but had an air of confidence, like someone used to being in command. Apart from that, he was clean-shaven, had a good haircut, and the expression on his face said 'I'm too busy and important to waste time having my photo taken'.

'Is this the man who took you to the flat?'

Siggi bent over the picture and studied it intently. Putting his hand over the lower half of the man's face, he tilted his head to the right and left while considering it. 'Yes. No. He didn't have his party clothes on.'

Freyja ignored the comment about his clothes. She wished now that she had Huldar's voice in her ear. What did the boy's response mean? Was it a yes or a no? Had Helgi taken the boy to his flat, then afterwards been murdered? If yes, what questions should she ask? 'Siggi, the man in the picture is called Helgi. He lives in the flat. Was it him who took you there?'

'Maybe.'

Freyja didn't want to put pressure on the child. Further questions were unlikely to do any more to clarify something he simply didn't seem to know. 'Did you go there by car?'

'Yes. Not in our car. It was mucky. Our car's clean.'

'Where did you get into the car, Siggi? Did the man pick you up from your house?'

'I don't know. I woke up and I was in the car. In the back.'

Freyja was silent for a moment. 'Did the man take you to the flat?' Siggi nodded, and Freyja left it at that. She moved on to the next question: 'Did he stay with you for a while?'

'He went away.'

'Did he hurt you or do anything to you? In the flat or in the car?'

Siggi hesitated, apparently searching his memory. 'No.'

Freyja was relieved. She could feel her shoulders untensing, but resolved nevertheless to call in a doctor once the interview was over. The boy would have to be given a medical examination. It was possible that he didn't want to talk about what had happened or had been told to keep his mouth shut. 'How long were you in the flat before we came along?'

'I don't know. A very long time.'

'Did you get there this morning or after lunch?' Freyja rephrased the question. 'Had you already eaten your lunch or only your breakfast?'

'I didn't have any lunch or any breakfast. It was night time.'

'You came to the flat at night?'

'Yes. Then the daytime came. But it was late because it's winter. In summer it's always daytime.'

'That's right.' Freyja considered what to ask next. Yet again she regretted not having put in the earpiece. A prompt from Huldar would have been welcome right now. Today's interview was absolutely crucial, because kids Siggi's age were quick to forget. By tomorrow his memory of the events would already have shifted or become scrambled. But the trouble was, she knew nothing about the circumstances of the murder, no specifics about when, how or where Helgi had met his end. 'Why didn't you leave the flat and go and look for help, Siggi?'

The boy hesitated again and started fidgeting before eventually answering, 'I wasn't allowed to. The man said so.'

Remembering how long she and Didrik had stood outside the flat, Freyja asked: 'You mean you weren't allowed to open the door?'

'No. The man said I mustn't open the door until the alarm clock rang. I had to wait with the clock until then. But I was allowed to sleep. And to drink the orange juice. I did a wee-wee in the toilet too. I was allowed.'

'What did the man say would happen if you didn't do what he told you?'

'I had to do what he said. Or Mummy would hurt herself. Mummy mustn't hurt herself. Not now.'

Without meaning to, Freyja blurted out: 'Why not?'

'She's got a baby in her tummy.' Siggi held his short arms out in front of him as far as they would go. 'Her tummy's this big.'

Assuming this wasn't an exaggeration, the boy's missing mother must be on the point of giving birth. Perhaps that was why nothing had been heard from her or the father. But unless she was lying in a delivery room, in the middle of her labour, this was bad news. Very bad news indeed.

A small hand tugged at Freyja's sleeve. She met the child's grave look. 'He's a bad man. Very bad.' He tugged her sleeve again, harder this time. 'You must find my mummy.' Then he let go and his head drooped. 'I don't want her to die.'

Chapter 7

The caretaker met Huldar and Gudlaugur at the door of the exclusive block of flats where Helgi had lived. He was a thin man in his fifties, still with a full head of hair, though his face was beginning to sag a little. He shook them both by the hand and, speaking in hushed tones, asked them to call him Doddi. At that moment a woman emerged from the lift, laughing loudly, a phone pressed to her ear. The caretaker shot her a dirty look as if taking exception to her cheerfulness. Perhaps he thought a funereal atmosphere would be more appropriate in the circumstances. But for now Doddi was the only person in the building who knew Helgi was dead. It had been necessary to tell him, and to bring home the seriousness of the matter by explaining that Helgi's death was being treated as murder. Since no keys had been found in Helgi's pocket, they needed the caretaker's cooperation to enter the flat and retrieve the recordings from the building's CCTV system.

When the woman had gone, they took the lift up to the top floor where Helgi's flat was located. They ascended in silence, all three keeping their eyes firmly fixed on the illuminated sign showing which floor they were on. At the top, a bell rang, the door opened and they got out. Instantly their awkwardness melted away and they found their tongues again.

'So you're not aware of any break-in?' Huldar had already

asked this downstairs but felt it wouldn't hurt to repeat the question. 'I'm assuming the building has several entrances?'

'None of the doors have been damaged and there's no sign that any of them have been tampered with. The door to Helgi's flat hasn't been forced either.'

'Did you know Helgi at all?' Huldar watched as the caretaker pulled out a bunch of keys and flipped through them.

'No, not really. But I used to bump into him in the corridor and I provided assistance when required.'

'Did he cause any problems?'

Shaking his head, the caretaker inserted a key in the lock. 'No, far from it. He was the quiet type, like most of the residents here.' The door opened and they stepped inside. The flat had been immaculate when Huldar had seen it earlier that day, but now it was a different story. Everywhere they looked they could see traces of fingerprint powder left by Forensics, and the furniture had been pushed aside, spoiling the overall design. Death had no respect for the departed.

'Did he get a lot of visitors?' Gudlaugur was looking around, his mouth slightly open. Huldar imagined that he himself had worn the same startled look the first time he'd set foot in here.

'I don't tend to notice that sort of thing. I'm a caretaker, not a doorman.'

Gudlaugur flushed slightly. 'Of course.'

The caretaker, who was not a doorman, realised that his answer had been a little brusque and tried to make up for it. 'I did meet him on his way in or out with other people from time to time. So he did have visitors. I just don't know how many.'

'Were they women? Men? Children?' Huldar walked further

into the room and noticed that the birthday present had vanished from the kitchen table. No doubt Forensics had taken it back to the station along with any other items that warranted closer examination.

'Mainly men. The occasional woman.'

'What about children?'

'No.' The man thought for a moment, then added: 'Actually, yes. I once saw him leaving the house with a man carrying a child.'

'A boy?'

'No, a girl. A toddler, no more than two years old.'

Huldar went over to the glass wall. Part of the reason for their return visit was that Forensics had forgotten to check whether the curtainless flat was overlooked by a nearby tower block or by any of the neighbouring flats. A quick glance established that it wasn't. They also needed to pick up the recordings from the building's CCTV system and to grill the caretaker for details of the deceased's lifestyle. 'Did he always live alone here?' Huldar asked, walking back over to the others. 'No girlfriend? Or boyfriend?'

Doddi shrugged. 'He's lived alone since he moved in. I know nothing else about his private life and I've no interest in prying.'

'When did he move in?'

The man furrowed his brow, thinking. 'About eighteen months ago, I think. No, less. Just over a year. Something like that. I can look it up afterwards, if you like.'

'Yes, please.' Huldar glanced up at the ceiling. 'Are there any security cameras in the flat?'

'Not that I'm aware of. But I'm not responsible for that sort of thing. I just look after the general maintenance and day-to-day running of the place. It's quite possible Helgi had them installed himself. It would have been a bit pointless seeing as we already have a very comprehensive security system. But of course it's up to the residents what they do in their own homes.' The caretaker's gaze travelled over the ceiling and down the walls. 'It doesn't look like there's anything in here, though I suppose he could have had hidden cameras.'

If so, Forensics hadn't uncovered any.

'We need to pick up the CCTV files. I've got a warrant for them.' Death might be no respecter of persons but judges, on the other hand, were great respecters of death. In cases like this, the police were almost invariably granted the warrants they applied for without a murmur.

'You won't need a warrant.' The caretaker had remained standing just inside the front door, apparently unwilling to step any further into the flat. 'You won't meet any opposition from me or the residents' association when it comes to providing assistance.'

Huldar smiled, privately hoping they wouldn't have to rely on the residents' association to solve the case. 'Thanks.' He looked around again before asking the next question. 'It wasn't you who rang the police to say there was a child in here?'

The caretaker shook his head. 'No. I'd have knocked on the door first if I'd heard anything strange. Helgi was a nice guy, so there'd be no reason to report something like that without checking with him first.'

'Do you know how he got on with the other residents? Any reason to think they wouldn't have shared your good opinion of him?'

'I wouldn't know. I've never had any complaints and his name's never come up at any of the residents' meetings. If anyone had wanted to raise an issue, that would have been their chance, as Helgi never attended himself. But then, hardly anyone does.'

Huldar nodded, guiltily conscious that he hadn't made it to a single residents' meeting in his own building. 'There aren't many flats that would be affected, are there? I'm guessing the sound insulation's pretty good here.'

'The kid would have had to scream his head off for the sound to carry. And even if he had, it would only have been heard in the flats on either side or on the floor below. But I happen to know that there's been nobody downstairs for the last couple of weeks. The owners are abroad.'

'Could they have lent out their flat?' Gudlaugur had got over gawping at the furnishings and turned his attention back to Huldar and the caretaker.

'No. They asked me to water the plants and keep an eye on the place. No one's been in there since they left. But I can take another look if you like, to make sure nothing's changed.'

Huldar handed the man his card. 'No rush. Just next time you get a moment, if you could let me know.'

They went back out into the corridor and knocked on the doors of the flats on either side. The occupants denied all knowledge of any phone call to the police, and said they didn't recognise Siggi when shown a photo of him. In the picture, he was sitting in Huldar's chair, gaping at the camera lens open-mouthed, as though he expected a unicorn to pop out of it. Despite this, it was a good likeness.

The neighbours echoed the caretaker's opinion of Helgi: perfectly pleasant, never caused any trouble. Wasn't at home much and didn't have many visitors. None of the people they talked to had noticed anything unusual over the last twenty-four hours either.

Huldar gave them all his card, in case they remembered anything later, and deflected their curiosity with the comment that it wasn't possible to say anything more at present. One man from further down the corridor wanted to know if their questions had anything to do with the child his wife had seen being taken from the flat, but he was fobbed off with the same response. If he'd been expecting to be given preferential treatment because his wife had witnessed the day's events, he was disappointed.

After interviewing the neighbours, they went down to the underground garage where Doddi showed them Helgi's cars. Both were in their spaces: a black Range Rover and a dark-blue Audi, parked side by side. The Range Rover had a thin layer of dust on it, which was consistent with the caretaker's comment that he didn't think Helgi used it much. Nothing of interest could be seen through the windows of either vehicle, except for a pair of leather gloves on the passenger seat of the Audi. They looked as if they belonged to a man, presumably Helgi himself.

'If you want to take a look inside them, I've got spare keys to both vehicles. Lots of the residents opt for that arrangement.' The caretaker had clearly meant it when he said he was willing to help. Huldar accepted his offer and once the car doors had been opened, pulled on a pair of latex gloves and set about searching the various compartments, the ashtrays, underneath the seats and in the boot. This resulted in nothing but two vehicle registration certificates, which he put back where he'd found them. There were no traces of cannabis in the ashtrays, no small white envelopes or bags of dope in any of the glove compartments.

Once Huldar had handed back the keys, the caretaker led them to the basement storeroom that went with Helgi's flat. When he opened the door, it was empty. Huldar noticed Doddi's look of puzzlement.

'I've never seen that before,' he said. 'Usually these storerooms are full to bursting with boxes and other junk, unless the flats are vacant.'

'Do you think it could have been cleaned out?' Huldar asked.

Doddi shrugged, unable to answer this.

The three of them walked back through the garage to the caretaker's office where the computer that stored the CCTV recordings was kept. As they passed one swanky vehicle after another, Huldar tried to tot up their value in his head but abandoned the attempt by the time he'd got to well over a hundred million krónur. He hoped the fact that the residents were so wealthy meant that the caretaker was well remunerated, but knew there was no guarantee of this. Especially not on the evidence of his office, which, in striking contrast to the rest of the building, turned out to be a windowless rabbit hutch containing an ugly old desk that had probably been bought for peanuts online. Apart from that, there was a dull-green filing cabinet that looked as if it dated from the sixties, and basic wall-mounted shelves full of folders. The ceiling was made of the same raw, exposed concrete as the garage. In comparison to this, Huldar's workstation in the corner of the CID offices looked like a managerial suite.

When the caretaker had finished copying the camera files onto a USB stick and handed it over, he let something slip that explained why he was being so obliging. 'Helgi gave me an extremely generous tip at Christmas. He said it was a bonus for the good job I'd done during the past year. None of the other residents have ever bothered to make a gesture like that. Oh, they'll say "Happy Christmas" if they bump into me, but otherwise they behave as if the holiday didn't apply to me.'

'That was nice of him.' Huldar didn't know what else to say.

'Anyway, I hope you find something on those recordings that'll help you catch the guy who did it. And I hope you don't dig up any dirt on Helgi. I'd like to think he was a good bloke.'

'We're not out to dig up dirt on the victim.' Huldar watched as the caretaker scribbled down the name of the contact at the security firm that maintained the system. He pocketed the note.

'There are quite a few cameras around the place but I'm afraid I can't tell you much about the files. The man at the security firm knows how it all works.'

Doddi stood up and escorted them out. He locked the office conscientiously behind him and, when asked, confirmed that he always kept it locked, which meant that no one could have got at the keys hanging on the large corkboard above the desk. Among them was the key to Helgi's flat, as Huldar had noticed when Doddi returned the car keys to the same hook. Logically, then, whoever brought the boy there must have used Helgi's own set of keys, which implied that it was almost certainly the killer. Unless the boy had been brought there by Helgi himself. The child's account had been ambiguous.

As they were saying goodbye in the lobby, the caretaker

suddenly seemed embarrassed, his eyes flickering shiftily away from theirs, which Huldar found odd given that they had been getting on perfectly fine up to that point. But all was explained when the man eventually blurted out: 'I know you're bound by confidentiality, but can you tell me what exactly happened? How and where he died and so on?'

Huldar clicked his tongue. 'Sorry, no can do.'

Chapter 8

Monday

'Can somebody sum up what we know about the victim so far?' Erla's question wasn't addressed to anyone in particular, merely projected across the open-plan office. She still had her coat on. Most people began the day with a coffee and a chat before getting stuck into work, but not her: she was on the job from the moment she walked in the door. Usually she'd have been the first person to arrive, too, but she'd stayed late the previous night.

Huldar watched as she strode over to her glass cage, trying and failing to make eye contact with her team, most of whom appeared suddenly very intent on their computer screens. The only head sticking up above the parapet belonged to Lína, whose red hair was tied back in a thick ponytail today. She had bobbed up the instant she heard Erla's voice. When Erla pretended not to notice her, Huldar waited for Lína to raise her hand, like one of the keen girls in his class at school.

Instead, Lína got up and set off in pursuit of Erla. Huldar looked round and met Gudlaugur's eye. The young man still had the desk opposite him, despite the cooling of their friendship. His apprehension mirrored Huldar's own. Huldar pushed himself to his feet, muttering: 'I'd better go after them.'

Thanks to his longer legs, Huldar caught up just as Erla entered her office with Lína hot on her heels, and witnessed the moment when his boss turned and realised that the student was right behind her. Erla's incredulous expression was confirmation that Huldar had done the right thing to follow them. You'd have thought she'd just spotted a piece of loo paper stuck to her shoe.

'What?' she snapped.

'I've been round and talked to everyone,' Lína said with breathless eagerness, 'and I've compiled a report of what we know so far about the deceased, Helgi Fridriksson.'

'Yes, thanks, I do know his name,' Erla said with heavy sarcasm. She took off her coat, hung it on a peg and sat down at her desk. 'Out with it, then.' But before Lína could begin, Erla rounded on Huldar: 'What do *you* want?'

'I was going to update you about the kid. Just thought you might be interested.' Huldar had spoken to Freyja earlier that morning, having rung her as soon as he was confident she'd be up. It wouldn't take him long to tell Erla everything they knew about the boy, since they were getting absolutely nowhere with tracing his parents.

Erla snorted and directed her gaze back to Lína. 'Fire away, then.'

Lína snapped to attention and held the page of notes up to her face. Again, Huldar was reminded of the keen girls at school. 'OK, so, the deceased was thirty-five years old and would have been thirty-six in December.'

'I see the case is about to be solved.' Erla rolled her eyes.

Lína blushed and the paper shook in her hands, but she went on doggedly: 'He graduated from the Commercial College with the third highest marks in his year.' She looked up from her summary, having apparently recovered from Erla's mockery. 'He must have been gutted. To just miss being top of your year like that. Not even second best. After all, there are no bronze medals when it comes to school-leaving exams. It must have been pretty demoralising.'

Huldar had a sneaking suspicion that Lína was speaking from personal experience.

Erla was too astonished to come up with a cutting remark. Instead she just stared at the young woman, who, oblivious to the impression she was making, peered back at the page, which was no longer trembling in her hands. 'Regardless, it was good enough to secure him a place at a respected university in America. According to his parents, he graduated three years later with a degree in finance, as one of the top students in his year, before moving to an even more respected university to do his master's. He subsequently took a job at an investment bank on Wall Street and stayed there until he changed direction and started working for a hedge fund, where he was in charge of buying and selling the creditors' claims that flooded the market following the collapse of the Icelandic banks. Since he was on a bonus contract, he'd made a killing by the time the proceedings were wound up. After that he seems to have had enough and moved back to Iceland just over a year ago. By then he was so wealthy he could afford to retire and live off his fortune for the rest of his days. Though of course he only lived for just over a year, so he never got a chance to see if his money would have lasted him into old age. Having said that, he was still managing his own investments.'

'Who stands to inherit?' Erla had pricked up her ears at the mention of money. It had already been obvious that the man had had an expensive lifestyle, but his wealth could have been illusory. However, since it now appeared he really was worth a packet, there was every chance that his murder had been motivated by money. People were prepared to kill for far lower sums than the billions of krónur he must have stashed away.

'Um . . ' Lína looked back at her notes. 'He's never been married and doesn't have any children in Iceland. So far, we haven't had a response from the American authorities to our enquiries. Of course, it was Sunday yesterday, and because of the time difference the working day hasn't yet begun over there, so we probably can't expect an answer until after lunch. But it would be surprising if he did have children in America as his parents aren't aware of any. In addition to his father and mother, there's one brother. The parents will inherit if it turns out he died intestate and didn't have any offspring. We'll need to talk to them again as the initial interview was taken when the news of their son's death was broken to them. According to the officers you sent round, the parents didn't feel up to talking much. Which is understandable.' Lína paused to snatch a quick breath before carrying on. 'We've also received details about the company Helgi set up to manage his assets. From what I understand, the situation's very complicated. Apparently several of the accounts and subsidiaries are in tax havens, so there'll be a delay before we can find out exactly how much he was worth – assuming we ever do manage to untangle his affairs. There are so many subsidiaries, offshoots and offshore companies with accounts all over the place. We're assuming the set-up is designed for tax evasion.'

'Meanwhile, our wages for investigating his murder are paid

out of the contributions of ordinary Icelandic taxpayers.' Erla snorted in disgust. 'Perhaps we should just send the case to Tortola and leave it to the police there to solve.'

Lína shuffled her feet, clearly unsure whether she was supposed to respond to this. In the end, she decided to let it go and continued reading her summary. 'Right, we've also requested information from his bank, credit-card company and telephone provider, most of which should be sent over today. We're still examining his computers and hopefully something will turn up there, though I haven't heard anything yet. They found one desktop computer and one laptop at his flat, but it's very probable that others will come to light when we search the office he rented in town. We're waiting for you to allocate the task to someone.'

Erla didn't reply to this. She wasn't about to discuss her staffing plan with Lína. 'Carry on.'

'OK. The man who examined the plank used as a gallows is fairly sure it can't have been transported to the scene on Saturday night. He says it's almost inconceivable that the perpetrator could have dragged along an object that heavy and cumbersome, while simultaneously forcing Helgi to walk through the lava-field. There would have to have been a second person involved, or he could have moved the plank there earlier. Then there's the question of whether you want to go on searching the area for the missing piece of paper that was nailed to Helgi's chest. Yesterday's search found nothing. No nail gun, no paper. And no sign of the victim's phone or keys.'

Since Erla didn't appear to think she owed Lína a response, a silence fell until, growing impatient, the younger woman coughed and continued: 'They've checked if Helgi had any connection to Bessastadir but it doesn't look like it. He didn't have any links to China either, from what we can see, though it's not impossible that he had dealings with Chinese clients during his time in America. The bank and hedge fund where he used to work should be able to help us with that. I understand you're planning to get in touch with them.' At this point Lína digressed from her dry recitation of facts to add a personal reflection: 'If you ask me, that's a sensible decision. It's more likely they'll respond to you than to a junior officer. Though perhaps you should consider asking someone even more senior, like the Police Commissioner himself, to request the information.'

Erla blew her top: 'How about the prime minister? Or, no, I know – the Pope! They're sure to get back to him.'

Huldar suppressed a smile. Lína had unwittingly touched a nerve. It had nothing to do with Erla's relative seniority or the question of whether she was important enough to avoid being put on indefinite hold if she rang an American bank. No, her touchiness was related to her linguistic abilities – or lack of them. Unusually for an Icelander, Erla was terrible at English; so bad that it was hard to see how she was hoping to conduct a conversation about Helgi's complex financial affairs. If she hadn't been so quick to flare up at Lína, she could have seized on the escape route that the young woman had inadvertently offered, and asked one of the senior officers to step in for her.

Instead, Erla changed the subject. 'What about Saturday evening? Have we got a clear picture of his movements yet?'

Lína dropped her eyes to her summary again. She hadn't blushed as much as usual at Erla's mockery; perhaps she was getting used to it. 'There are still a few gaps but what we know so far is that he went out to dinner. His parents said he was planning to meet some old school friends, who we haven't interviewed yet. The receipts in his pockets show that he took a taxi from his home at 7.30 p.m., then paid a restaurant bill at 10 p.m. From the receipt it appears that he was paying for himself and three other people. There were also receipts for drinks at the 101 Bar. The last transaction on his credit card was from there. After that we lose sight of him. There are no more card payments, so it doesn't look as if he went anywhere else, unless he paid for further drinks or food with cash. As you'll remember, his wallet was full of money, so it's possible. Or perhaps he didn't buy anything else. Hopefully we'll be able to get an answer soon, because the CCTV from the city centre is ready for analysis. We're still waiting for you to assign the job to someone. Oh yes, and we got a message from the pathologist about the post-mortem. He'll be ready soon and wants you to give him a call.'

Erla sighed. 'That's all we bloody need. Why couldn't he just name a time?' When Lína failed to leap to the patholo-gist's defence, Erla asked instead: 'What about the CCTV from his building? Any problems?' Huldar had dropped by Erla's office when he'd taken the files back to CID the previous evening, and filled her in on what he and Gudlaugur had learnt during their visit to Helgi's apartment block. When he had gone home an hour later, she had still been hard at it. From the team's central attendance record, it was clear that she hadn't gone home until around two in the morning.

Lína nodded and Huldar seized the chance to take over. Although he hadn't made notes like Lína, he was more or less up to speed with the progress of the investigation and knew she could have nothing to add. 'I'll go through the recordings if you don't have anyone else in mind. I'm familiar with the building and probably in a better position than anyone else to recognise the boy. With any luck the CCTV footage will establish when he arrived and who brought him. I've got the name of a contact at the security firm that installed the system.'

Erla didn't reply to his offer, which Huldar chose to interpret as assent. She switched on her computer and stared at the screen as it was booting up. 'Have they found the boy's parents yet?'

'No.' Huldar decided not to complicate his answer with any explanations, just state the bald truth.

'I see.' Erla looked up from the screen. 'So you barge in here before anyone else basically to tell me that there's no news about the kid?'

He resisted the temptation to point out that Lína had got in ahead of him. 'We're doing all we can. I've been speaking to the National Register and they're going to check if there are any children called Sigurdur of the right sort of age living in Reykjavík but registered elsewhere. Gudlaugur's already got hold of the parents of eleven of the sixteen relevant Sigurdurs living in Reykjavík and none of them are missing their son. He's going to keep trying the parents of the other five boys. Since the kid says he has a mother and a father we're bound to track them down in the end. Maybe they're one of the couples we haven't been able to get hold of yet. Or they're druggies, totally out of it somewhere, though none of the parents in question crop up on any of our lists of addicts. And, for what it's worth, the boy shows no signs of having grown up in a problem home.'

'Maybe his grandparents step in when necessary. It's not unusual.'

'Yes, possibly.' Huldar was sceptical, though he couldn't come up with any good reason why.

'Where's the boy now?'

'He's been taken into temporary care by social services. That's where he spent the night. I rang this morning to see if he'd said any more about his parents, but no luck. Seeing as no one's reported him missing, either they're not aware he's gone or they're in trouble of some kind. And in that case, we have to consider the possibility that they've fallen victim to the same person who killed Helgi.'

Erla nodded thoughtfully. 'That's occurred to me too, of course. As well as the chance that they were responsible for the murder, assuming the kid was right when he said Helgi might have brought him to the flat – in the middle of the night. Which would have been after Helgi's night out on the town? Or before he went out?'

Huldar couldn't answer this, so Erla asked instead: 'How's the timeline coming along?'

Lína jumped in at this point, pleased to be able to answer. 'We're working on it but there are still quite a few gaps, including the precise time of death.'

Ignoring her, Erla returned to grilling Huldar about Siggi. 'What about the person who rang to tip us off about the boy? Have we identified them yet?'

'No. The call was made to emergency services but the number was withheld, and no one saw any reason to try and trace it. The sad fact is that children's services receive around ten thousand similar calls every year, and although most don't go through the emergency number, it's not unheard of. It's a bit odd that none of the neighbours will admit to making the call. Mind you, given the state-of-the-art insulation, I'd be surprised if a bit of crying would have been overheard next door, let alone in the flats further down the corridor. It's also rather suspicious that the phone call came such a short time before the boy's alarm clock started ringing. He'd been told not to open the door or answer the phone or make any noise until the alarm had gone off. Maybe it was just a strange coincidence, but I don't buy it.'

Erla frowned. 'We'll go over all that later at the meeting.'

Lína cleared her throat. 'There's one thing I think you should look into.'

'I can't wait.' Erla's expression said the exact opposite.

'The choice of location. Why the Gallows Rock? Surely we need to ask ourselves that?'

'Do you really imagine you're telling me something I don't know?'

'No.' Bright red spots appeared on Lína's cheeks, but she ploughed on anyway. 'If it's OK with you, I'd like to see if I can find any possible links or reasons why that particular spot was chosen.'

'Fine. Whatever.' Erla turned her attention back to her computer screen without another word. Huldar took the hint: *Thanks. Now get lost.* He exited smartly, giving Lína a sign to follow suit. Otherwise she was perfectly capable of standing there until Erla threw her out.

Huldar's eyes were dry from staring at the screen. After blinking a few times, he clicked on the next file. He'd been hoping to find what he was looking for in the footage from Helgi's building before his next meeting with Erla, but it wasn't looking promising. The problem was the sheer number of security cameras in the apartment block. No doubt this excessive coverage helped to give the residents peace of mind, but far from improving their security, it simply got in the way of processing the information the cameras contained. There were so many files that it took him ages to work out which area he was looking at, because they weren't numbered according to any system he could understand. The employee from the security firm who was in charge of the codes wasn't answering his phone and apparently no one else there could help.

Nevertheless, Huldar had managed to find a clip showing Helgi leaving the building by the front door. Since they already knew what time his taxi had arrived, this had simplified the search. But nothing was known of Siggi's movements, which made things much trickier. And to complicate matters still further, the building had three separate entrances, one at the front, one at the back and a third via the underground garage. Huldar had already fast-forwarded through the footage of the front door without spotting a single child. He had yet to locate the files relating to the other two entrances.

The image of yet another corridor appeared on screen. They all looked identical to him: all furnished with those giant exotic plants that Huldar hadn't seen for sale at any garden centre; they looked as if they'd been ripped up by the roots from some endangered rainforest. The residents did nothing to personalise their flats, either: they all had identical doormats and it was impossible to read the numbers on the discreet labels in this low-res recording. Huldar clicked on fast-forward in the hope that this was the right floor. He was beginning to despair when he saw a door open and a familiar face appeared in the gap. As far as he could tell, it was Helgi, though he looked a lot healthier than the man he'd seen on the pathologist's table.

Huldar paused the picture, rewound a bit and noted down the time when Helgi had appeared in the frame. It was just before half past seven, so presumably he was on his way down to the taxi that would take him to the restaurant. Helgi strode along the corridor, but instead of heading straight to the lift, he went in the opposite direction, towards a round hatch in the wall, which must be the rubbish chute. There he paused to tear a piece of paper to shreds, before opening the hatch and chucking in the scraps. He slammed the hatch, then opened it again, apparently in order to slam it even harder. His behaviour suggested that the piece of paper had annoyed him. Huldar rewound and enlarged the image in the hope of seeing exactly what Helgi was holding. He thought he could make out an envelope as well as a piece of paper, but couldn't be sure. It was probably just some post that had got on his nerves, but you never knew. Anyway, at least this proved that Huldar had hit on footage from the right floor.

Feeling pleased with himself, he double-checked the date, just to be on the safe side. After fast-forwarding for what felt like ages without any sign of the boy, his conviction that he was getting somewhere began to fade. Finally, though, Siggi popped up in the frame – at quarter past three on Sunday morning.

Huldar slowed the playback and called out to Gudlaugur, keeping his voice as low as possible. The last thing Huldar wanted was the whole team breathing down their necks. Once Gudlaugur had come round the desk, he rewound a bit and together they watched as the boy was led to Helgi's flat.

Unconsciously, they both bent closer to the screen but it didn't help: the face of the man holding Siggi's hand remained hidden. He had his hood up and was wearing a baseball cap underneath. Only once did they catch a glimpse of his profile, only to realise that he had a cloth or scarf tied over the lower half of his face, like the baddie in a Western. At this point it dawned on Huldar why Siggi had put his hand over Helgi's nose and mouth when asked to identify him from a photo. Obviously the man had been aware of the CCTV cameras and taken precautions to conceal his identity. Although Huldar knew it was unwise to leap to conclusions, he was fairly sure this wasn't the first time the man had been there. He must have visited before to scope out the cameras.

Despite the disguise, the figure was unmistakeably a man. It should be possible to work out his approximate height relative to the boy. He was of average build, neither fat nor unnaturally thin. His clothes were similarly unremarkable: jeans, a mid-length anorak with a hood, and trainers. They could identify the brand of those, at least. However, none of this was enough to establish whether it was Helgi or someone else entirely. Perhaps the man's face would be visible in other clips, as he entered the building or climbed the stairs, for example. But if he wasn't a complete fool, he'd have hidden his features before entering the building.

They watched the man pull a bunch of keys from his pocket and insert one in the lock. It took him a while because he was hampered by his thick gloves. While this was going on, they could see Siggi staring around with a dazed expression. His attention seemed to be caught by the large plant container, and he gaped at it for a while until, apparently bored, he yawned and turned back to his companion.

The man managed to open the door, but instead of going inside, he bent down to Siggi and remained stooping for a moment. They couldn't tell if his lips were moving because of the cloth, but, as Siggi nodded, it seemed likely. Then he straightened up and both figures disappeared through the door. Before Siggi vanished from sight, he glanced back and stared straight into the camera lens for a split second, as if looking Huldar and Gudlaugur in the eye.

Huldar paused the recording. 'What do you reckon? Is that Helgi?'

Gudlaugur released the breath he'd been holding. 'I just can't tell. But those aren't the clothes he was wearing when he died. If it is him, he obviously didn't want to be recognised, which is a bit odd considering that he was taking the boy back to his own flat. Why didn't he take the kid somewhere else if he didn't want to be identified?'

Huldar started uploading the file to the shared drive. He wanted to get it to Erla and let her know that he'd managed to pinpoint the time of Siggi's arrival and Helgi's departure, and that Helgi had thrown something away in an apparent fit of temper. 'That depends on what the boy was doing there. I just can't come up with any rational explanation. And neither can anyone else, from what I hear.'

Gudlaugur hovered at Huldar's side, showing no signs of returning to his own desk. Huldar, who was getting a crick in his neck from looking up at him, prompted: 'What?'

'Did Erla happen to mention who she wants to go through the CCTV from the city centre?' The question sounded casual but Huldar knew his colleague well enough to realise there was more to it.

'No. Why do you ask?'

'No reason.' Colour rose revealingly in Gudlaugur's face.

'Oh, come on. Out with it. Why do you want to know?'

'I was just hoping I might get the job. I don't really feel like traipsing around the lava-field at Gálgahraun on a wild-goose chase, or having to rummage around in the dustbins at Helgi's building.'

'I see.' Gudlaugur's mention of Gálgahraun reminded Huldar of the state the young man had been in at the crime scene yesterday morning. 'You weren't by any chance out yourself on Saturday night?'

Gudlaugur's colour deepened, the flush reaching up to his hairline. 'That's not the reason.'

'No, sure it isn't.' Huldar had hit the nail on the head, though he took no pleasure in the fact and had no wish to rub Gudlaugur's nose in it. 'We should be able to fix it for you to get the job. There aren't that many of us left.' The Chinese delegation hadn't only created problems regarding the discovery of the body, it had also caused a staffing shortage, since so many officers were needed for security duty. 'Anyway, I thought your ankle was playing up?'

'What?'

'You know, after you sprained it in the lava-field yesterday?' Gudlaugur was being so slow on the uptake that Huldar was forced to spell it out for him. 'Pity your injury will get in the way of you doing anything that requires a lot of walking. Maybe Erla could find you something to do here at the station. Like watching CCTV footage. You get me?'

Gudlaugur nodded. The blood that had coloured his cheeks was beginning to recede. 'Of course, yes, thanks.' He set off with an exaggerated limp in the direction of Erla's office.

Chapter 9

Heidrún folded the newspaper and pushed it away. As usual, there was nothing of interest. A recent poll showed that support for the various political parties had shifted by a small number of percentage points; tourists caught short by the lack of toilet facilities continued to scandalise the Icelanders by doing their business on private property, and China's foreign minister was enjoying his visit in spite of the weather. Apart from that it was nothing but press releases masquerading as news. This was probably just as well since she only had time to scan the headlines. The demands of her job meant she couldn't immerse herself in the papers any more than she could surf the net.

For now, the four children in her care seemed perfectly content playing with the worn old toys scattered across the floor. They made do with the faded wooden bricks, the Barbie doll with the hopelessly matted hank of hair, and the toy road with its badly fitting pieces. That's all there was. The usual toys had all been sent off to be sterilised after a boy had been diagnosed with measles. He was now in hospital and Heidrún hoped this would bring it home to his mother how foolish it had been to refuse to get her son vaccinated. It was ironic, since she seemed perfectly happy to expose him to rampant drug abuse at home. But Heidrún doubted the message would get through.

The official care home had far exceeded its maximum capacity of twelve children and, since there was no sign of the new accommodation supposedly in the works, social services had resorted to renting this flat to house the overspill when necessary. Although not particularly large, it could accommodate up to six children, but the funding only stretched to cover a single carer on duty. Not only did this make life difficult when there were more than two charges, but Heidrún missed having adult company when she did her shifts here. Still, the situation was only temporary, like the placements themselves.

Heidrún watched the children play. The differences in their ages meant there was no apparent logic to their game. The only girl in the group, who, at seven, was the oldest, had appointed herself as mediator, handing out the toys as she saw fit and making sure they were regularly rotated so none of the younger kids got bored or jealous. She was clearly used to the role, for the sad reason that her mother was an addict. According to the social workers' reports, she did everything she could to make the situation at home look better than it was, in order to give the impression that her mother was coping. Once, when social services knocked on the door, they found that she had picked a dandelion in the garden and stuck it behind her unconscious mother's ear. She had only been four years old at the time. From her child's point of view, the flower had made her mother look pretty, clean and sober, like other mothers: capable of looking after her, in other words. But the social workers hadn't been fooled and the little girl had become a regular guest in care. The tragedy of it was that Heidrún had been working in the city's care homes for long enough to remember the girl's mother at the same age, in the same heart-rending predicament.

The four children playing on the floor were recent arrivals. It was often like that over weekends. The girl had been brought in on Saturday lunchtime after her mother had over-dosed on Fentanyl and been taken to hospital. As the child's extended family were no more reliable than her mother, temporary care was the only answer. The two brothers, one two, the other five, were in much the same situation. They'd been brought in later on Saturday afternoon when no other solution could be found. Their parents were alcoholics rather than junkies.

It was obvious that the fourth child, Siggi, came from a very different background. His clothes were clean and it hadn't been necessary to start by washing him, combing the tangles out of his hair, cutting his nails or dressing him in borrowed clothes. He was trusting, looked you straight in the eye and ate the food that was put in front of him without protest. He even put the lid down on the toilet after he'd been for a pee. According to the man who had brought the boy in, he had been taken into temporary care because they were unable to track down his parents. Nothing more was said but it was clear to Heidrún that if the parents were addicts, they must be very unusual ones.

The children were showing signs of growing bored. The younger brother started bashing Barbie's head on the floor and the girl tried in vain to stop him, upset by the violence. Seeing that she was becoming more distressed with every blow, Heidrún stepped in. 'Right, kids. You must be getting hungry. How would you like something to eat?' It was still ten minutes until lunch but it would take them a while to help her lay the table and get seated. By the time they'd done that, hopefully it wouldn't be too long before the food arrived.

Heidrún got to her feet and scooped up the younger brother, who was still holding the Barbie and now started bashing her with it. She had to prise off his fingers one by one before she could get it away from him. As the doll dropped to the floor, he started bawling but calmed down when Heidrún carried him into the kitchen. By the time she had settled him in the high chair at the kitchen table, Barbie had been forgotten.

The girl and the older brother trailed into the kitchen after Heidrún but Siggi stayed put. Heidrún interpreted this behaviour as further evidence that the boy came from a good home. He took it for granted that he would be fed when he was hungry, so preferred to carry on playing now he had all the toys to himself. Whereas the other children, afraid of being forgotten, clung to her heels.

'What's for lunch?' The girl stared at the bare kitchen table, the disappointment on her face revealing that she didn't hold out much hope of getting anything to eat. The poor kid was so thin, it obviously wouldn't be the first time she'd gone without a meal. Heidrún had needed to take in the elastic on the tracksuit bottoms the little girl had borrowed.

'Rice pudding.'

The girl cheered up but then, worry shadowing her face again, asked if there would be cinnamon sugar. When Heidrún said yes, it was as if a weight had been lifted off her shoulders. She even started humming a tune as she took the bowls to lay them on the table. Heidrún, judging the older brother too young and clumsy to be entrusted with anything breakable, handed him the plastic beakers for their milk and four spoons. When the children had finished, the table looked as if there had been a minor earthquake: everything was more or less in the right place, but a little askew.

Heidrún called Siggi, who appeared a moment later and took his place at the table. He seemed a little dejected as he stared into the empty bowl in front of him. 'I want to go home,' he said dolefully.

The girl, who was sitting next to him, put a hand on his shoulder, leant over and said kindly: 'You can go home soon. We always go home again, but sometimes not for a little while.' The older brother, who was sitting opposite, nodded vigorously.

Heidrún was about to change the subject, before the children could become too downhearted, when the bell rang. She had to go and open the door for the delivery, and by the time she got back, it was too late. The older children were looking tearful and even the smell of food didn't cheer them up. Their chatter broke off as she entered the room.

'What were you talking about, kids?'

'Nothing,' the older three answered in unison, while the youngest banged his plastic beaker with his spoon and stuck out his tongue. 'Oh, really? I thought I could hear you talking.' Heidrún took the rice-pudding container out of the bag and began serving up. 'Is it a secret?'

The older brother couldn't restrain himself. Squirming in his seat, he said in a rush: 'Siggi says his mummy's lost. He says the bad man's taken her.' A pause for breath, then he went on, just as insistently: 'So he can't ever go home, can he?'

'Eat your food now,' Heidrún said. 'You shouldn't be saying silly things like that. Of course Siggi's going home again, just like the rest of you.'

'But he said the bad man kills people.'

'Now, now. There is no bad man.' A familiar ringtone sounded from the playroom and Heidrún hurried out to fetch her phone, hoping the children wouldn't carry on this conversation while she was out of the room. It turned out to be her sister, wanting to know if she'd received an invitation to their brother's ex-wife's fortieth birthday party. While she listened to her sister's exclamations of disapproval, Heidrún's wandering gaze alighted on the Barbie. She cut short the conversation, promising to call back later.

Having pocketed her phone, she went over to the clothes airer standing by one of the windows. This morning she had hung two dishcloths and a threadbare towel over it, but now these had been joined by the doll. She was dangling just above the floor, her tiny plastic feet, shaped to fit high heels, pointing downwards as if they were desperately scrabbling to reach the parquet floor. A piece of string, taken from the car that the youngest children liked to tow around, had been wound round her neck and tied to the clothes airer. Only Siggi could have done this since he had been the only one left in the room.

Although he couldn't have meant to, it looked as if the little boy had deliberately hanged the poor old Barbie. The effect was oddly disturbing. Heidrún untied the string and the doll fell to the floor. Silly as it was, she felt better after that, and even more so once she'd unwound the string from around Barbie's long neck. Having tidied her away in the toy box, Heidrún tucked the string into her pocket. The little girl, who was understandably over-sensitive when it came to any kind of violence, would be upset if Siggi repeated the game.

Heidrún went back into the kitchen to find that an ominous hush had fallen. She wondered if she should ask Siggi why he had done it but was immediately distracted by a much more pressing problem, far more serious to the children than the execution of a Barbie doll, the existence of a bad man, or the question of who would or wouldn't be allowed to go home. There was no cinnamon sugar: the caterers had forgotten to include it.

Chapter 10

Thormar was at the restaurant already, his gaze fixed on the door. It was quarter past twelve and there was still no sign of his friends. The meeting had been his suggestion, as had the time and place. It was suitably dark in here and most of the clientele were foreign tourists. Far more sensible than meeting in the woods on Öskjuhlíd Hill, that classic spot for Icelandic skulduggery, where anyone who saw them was bound to be suspicious. At least there was no chance of any locals wandering in here.

The interior designers had pulled out all the stops to come up with a style that could best be described as 'post-modern tourist trap', featuring stuffed puffins, large framed posters of volcanic eruptions and mediocre paintings of the hot springs at Geysir. The staff had been forced into traditional Icelandic *lopapeysa* jumpers and Viking helmets with yellow plastic horns. The menu hadn't escaped the designers' attentions either and clearly wasn't aimed at locals. The version Thormar had been given was in English. He got an odd look from the waitress when he asked if she had one in Icelandic. Apparently the answer was no.

Finally the door opened to admit Tómas, after which Thormar was no longer the only customer without a backpack. His suit, smart coat and thin scarf revealed that, like him, Tómas had slipped out of work to be there. He was an economist at the Central Bank, and looked like an ambitious young man on his way up – though for all Thormar knew he could have reached a plateau. It was the sort of thing you could only see in hindsight.

The door had barely closed behind them before it opened again to reveal Gunni, also in a business suit, looking, if anything, even smarter. He worked in finance and was always sharply attired, except on dress-down Fridays.

They were all here – all apart from Helgi, that is. But Thormar was fairly sure he wouldn't be coming.

'What the hell is this place?' Gunni loosened his scarf and chucked it into the booth. 'You can hardly move for top-class restaurants around here and you go and suggest this dump. What's going on?'

Thormar didn't want to explain. He was afraid they wouldn't take the video seriously; afraid of looking like an idiot, a pussy. Instead of answering, he started passing round menus. This did nothing to lessen Gunni's incredulity. 'Jesus. Is there anything edible among this shit? A Viking burger? What the . . . ?'

For once Tómas said nothing. He studied the menu with an intensity normally reserved for reading the sales contract on a house. This was so out of character that Thormar took it as a sign that he shared his fears. Unlike Gunni.

'How did the birthday party go?' Tómas put down his menu without saying what he was planning to order. 'Dísa was completely knackered when she got home. So was Silla.'

'Oh, fine, good.' Thormar refrained from asking how the hell Tómas's wife Silla could have been knackered when she'd done nothing all afternoon but sit on her arse gossiping and being waited on hand and foot. His daughter Dísa, in contrast, had torn around the flat like a mad thing, burning up more energy than a gym-goer in January.

Gunni, being childless, hadn't the slightest interest in kids' parties.

'Mate, what are we doing in this shithole? Seriously?' Having surveyed the other customers in disbelief, Gunni turned back to his companions.

'Just because, all right?' Thormar knew how absurd it would sound the minute he admitted that he was worried their conversation might be overheard or that they were being bugged. 'It's no worse than anywhere else and we're less likely to be interrupted every few minutes by your mates.' Gunni collected club memberships like nerds collect stamps. Golf club, hunting club, Round Table, cigar club, cookery club, wine-tasting club, running club, in addition to volunteer work for whatever political party he happened to be supporting at the time. He couldn't move without bumping into a fellow member of one of these associations.

'Well, I'm going to have the Glacier Sandwich.' Typical Tómas. He always tried to avoid any kind of confrontation or unpleasantness. With this intervention he was hoping to prevent a row from brewing between Thormar and Gunni. If all else failed, he could be relied on to come up with a remark about the weather. 'Aren't you two going to make your minds up? The waitress looks like she's heading our way.'

Gunni rolled his eyes. 'I don't want anything.'

A *lopapeysa*-clad waitress came to stand at the end of the table. Her helmet was on crooked and she straightened it, smiling shyly, seeming embarrassed to encounter other

Icelanders while wearing this costume. Her pen and note-book poised, she asked what they'd like, then scribbled down their orders. Thormar wasn't remotely surprised when, contrary to his declaration that he didn't want anything, Gunni ordered the day's special with a show of indifference. Nor was it unexpected when he asked for a large beer as well.

They watched in silence as the willowy girl walked away. When they turned back to each other, Thormar decided to broach the subject. If he didn't do it now, he risked missing his chance. The moment the food arrived their attention would be distracted, and the lower the level of beer in Gunni's glass, the less he would care. It was hard enough to get him to take anything seriously when he was sober. And the instant they finished eating, the others would be impatient to leave, so it would be pointless trying to raise the issue then. 'Have either of you heard from Helgi?' he asked.

Neither of them had, though it transpired that they'd both tried to get hold of him. Thormar had been expecting this, but he was still disappointed and could feel his anxiety growing. 'Do you think it could have anything to do with the video?'

Gunni spluttered into his glass. 'Are you crazy? That was just some hoax. Something off the internet.'

'The man looked like Helgi to me. He was the spitting image of him.' Thormar had meant to leave it to one of the others to point this out. He didn't want to risk being called gullible. 'Did neither of you notice?'

Tómas shrugged and answered noncommittally: 'At first I thought it was him, but then I wasn't sure. It wasn't exactly high-definition. Wasn't it just some hoax, like Gunni said?

Something Helgi posted because it looked like him? Wasn't that the whole joke?'

'Then why isn't he answering his phone?'

Gunni rolled his eyes heavenwards again. 'Are you kidding, man? You know Helgi's always abroad. He's probably on a plane with his phone off.'

'In that case, where can he be flying to? SpaceX hasn't started offering commercial flights yet. Helgi's phone's been switched off for at least thirty-six hours, so he'd have landed by now if he was travelling anywhere on Earth. I started calling him at lunchtime yesterday and I tried several times overnight as well.' Thormar read in Tómas's eyes that he shared his concern, though he wasn't admitting to it. But seeing that Gunni wasn't convinced, he persisted: 'He didn't mention anything about going abroad either. In fact, he said he was going to drop off a present for Hallbera before the party yesterday, but he never turned up.'

Silence fell. After a few moments it was broken by Gunni. 'It is a bit strange, but there has to be some explanation.'

'Well, what is it, then? It's not funny and I can't see the point of the post. We didn't set up the forum for shit like that.'

Tómas seemed to have given up hope that the conversation would move on to the footie. Putting down his knife and fork, he took out his phone. 'I tell you what I found odd . . .' He paused, fiddling with the screen, then held it up to them and asked: 'Who's this *administrator* who uploaded the video?'

The phone was passed round. Gunni barely glanced at it before handing it on to Thormar and taking a mouthful of beer. 'We've all got admin status,' he pointed out. 'It must have been Helgi, like I said. Some kind of sick joke.' He drank again, then wiped the froth off his upper lip.

'But why Helgi?' Tómas said. 'It could just as well have been one of us. Like you say, we're all registered as administrators.'

They all talked over each other in their haste to deny responsibility. Thormar was still staring at the screen. 'Tommi's right. How come the post is by an *administrator*? If Helgi or one of us was responsible, our username would have appeared. It shouldn't be any different from the other stuff we post.'

He held out the phone and Gunni took it, frowning. Finally it seemed to be sinking in that something was wrong. They watched him tapping the screen, then he looked up and his usual careless air had vanished. 'What's going on?'

'What?' Tómas was the first to grab the phone. 'Jesus.'

Too impatient to wait, Thormar demanded: 'What? What is it?'

'There are five users registered on the forum. Us three, Helgi, and someone with the username *administrator*.' His face drained of colour, Tómas passed the phone to Thormar.

Thormar stared at the screen. There it was, in black and white, on the admin page: five people had access. But that wasn't right.

'When did this extra user turn up?' There was a tremor in Tómas's voice but none of the others were surprised: they shared his anxiety.

Thormar searched the editing interface and licked his lips nervously. 'Just over a year ago. You wouldn't notice unless you checked the admin page and I haven't looked at it since we set up the forum. How long ago is that? Ten years?'

'Something like that. I've had no reason to check the admin page either. How can it have happened?' Tómas reached for his phone but Thormar held it away so he could keep looking. Tómas asked again, sounding angry. 'Who granted this guy access?'

'Guy? It could be a woman.' For an instant a knot of cold fear constricted Thormar's stomach. Surely Sigrún or one of the other wives hadn't found out about the site? A moment later common sense kicked in, telling him there was no way she would have stayed silent about it for a whole year if she had. He searched for information but couldn't find it, which was hardly surprising since the page had been deliberately set up to protect the users' anonymity. 'There's no indication as to who gave him – or her – access. No name, email or anything else. But whoever it is has been lying low for a whole year. They haven't posted anything except this video.'

'What about viewing stuff, though? Have they been looking at what we've posted?' Tómas voiced the question that was on all their lips. The forum was strictly for their eyes only.

'I can't tell.' Thormar gave up and handed the phone back to Tómas. 'But whoever it is must have seen our posts. It goes without saying.'

None of them could speak. They were all thinking the same thing; all mentally reviewing the material they'd uploaded. For the entertainment of their friends – absolutely no one else.

Thormar's fear about what had happened to Helgi had been replaced by fear for himself. If the forum went public, he was done for. Both professionally and personally. The same applied to the others. Helgi too. Even his money wouldn't be able to shield him from the resulting shitshow.

They were still sitting there in silence when the waitress in the silly costume returned with their food. None of them had any appetite and when they left, such was the gravity of the situation that there was still beer in the bottom of Gunni's glass.

Chapter 11

The post-mortem was over and Huldar congratulated himself yet again on having successfully dodged it. Erla had taken Lína along instead and, judging by the colour of her face, it seemed Erla had finally managed to jolt her composure. She was always pale but now she was positively ashen.

'Drink this. You'll feel better.' Huldar handed Lína an ice-cold Coke from the vending machine. He wanted to know what had emerged from the post-mortem and thought he'd learn more from Lína with her fantastically retentive memory than he would from Erla. He watched her swig the Coke, waiting until she put down the can before starting the interrogation.

'Well, what did we learn?'

'Ugh. A lot of things I'd rather not know. But the most significant was that they found Flunitrazepam in the urine sample they took from Helgi yesterday. They're waiting for the blood test to provide a more accurate reading but the pathologist expects it to confirm the results.'

The drug was better known by its brand name Rohypnol, the 'date-rape drug'. It was a sleeping pill with unfortunate side effects, often implicated in rape cases, although its presence could rarely be proved. Personally, Huldar would rather lie awake all night with insomnia than allow himself to be knocked out by a so-called rape drug.

Lína proceeded to lecture him as if she were the experienced cop and he the rookie. 'The drug is a sedative-hypnotic, almost ten times stronger than Valium. It starts to work about twenty minutes after being ingested and the effects peak after two hours. They last for around four to six hours, but the influence can be felt for up to ten hours after the drug is taken. Sometimes longer. Not that this would have applied to Helgi as he died while the drug was still active.'

Huldar raised his eyebrows. 'Did you learn all that on your course or did you manage to take it in during the post-mortem?'

Lína looked embarrassed. 'During the post-mortem. I only survived by focusing all my attention on what the pathologist was saying – as long as it wasn't anything to do with saws, scalpels or forceps.' She shuddered. 'Excuse me if I'm concentrating too much on the details but it helps me to stay detached.'

Huldar smiled. 'I understand – better than you think. I can't stomach post-mortems either. Next time I'll try your method. Maybe I'll even learn something. Usually I'm too busy trying not to throw up into the victim's chest cavity.'

Lína seemed relieved to hear that she wasn't alone in her squeamishness. She smiled at Huldar before resuming her report. It was a vivid, pretty smile, in stark contrast to what she was saying. 'In other words, Helgi was under the influence of the drug at the time of his death. Which means it would have been relatively easy for his killer to get him to the site. He would have obeyed orders without protest, as long as the dose wasn't too high. If it was, he'd have been half paralysed and his murderer would have had to carry him.'

'How would somebody find out the appropriate dose? Can

you google it? I doubt the manufacturer's instructions include information on how much to give someone to turn them into a zombie.'

'I don't know, but I can check. Researching is what I do best.'

'I don't doubt it.' Huldar grinned at her. 'If Erla hasn't already given you a job, it would be great if you could do that. Anyway, back to the post-mortem. What else?'

'The pathologist estimates that Helgi died between half past two and three o'clock on Sunday morning.'

Huldar stroked his jaw, the harsh stubble reminding him that he'd forgotten to shave. Too bad, it would have to wait. He wasn't surprised that the time of death couldn't be pinned down any more accurately. Practically the only way to get a precise answer was if the victim died in front of another person, preferably a doctor. 'Siggi popped up on the CCTV footage at quarter past three. So it can't have been Helgi who took him to the flat. He would have been hanging from a noose on Álftanes by then, not only doped up on Rohypnol but dead.'

'And not just doped up. According to the pathologist he was drunk at the time of his death, too. He would have been really out of it on a combination of Flunitrazepam and alcohol.'

'How drunk exactly?'

'He had a reading of 1.2 per mille. Drunk, but not totally intoxicated. According to the table I found online, in that state his speech would have been slurred and his reasoning and judgement impaired. His ability to control important motor functions would also have been affected.'

Huldar was familiar with the condition – more familiar

than he was prepared to admit to this bright-eyed, no doubt clean-living, young woman. 'How did the pathologist reckon the Rohypnol entered Helgi's bloodstream?'

'He couldn't find any puncture marks, so it's unlikely to have been administered by injection. The contents of his stomach showed that . . .' Lína's mouth twisted involuntarily and she paused for a moment to collect herself before carrying on. 'Apparently Helgi had vomited, so his stomach contents weren't as complete as they'd have liked. But what remained was consistent with what he'd ordered at the restaurant, and there was nothing to indicate that he'd eaten again later that evening. Given that he left the restaurant at just past 10 p.m., the drug can't have been in his food. It starts to take effect after twenty minutes and, if it had, he wouldn't have been capable of buying drinks at 101 Bar. The pathologist thinks his drink was probably spiked, which is the usual method of slipping someone the drug. He says it's not impossible that Helgi took it deliberately. But I don't believe that for a minute.'

'He could have thought he was taking something else – Ecstasy, for example. Or meth or coke, if it was in powder form. But he's unlikely to have made that mistake if he was a habitual user.'

'Hmm.' Lína didn't give the impression of being familiar with drug culture. She looked more like the type who drinks one beer, then orders another only to find she can't finish it. So it was only natural that she should be unconvinced. He could guess what she was thinking: why would a wealthy man like Helgi, who had everything he wanted, mess up his life with dope? In time she would learn that it wasn't quite that straightforward. The most unlikely people fell into the trap of taking drugs to fill the void in their lives, many realising too late that their habit only exacerbated the emptiness.

'Anyway, what was the cause of death? Hanging?'

'Yes. Asphyxia caused by the noose around his neck. The nail in his chest hadn't penetrated any vital organs. It would have been horribly painful but not fatal, unless he developed an infection.'

'Nasty.'

'Yes.' Lína shuddered again. 'I can't begin to describe what it was like when the pathologist pulled out the nail. There was this sucking sound . . .' She broke off.

'That's quite enough of that, thanks.' Huldar had absolutely no wish to hear the grisly details. He hadn't dodged the post-mortem only to be forced to listen to the audio version. 'Anything else significant come to light?'

'No. Except that Helgi was in great shape and very healthy. He seems to have taken good care of himself.'

'What a waste of time that turned out to be.' Huldar resisted the temptation to add that Helgi would have done better to take up smoking than to sweat it out in the gym.

Lína's face suddenly lit up. 'Oh. And another thing. It's got nothing to do with the post-mortem, actually, but I looked into the history of the murder scene. Both the Gallows Rock itself and the surrounding area, in case there was any connection.'

'And what did you find out?'

Lína smiled. 'Loads. Too much, probably.' She picked up a printout that had been painstakingly formatted like the summary she had read out to Erla earlier. 'Right, the Gálgahraun lava-field is part of Búrfellshraun, which is believed to have formed about eight thousand years ago.'

Huldar was privately amused. He knew he ought to point out that this was hardly relevant but he didn't want to spoil her moment since she seemed so pleased. Better let her finish reading, then borrow her pen and cross out anything superfluous before she presented it to Erla. Unfortunately, there would be nothing left if all the information was of this type.

'Anyway. The lava-field derives its name from the cleft rock where we found Helgi: the "Gallows Rock", where criminals were supposedly hanged and interred under piles of stones. Although there are no written records of executions being carried out there, apparently it was used for judicial punishments back in the days of the Kópavogur Assembly. The rocks are visible from Bessastadir, so the Danish king's representative could watch without having to leave the house. Handy.' Glancing up, she smiled apologetically. 'Erla already mentioned the bit about executions on Sunday. Sorry.'

'No problem. It never hurts to repeat things. Carry on.'

Heartened, Lína continued reading. 'The lava-field is extremely rugged, full of craters, ridges, fissures and jumbled rocks, as you'll remember.' She paused. 'I also checked out people and events linked to the area, both online and in the police database.'

'And what did you find?'

'Various things. The lava-field's best known for the fact that Jóhannes Kjarval painted countless pictures of it.' Seeing that Huldar was distinctly underwhelmed by this information, Lína added: 'I realise that's not really relevant in this case. But there's more.'

Huldar crossed his fingers in the hope of finally hearing something relevant.

'The area crops up several times in the police database. In October 2013 a number of protestors, calling themselves "Friends of the Lava", were arrested while trying to block the construction of a road through the southern end of the lavafield.'

'Did Helgi have any connection to the protestors?'

'No. Not that I can see.'

'Go on, then.' Huldar was beginning to despair. There would be practically nothing left by the time he'd crossed out the irrelevant parts.

'OK. In the last twenty years, three bodies have been washed up on the coast near the Gallows Rock. Eighteen years ago a sixty-year-old man, who had walked into the sea on the southern shore of Skerjafjördur, turned up there. Or rather his coat, shoes and wallet were found there. He'd been suffering from serious depression and the circumstances surrounding his death were not regarded as suspicious. Five years ago a young woman was found on the shore. She's thought to have entered the sea in Fossvogur. She was also struggling with depression, but had so much alcohol in her blood that her death could have been an accident rather than suicide, though the latter's more likely. Her body showed no signs of violence and her belongings were found at the top of the beach. Then, three years ago a man of twenty-eight was washed up there. He'd drowned while swimming in Nauthólsvík Cove and the current swept him over to Álftanes.'

'Two suicides and one drowning.'

'Yes.'

'And we have no reason to believe that any of these deaths were suspicious?'

'I'd need to look into the cases in more detail. But the

conclusion of all the investigations was that there was no reason to suspect foul play.'

'Anything else?'

'Yes. One more recent case.'

'Which is?' Huldar's interest was roused. Perhaps Lína had discovered a lead after all.

'The police were called there last spring in connection with the illegal collection of eiderdown. Down theft, in other words.'

'Down theft?'

'Yes. There was a dispute between the local landowner and a man taking eiderdown from nests on his property without a permit. The thief was arrested and the case was sent to the prosecution service. It doesn't look as if it went any further, though. At least, it never went to court and no fine was issued.'

'Don't tell me Helgi was one of the men involved?'

Lína's face fell. 'No, unfortunately. I can't see any link. But guess what?'

'What?'

'The Gálgahraun lava-field borders a property called Selskard, which belongs to the family of none other than Bjarni Benediktsson, the ex-prime minister.'

Huldar found himself at a loss for words. Rubbing his jaw, he wondered which party Lína supported. Young, heart in the right place, keen. If she hadn't been training to join the police, he'd have had her down as a Left-Green. 'I think we can rest assured that Bjarni Benediktsson didn't have anything to do with this, Lína. Or any other member of his family either.'

'I know that.' Lína sounded annoyed. 'But Helgi was an

investor and there are potential building sites on the property.
Perhaps the killing had a political dimension.'

Huldar dismissed this far-fetched theory. 'Do you mind if
I go through and cross out the bits I think you should drop
before you give this to Erla?'

Lína handed him the report and watched in dismay as he
put a line through the bulk of the text. All that was left was
the information from the police database. The two suicides,
the drowning and the protest by the Friends of the Lava.
'There you go. You'll thank me later.' He grinned at her but
received no smile in return.

Gudlaugur had tilted his monitor. Only slightly, but just
enough to prevent passers-by from seeing the screen. Erla,
taken in by his fake limp, had given him the job he'd been
angling for.

'Any sign of Helgi?' Huldar dropped heavily into his chair,
trying not to spill his brimming coffee. The question he really
wanted to ask was whether Gudlaugur had come across any
footage of himself.

'No. Not yet.'

Huldar guessed that although it would have made more
sense to track Helgi from the bar, Gudlaugur would have
begun by checking the CCTV from cameras close to the clubs
he himself had visited that night, hoping that his and Helgi's
paths hadn't crossed. The clubs he remembered, anyway.
Going by the state of him on Sunday morning, he was bound
to have a few gaps in his memory. Huldar sipped his coffee,
then thought what the hell. 'Have you spotted yourself yet?'
he asked. 'The unexpurgated version?'

Gudlaugur was not amused. 'I'm not looking for myself.'

'No, right. My mistake.' Huldar had to suppress a smile as he took another sip. He couldn't deny that it was a pleasant sensation to watch someone else squirming for a change. 'Tell me one thing. I promise to keep my mouth shut, but what are you going to do with the clips you turn up in?'

'I don't suppose we'll have been at the same bars, so if I do turn up, it's unlikely the victim will be anywhere near.' When Huldar didn't comment, Gudlaugur hastened to add: 'What I mean is, he was loaded, whereas I have to watch every króna. He's sure to have been in the more exclusive bars.'

'That's where you're wrong.' Huldar jumped at this chance to spin out the conversation. 'When people are drunk, they're happy to slum it. They just want to go where the action is. And that's usually where the younger, less well-off crowd hangs out. I wouldn't be too confident, if I were you.'

'I'm not worried about turning up on camera with him. Believe me.'

'Fine. In that case, what's that pub you're checking out? I thought you were meant to be searching the exclusive bars for Helgi?'

Gudlaugur hesitated. Lying didn't come naturally to him. In the end he tried to wriggle out of it by firing back at Huldar: 'Does it matter?'

'Nope. Just curious. I don't spend much time in swanky bars, so I was wondering if I'd recognise the one you're looking at.'

'I very much doubt you'd know it.' Gudlaugur lapsed into silence. All that could be heard was the clicking of his mouse. Then he pushed back his chair and got up, saying he was going to fetch a coffee.

'Don't forget to limp.' Huldar smirked as he watched his colleague hobble over to the coffee machine. Gudlaugur kept glancing over his shoulder, clearly worried that Huldar was going to sneak a look at his computer. But the thought hadn't occurred to him. He didn't need visual confirmation that he was right about what Gudlaugur was up to. When Gudlaugur came limping back, he was still sitting in the same place, feet up on the desk, nursing his coffee cup. And there he stayed as Gudlaugur clicked his mouse, resumed the playback and shortly afterwards emitted a groan.

Clearly, he had found himself on film and, by the sound of it, Helgi was there too.

At first, Huldar pretended not to have noticed. He sat there, wondering how he ought to react. Then, slapping his hands on his armrests, he stood up, went round to Gudlaugur's side and said: 'Show me.'

Gudlaugur had hastily closed the window on his screen. 'Oh, look, it was nothing important. I think Helgi walked past. Alone. It's irrelevant apart from charting his movements for the timeline. We're bound to come across more sightings. There are about forty cameras downtown, on top of all the ones in bars that they're still collecting footage from.'

'Show me,' Huldar said again, firmly but without heat. He wasn't angry, he just wanted to stop Gudlaugur from doing something foolish that could get him into trouble later on.

Gudlaugur opened his mouth to object, then shrugged and maximised the window again. A view of Laugavegur high street in weekend mode appeared on screen. The camera was angled to show the pavement on the southern side of the street, up to the corner of Klapparstígur. The digital display showed the time as 1.30 a.m.

To begin with, there was no sign of Helgi. People swarmed past, in various states of intoxication and dishevelment. The interaction between those who stopped to talk to one another was wildly exaggerated, like actors in a children's TV show. Arms waved, people staggered backwards with roars of laughter. The fact that it was the middle of winter didn't seem to cramp their style one bit, but then the weather had been unusually good for the time of year: cold and dry with not a breath of wind.

The man who had just entered the picture stopped dead and turned towards a young woman walking alone down the pavement. As he did so, his face became visible and Huldar agreed with Gudlaugur that it was definitely Helgi. The woman who had caused him to stop in his tracks was slim with long blonde hair. It was impossible to tell what passed between them but their brief exchange ended with each going their separate ways, she towards Lækjartorg Square, he towards Hlemmur.

Huldar saw Gudlaugur's fingers fidgeting on the mouse as if he wanted to stop the video. At that moment he appeared on screen with his arm around another man. They paused to exchange a passionate kiss before continuing on their way and vanishing from view. Their behaviour was no different from that of the other revellers; they were obviously a bit the worse for wear and having a good time.

Gudlaugur stopped the recording. Neither of them said anything until Huldar finally broke the embarrassed silence. 'That's nothing, mate. If I'd been downtown with a woman on my arm there'd have been a lot more going on, I can tell you. Don't worry about it.'

'I'm going to delete it. From the moment Helgi carries on

walking up Laugavegur. The bit with me in it doesn't add anything.'

'You don't know that. One of the people in the shot could turn out to be the killer, trailing Helgi. Not you of course, or the bloke you're with, but one of the others.' Huldar waved at all the other frozen figures on screen. 'It wouldn't be a good idea to tamper with the file, Gudlaugur. Don't do it.'

Gudlaugur slowly shook his head in resignation. 'Great.'

'No, not "great". Shit. Just as shit as if it was me, drunk, with my arm round a woman. Or Erla. Or any other member of the team. It's embarrassing, but no more for you than anyone else. Even a dope like me can see that.'

Gudlaugur didn't answer. What was there to say?

Chapter 12

Erla watched the recording expressionlessly. Then rewound and watched it again, still with the same poker face. Afterwards, she looked up and met Huldar's eye. 'And? Is this supposed to be a problem?'

Huldar shrugged. 'Not in my opinion and clearly not in yours either, but Gudlaugur's uncomfortable about it and I can understand why. I wouldn't want the whole department to see me drunkenly snogging some woman.'

While Erla watched it for a third time, Huldar shifted from foot to foot in front of her desk. He always found it excruciatingly embarrassing to discuss anything to do with sex or relationships with Erla, given their history. But right now it was more important to help Gudlaugur.

'I don't understand why he's being so squeamish about it.' Erla pushed her mouse away. 'Being gay's not an issue any more in Iceland. Maybe you should point that out to him. Seems to me like he's the one with the problem.'

'Not everyone in the department has moved with the times, Erla. You must know that some of the guys are still total Neanderthals. I expect they're the ones Gudlaugur's worried about. It would only take one or two of them to make his life hell, even if the rest of us aren't bothered.' He avoided mentioning Jóel, though that prick was the main offender. If

Jóel discovered Gudlaugur's weak spot, he'd lose no opportunity to make his life hell.

'Yeah, yeah, I'm well aware a few of the lads still take the piss, but, as far as I can tell, it doesn't go that deep. I'm sure they'd make an exception for Gudlaugur. After all, he's one of us.'

Huldar disagreed but knew he had to tread carefully. Anyway, prolonging the conversation was unlikely to achieve anything since people rarely changed their minds during an argument, himself included. And Erla was so pig-headed that she was more likely to defend her position with all guns blazing than to admit to seeing sense.

When he didn't protest, Erla said: 'Look at it this way: if the situation's as bad as you say, it's better to get it out in the open. If everyone hides their sexuality, nothing's ever going to change.'

'I think Gudlaugur should be allowed to choose when and how he comes out to his colleagues.' When Huldar had told Gudlaugur that he couldn't care less if he wanted to stay in the closet, Gudlaugur had retorted furiously that just because he didn't choose to discuss his sex life with his colleagues, that didn't mean he was in the closet. It was simply none of their business. Huldar could understand that attitude. Personally, he had zero interest in hearing about his workmates' private lives and even less in sharing the details of his own. Seeing that Erla remained unconvinced, he added: 'All right then, have you considered this? There are around seven hundred police officers in Iceland, about five hundred of whom are men. How many do you know who are openly gay?'

'I know about three. Or four.' Erla seemed irritated at not being able to name a higher number. 'But then I don't know them all, Huldar. Any more than you do.' She paused. 'It doesn't exactly make my life easier that Gudlaugur appears so soon after Helgi exits. You do realise we'll have to watch the recordings to check if someone was following Helgi? So I can't agree to deleting the footage. Gudlaugur will just have to accept that the interests of the investigation take precedence over his right to privacy. I'm sorry but there it is.'

'But—'

'No *buts*, Huldar. We're investigating the murder of a rich investor who seems to have been well liked. When the story goes public, the media spotlight will be trained on us, so we'd better have done everything by the bloody book. "Wealthy financier in gruesome gallows execution." Can you imagine the sensation? The media will be falling over themselves to report that, rather than some dull footage of the Chinese foreign minister waiting for a geyser to blow. The only reason the switchboard isn't jammed with calls is that the original verdict was suicide and the official story hasn't changed yet. But now the post-mortem's over, we can't hide behind the uncertainty any longer.' Erla folded her arms, staring Huldar in the eye. 'The inquiry has to be beyond reproach. I'm not budging on that. Unlike you, I want to hang on to this job.'

Huldar couldn't argue with any of this. But perhaps a compromise was possible. 'Simple solution: let Gudlaugur carry on viewing the footage. If it turns out that Helgi was being followed and the individual in question turns up at the same time as Gudlaugur, he'll just have to live with it.'

Erla mulled this over for a moment.

'Besides, he's ideal for the job. His ankle's killing him, remember?' Huldar lied smoothly.

Erla pursed her lips. 'I suppose we could get away with that. But if—'

'Understood.' Huldar quickly changed the subject before she could have second thoughts. 'Did Lína tell you what she's found out about the area from the police database?'

Erla sighed and tutted. 'Yes, she did. I don't know what to say. We're so short-staffed, we need to focus on the here and now. "Friends of the Lava"?' Her face suddenly split into a grin. 'Seriously? What the fuck?'

'Yeah, I'm with you on that one. But what about the bodies washed up there? There could be a connection.'

'I took a quick look at the cases and I have to say I'd be surprised. No one flagged them as suspicious at the time and I can't see how they could have anything to do with Helgi's murder. We could ask his parents if he knew any of the people involved but, if not, there's no point wasting any more time pursuing that angle.' Erla glanced at the clock on the wall. 'Speaking of which, I'm due to meet them now. You'd better come along.'

Huldar refused coffee for the fourth time since they'd arrived at the home of Helgi Fridriksson's parents. Erla followed suit. It was the mother: whenever a silence fell between questions, she'd jump in with the offer of coffee. She was staring at them unseeingly, too distraught to take anything in – all the lights on but nobody home. 'Are you sure? Quite sure?'

'Quite sure, thank you.' Huldar summoned up the same polite smile with which he had refused all her previous offers. Erla didn't say anything.

The four of them were sitting in the living room. Fridrik, Helgi's father, was an engineer and his mother, Thórhildur, a kindergarten teacher. They were both visibly shattered: her eyes were puffy with weeping; his hair was sticking up in tufts, his cheeks covered with grey stubble. Their home appeared very ordinary, showing signs of neither affluence nor poverty – except in the living room. Huldar and Erla were perched on a singularly uncomfortable leather sofa that had evidently been designed to please the eye rather than the backside. The couple sat facing them in matching chairs that looked no more forgiving. The furniture didn't seem suited to them, any more than the other stuff in the room, which bore the signs of having been chosen by a much younger person, particularly the kitschy cartoon-like paintings. Huldar was convinced Helgi must have been responsible for those. And there was no question that he had been behind the fantastically expensive music system gathering dust in the corner, with incongruously large speakers, out of all proportion to the modest-sized room.

From what Huldar and Erla had seen so far, the rest of the house couldn't have shown a greater contrast to this decor. It reminded Huldar of his parents' place; they were the same sort of generation. He had spotted a glass cabinet in the dining room containing wine glasses and tasteless figurines that would no doubt end up in a charity shop once the couple were no more. The walls were hung with a few small landscapes and a calendar displaying a long-passed month. Framed photographs, vases and pointless bowls were arranged on the sideboard and shelves; a lifetime's accumulated tat.

Huldar forced his gaze back to the grieving couple, but it kept straying to the music system in the corner. It was a strain to concentrate when all he wanted to do was go over there, put on some music and crank up the volume full blast.

The couple had supplied them with the names of the friends they believed Helgi had been planning to meet on Saturday evening. Erla had jotted them down: Thormar and, in the case of Gunnar and Tómas, their nicknames, Gunni and Tommi, which seemed to come more naturally to Helgi's parents. They were all old school friends of Helgi's, who had stuck together over the years. Helgi had eaten lunch with his parents on Friday – a good, traditional Icelandic meal of rice pudding served with steamed rye bread. Helgi's father gently stopped his wife when she started itemising everything her son had put on his bread. They hadn't seen or heard from him since, though Thórhildur hastened to add that this wasn't unusual. Several days often passed without their being in touch. This was because he was so busy, she explained. If he wasn't on business trips abroad, he was dealing with clients here at home. The couple were under the impression that he spent as much time abroad as he did in Iceland. For example, when he came round for lunch he had just returned from a week-long trip to New York. They disagreed about whether he had got home that Friday morning or early the day before. Although the information was unlikely to be of any relevance, Erla noted it down.

Apart from this, the conversation hadn't provided much new information. In between breaking down in tears, Helgi's parents had simply confirmed what the police had already discovered, though they were able to add a few personal insights that couldn't have been found online or from a computer database. The descriptions rang true when they related to Helgi's childhood but became less plausible when they touched on his adult career. No wonder – their son had left home and gone abroad straight after school, just on the cusp of adulthood.

They were able to give detailed accounts of Helgi's friendships during his teenage years, and the three men he'd met on Saturday evening loomed large in these. The stories all revolved around what a good, handsome, intelligent boy their son had been and how he had excelled in every arena, both academically and socially. If anything, the couple seemed to feel that his friends hadn't been his intellectual equals, and on the handful of occasions when Helgi had gone off the rails, the parents were inclined to blame them. They drank too much, smoked, played computer games and skived off school, dragging Helgi down with them. His youthful indiscretions were so trivial that Huldar wondered why on earth his parents would think they were even remotely relevant to the inquiry, until, belatedly, he realised that the couple simply couldn't bring themselves to talk about the present. The past was neutral ground where nothing really bad had happened and any problems had been solved.

The parents had brought out their old photo albums, which were now spread over the coffee table or on Erla's and Huldar's laps. Neither of them had the slightest interest in seeing pictures of Helgi growing up but, suppressing their impatience, they accepted one album after another and tried to smile from time to time as they turned the pages of photos showing a boy with a gappy grin and later with braces on his teeth. Many also featured Leifur, the younger brother, either on his own or with Helgi. The pictures seemed mainly to have been taken on special occasions, like Christmas, birthdays and summer holidays, as was common in the days before

smartphones; before all occasions became of equal importance.

'How did the brothers get along?' Huldar looked up from
a photo of Helgi and Leifur sitting on a sofa, beaming from
ear to ear. Both had Christmas presents in their laps and were
clearly itching to tear off the wrapping paper as soon as the
picture had been taken.

'Helgi and Leifur, you mean?' Fridrik's question was redundant. Which other brothers could Huldar be talking about?
He nodded and the man continued: 'Well, badly and everything
in between. They used to fall out sometimes, especially when
Helgi hit adolescence. Leifur used to really get on his nerves
because he was still a child. But their relationship improved
later. They're . . . they were . . . very different types, and they
probably wouldn't have had much to do with each other if
they hadn't been brothers. But ultimately they got on all right
despite their differences, as siblings usually do.'

'Where's Leifur now? Is he in the country?'

The couple exchanged glances, their grief giving way to
anger. The wife answered first. 'Don't go thinking that Leifur
had anything to do with it. That's so ridiculous it might make
me refuse to tell you where he is. The last thing he needs is
for you to start harassing him with absurd suspicions.'

'I assure you, that's not our intention. We simply want to
talk to him. It's possible that Helgi confided in him about
things he didn't share with you. That's all we're interested
in. For now.' Erla lowered her voice towards the end of this
speech, so the final words were barely audible.

The sadness returned to the couple's faces. 'Of course
Leifur's in the country. Where else would he be?' The woman's
hand darted up to wipe her eyes, then fell back into her lap.

'He doesn't go abroad much. He's a sports teacher and can't get away during term time. And even if he had been away, he'd have caught the first plane home. He wouldn't have stayed away when something like this happened.'

'No, of course not.' Erla and Huldar both turned their attention back to the photo albums. They would get Leifur's phone number and address at the end of the visit but it was clearly better to back off for the moment.

The album on Huldar's knee was full of pictures from Helgi's sixth-form days. Since these were more recent, he no longer had to fake an interest. Huldar asked Helgi's mother to point out the friends who'd been with her son on Saturday evening and she seemed relieved at being asked to do something that didn't require too much of her. Meanwhile, Erla was stuck irritably flicking through an album containing pictures of Helgi as a three-year-old and Leifur as a newborn baby.

A weathered finger with a dark-red nail picked out the adolescent faces of the three boys, one after the other – Gunni, Tommi and Thormar. Still childishly gangly and awkward.

'Is any of them a carpenter, by any chance?' Huldar asked, thinking of the nail gun and the plank that had served as a gallows. Helgi's parents shook their heads, puzzled. When Huldar followed this up by enquiring if any of them were good with their hands, Helgi's father smiled and said quite the opposite. Huldar quickly returned to studying the pictures, to forestall any questions about why he wanted to know.

As he turned the pages full of photos of almost indistinguishable teenagers, Huldar recognised the type: ordinary, rather geeky boys, holding zero attraction for the opposite sex. The poor kids looked as if they knew it, too, all except the one Helgi's mother had identified as Gunni. He appeared to have the most self-confidence, and wore trendier clothes than his mates. Plainly the cool guy in the group.

At the other end of the spectrum was Tommi, the smallest, who always looked ready to melt into the background. Perhaps he'd been desperately hoping for a growth spurt and didn't want to be caught on film until he had. Helgi and Thormar looked so alike that Huldar found himself mixing them up. Similar colouring, similar height, wearing their fringes over their eyes in a vain attempt to hide the acne on their foreheads.

Girls rarely featured and when they did it tended to be in class pictures taken by a professional photographer or in photos from school socials. In the latter the girls were always in the background, never beside Helgi or his mates.

'Did Helgi ever go out with any of these girls?' Huldar turned the album, open at one of the class pictures, to Thórhildur.

'No. He wasn't interested. He didn't have a very high opinion of them.'

Huldar couldn't see anything wrong with the girls smiling into the camera. They looked attractive enough. He suspected that Helgi and his friends had fancied the girls but their feelings hadn't been reciprocated. But perhaps he was wrong. He glanced up. 'Was your son by any chance gay?'

The couple seemed more in tune with the times than Huldar's colleagues since they didn't appear remotely fazed or affronted by the question. Thórhildur's reply sounded perfectly genuine: 'No. I'm pretty sure he wasn't. He'd have had no reason to hide it from us if he was, but he never mentioned it.'

Huldar and Erla turned back to the albums but nothing they saw was likely to further the investigation. Erla had less patience than Huldar with the grieving parents' reminiscences. She wasn't here in the role of counsellor. When Thórhildur took out yet another album, Erla said rather curtly: 'I think it's pretty clear that your son's early years aren't going to help solve the case. I'm sorry to dismiss the photo albums, but could you tell us about something more recent, like any relationships he's had in the last few years?'

Huldar smiled apologetically and tried to soften this by adding: 'We believe the killer had some connection to Helgi. We also think he may have had a grudge against your son. But it's highly unlikely to have had anything to do with his school days. One possibility is that Helgi had a girlfriend, or had been seeing a woman, with a jealous ex or a stalker.'

Fridrik answered as soon as Huldar had finished, glancing at his wife as he did so, as if to check her reaction. Her mouth was shut in a tight line, apparently in offence at Erla's brusqueness. 'Helgi wasn't in a relationship. Not recently. Not that we know of. He used to take women out when he came home on visits, while he was still living abroad, and after he moved back to Iceland too, but it was never the same woman. He hadn't settled down yet – and now he never will.'

Erla muscled in, as if afraid this last comment would trigger another flood of tears. 'Did you meet them or did he tell you about them? You don't happen to know any of their names?'

The couple looked oddly embarrassed. 'No, actually. He never discussed his love life with us,' Thórhildur said. 'After he left home, we used to see pictures on his friends' Facebook pages of Helgi out on the town. Sometimes with women. But the relationships weren't serious, as far as I know. At least, he never introduced us to any of them.' She flashed a look of appeal at her husband, in case he could add anything.

But clearly he could only agree with his wife. 'He didn't discuss his love life with me or his mother. Don't get me wrong – we had a good relationship with him. Both when he was living in America and after he moved home. It's just that we never discussed his private life.'

At this point Huldar felt compelled to chip in, to help dispel their embarrassment. 'I can understand that. I don't discuss my love life with my mum and dad either.' He stopped short of saying that it would probably finish them off if he did. 'I think that's quite common. In any case, I'm sure we can trace some of the women from the Facebook pages you mentioned, or maybe his friends can help. So don't worry.' Seeing the couple's relief, Huldar asked: 'Did Helgi stay with you when he was visiting from New York? Before he moved home for good, I mean.'

Thórhildur smiled. 'No, he didn't. He had a flat here.'

Huldar nodded. Of course the man hadn't camped on his parents' sofabed as he himself was forced to do whenever he visited his family out east. It was a pity, though; if Helgi had stayed at home, his parents might know more about his life. 'So, as far as you know, there hadn't been any trouble over a woman recently? Nothing you noticed from his behaviour, even if he didn't discuss it?'

When the couple said no, Huldar handed over to Erla again, who was quick to fire off the next question: 'What about his business? Could someone have felt they'd been ripped off by him?'

'No. Helgi wasn't involved in the banking crisis. We've

already told you that. He was working in America until last year.'

'He went abroad with nothing and came back one of the richest men in Iceland,' Erla went on. 'We understand he made a packet out of creditors' claims connected to the failed banks. There would probably have been domestic claims among those. He made a fortune – others lost out. While that sort of thing's not necessarily dishonest, it doesn't alter the fact that people are going to be sore about losing everything. Did he ever mention receiving threats or getting into disputes as a result?'

'No. Never. But then he didn't discuss money or his job with us. All we knew was that he was doing well. That was obvious.'

'You haven't heard any rumours – any complaints, for example? Like snide comments below pictures of him on social media?'

Huldar wondered if Erla had failed to notice that pretty much everything online attracted nasty comments. But the couple merely shook their heads. And no one had badmouthed their son in their hearing.

'Do you know if your son knew or had any connection to a man called Dagur Didriksson, who died about eighteen years ago? He'd just turned sixty at the time of his death.'

The couple shook their heads, looking mystified. 'No, why do you ask?'

'There are some angles we need to eliminate from our inquiries. If you could bear with us.' They nodded and Huldar went on. 'What about a young man by the name of Olgeir Magnússon, who drowned three years ago while swimming at Nauthólsvík? He was close to Helgi's age – only a year younger.'

'No, I don't recognise the name.' Helgi's father looked enquiringly at his wife, who shook her head.

'OK. What about a young woman called Maren Thórdardóttir? She died five years ago and was six years younger than Helgi.' The parents' answer was the same: no, they'd never heard of her. That left only one question. 'I don't suppose your son was ever involved with the Friends of the Lava?'

'The Friends of the Lava?' Incredulity briefly banished the grief from the couple's faces. 'You mean the people who were protesting against the road through the lava-field?'

'Yes, them.'

'No. Definitely not. Helgi was living abroad at the time and anyway I assure you he hadn't the slightest interest in roads in Iceland.' Helgi's mother couldn't have been more emphatic.

Erla jabbed Huldar hard in the thigh under cover of the photo album she was holding. He was glad he hadn't mentioned eiderdown theft or possible links to the former prime minister, Bjarni Benediktsson, or she'd probably have bored a hole in his leg. Getting the message, he changed tack and slid the picture of Siggi across the table. 'Do you recognise this boy?'

The couple bent over the picture, then raised their heads, looking uncomprehending. 'No. Who is he?'

'His name's Siggi. Short for Sigurdur.'

'It doesn't ring any bells. Whose son is he?'

'We don't know. His mother goes by the nickname of Systa and his father's known as Sibbi.'

The couple looked even more baffled – or at least Fridrik did. Thórhildur had picked up the photo and was studying it closely.

'Do you recognise him?'

'I have the feeling I might have seen him somewhere.' She frowned over the picture, then put it back on the table. 'No, I'm getting confused. I don't recognise him.' She drew back her hands. 'But I don't understand. What's this little boy got to do with what happened to Helgi?'

Erla answered honestly. 'We don't know. He may not have any connection.' She paused. Huldar could tell she was weighing up whether to confide in the couple. She'd wondered aloud about the wisdom of this before the visit. But finally she made up her mind. 'He was found in Helgi's flat. The day your son's body turned up in the lava-field.'

'What?' Judging from Fridrik's reply and the startled look on the mother's face, the couple obviously thought they must have misheard. Thórhildur's right hand clasped her throat and she asked, 'What do you mean?'

Their astonishment didn't come as any surprise. 'We're trying to find out what the boy was doing there,' Erla told them. 'If you have any information that could help, we'd be very grateful. For example, could he be the son of someone Helgi knew? Do any of his friends have children?'

'Er . . .' Fridrik looked lost but his wife was obviously better informed.

'I've never heard of anyone called Systa or Sibbi among Helgi's circle. Some of his friends are married and have children but none of them are called Sigurdur – or Siggi – that I'm aware of.'

'So he talked to you about his friends' kids, did he?'

'Well, not exactly. But while he was abroad I took care of buying presents for him when his friends had babies. And after he moved home I carried on choosing gifts whenever he was invited to a child's birthday, because he knew nothing about kids. It was the same with Christmas and his friends' weddings and birthdays. He always asked me to help pick out the gifts, so I know how incredibly generous he was.' Thórhildur's chest heaved and she closed her eyes for a moment, as if to stop herself breaking down, before adding: 'I used to choose the cards and write them for him as well. I don't remember any for a boy called Sigurdur.'

'Did you buy a present recently for someone called Hallbera?' Huldar asked, thinking of the parcel on Helgi's kitchen table.

'Yes.' Tears began to slide down Thórhildur's cheeks. 'Last week. Her birthday was this weekend.' Her voice wobbled. 'I didn't think for a minute that it was the last gift I'd ever buy for Helgi. In fact, I was dreading the children becoming teenagers, because that age group is so difficult. I needn't have wasted my time worrying about that.'

A silence fell that lasted until she moved her hand involuntarily as if to make yet another offer of coffee, at which point Huldar hurriedly intervened. 'Any enemies or tensions unconnected to a girlfriend or work? Anything you can think of in the past or more recently?' The moment he'd said it, he could have kicked himself for referring to the past, afraid this might encourage them to start reminiscing about bad feelings caused by a burst football or a stolen bike. But he needn't have worried.

'No.'

'And Helgi never fell out with any of his friends?'

'No,' his mother said firmly, before immediately qualifying this. 'I mean, nothing serious. They always made it up in the end.'

'Nothing recent, in other words?'

'Not that I remember.' It was Fridrik's turn to sound certain.

Thórhildur backed this up. 'Nor me. At least, all his friends are on his Christmas list this year, so nothing can have come up in the last few months.'

Erla frowned and pounced on this. 'What do you mean? Have you removed names from the list in the past?'

The woman looked a little flustered. Running a hand over her hair, she tried to sit up straight in the incongruous leather chair. 'Only once. But that must have been a storm in a teacup because he was back on the list the following year.'

'Which friend was that?'

'Thorri – Thormar, I mean.'

Huldar and Erla automatically looked down at the open photo albums. They recognised the name because Thormar had been in many of the pictures. And, in contrast to the other boys, Helgi's mother hadn't criticised him. On the contrary, she had smiled, referred to him approvingly and twice dropped into the conversation that he was a dentist now. 'This is the same Thormar you said was still his best friend?'

'Yes.' Thórhildur pursed her lips, as if regretting having raised the subject. 'But it was nothing. Like I said, they made it up again.'

'And you have no idea what caused them to fall out?' Huldar reached for another of the albums and leafed through until he found a picture of Helgi with Thormar. It appeared to have been taken when Helgi passed his driving test, since he was proudly holding up his certificate and brandishing a set of car keys, a broad smile on his face. Beside him, Thormar stood grinning from ear to ear, his arm draped over Helgi's shoulder, giving the impression of two best mates who couldn't wait to take the car out for a spin. Huldar was struck once again by how alike they were: two rather gangly nerds, now in possession of a set of wheels, totally unaware that in a few years' time their currency would have rocketed with the opposite sex. Although dentists couldn't compete with rich investors, they were still regarded as a good catch in Reykjavík's social scene.

'No. Helgi didn't want to talk about it and I didn't push him. Like I said, it can't have been anything serious. This was about four or five years ago, so I'm sure it has been long forgotten. At least, they made up and have been best friends ever since.'

'Is Thormar married, or in a relationship?' Erla was probably thinking along the same lines as Huldar: that Helgi might have tried it on with his best friend's wife. It happened, especially when people were drunk, as Huldar knew only too well. And the consequences could be disastrous. His thoughts shied away from the memory.

Helgi's mother didn't cotton on, however, and answered without making a face or repeating the spiel about her perfect son who could do no wrong. 'Yes, he is. His wife's called Sigrún. She's a lawyer, a few years older than Thormar. They've got one daughter, Hallbera, whose third birthday it was last weekend, but Sigrún's also got a teenage son from a previous relationship.'

The little girl obviously couldn't be Siggi and the stepson was too old to be of interest. It was time to say *right, well* . . . Erla closed the album, put it down on the coffee table and said the magic words: 'Right, well . . .'

Chapter 13

Freyja slammed the driver's door and opened the rear one to get Saga out of her car seat. When she ducked inside she came face to face with her brother, who had just opened the door on the other side to do the same thing. Smiling in embarrassment, Freyja backed out. It would take her a while to get used to the fact that she was no longer Baldur's stand-in: he could take care of the parenting himself – most of the time. Freyja still got Saga to herself in the evenings and overnight during daddy weekends while Baldur was subject to the halfway-house curfew. In a few months he'd take over there as well, and Freyja would be relegated to the position of auntie. She wasn't looking forward to it.

'Well, what do you think?' Baldur settled Saga on his hip, closed the car door and nodded up at the block of flats where his friend Tobbi lived. 'Smart, isn't it? Maybe I should live here and let you stay on in my flat.' He winked at her. It would never happen: he was too attached to his place, particularly the insulated storeroom with the heat lamps.

Freyja smiled, then turned to examine the building. Her jaw dropped a little when she saw how upmarket it was, but she quickly closed it so Baldur didn't notice. Then her gaze wandered to the car park, full of new, expensive-looking models. This couldn't be right: the rent Tobbi was asking would barely cover a windowless broom cupboard in the suburbs.

Baldur swore it was true, however, and told her not to look a gift horse in the mouth. According to him, Tobbi had received notice that he was to start his sentence in ten days' time. When Freyja asked how long he would be in prison for and what he'd done, Baldur replied one and a half years, if he behaved himself, but omitted to mention the crime. When Freyja pressed him, he pretended to have forgotten. She gave up. After all, what relevance did it have? It wasn't as if she'd be expected to take over the reins of Tobbi's criminal activities while he was behind bars.

'What do you think, Saga? Would you like to come and visit Auntie Freyja here?' Baldur pointed at the building, but instead of following the direction of his finger, his daughter stared at a seagull circling overhead. As usual, her expression was unreadable. Anyone who didn't know her would think she was sulking or cross with the bird, but Freyja knew better. Saga wore this scowl regardless of whether she was eating an ice-cream or having an injection. The closest she ever came to smiling was at Baldur's dog Molly. Especially when Molly misbehaved, as happened all too often.

Freyja stopped dead. 'Shit, Baldur. What about Molly?'

'What about her?' Baldur stared at her in surprise.

'Who's supposed to look after her overnight if I move in here while you're at the halfway house?'

Baldur waved away her fears. 'Don't worry about it. She can stay here till I get out,' he said airily. 'Tobbi won't be bothered about a dog.'

But Molly wasn't just any dog. She was easily the equivalent of two or three – four, if you were talking about small dogs. 'But it's not up to Tobbi. What if dogs aren't allowed in the building?'

'Oh, please. Relax. It's none of the other residents' business. If it comes to that, I don't suppose you're allowed dogs in my flat. But who gives a toss?'

Freyja didn't like to point out that there was bound to be a world of difference between the tolerance threshold of Baldur's rackety neighbours and the kind of people who lived in this building. She could have pointed out, too, that Baldur was an expert at wrapping people around his little finger. If anyone came round to complain about Molly, they'd be putting their name down for one of her puppies by the time they'd been exposed to the full force of Baldur's charm. Freyja was too stiff and awkward to pull this off. The only man she'd managed to charm in recent memory was Huldar, which was unfortunate as they were like Tetris blocks: their ability to click depended on which way they were facing. In the horizontal, they fitted together perfectly, but it was a different story in the vertical.

'This has to work out, Baldur.' Freyja held the front door open for her brother and his daughter. 'Or we'll be stuck with each other for good.'

'No worries. Of course it'll work out.' Baldur found the correct doorbell, planted himself in front of the small lens and waved when his friend's voice emerged from the entry-phone.

'Yo!'

From the style of his greeting, Freyja deduced that Tobbi's crime was more likely to be related to drug dealing than white-collar fraud.

A buzzing sound from the lock drowned out Baldur's reply

and they went inside and climbed up to the first floor. Just before he tapped on the door, Baldur said in a quick aside: 'Don't make a fuss about looking after his pet for him. It's the condition of renting the place.'

The door opened before Freyja could say a word. The timing of this revelation was no coincidence. It had to be the reason for the unbelievably low rent. Tobbi wasn't saving himself the cost of renting a storage unit for his belongings as Baldur had claimed. No, she was going to have to look after some animal. How bad could it be? she reasoned. A cat or dog? It could hardly be something small like a hamster. Maybe it was a deranged parrot that would keep the tenant awake all night with its swearing. Freyja braced herself for the worst.

'A poisonous snake! Are you mad? How could you dream I'd look after a poisonous snake?' Freyja looked down at the dressy trousers and shoes she'd worn to make a good impression on Tobbi. What a joke. She'd have been better off in a safari suit.

'It's not poisonous,' Baldur protested as he pulled into the drive of the Children's House.

'Yes, it is. You saw it for yourself!' Freyja glanced, irritated, at the dashboard clock. She had popped out in her lunch hour to view the flat and was now cutting it fine, but Baldur acted as if he had all the time in the world. He was supposed to be at work himself, as this was one of the conditions for finishing his sentence at the halfway house, but he had fixed something up with one of his unscrupulous friends. As a result, he was fancy free, in spite of the paperwork proving otherwise. Still, he had redeemed himself in Freyja's eyes by devoting the time to his daughter rather than to plotting his next dodgy deal.

'Freyja, it's a python. They're not poisonous.'

'Jesus. Like that's any better! Pythons can squeeze people to death.' Freyja undid her seatbelt as the car came to a halt. 'In case you hadn't noticed, they're also illegal in Iceland. I wouldn't be surprised if pythons topped the list of banned pets.'

'Calm down.' Baldur let go of the steering wheel. 'Think about it: it's not that bad. The python has a room to itself and only needs to eat once a week. It spends pretty much its whole life asleep. You won't even notice it. It's not like you have to take it out for a walk or anything, just feed it and clean out its cage from time to time. That's all. And in return you get the flat for peanuts.'

Freyja felt her skin crawling. She tried not to think about the feeding procedure or what was on the menu. She'd managed to control her features in front of Tobbi, who had turned out to be reassuringly normal, in spite of his creepy pet and no doubt colourful criminal record. Freyja hadn't wanted to put him off by screaming when he opened the door to the snake's room, or throwing up when he described its eating habits. She didn't want him to find another tenant until she'd made up her mind one way or another. On the plus side, it was a fantastic flat; on the minus, it came with a bloody snake attached. She couldn't decide which held more weight. 'Look, I can't talk now, Baldur. I'm late for work. And I need to think about it.'

'Don't think too long. Tobbi needs a tenant asap.'

'I know.' Freyja twisted round to Saga and blew her a goodbye kiss. Saga's perma-scowl didn't shift, but she did raise one hand and waggle her stubby fingers in a kind of wave. It had come as absolutely no surprise to Freyja that her little niece had lit up with pleasure at the sight of the snake.

'You won't do anything stupid like report it to the cops? It would destroy Tobbi. He loves that python like a baby.' Baldur ducked his head to peer out at Freyja.

'Of course not.' It genuinely hadn't occurred to her. Although she was by nature honest and law-abiding, she had got used to making exceptions for Baldur. She didn't hold him to the same standards as other people, including herself. He was her brother; the only relative who mattered to her. Apart from Saga, that is. 'I'll call you later.'

Freyja closed the car door and went into the Children's House. She hoped the women she worked with would have forgotten why she'd gone out, as she was in no mood to gush enthusiastically about the flat.

Freyja raised her eyes from the screen, deep in thought. Once she'd got through the backlog of interviews with charges under the protection of the Children's House, she had returned to her office and started scouring the Child Protection Agency's records for boys Siggi's age called Sigurdur. No doubt someone else had already looked, but she didn't let that stop her. She wanted to see the results with her own eyes.

Before she started, though, she had spent a bit of time browsing for information about keeping snakes as pets. Desperate as she was for somewhere to live, the idea of cohabiting with a snake filled her with anxiety. Not so much for herself but for Saga. Would it be safe for a toddler to stay if there was a python in the flat? When she googled, the sheer number of results surprised her. It seemed snakes were quite popular pets and there were loads of enthusiastic python owners out there, eager to share their experiences. Freyja learnt that it was reasonably safe to keep a python, as long as it wasn't more than two and a half metres long. Freyja hadn't a clue how long Tobbi's snake was since it had been coiled up when she saw it. Going by the size of the cage, though, it was no baby. Freyja decided to get Baldur to ask Tobbi how long the python was and, if he couldn't answer, she would march over there herself with a tape measure.

She didn't usually have time to waste on personal stuff at work but for once she was actually on top of things. Since Baldur had transferred to the halfway house, he had been spending a lot of time at home in the flat during the day, which meant that she had been staying on longer at work. As a result, she was usually met by a clear desk in the mornings. No reports, open files, loose papers or half-drunk cups of coffee. No heap of pens. Her desk looked as if she was starting a new job. It wasn't that she was avoiding her brother, she just wanted to give him space. It was his flat after all and she felt almost like a squatter there. Baldur needed some time alone to get used to his newfound freedom, too. She was hoping he would use the peace and quiet to turn his life around and go straight in future, but had to acknowledge to herself that he was far more likely to use the breathing space to think up new, improved scams.

Thanks to her browsing, she was now much better informed about snakes, but Siggi remained elusive. She had found several boys of that name in the social services records but none were the same age as him. Although she had been hoping to find his full name and an explanation of his circumstances, she wasn't really surprised at her lack of success. If there had been anything on the system, someone else would have found it already.

There was nothing in Siggi's behaviour to suggest neglect or maltreatment. Quite the opposite. Remembering the picture he'd drawn at the police station, she wished she'd been there to observe as he had probably chattered away to himself as he worked. Unfortunately, though, he'd done it while she had popped to the ladies', so she'd had to make do with the boy's explanation of what the picture showed. With her analyst's eye, she deduced that his mother was the central figure in his life. Siggi had made her the biggest, and taken the greatest care over her picture. He was the smallest and his father had been in the middle. Both the mother and Siggi were portrayed smiling, whereas the father had a straight line for a mouth. God, she hoped nothing bad had happened to the parents.

Still, it appeared unlikely, if Huldar was to be believed. He and the young policewoman had turned up at the flat in connection with a murder inquiry. So far all she knew was that the victim, Helgi, had owned the flat where Siggi was found. Nothing had appeared in the news yet: most of the domestic bulletins over the last twenty-four hours had focused on the official visit by the Chinese delegation, showing footage of the foreign minister visiting local landmarks including a geothermal power station, the ancient parliament site at the Thingvellir National Park, Höfdi House, the presidential residence at Bessastadir, the hot springs at Geysir and an unnamed farmhouse. He and his retinue were making valiant efforts to appear interested but they weren't fooling anyone. You had to sympathise – it had obviously been a packed programme.

Her thoughts were interrupted when the door of her office opened to admit the director of the Children's House. The woman asked if she was disturbing her and Freyja answered honestly that she wasn't. 'We've just got the results of the medical examination of the little boy found in the flat,' the director said. 'The child hasn't been subjected to any kind of sexual or other physical violence.'

Freyja skimmed the report. She'd already heard the verbal version and there was nothing new here. Her boss stood over her while she was reading, apparently waiting for a response, but what was there to say? Siggi had no injuries. Certain parts of the body are more likely to display evidence of violence that is very unlikely to have resulted from an accident: the insides of the arms and thighs, for example, as well as the back, sex organs and bottom. These areas had been carefully examined but nothing had been found: no new injuries and no scars of older wounds. The X-rays had told the same story: no fractures, whether recent or earlier; no healed breaks.

But violence against children wasn't limited to physical or sexual abuse. Neglect and mental cruelty don't show up on an X-ray or on a child's limbs. In her career, Freyja had encountered countless victims of mental cruelty, so she was all too familiar with the behaviour indicative of such cases. Some children were subjected to chronic stress, others to intermittent incidents of escalating seriousness. In her professional opinion, Siggi didn't fit the profile. But of course you could never be sure. Children were affected differently by this kind of trauma and some fared better than others, demonstrating an ability to call on mysterious inner reserves of strength.

What was atypical was the fact that Siggi didn't seem

particularly anxious or upset at his parents' absence. Most children would be inconsolable but she didn't remember seeing him so much as shed a tear. That could have been due to the circumstances, of course: it didn't take much to distract young children and for them police officers were a big deal. It was possible that Siggi had been too preoccupied by all the bustle around him. He might have broken down later, in the relative peace and quiet of the care home.

Freyja thanked her boss, who left the office. The moment she'd gone, Freyja picked up the phone and rang the foster home. Her call was answered by a woman called Heidrún, who knew at once which case Freyja was referring to, since she'd been there when Didrik had brought the boy round the previous evening.

'I was wondering if you'd noticed any sign that Siggi was missing his parents?'

'He hardly mentions them,' the woman replied. 'But that's not unusual. We try to entertain the kids and keep them happily occupied. Actually, he did mention his mother to the other children when I was out of the room. Apparently he told them the bad man had taken her. Of course, that's the kind of thing a little kid like Siggi would think. It doesn't necessarily mean he's referring to a particular man.'

'What about tears or other symptoms of distress? Was he upset at bedtime last night, for example?'

'No, he wasn't. He just fell asleep. Quite soon after his head hit the pillow.'

'That's odd. I'd have expected him to show signs of anxiety.'

'Yes. You'd have thought. But, like I say, we've seen this kind of reaction before. Some kids simply adapt more easily than others. Siggi strikes me as the trusting type; I get the feeling he thinks it's all going to be fine in the end. He seems to believe it when we tell him it's only a matter of time before his parents come to fetch him.' Heidrún was silent a moment, then asked: 'Have you heard any news about how they're getting on with tracing them?'

'No. I don't think they're getting anywhere.'

'How strange.' The woman paused again, then said: 'Talking of strange, I did notice one thing about the boy's behaviour that was a bit odd. It might not be important but I think you should know.'

'Oh? What's that?'

'He hanged a Barbie doll. Maybe he didn't mean to; maybe she was supposed to be lowered on a rope from a helicopter or something. Only, when I asked him, he flatly denied that he'd done it. But the thing is, it can't have been any of the other kids. The fact that he lied about it struck me as even stranger than executing the doll in the first place. The boy's so sweet and well behaved otherwise; it seems out of character for him to tell lies. His drawings are quite violent as well – covered in red scribbles. When I ask, he tells me it's blood.'

Freyja raised her eyebrows. 'Really? He drew a picture while he was at the police station but that was very ordinary, just him and his parents. Mind you, he only had two crayons to choose from. Perhaps he would have added some blood if he'd had a red one.'

After she'd hung up, Freyja sat there, thinking. Was it possible that Siggi wasn't as unconcerned about his parents' whereabouts as he seemed? Perhaps the drawings provided an outlet for his anxiety. Or could the poor kid have witnessed something he wasn't telling them about?

Freyja's mobile phone rang. When Huldar's name flashed

up on screen, she grimaced briefly, unsure if the call would be related to the investigation or yet another attempt to invite her out for a meal.

'Hi. How would you like to come for a drive?'

Before Freyja could say no, he elaborated, and she instantly accepted his offer. The plan was to drive Siggi around town in the hope of finding his home. They'd drawn a blank after tracking down all the Sigurdurs of his age with fathers whose names began with an S. Before they widened the search, they thought it was worth trying this method. The Child Protection Agency had given the green light and agreed that Freyja should go along as their representative, since no one else was available.

Freyja rang off and began to get ready. As she zipped up her jacket, she realised she was almost disappointed that Huldar hadn't tried to flirt with her.

Hastily pulling herself together, she left the office.

Chapter 14

The car stopped at a red light. Siggi turned away from the window to stare at the back of Gudlaugur's head in the driver's seat. Huldar winked at the boy encouragingly from the passenger seat. Siggi's excitement at being allowed to ride in a police car had faded now that they'd been driving around for over an hour. They'd been hoping he would spot something familiar that could help them identify the area he lived in but the only things he had pointed out were landmarks everyone knew: the Laugardalur swimming pool, the Kringlan shopping mall, Hallgrímskirkja Church and the great glass dome of Perlan.

At first they had concentrated on neighbourhoods that fitted his description: no views of Esja, Hallgrímskirkja or the sea. Freyja had lost count of the streets they had crawled up and down to no avail. The boy watched as they passed houses, blocks of flats and terraces, but didn't recognise any of them. It turned out that he wasn't old enough to see the similarities between certain types of building and the one he lived in, something that could have narrowed down their search. There were only two categories: his house or not his house.

They had tried driving into Kópavogur, the town immediately to the south, in case the boy thought it counted as Reykjavík, but when they got there he only seemed more bewildered. He didn't even recognise such obvious landmarks as the Smáralind shopping centre or the Toys R Us store.

'Can I have an ice-cream now?' Siggi looked hopefully at Freyja, sitting beside him in the back.

'Soon. We just need to check a few more streets and when we've done that we'll get you an ice-cream. With sauce.'

The boy smiled and turned back to the side window. He was sitting on a cushion that raised him high enough to see out. 'I want to go to Florida. To Disneyland.' This was clearly a test to discover how far he could get with his wishes. From ice-cream with sauce to Disneyland. It was a bit of a leap.

'Nice try, Siggi, but we can't take you there, I'm afraid,' Freyja laughed. 'But you can have an ice-cream.'

'Can you see your house anywhere, Siggi?' Gudlaugur grabbed the chance, while the car was held up at the lights, to peer over his shoulder at the boy. They had asked him the question so often that it was getting ridiculous. Siggi already knew the purpose of their drive.

'No.'

Gudlaugur turned back to face the front, the lights changed to green and they pulled away.

'My mummy's not allowed to drive.' Every now and then the boy would pipe up with scraps of information about his life, none of which had any bearing on their quest. But Freyja always tried to get him to expand on what he said in the hope that something useful might eventually emerge.

'Why's that, Siggi?'

'Her tummy's so fat. The baby inside is so big the steering wheel could pop her tummy if she brakes.' The boy continued imaginatively with his account, making a face and clasping his own stomach.

'Oh yes, of course.' Freyja tried to hit on something that could provide them with a lead. 'Does your daddy drive her when she needs to go somewhere?'

'Yes, sometimes.'

'Are you allowed to go with them?'

'Yes, always. I'm not allowed to stay at home on my own.'

'Where have you been with them? Can you remember?'

'Once we went to the hospital.'

'Of course. Was the doctor looking at your mummy's bump?'

Siggi stared at Freyja in surprise. 'How did you know?'

'Because when mummies are going to have a baby they often go to see the doctor. They have to make sure everything's all right.'

Siggi frowned. 'Not that kind of bump.'

'Oh? What kind, then?'

'A bump here.' Siggi pointed to his temple. 'The bump made her be sick. In the car.'

'Oh really? What happened?' Freyja was careful to phrase the question vaguely so as not to influence Siggi's reply, since information about the injury could come in useful. The Reykjavík A&E must keep records they could use to trace the woman. There couldn't be that many pregnant women who had been brought in with a lump on the side of their head. If she had gone to her GP, though, the task would be more challenging, since there were any number of doctor's surgeries in the capital area and no central records system.

'She hurt herself.'

'Oh dear. How did she hurt herself?'

Siggi shrugged and stared unseeingly at the houses lining the street. 'She just did.'

Freyja decided to leave this for a moment and pursue another angle. 'Did the doctor help her?' Again the little boy shrugged. 'Did she get a plaster?'

'No.'

'When was this?'

'A long time ago.'

Freyja's smile was growing strained. Four-year-olds had a very abstract concept of time. They could understand 'before' and 'after', but when they said something happened yesterday, it could just as well have been several days or even a week ago. There was little chance, then, that Siggi would be able to tell them if the incident he was describing had taken place last month or six months ago. 'Were there cartoons on TV in the morning?' As the Icelandic TV stations only showed cartoons in the morning at weekends, perhaps they could narrow it down to a weekend. Thinking about her phone conversation with the woman from the care home, who had mentioned the boy's lie about the Barbie doll, Freyja hoped he hadn't made the story up.

'No.'

Freyja hid her disappointment. 'Was it at Christmas, then?'

'No.'

'Was Christmas over?'

Siggi looked thoughtful. 'Yes. I gave Mummy a scarf for Christmas. It's pink. But it got blood on it in the car. And it wouldn't come out. Now the scarf's got blood on it.' From his expression, she gathered that this made the scarf a great deal more interesting.

'Was she wearing the scarf with blood on it at the New Year's fireworks?' Freyja saw Huldar twist round in his seat, as eager as her to hear the answer.

Siggi took a moment to think about it. 'Yes. Daddy didn't want her to wear it to the bonfire but she did anyway. He got cross. He's always getting cross.'

That was as close as Freyja was going to get. The woman was given the scarf for Christmas and it got stained with blood from a wound that caused her to go to A&E. The blood-stain was on the scarf on New Year's Eve. This time frame would have to do. 'When your mummy went to hospital, did she go to A&E?'

'I don't know.'

'Did you go with her?'

'Yes. But I waited outside. With Daddy. We weren't allowed to go inside because we weren't hurt. Only Mummy.'

'Were there lots of people waiting outside like you?'

'Yes. And some of them were drunk.' Siggi studied Freyja's face to see how she would react to this shocking news. 'Daddy said so. One man even had some beer.'

The boy had to be describing A&E. Drunks rarely stumbled into GPs' surgeries.

Huldar raised his fist and lightly punched the roof of the car in a muted gesture of triumph. They'd probably got their vital clue. No need to drive round any more neighbourhoods, watching the boy staring blankly at endless rows of houses.

'Right then, Siggi. How about that ice-cream?'

Didrik from the Child Protection Agency was waiting for them at the care home. He was sitting in the poky little office with a mug of coffee. By the time they had all crowded in there you couldn't have fitted even a small child in as well. But they put up with the cramped conditions; it was the only place they could close the door for a bit of privacy.

'Nothing?' Didrik asked Freyja once the small talk had petered out. She couldn't help thinking how incredibly hot he was. The first time she'd met him his beard had struck her as affectedly hipsterish, but now she found the waxed tips of his moustache rather cool. His haircut, too, with the shaved sides and the mop of longer hair heavily gelled on top of his head. She'd even got used to the ring through his nose. If you got a man like him into bed, he wouldn't be remotely disturbed by the presence of a snake coiled up in the next room. The lemongrass fragrance that hung around him did things for her as well. Though not for Huldar, evidently; he had wrinkled his nose when they shook hands and now seemed to be sulking.

To be fair, she had to admit that a snake in the next room was unlikely to put Huldar off his stride either. Or even a snake under the bed – or indeed in it, for that matter.

Didrik repeated his question. 'Really nothing?'

'We didn't find his house, unfortunately. But he did let slip some information about his mother that we're hoping will be useful. It remains to be seen.'

Huldar seemed impatient with this exchange. Pulling something from his pocket, he held it out to Freyja. When she saw that it was a measuring tape, she was momentarily thrown, thinking he must somehow have got wind of the python and was offering to help establish its length. But her fears were unfounded.

'I need to find out how tall the boy is,' Huldar said abruptly. 'Does one of you have to be present while I do it?'

Didrik shook his head and Freyja copied him.

Huldar went out without another word, Gudlaugur following on his heels. Freyja had nothing against being left alone with Didrik. He had a uniquely soothing presence, a sort of 'I-was-born-cool' aura. Freyja had always been attracted to this type; to people who were too comfortable in their own skins to display the kind of spite or negativity that was all too common these days. She caught herself dropping her gaze in search of a wedding band and smiled privately when his only ring turned out to be a large silver skull. Surely no one, however little they cared for convention, would exchange skull rings when they got married?

Didrik didn't notice Freyja's interest in his hands. He sipped his coffee unhurriedly, then said: 'I need to fill out a report. Do you know how the cops are getting on with locating his parents? Otherwise I'll just have to describe the circumstances he was found in and the carer's statement about his behaviour and developmental level. My bosses don't care if he can tell yellow from green: all they want to know is whether we need to look at more permanent solutions for him.'

'They're not making much progress. But it's possible A&E have information that will enable the police to identify his mother. That's all I know, I'm afraid.' Freyja wished she could give him something to help with his report. She wished even more fervently that he would ask her out. It was far too long since she'd been on a date that hadn't ended in an awkward handshake and unspoken hopes on both sides that all talk of being in touch was a polite fiction.

'Strange business.' Didrik reached for his mug again and his sleeve pulled up a little, revealing a glimpse of his tattoos. From under his cuff peeped the yellow outstretched talons of the eagle that had so fascinated Siggi. Ready to snatch its prey and never let it go. The claws vanished as Didrik raised the mug to his lips. 'Want to see?' He handed Freyja a sheet of paper with the carer Heidrún's report.

Freyja skimmed the text, which was consistent with the conversation they'd had on the phone earlier. There was a brief statement about Siggi's drawings being unusually violent for a four-year-old. No attempt was made to explain this, beyond suggesting that it was possible the boy had been allowed to watch unsuitable TV programmes. Apart from that there was nothing to indicate problems at home. The boy was neat, clean, and dressed in clothes that were appropriate for the season. There were no cavities in his teeth or build-up of wax in his ears, and his hair and nails had been trimmed. His face bore no signs of foetal alcohol syndrome, and his physical development indicated that his nutritional needs had been met. His body showed no visible signs of violence apart from grazes on the palms of his hands, which Siggi accounted for by saying he'd fallen over in the play-ground. His language level was normal for his age and he had no problems communicating with adults or other children. His mental development was also normal. He displayed no signs of stress or misery, except in relation to his parents' absence. In other words, it was extremely unlikely that the boy had experienced anything other than a good, stable upbringing.

Didrik took the report back from Freyja. 'Could they have left the country? Gone on holiday, for example? Left the boy with a babysitter and something's gone badly wrong? Or gone for a drive in the countryside and rolled their car somewhere that can't be seen from the road?'

Freyja shook her head. 'I don't think so.'

But Didrik hadn't given up on possible theories to explain

the parents' disappearance. 'What about poison? Could they have lost consciousness as a result of breathing in toxic fumes, or from food poisoning, and be lying at home in a coma?'

'All I can say is, judging by the trouble we're having finding the boy's home, there's a risk the story's not going to end well. I just hope I'm wrong.'

Although Didrik wasn't in possession of the full facts of the case, he clearly feared the same as her: that Siggi's parents were either unconscious or worse.

The door opened and Huldar and Gudlaugur re-entered, forcing Freyja to budge up, closer to Didrik. She could feel the warmth radiating from him through his thin jumper and hoped the detectives wouldn't be off again straight away. But her wish was not granted.

'Right, we've measured the boy and we need to get going. Can you sort out a lift for yourself, Freyja?' Huldar seemed to have some trouble coming out with this last part and avoided looking at her.

Before Freyja had time to say she'd take the bus, Didrik jumped in: 'I'm in a car for once. I can drop you off.'

This couldn't have suited Freyja better, though she was careful not to make her pleasure too obvious. She'd have been happy to sit on the carrier on the back of Didrik's bike if necessary. Huldar was transparently annoyed.

Chapter 15

The atmosphere in A&E was subdued. People were sitting hunched on plastic chairs, apparently resigned to the endless waiting. Most were poring over their phones, but judging from the boredom on their faces, they had already exhausted the outermost limits of the internet. Almost all of them looked up as Huldar and Gudlaugur walked over to the reception desk and announced that they were from the police. A spark of interest lit their eyes, then faded again as the officers were immediately shown through. No arrests, no drama.

Once inside, Huldar and Gudlaugur were faced with an empty corridor, lined with the closed doors of examination rooms, interspersed with bits of portable equipment and a variety of trolleys, ready for use. A door opened but the nurse who emerged didn't so much as look at them, just bustled straight into the next room, almost at a run. Evidently, the long wait out in reception was not caused by any slacking from the staff.

'I need to get back to the station. Where's the doctor?' Gudlaugur had been on edge ever since Erla had sent him and Huldar out to comb the streets with Siggi.

'Perhaps she's busy operating on an open fracture. I saw on the news that yet another tourist has tumbled down a mountain. We could be here all day.'

Seeing Gudlaugur's look of horror, Huldar regretted teasing him. He thought he knew why his colleague was so twitchy: he still had to finish going through the CCTV footage from the city centre before tomorrow morning's progress meeting and was afraid that Erla would allocate the job to someone else if he wasn't back at his desk soon. Well, it was his fault for forgetting to limp in her presence. 'We'll be back before you know it,' Huldar reassured him. 'Don't worry – Erla's not going to hand over the CCTV to anyone else. We're still so short-staffed.' This was true. Erla was having so much trouble finding people to delegate to that she'd had to take on a number of tasks herself, which meant she had no time to provide supervision. She'd just taken a statement from Helgi's brother Leifur, which according to her had been a complete waste of time. He'd told exactly the same story as the parents: Helgi had no ill-wishers, didn't know Siggi, and had no connection to the bodies washed up from the sea.

Nothing they did seemed to get them any further. But now, with luck, they might finally have reached a turning point.

Before Gudlaugur could reply, Huldar felt a tap on the shoulder and turned to see a middle-aged woman standing behind him, wearing a white coat over scrubs. She was thin and weary-looking.

When it turned out that this was the doctor they were supposed to be meeting, they introduced themselves, smiling politely. Her handshake was firm and warm. Once the pleasantries were out of the way, she said: 'I've only got quarter of an hour max, so I suggest we get straight down to business.' Without more ado, she showed them into a room containing a small desk with a computer and two visitors' chairs. There was a moment of awkwardness as the men tried to arrange their long legs in the limited space.

'We've gone over the records based on the information you gave us.' The woman laid her hand on some printouts beside the keyboard. Her nails were cut to the quick and she wore no rings or other jewellery. 'We're meant to be looking for a pregnant woman who came in with a head injury between Christmas and New Year, correct?'

Conscious of the need for haste, Huldar and Gudlaugur nodded without speaking so as not to waste any of her precious time.

The doctor nodded back. 'Then I think we've found the woman you're after.'

Huldar felt this justified opening his mouth. 'Great. That's great.' Finally, finally they were getting somewhere.

Ignoring his delight, the doctor went on: 'Though we can't be sure she's the person you're looking for, she's the only patient who fits your description.' She shot a glance at the printouts, picked up the top sheet and began to read in a mechanical voice: 'The incident we believe to be the one in question occurred on 27 December and involved a head injury resulting from a blow. The woman had significant bruising around a bleeding wound above her right temple, accompanied by nausea and a headache indicative of concussion. The wound required five stitches and the patient was kept in under observation until we could be sure the concussion wasn't serious and that there was no cranial haemorrhaging. We also ran tests to make sure her unborn child was unaffected. Once we'd established that there were no complications, she was discharged, some four hours after she came in. She was advised to take it easy and to get in touch immediately if she experienced any dizziness. Also if her headache or nausea returned or she became confused. But we didn't hear from her again. I can't see from our records when or where her stitches were removed, so I assume she'll have gone to her GP for that.'

Huldar shifted restlessly in his chair. He wasn't interested in the woman's injuries, only in her name. He had already decided to ask Gudlaugur to drive on the way back so he could get straight down to looking Siggi's mother up online. 'I see.' But he had no chance to press the doctor for a name before she resumed speaking:

'Before going any further, I should tell you what caused her injury.'

Huldar sighed under his breath but managed to nod and put on a show of interest.

'According to the woman, she walked into a cupboard door. I was on duty that evening and examined her.' The doctor paused briefly. 'I was and remain convinced that this explanation was untrue.'

'Untrue?' Gudlaugur prompted, though he and Huldar both knew perfectly well what the doctor was implying.

'Yes, untrue. The contusion was round and nothing like the type of injury you'd get from walking into a door. If I had to guess, I'd say a glass had been thrown at her. Or deliberately smashed over her head. That would explain the cut, which was caused by a sharp object. I've yet to encounter a spherical cupboard door with razor-sharp edges.'

Huldar supplied the obvious conclusion: 'Domestic abuse.'

'Yes, very probably.' The doctor looked up from the

printout. 'A classic case, in my opinion, though the woman wouldn't admit it. Unwillingness to make eye contact, unconvincing story and the faint signs of other, older injuries that she couldn't adequately explain – I could mentally tick all the usual boxes. She even displayed signs of relief, which is characteristic for this type of victim. They've known for ages that a new attack was imminent and once it's over, there's a brief respite where all is sweetness and light and they can temporarily let down their guard. The worst is over, for the moment.'

The doctor's forehead creased into deep, horizontal lines. 'I've heard it described as being like an earthquake. Tension builds up until it's released with a bang. Then the process starts all over again.' She picked up another page and ran her eyes down it. 'As is usual in these cases, I sent her for a screening interview but all her answers were designed to cover for her husband. It's pretty standard.' She put down the papers. 'Of course I could be wrong – I can't rule that out. These cases are complicated. Anyway, I thought it right to let you know.'

Since the information could prove important for establishing what had happened to Siggi's mother, Huldar's interest was piqued. Her name could wait. In the circumstances, the person most likely to be responsible for the woman's disappearance was her husband. It was no secret that every other murder in Iceland was linked to a domestic. He only hoped Siggi's mother wasn't about to become another statistic. 'We understand that her husband came in with her. And her young son as well. Did you talk to the man?'

'Yes, briefly. The wife wanted him to come into the examination room with her but I put my foot down. I suspected immediately that he'd attacked her, and of course it's pointless carrying out a screening interview with the abuser present. She had to accept my decision but was very ill at ease, presumably afraid that her husband would take it badly if he had to wait outside. Naturally I didn't give the real reason when I stopped him from coming in. I used the little boy as an excuse, saying it wouldn't be suitable for him to be present, and the man seemed to accept this. The patient calmed down after that.'

'And that was your only interaction?'

'No. I had a word with him when she was discharged, explaining the warning signs he should look out for and stressing that his wife needed peace and quiet for the next twenty-four hours.'

'You didn't mention your suspicion?'

'Yes, I did. I told him that I was sceptical about his wife's version of events, but left it at that. He had their son in his arms at the time. It looked as if the little boy had fallen asleep while they were waiting but I couldn't see his face and didn't want to speak any more plainly in case he was awake and listening. Anyway, there wasn't much I could say to the man that he didn't already know. If abusive partners won't change their behaviour for their family – for the people closest to them – they're hardly likely to do so because we order them to. But he was shaken. I allowed myself to hope that the fear of being exposed might have some effect. I suppose that was naive of me.'

Huldar handed her the photo of Siggi. 'Is this the boy?'

The doctor took the picture and looked at it briefly. 'I'm afraid I don't know. I never saw his face.' She gave it back to Huldar, who returned it to his pocket, disappointed.

'You didn't report it?' he asked.

'No, I didn't. We respect the confidentiality of our patients and only report incidents when we believe the person in question or those close to them might be in danger.' The doctor took a deep breath before adding: 'Since you're here, I assume my judgement must have been at fault.'

'It looks like it, I'm afraid.'

'In my defence, it was the woman's first visit to A&E. The older marks I saw during the examination were faint bruises, and one patch on her scalp where she had nothing but stubble. I concluded that her hair had been pulled out in a recent struggle. But those injuries weren't nearly as serious as the blow to her head. You see, domestic abuse often escalates. When it gets more serious, the victims sometimes see the light. They're forced to face up to the fact that things aren't going to improve, only get worse. I thought the woman had probably reached that stage, though she wouldn't confide in me.'

The doctor didn't need to make excuses to Huldar. He was all too aware that domestics weren't cut and dried. The relationship between victim and abuser made them far trickier to deal with than most of the crimes that reached the police. Huldar was no expert, but he did know that victims tended to be torn by conflicting feelings that were hard to untangle: fear, anger, love, hate, guilt, self-accusation, anxiety, contempt and shame. This muddied the waters and made it almost impossible for the victim to report their spouse to the police and leave them. Instead, they tended either to put up with the situation or cling to the deluded hope that things would eventually start to get better.

Huldar decided to make things easier for the doctor. The

blame wasn't hers or due to any failing by A&E. 'We're not at all sure that her disappearance is linked to her husband,' he said. 'We're not even sure she's missing. We just can't find her.'

The doctor looked back at the report. 'If my calculations are right, she must be more than eight months pregnant.' She raised her eyes to Huldar. 'If she really is missing, I hope you find her as soon as possible.'

'So do we.' Huldar pulled a notebook out of his coat pocket and opened it in the middle. Although it was dog-eared, its pages were still completely blank. He usually trusted his memory, leaving it to others to make notes, but there must be absolutely no risk of forgetting Siggi's mother's name. 'If I had the woman's name, we could get on with tracking her down.'

The doctor made a face. 'I'm sorry, I can't give you that information without a warrant. You know that. The police can't just walk in and start demanding details about our patients. We're bound by confidentiality. Although I've spoken openly about the patient's circumstances, that's because she was anonymous. I have to draw a line somewhere.'

Gudlaugur frowned. 'I don't understand. Can't you just report it as domestic abuse and solve the problem that way? You're allowed to do that if you believe there's good reason.'

'Not unless I can support my decision. But I can't do that now, more than six weeks after the event. Any deviations from the rules are taken very seriously. We're short-staffed enough without my being temporarily suspended while the matter's under investigation.'

'But this is an emergency.' Gudlaugur wasn't ready to give

up without a fight. Although judges were usually accommo-
dating in murder cases, there was bound to be a delay while
the formalities were taken care of. Search warrants, phone
tapping and the handing over of bank details were one thing,
but sensitive private details like patient records were quite
another. Especially when the police couldn't be positive that
they had the right person. The wait was likely to waste
precious hours and a warrant might even be refused.

'If I were to describe it to the ethics committee, your emergency would sound like this: the police were looking for a
woman but didn't know if she was actually missing or what
her name was. They claimed she'd come to A&E between
Christmas and New Year but weren't quite sure. Despite this,
I handed over the details and name of the woman I thought
might be the right one. Without being absolutely sure.' The
doctor stood up. 'No. I'm sorry but I'll need a warrant.' She
pushed the papers into the middle of the table. Before
Gudlaugur could object further, she added: 'But as this is
urgent – despite all the holes in your account – I'll consult
the doctor in charge of this shift. He may see it differently,
though I doubt it. If you could just wait here.'

When she reached the door, she turned and looked briefly
back at the desk. Then she went out.

Huldar smiled and reached for the printout. Gudlaugur
raised his eyebrows, scandalised, though he made no attempt
to prevent him.

'Sigurlaug Lára Lárusdóttir.' Huldar put the papers back
on the desk. He wasn't interested in anything else. At long
last.

When the doctor came back it was to say that her superior
had refused their request. She shook their hands again in

parting and didn't seem remotely surprised when Huldar bestowed his warmest smile on her and thanked her sincerely for her help.

As they stepped outside into the car park, he chucked the keys at Gudlaugur. 'You're driving.'

Chapter 16

Huldar had never set foot in a family home like it. It wasn't the furniture, the interior design or the view – none of which were in any way remarkable – that brought him up short, it was the fact the place was immaculate, like a show home. There wasn't a speck of dust or the least bit of clutter anywhere. Even the tea towel in the kitchen looked as if it had been folded with the help of a ruler. The contents of the cupboards were neatly organised in perfectly straight rows. The fridge looked as if it had just been installed: no dried milk stains from leaky cartons, no shrivelled lemons or slimy lettuce leaves in the vegetable drawer.

Although Huldar disliked mess himself, this apparent mania for order made him uneasy, not least because a child lived here. His five sisters all had kids – one had four – all boys like Siggi, and Huldar couldn't remember ever leaving their homes without limping from treading on a Lego brick. But Siggi's toys were all in his room, carefully stowed away in a box or systematically arranged on a small set of shelves. Even his clothes were folded away in drawers or hanging in the wardrobe. There were no odd socks lurking in a corner or under the bed. In fact, the only sign that this wasn't a display room in an Ikea store was the boy's unmade bed.

The extraordinary tidiness immediately put Huldar in mind of Helgi's flat. In both cases everything was in its place, every surface shone, like crime scenes à la Marie Kondo. But there the similarity ended. Everything about Helgi's apartment spoke of wealth, whereas here it was immediately obvious that money was tight.

'Looks as if the boy was taken from his bed while he was asleep, which is consistent with what he told us.' Huldar raised a latex-gloved hand to the globe on the white-varnished chest of drawers and watched it spin. It came to a halt with the Mediterranean facing him. Someone had drawn a circle in red felt pen round the island of Majorca. 'To go by the rest of the place, you'd expect his bed to be made every morning without fail.'

'Hmm.' It was unclear whether Gudlaugur's mumble indicated agreement. He was down on all fours, peering under Siggi's bed. He'd thought he was safe after they'd got back to the office but he hadn't been poring over the CCTV footage for long before Erla had secured the search warrant and dragged them both out again.

Huldar had been delighted but Gudlaugur had taken it badly, though he calmed down a bit when Erla gave him the green light to finish watching the recordings after work. At least she wasn't planning to give the job to anyone else, though it did mean Gudlaugur would be working late.

'Is your place this spotless?' Huldar opened a drawer containing the boy's T-shirts. Top of the pile was one sporting a cartoon of a plump dinosaur with a broad smile plastered across its face, red cheeks and a flower in one claw. About as far from reality as you could get.

'No. No way.' Gudlaugur got to his feet. 'There isn't even any fluff under the boy's bed.'

Lína appeared in the doorway, looking as perplexed as

them. She'd been searching the bathroom-cum-utility room. 'What's with this place?'

Gudlaugur shrugged but Huldar replied: 'Either they've had professional cleaners in or one or both parents are obsessed with hygiene.'

'There isn't so much as a toothpaste mark in the sink. The mirror looks like it's been polished and the toilet like it was put in this morning. I get the feeling nobody lives here at all, that it's just for show.'

Huldar surveyed the room. 'Or, alternatively, someone's scoured the place from top to bottom to hide the evidence of whatever happened here.'

They'd found the address as soon as they entered Sigurlaug Lára's name in the National Register. It had turned out to be a block of flats in Grafarholt, a new suburb on the eastern outskirts of the city. Siggi's description hadn't been entirely accurate since there were glimpses of the sea and also of Mount Esja between the neighbouring buildings, though a large block hid Hallgrímskirkja's distinctive spire. They hadn't visited this district during their drive around the city, as it hadn't seemed to meet the criteria. Gudlaugur, unimpressed by the little boy's mental acuity, had muttered darkly that he doubted it would have made any difference. But then he had been extremely wound up when he said it. There was no point reminding him that, according to the National Register, the kid was only four years and two months old.

Erla hadn't pressed Huldar for details when he passed on Sigurlaug's name with the comment that he couldn't reveal his source. Apparently she still trusted him enough to take him at his word when he said it was better she didn't know. In return, he hadn't asked her how she was planning to account for their success in her application for a search warrant. Perhaps she'd just left that part blank and stressed that finding these people was a matter of life or death. The warrant had certainly been issued with record speed.

The entry in the National Register helped to explain why they'd had no luck in tracing Siggi's family. Despite having the nickname Sibbi, the boy's father was called Margeir – it didn't even begin with an S.

Erla had hit the roof when this came to light. She couldn't for the life of her understand how someone called Margeir could have a nickname like that. She bawled out everyone within range, directing the worst of her wrath at Lína, although the intern hadn't expressed any opinion on the matter. But Lína took it on the chin, even when Erla started making disparaging comments about her name. At this point Huldar had intervened, unable to stand by any longer, with the result that Erla had turned her ire on him instead. But then he was used to it. In the end she had simmered down, and her mood had shifted to jubilation when the news came through that a search warrant had been issued.

Although they'd had to carefully fudge the explanation of how they'd come across Siggi's mother's name, they had been able to provide other information in support of their request. Before submitting the application they had talked to Sigurlaug's mother and also to the parents of her husband, Margeir Arnarson, who had said they weren't in touch that often so they hadn't been concerned at not hearing from their son for a few days. It was a different story with Sigurlaug's mother. She said she'd been a bit worried as she hadn't heard a word from her daughter since Saturday, which was out of character. Usually she heard from her every single day without fail.

When the police asked if she'd tried to call her daughter, the mother explained that she hadn't because she'd been afraid Margeir would answer. And he would *not* be pleased to hear from her. Phone calls to the couple's closest friends, whose names were provided by the parents, told the same story. No one had heard from Sigurlaug or Margeir for several days, though the friends also mentioned that they didn't see that much of them any more. Sigurlaug's mother's statement provided the strongest grounds for a search warrant. Along with Siggi, of course. Everyone the police spoke to agreed that both parents adored their son. No one believed for a minute that they would have deliberately abandoned him. And no one knew of any links between his parents and the murdered man, Helgi.

Huldar looked around the child's immaculate room again. There was no reason to linger as he and Gudlaugur had been through everything. 'I don't think we'll find anything here. It's possible Forensics will spot something when they go over the place with Luminol, like traces of blood-stains that have been wiped away. We'll get them to test the headboard and bed frame for fingerprints as well, in case the person who took the boy touched them. I'd be surprised, but you never know.' The building had no security cameras to show them who had carried the sleeping boy from the flat. There was no CCTV in the area either, so no chance of identifying the car that had taken the child away.

'They've searched the master bedroom,' Lína announced. 'Everything's as pristine there as it is everywhere else. The bed's made as well. Do you want to take fingerprints from it anyway?'

'That's for Erla to decide. She'll have to come back inside

soon.' Erla had been in the middle of supervising the search when her phone had rung and she stepped out into the corridor to answer it. Huldar suspected the call was from her bosses, who had been keeping an eagle eye on their progress since the news had started filtering out into the media that afternoon. He didn't suppose this would do anything to improve her mood.

The only potentially interesting material discovered during their search had been deposited on the sitting-room table: a scarf with brown stains on it, believed to be Siggi's Christmas present to his mother. Two laptops – one white, one black. Two folders containing carefully organised home accounts. Some post that had been found torn to pieces in the bin. Sigurlaug's passport and a handbag containing her credit and debit cards and driving licence. In addition to these, there was a china vase, broken into three pieces, that had been found at the back of a cupboard, which might possibly have been used in a struggle; although, if so, it was hard to believe it would have been tidied away like that. The cupboard was full of other smashed ornaments and crockery, and snapped necklaces, which seemed to have been put away to be mended later. Everyone had a drawer or shelf like that. But Siggi's family appeared to be clumsier than most. The objects would all be sent to Forensics in case any of them bore the fingerprints of the person responsible for the family's disappearance. This was clutching at straws, however, and showed just how little they had to go on.

It was far more likely that these breakages were evidence of the long-term domestic abuse that the A&E doctor had suspected.

'Can I have a go at piecing together the torn-up post?' Lína was standing over the table where the evidence had been collected, examining the scraps of paper from the bin. 'I won a jigsaw-puzzle contest at school.' She held up her hands to show that she still had her latex gloves on.

'Be my guest.' Huldar reached for a stool from the bar that divided the kitchen from the dining and sitting areas. 'Just don't let Erla catch you at it, or she'll give you the job of sifting through the rubbish from Helgi's building to find whatever he tore up. I gather it's all been brought to the station and there's a ton of the stuff.' He sat down, contemplating the gleaming wall tiles above the cooker. He doubted the husband had been responsible for the obsessive cleaning.

'They're letters from the bank. And one from the company they got their car loan from.' Lína carried on fitting the scraps of paper together. 'Shit. They were up to their necks in debt. They were about to lose their car. And as if that wasn't bad enough, they were about to default on their mortgage too.'

'Lots of people are in that situation but they don't all vanish, leaving their child in a stranger's flat,' Gudlaugur said scornfully. He hadn't changed his opinion where Lína was concerned.

'Oh, come on. When people are on the point of losing everything, it's bound to affect their behaviour, so the information's obviously relevant.' Huldar shouldn't need to tell Gudlaugur this. 'Someone had better ring the loan company and find out if their car's been repossessed. That could explain why it's not parked out the front.' Before entering the building they had searched the nearby parking spaces for a white Yaris, with no luck.

The door opened and Erla came back in. 'Finished? Can I call in Forensics?'

'Yep, I reckon so.' Huldar tried to tell from Erla's expression whether the phone call had put her under even more strain or had been constructive for once. But her face was unreadable. 'The couple seem to have been on a fast track to bankruptcy.'

'Huh. You don't say?' Shoving her phone in her pocket, Erla went over to the table where the post had been pieced together. She didn't ask who had done it and Lína had edged discreetly away as soon as she appeared. 'That puts a whole new light on the matter. Maybe we're looking at suicide.'

Huldar was suddenly struck by an idea. 'Has the body from Gálgahraun been formally identified yet?'

'Yes, the victim's parents took care of that earlier. Why do you ask?' Erla glanced up from the jigsaw puzzle at Huldar.

'Oh, I just suddenly wondered if the man we found could have been Margeir – with Helgi's wallet in his pocket. The whole thing could be a misunderstanding and the rich guy could be bathing in champagne somewhere in the Caribbean right now, without a clue that we think he's dead.'

'No. It was him all right. If this couple have killed themselves, their bodies haven't been found yet.'

'I don't believe a woman would kill herself when she was eight months pregnant.' From her haunted expression, Lína appeared to be picturing the scene. 'The child could be born while she was in her death throes and no mother could face that.'

Gudlaugur snorted at this but Erla ignored him. 'I reckon you're right. It's not hard to find a good home for a newborn. If she'd been contemplating suicide, the woman would have waited. I find it more likely that her bastard of a husband battered her once too often and finished her off.'

'Well, there's no sign of that in here.' Huldar ran his eyes round the room. 'Though I suppose he could have cleaned up after himself. The flat's unnaturally spotless. Mind you, if you were cleaning up after a murder or a violent attack, you'd hardly waste time folding laundry. Still, Forensics should be able to establish that once and for all. We're left with the mystery of where the couple are now, dead or alive.'

'And who killed Helgi.' Erla gestured to the collection of objects on the table. 'You didn't find anything connecting them?'

'Nope, not a thing. Though of course we haven't looked at the computers. Perhaps something'll come to light there. Or in their phone records, once we've examined them.'

'What about mobiles? Any sign of them?'

'No, none.' Sigurlaug's phone hadn't been in her bag. They had found chargers, their wires neatly coiled, on each bedside table, but no phones connected to them. It was odd that Sigurlaug's mobile was missing, given that her bag and bank cards had been left behind. The presence of her handbag was a strong clue that she hadn't left the flat voluntarily but it was impossible to guess why the person who abducted her should have taken her phone. Especially since these days even a child would know that phones can be traced if they're switched on. Unless, that is, she'd managed to take it with her without her attacker realising. But in that case why hadn't she used it to call for help? It didn't look good. Her husband's wallet, perhaps significantly, was nowhere to be found.

'I was asked to fetch some clothes for the kid. Could one of you pick some out before we leave? It looks like he may be going to stay with his grandmother.' Erla waited for someone to volunteer but they all kept quiet. In the end,

Huldar heaved himself up off the bar stool and agreed to do it. He had a horde of nephews, after all.

Having got a bag from Erla, Huldar went back into Siggi's room. He began by putting in plenty of underwear and socks, taking care not to make a mess, influenced by the excessive neatness of the drawers. Then he picked out a few tops, including the T-shirt with the dinosaur on the front, and three pairs of trousers. Finally, he put in a pair of pyjamas and reckoned that would do. Hopefully they'd find the boy's parents before he ran out of clothes.

Huldar's gaze returned to the bed, then wandered round the room again. The rabbit the boy had mentioned was nowhere to be seen. It hadn't turned up in Helgi's flat either. Perhaps the boy had taken it with him and dropped it in the abductor's car, though, from Huldar's memory of his days in the regular police, that seemed unlikely. He had occasionally been involved in helping to remove children from problem homes and if the kids had a favourite cuddly toy, nothing could prise it out of their clutches once they found themselves in unfamiliar surroundings.

Something didn't add up here. Huldar corrected himself: nothing about this added up. Not a single damned thing.

Chapter 17

Siggi was sitting in a chair facing his grandmother, colouring as if his life depended on it. The woman was a tall, thin sixty-year-old, with a straight back and clear eyes. Her face was healthily tanned but the skin at her neckline was snow-white, suggesting that she was the outdoorsy type, a walker or golfer, rather than someone who made a beeline for the sun-lounger the moment the clouds parted. She looked ten years younger than she was, only her hands giving her true age away. Her name was Margrét, but she had asked Freyja to call her Magga.

Freyja noticed the small telltale signs that Margrét had made an effort for this meeting, like the hastily applied lipstick in a colour that didn't suit her – perhaps she'd bought it in a hurry on the way here.

'I'm speechless. I mean, I'd heard rumours about your inhumane policies, but it never occurred to me that they were true.' The woman's gaze left Freyja and strayed back to her grandson.

'I'm afraid there are guidelines that have to be followed. I assure you it's nothing personal.' Freyja had been landed with the unenviable task of breaking it to Margrét that Siggi wouldn't be allowed to go to her yet. Various formalities had to be taken care of first, formalities that were necessary in order to protect the interests of the children who ended up in the hands of social services. When the child's close relatives were involved, it could appear unfair, giving the impression of a cold, uncaring system.

This was far from the truth, but the present case was undeniably unusual, if not unparalleled. Normally, either one or both parents were available to give their consent for the arrangements. 'They're looking for a temporary solution, which should hopefully work out in your favour. You won't have to wait long for the decision. The people involved know how urgent it is.' Freyja had to phrase this carefully in front of Siggi. Although he didn't appear to be taking an interest, he was nevertheless listening.

'You say they need to inspect my flat.' The boy's grandmother glanced round at the shabbily furnished living room of the temporary care home. 'Is that some kind of joke? I mean, who inspected this place?' Her eyes lingered on the battered toys that lay strewn over the floor where the children had abandoned them.

Freyja chose not to answer this. The question had been rhetorical anyway. She looked at Siggi, who was now scribbling in red crayon over the head of the matchstick figure he had drawn. 'Have Siggi's pictures always been like that, Magga?'

Margrét turned to watch her grandson scribbling furiously until the matchstick figure's head had been completely obliterated by red lines. Then she looked back at Freyja, her face puzzled. 'I've never seen him do that before, but I have to admit I haven't had much contact with him over the last year. Much less than I'd have liked or my daughter would have chosen.'

'What prevented you?'

The woman silently mouthed: 'His father.'

'I see.' Freyja asked Siggi: 'What's the red meant to be?'

The boy stopped his colouring and raised sleepy eyes to Freyja. 'I'm not telling.'

'I see.' Freyja smiled. 'Who's the picture of, then? You can tell me that.'

'Mummy.'

There was a sharp intake of breath from the boy's grandmother. At that moment the carer put her head round the door and asked if Siggi would like some hot chocolate and doughnuts with the other kids. The boy accepted the offer and, climbing down from his chair, went out of the room with her. He had seemed pleased to see his grandmother but his pleasure had been muted and wary. He had soon wriggled free of her affectionate embrace, preferring to sit on a chair on his own and draw.

'He'll be back, don't worry.' Freyja thought the woman looked afraid that Siggi had gone for good and that next minute she herself would be shown the door. 'We can talk freely now. I get the feeling you want to tell me something that's not suitable for his ears.'

Margrét closed her eyes and rubbed her forehead. 'What do they think has happened to my daughter?'

'To be honest, I don't know. I'm not from the police. I expect they've got some theories they're working on but they haven't shared them with me. At least you can be comforted by the fact that they're making it their number one priority to find your daughter and her husband.'

'I couldn't care less about Sibbi. They needn't bother looking for him at all as far as I'm concerned. I want them to find Systa.' Margrét coughed and lowered her eyes to the table. 'Alive.'

So Margrét was no fan of her son-in-law. After learning that the man was suspected of being abusive, Freyja wasn't surprised. The information had reached her via the Child Protection Agency, who had been alerted to the situation by the police.

Although Freyja had no say in what would become of Siggi while the search for his parents was going on, she had been asked to help out in other ways, such as informing his grandmother that she would not be able to take him home with her at present, and to answer any questions the woman might have. If Margrét showed signs of wanting to talk or unburden herself, Freyja was to provide a listening ear. Given the circumstances, there was no call to be stiffly professional towards the understandably distraught woman.

The request to speak to Margrét had come in towards the end of the afternoon. Although it was a fairly minor part of the investigation, Freyja had, as always, welcomed the opportunity for more work. Children's services were so overstretched these days that her willingness to do overtime would end up making her the most popular girl in the system. Then again, if she agreed to rent Tobbi's place, her money problems would be a thing of the past and there would be no more need to take these extra shifts. That damned snake wasn't all bad news.

'I understand that your son-in-law is suspected of having been abusive towards your daughter. Has it been going on long? From the beginning of their relationship, perhaps?'

'I don't know when it began. It may well have been like that from the beginning. They started seeing each other six years ago but Systa broke things off after a year. He went running after her, though, begging her to take him back, and after that it was on and off for several months until Systa got pregnant. Then they moved in together and got married. I wish she'd stuck to her decision to leave him but then she wouldn't have had Siggi. It's complicated.' The woman looked up, wiping her eyes. After a moment, she got a grip on herself, gave a little cough, and went on: 'But it's easy to be wise in hindsight. I first began to notice something was wrong about three years ago, after Siggi was born. Systa would never admit it, so I had nothing solid to go on, except that I know when she's lying. I brought her up on my own and I could always read her like an open book. But despite that it took me a while to cotton on. It had just never occurred to me that she'd end up in a relationship like that – a strong, clever girl like her. But I've since learnt that it happens to all kinds of people.' Deep lines of worry appeared between her brows. 'As you can imagine, I keep asking myself if there was something I could have done. I don't know what, though. I tried to talk to her often enough. Perhaps I should have called the police and reported my suspicions. Then maybe I wouldn't be sitting here now.'

There wasn't much Freyja could say to this. Hovering in the air between them was the unspoken fear that Sibbi had beaten her daughter to death. They both glanced inadvertently at Siggi's drawing. Freyja hoped Margrét wasn't thinking along the same lines as her: that the boy could have witnessed the incident. 'Siggi says his mother's a teacher.' Freyja was careful not to refer to Systa in the past tense. 'If I understood him right, she chose to stay at home and look after him. Not many Icelandic mothers take four years off for maternity leave. Mind you, Siggi seems to have benefited from it. He's obviously been very well brought up.' In spite of his apparent indifference to the whereabouts of his parents, and his gory drawings.

'Systa never meant to be on maternity leave for four years. She'd only been teaching for three before Siggi came along, and she was really enjoying it. If you ask me, it was Sibbi who refused to let her go back to work.'

That would make sense. If abusers could find a way of isolating their victims, it was much easier to hide the evidence of their violence and reduce the risk that someone would intervene. But it would be unprofessional to voice these thoughts aloud. After all, Freyja didn't know the details. 'Siggi said his mother was planning to begin teaching again when he started at kindergarten. But presumably that won't be possible until the new baby is old enough.'

'Systa's often talked about going back to work. After Siggi was born she couldn't wait to get out of the house. She did actually start teaching again the autumn after he was born, when he was only eight months old. She'd got him a place with a childminder and everything. Then two months later she quit her job and never told me why. I kept asking her but gave up in the end when I saw what a strain it was for her to lie to me about it being her decision. It wasn't true: I'm sure of that. Sibbi was behind it. I can see that now.'

Again, Freyja carefully refrained from comment. There were all sorts of possible reasons for Systa's decision that wouldn't necessarily have involved her husband: post-natal depression, for example, or job-related stress. 'Well, let's hope she decides to go back to work after her maternity leave this time. There's always a need for good teachers.'

Margrét brightened up slightly, but then her face fell again. 'When do you think they'll find her? She could give birth any time. What'll happen to the baby if she's being held prisoner somewhere?'

Freyja laid her hand on Margrét's bony one. 'There's every likelihood that your daughter and her baby will be fine. Remember, the odds are just as high that everything will turn out all right.' Freyja based this on the simple statistic that either it would go well or not, 50/50 – using the same logic with which she had failed her probability test back in the day.

Her attempt at kindness backfired. Margrét's eyes filled with tears and she had to pull back her hand to wipe them away. Freyja hurriedly went on talking to give the woman a moment to recover: 'What about Sibbi? Siggi told me he was an electrician. Is he in work?' Freyja thought he probably must be, or the little boy would show more signs of coming from a problem home. If both his parents had been hanging around the flat all day, he was bound to have witnessed beatings, deliberate humiliation, screaming, shouting and whatever else Sibbi might resort to. Whereas if his father was at work during the day, it was possible that he was able to control himself until after the boy had gone to bed. That might explain why Siggi appeared so placid and free from stress. He was still so young that it would be possible for his parents to conceal a lot from him. But if the situation continued, sooner or later he would start to pick up on it. For all their innocence, children were no fools.

Margrét sniffed and shuddered. Then, wiping away a tear with the back of her hand, she answered Freyja's question. 'He was in full-time work until about six months ago. Now I gather he takes on odd jobs when they come up. He isn't speaking to me so I know nothing about his life apart from what I hear from Systa. But we don't often discuss Sibbi on the rare occasions when I get to see her. I have absolutely no wish to talk about him.'

'Did you fall out with him?'

'Yes, you could say that. Just over a year ago I told him bluntly that I was sure he was mistreating Systa. They'd gone on a trip to Majorca that they'd been planning for ages, but when they came home it was obvious that he'd taken his fists to her. Before they went away things had seemed unusually good between them, but that obviously didn't last because she came back from the holiday with two black eyes and bruises on her neck. She made up some lie about having fallen off her bike but it was blatantly obvious that her injuries weren't the result of a fall. I couldn't stomach it, so I confronted Margeir and he went berserk. I thought he was going to go for me, but in the end he just threw me out of their flat and banned me from having any further contact with my daughter. Systa's too frightened to stand up to him, so we have to meet in secret. That worked all right while Sibbi was employed full-time but we've seen a lot less of each other since he was sacked.'

A teacher stuck at home being a housewife; an unemployed electrician – two professions that were always in demand, especially in the current economic climate. When Freyja had needed an electrician a month ago, she had been advised to put her name down for a course on the grounds that she'd probably have qualified herself before she managed to get one to come round. 'Once she's found, I hope your daughter will manage to sort out her problems. Now that children's services are involved, they'll be able to provide her with help and counselling, to empower her to take control of her own life and provide her little boy with a safe environment to grow up in. That's part of our job, since it's in the child's interests.'

'Counselling, huh?' The woman emitted a short, bitter laugh. 'I think a contract killer would be more use. There's nothing wrong with Systa: Sibbi's the problem. With him out of her life, she'd be fine. But as long as he still draws breath and is living in Iceland, she'll be frightened and permanently on edge. With good reason. He either needs to change or to get out of their lives. But he won't change. Adults never do.'

There was something in what Margrét was saying – apart from the nonsense about contract killers, of course. 'The solution to your daughter's problems doesn't have to be as drastic as you think.' Freyja gave the woman a friendly smile. After all, people often said stuff they didn't mean in circumstances like this. She changed the subject. 'Do you have any other children who can support you while you're waiting for news?'

'Yes, a son, Dadi – Systa's older brother. He's at work at the moment and I'm waiting for him to finish before I break the news to him. I'm not looking forward to it.'

'No, it's no fun being the bearer of bad news.' Freyja was glad to hear the woman had someone to turn to. 'Is he aware of what's been happening to his sister?'

'Yes. That's partly why I'm dreading telling him. Of course he couldn't accept the situation and he tried talking to her, and to that bastard Sibbi, but it didn't go well. He ended up being frozen out like me. But he found it harder to forgive his sister for putting up with the situation. Their relationship hasn't recovered because he wasn't prepared to meet her in secret.'

At that moment Siggi came back into the room with a

brown cocoa moustache on his upper lip. The carer appeared in the doorway behind him and told him to say goodbye to his grandmother as she was going home now. The boy accepted this news without any tears or other evidence of distress. He simply went over to her and accepted a kiss and a cuddle before he freed himself and went back to the carer, pausing in the doorway to turn and wave. Then he was gone.

His grandmother was left, her arms suspended in the air, as if expecting her grandchild to come running back to her.

Chapter 18

Huldar's stomach was rumbling so loudly that it was distracting him from work. He'd tried to fob it off with coffee but it had seen through this cheap trick and redoubled its protests. The only answer was to feed the damned thing, so he got to his feet and asked Gudlaugur if he wanted to go for a quick burger. Gudlaugur declined the offer without even looking up from his screen. He'd been glued to it ever since they got back to the station, where he'd found a whole new batch of CCTV from the city centre waiting for him. Although he needed to finish editing together the videos in which Helgi appeared by tomorrow morning at the latest, he had brushed off Huldar's offer of help. Well, that was his problem.

Huldar went to let Erla know that he was going to grab some food. Most of the others had already gone home; the only detectives still there were either single like him or older men whose kids had grown up. All the young fathers had left for the day, as had the single guy with the cat. But, needless to say, Lína had stayed behind, radiating satisfaction over the urgency and sheer number of tasks that remained to be completed. Huldar wanted to warn her not to appear too eager since Erla still hadn't allocated the job of going through the rubbish, but she looked so happy as she sat focusing intently on her computer screen that he couldn't bring himself to spoil her pleasure. It was a long time since he'd seen anyone in this office emanating such an air of contentment.

He tapped on the door to Erla's office and opened it without waiting for a *Come in*. Erla rarely bothered to respond anyway.

The door bumped into the back of the man who was standing just inside, as far away from Erla's desk as possible, forcing him to move up, closer to her. Huldar vaguely recognised the guy. Young and painfully shy, he hovered awkwardly as Erla introduced him as Geir from IT.

'Found anything yet?'

Geir turned to Huldar, apparently thankful to speak to him rather than Erla. 'Yes, some pretty interesting files on the desktop computer from Helgi's flat.'

'Oh come on, just spit it out. What's in the files?' Erla glanced irritably at Huldar. 'He's been standing here for five minutes, blithering round in circles. I can't get any sense out of him. Perhaps he's like one of his computers: needs a bit of a kick to sort him out.'

'Kicking is no way to treat a computer.' Geir found his tongue at last, deeply affronted on behalf of all the microprocessors and motherboards in the world. 'They're not like a jammed vending machine.'

'For Christ's sake, how many times do I have to ask? What's – in – the – bloody – files?'

Geir braced himself. 'Sex videos.'

'Jesus. Why couldn't you say so straight away?' Erla shook her head, exasperated. 'What kind of sex videos?'

'Homemade ones, we think.'

'Homemade? How can you tell?'

'Because that's what they look like.' Geir shot a look at Huldar in a transparent plea for help but Huldar was no more eager than him to explain to Erla the difference between homemade sex tapes and the kind of stuff churned out by the porn industry. Geir was on his own. 'Well, er, the action always happens in the same room, in the same bed, filmed from the same angle. Same headboard, different sheets. There's no camerawork to speak of – just a fixed point of view – and the sex is over too quickly for a professional job.'

'Are you saying there's no short porn?' The two men looked at Erla uncertainly. She didn't appear to be joking.

Geir threw another despairing glance at Huldar, who merely smiled and prompted him: 'Go on. Enlighten us.'

The young man cleared his throat. 'I wouldn't know. But I think the man in the videos is Helgi himself, though I can't be absolutely sure.'

Huldar guessed that Geir's uncertainty on this point was because all his attention had been fixed on the women. When he himself watched porn, he studiously avoided looking at the men – they were only there as props.

'Unfortunately,' Geir added, 'they appear to have been shot on a camera that wasn't connected to GPS or we could have identified the location from the metadata.'

'Metadata?' Erla raised an enquiring eyebrow.

'That's what they call the information that accompanies the file. The format's not always the same but generally it shows the date when the file was created, the last time it was updated, what program was used, and so on. But like I said, we've nothing like that to go on in this case. The camera wasn't connected to the internet or GPS.'

'Just our luck. How many videos are there?'

'Thirty-five in total. The oldest is from about two years

ago; the most recent was made just over three weeks ago. But there could be more.'

'Were the files locked?'

'No. The computer wasn't even password protected. People are often unbelievably careless with their home computers. His work PC and laptop were locked but we managed to get into them anyway.'

'Did he have the same sort of files there?'

'Not that we've found so far.'

While Erla was pondering this information, Huldar slipped in a question of his own. 'Could it be more than one man, seeing as you're not sure it's Helgi?'

'No. The man's instantly recognisable in all the videos, though you hardly ever see his face. He's got this large white patch on his lower back. Like the scar from an old burn or something. You can't miss it because he's got his back to the camera most of the time.'

Erla reached for the pile of papers on her desk and leafed through them until she found what she was looking for. Extracting a report of some kind, she ran her eyes down it. 'It says here in the post-mortem report that Helgi had an oval patch of unpigmented skin, measuring five by ten centimetres, right across the lumbar region, probably caused by vitiligo – whatever that is.' Erla laid the report back on the pile. 'So it definitely was Helgi. What about the woman? Is she always the same too?'

'No. It appears to be a new woman every time, though they're all the same type.'

Geir began to sidle towards the door but Erla stopped him in his tracks. He turned back with a martyred look. Huldar doubted the staff in IT had exactly been competing for the job of discussing porn with Erla. They'd probably drawn straws and this poor sod had lost.

His ordeal showed no sign of ending as Erla grilled him for his opinion on why Helgi had kept these videos on his computer. Geir tried to get out of it by claiming ignorance but Erla wasn't about to let him off the hook. She asked if the men who made this sort of video usually kept them for their own private consumption or whether it was common for them to sell that sort of material, and, if so, where. Geir disclaimed all knowledge of the subject, but Erla persisted, asking if he thought the films had been made with the knowledge and permission of the women involved. The answer was a shrug. It was the same when she asked if he thought Helgi himself had been aware he was being filmed. Then she interrogated Geir about whether the sex in the videos was in any way kinky or within the normal range. But by now he had had enough and referred her to the Sexual Offences Unit. IT's expertise lay in analysing data – in files and online transactions. He reeled off the details of the file path on the server where he had transferred the videos for further analysis.

This done, he made for the door again, but not before Erla got in a final question, asking if he'd made sure the area on the server was locked. His eyes flickering evasively, he admitted that it hadn't occurred to him, but he'd remedy that immediately and email Erla the password.

Once he had gone, Huldar went over to the glass wall that separated Erla from her underlings. Most of the detectives still at work were glued to their screens with unnatural attention. It seemed the IT department's discovery had already leaked out, but Huldar wasn't about to tell Erla that. She was stressed enough as it was.

Hearing her speak, he turned.

'I'm assuming you have a little experience when it comes to porn.' Erla corrected herself: 'Sorry, I didn't mean *a little* – that was a slip of the tongue.'

'Is that a question or an observation?' Huldar wasn't about to share his porn-viewing habits with her.

'An observation.' Erla leant back in her chair, folding her arms across her chest. 'By the way, how are you getting on with collecting background on the boy's mother?'

'Pretty well. Though she seems to have dropped out of contact with most of her friends and relatives over the last couple of years, so the people I've got hold of so far haven't been able to tell me much. Her mother and brother are convinced that her husband was abusive and the friends I've talked to suspected the same thing. But no one's heard it from Sigurlaug herself, which isn't really surprising. She's not the first victim to cover up what's happening. I still need to pull it all together and send you a summary. Then you can choose who you want to call in for a more in-depth interview.'

Erla didn't seem particularly enthusiastic at the prospect. 'So you're available for other jobs, then?'

'Yes. I was going to nip out for a bite to eat, though. Maybe even call it a day.'

'Just hang on a minute. I'm going to forward you the location of the videos – and the password as soon as it arrives. Before I hand the recordings over to Sexual Offences, I'd like your opinion of them. I want someone here in the department to be familiar with the contents but I'm not the right person to judge the material. Pay special attention to whether the women seem aware of the camera – Helgi too.'

Rather than draw Erla's attention to the fact that a good

Gallows Rock

proportion of her male subordinates had already got an eyeful of the material, he nodded. It wasn't a prospect he relished but he agreed because it was wiser than objecting. In light of their shared past, he had no wish to prolong any conversation with her that involved sex. It remained an incredibly sore point between them. Their ill-advised one-night stand had led to a sexual-harassment inquiry by Internal Affairs and the ensuing process had been no fun for either of them. Their working relationship had never fully recovered from the event and its aftermath.

It was better to obey and get the hell out of her office. That burger would just have to wait.

After watching six videos of varying lengths, Huldar was getting cramp and had to stand up and stretch. His colleagues had lost interest in their screens now that the files had been locked and the atmosphere had reverted to normal. Some were rattling away on their keyboards, others talking on the phone, others frowning over documents or conferring with each other. Though none of them could be described as eye-candy, Huldar found the sight of them infinitely preferable to the distasteful task of watching Helgi humping a succession of women.

He shook himself, then noticed Gudlaugur watching him over his monitor. 'God, I'm in no hurry to request a transfer to Sexual Offences.'

'Bit grim, is it?'

'I don't know what it is. Perverted. Sleazy maybe.'

'In what way?'

'Well, sleazy if it was done without the women's consent. Maybe sordid is the word I'm looking for.'

Gudlaugur must have been bored to tears with watching the CCTV because he kept up a flow of questions: 'Does it look to you like that's what's going on? Are they unconscious? Knocked out by booze or Rohypnol?'

'No, far from it. Drunk, maybe, but perfectly aware of what they're doing. They just don't seem to know about the video. None of the ones I've seen have looked into the lens, except by accident. They make no attempt to present a flattering angle to the camera. The only one who seems conscious of trying to look good is Helgi.' Huldar reached for his coat. 'Not that I know how a woman would behave if she'd volunteered to be filmed, as it's not something I've done myself or have any desire to. But I've lost count of the women I've seen posing for selfies, and I'm guessing they'd behave the same way if they knew they were being recorded. None of them appear to be pouting for the camera.'

Gudlaugur shrugged noncommittally. 'Who are they? Any familiar faces?'

'No, but I haven't seen all of them yet. Given how many videos there are, it's not unlikely I'll come across someone I recognise sooner or later – assuming they're all Icelanders.' Huldar pulled on his coat. 'If not, their names might help. The files are all labelled with the women's first names and the date. Of course, he could have called the files stina060517 or greta261116 at random, but I doubt it.'

'What did he do with the files? Could other people see them?'

'The IT department are going through his emails. Apparently he had several social media accounts under aliases. With any luck they'll be able to find out if he shared the videos. But maybe he just wanted them for himself: a private collection to wank over in his old age.'

'He could have posted them on foreign porn sites.'

'Why would he do that?' Huldar took the cigarette packet out of his pocket and peered inside to see if he was in luck. Aha, one left.

'To show off, maybe. Or humiliate the women. Isn't revenge porn the big thing these days?'

Now that Huldar had the packet in his hands, he was overwhelmed by a craving for nicotine. 'I don't believe it was revenge porn. If we're reading his relationship history right, he was mostly into one-night stands. Revenge porn tends to be associated with break-ups but, as far as we know, he never had a long-term relationship.'

Gudlaugur didn't say anything in response to this, so Huldar went out for a smoke. But the sense of wellbeing that had spread through his veins quickly evaporated when he sat down to watch the videos again. Yet another arse, breasts, long blonde hair. The women could all be sisters. Evidently Helgi had a type.

There was no clue in the videos themselves about where the encounters had taken place. No view from a window, and the room was very ordinary; no different from tens of thousands of other white-walled Icelandic bedrooms. The only fact he could be sure of was that it wasn't either of the bedrooms in Helgi's luxury pad.

The video came to an end and Huldar clicked on the next: disa071017. It was no surprise to discover that Dísa resembled Stína from the last film. And Sigrún from the one before. A new girl in the bed but otherwise no change. Same positions and tempo, same facial contortions, but then the 'director' was the same too: Helgi. He usually kept his back to the camera, as Geir had said, but occasionally the couple would roll over, revealing a fleeting view of Helgi's face. Nothing too clear, though. But the pale oval patch of skin on his back was unmistakeable every time, so there was no reason to doubt that it was him.

The monotony wasn't limited to the visuals; it applied to the soundtrack as well. Intermittent moaning and groaning that intensified as things came to a climax. Huldar tore off his earphones and pressed 'Pause'. He'd had enough for now.

'Where are you off to? I thought you'd just had a smoke?' As if to avoid sounding too interested in Huldar's movements, Gudlaugur added quickly: 'In case Erla asks.'

'In the unlikely event that Erla shows any interest in my whereabouts you can tell her I'm going to have a quick word with the Sexual Offences team.'

This answer seemed to satisfy Gudlaugur, who turned back to his CCTV.

The coffee was better in Sexual Offences. Huldar sipped appreciatively from the plain white cup, which he was told was standard there. Personal mugs with silly slogans and jokes were discouraged, in case they featured the kind of tasteless sexual innuendoes that would be totally inappropriate in this department.

'So you think this bloke Helgi's murder might be connected to his homemade porn videos?' The officer sitting across the round table in the Sexual Offences Unit coffee room was one of the two men still there after hours. He was an old colleague, who had requested a transfer for a change of scene. According to him, he had found that here all right. 'If so, it'll be a first for us here in Iceland.'

'I've no idea if there's any link. But it's the only thing we can find on the guy that's . . . well . . . not exactly squeaky clean.' Huldar took another sip of coffee from the carefully neutral cup. 'The idea of "revenge porn" has come up, but in my opinion it doesn't really square with what we know about the murder victim. He'd never been in a relationship, so he had no reason to take revenge on an ex-girlfriend. I don't think it's worth wasting much time on that angle myself.'

'You do realise revenge isn't the only motivation for disseminating this kind of material? That's why they've started referring to it as "non-consensual porn" rather than revenge porn.' The weary look in the man's eyes suggested that the change of scene he'd claimed was so great had its downsides after all.

'Sure.' Huldar put down his cup. 'But it doesn't look to me like the guy made these videos to flog them to official porn sites, or amateur ones for that matter. He didn't need the money, believe me.'

'We're not only dealing with revenge or profit here.' The officer opened the laptop he'd brought along. 'There are countless websites set up for sharing this kind of material. Some are especially dedicated to Icelandic women – or girls, rather. We're usually talking about girls or very young women. How old are the women in your videos?'

'I don't know exactly but I'm guessing under thirty.' Mentally he reviewed the images of Helgi's identikit sexual partners. They had all looked closer to twenty than thirty, but mercifully none had appeared to be underage.

'Any woman over thirty is considered past it on the majority of these sites.' The man tapped on the keyboard, then turned the screen to Huldar. 'See for yourself.'

Huldar leant forwards. At the top was a banner featuring the Icelandic flag and below it a rather primitive interface where users could exchange messages. All the posts appeared to be about Icelandic girls. Most of the threads started with a user posting an ordinary photo of a named girl and asking if anyone out there had naked pictures of her. This resulted in a slew of comments about the girl in question – whether she was fit, a slut, hot and so on. Sometimes photos would turn up in which the girl was topless or even naked and these were shared to general rejoicing. If none could be found, a popular question was whether anyone could use photoshop to render the clothing in the innocent image transparent. This invariably resulted in a series of attempts by the users to digitally alter the pictures to remove the girl's clothes.

'What the hell is this shit?' Huldar bent closer to read the URL. He came away none the wiser. 'Never heard of it.'

'No, that's hardly surprising. You're too old. The users are mainly very young men or teenagers. Of course there are some older users, but not many. Or so we believe. It's proving a bloody nightmare trying to track them down. The site doesn't cooperate with the police.'

'Is it on the Dark Web?'

'No. This particular site is on the Deep Web.'

'What's that?'

'The Deep Web's what they call content or sites that don't show up on ordinary search engines. The bulk of the content is illegal or immoral in some way. The Dark Web that you mentioned is part of the Deep Web, but its content is even better encrypted. This site is only on the Deep Web. That means a search for it wouldn't yield any results: you have to know the exact address to find the site. If it was on the Dark Web you'd need special access as well as a Tor browser to hide your IP number. Apart from that, the same applies to both web areas. Conventional search engines don't have access to the material stored there. That said, the Dark Web's full of this kind of shit too, including Icelandic stuff.'

'So my guy could have posted videos of himself on a site like that and shared them with other users in exchange for their homemade porn, or just out of some weird exhibitionist urge to get it out there?'

'Yes, for example.' The officer took back his laptop and snapped it shut. 'If the recordings found their way onto any of the Icelandic file-sharing platforms, he'd almost certainly have included the women's names. That's part of the whole kick – to identify the victims by name.'

'Why?'

'Originally it was probably done in an attempt to prevent users from posting pictures of foreign girls they'd pulled off the net and claiming they were Icelandic. Part of the thrill is being able to track the girls down on social media. The whole thing's twisted.'

'You're telling me.'

'Did he have the women's names?'

'Yes. Their first names, anyway. Probably their patronymics too. How do I find out if that's what he was up to? Sharing the videos, I mean. Please don't tell me I'll have to trawl through all these sites.'

'Want my advice? Take the file names down to IT. They'll be much quicker than you. Not only that but they have access to search engines that can comb the Deep and Dark Webs. Leave it to the experts.'

This made good sense to Huldar. He had little patience with surfing the net as it was, and absolutely no desire to extend his browsing to these subterranean worlds. 'They've already got the files and they're looking into them. I'll ask them to check out the Deep Web while they're at it.'

'Good. But bear in mind that just because they don't find anything, that doesn't mean it's not out there. The Deep Web's not called that for nothing – it's practically bottomless. If the file names have been changed and the content descriptions don't include any of the usual keywords, the search won't achieve much. In fact, you'll probably only find the videos if they were posted on one of the Icelandic file-sharing platforms we already know about. But send us the file names too, just in case they crop up on our radar or it turns out we're already aware of them. Women sometimes approach us wanting to press charges when they discover that sexual images of them have been posted on sites like that. But teenage girls mainly just stick their heads in the sand or issue vain threats under their pictures on the websites. All that does is encourage the bastards. The sad thing is, we're not much more effective ourselves because it's so difficult to identify the user sharing the material.' The man wore a defeated look. 'It's almost impossible if they've made any sort of effort to cover their tracks.'

Huldar went back upstairs in a sombre frame of mind. Before picking up where he'd left off, he wondered if there was any point in trying to find out if the videos had been shared. Even if they had, it was hard to see how this could be linked to Helgi's murder. None of these leggy blondes looked like the violent type.

Chapter 19

Didrik hadn't taken the bait and invited Freyja out for dinner when she rang him to report back on her conversation with Siggi's grandmother. Nor had he suggested meeting at a bar or given any other hint that he reciprocated her interest. This was a blow, but hardly the end of the world. In fact, it was probably just as well, since she couldn't have accepted an invitation for a date that evening – or any other in the near future – because of Saga. Baldur had talked Fanney into letting him have his daughter for a bit longer, which meant that she was Freyja's responsibility once he reported back to the halfway house. He had to go in for supper between six and seven, and remain on the premises overnight, from 11 p.m. to 7 a.m. And Saga didn't really fit into Freyja's idea of a romantic evening with a hot date.

The little girl seemed to read Freyja's mind as she sat beside her in yet another high chair at yet another restaurant. Scowling, she went on poking her finger into the small bowl of tomato ketchup. Saga was a fussy eater. Freyja had cooked a healthy meal for her earlier but she might as well not have gone to the trouble. Saga had merely pushed her food off the tray of her high chair into Molly's waiting jaws. Then, inevitably, when it got to bedtime, the little girl had been too hungry to sleep, so Freyja had resorted to dressing her again and taking her out for supper. She had opted for a burger joint, against the express wishes of Saga's mother Fanney, who wanted her daughter to eat nothing but organic food, preferably sugar-free too. Sometimes, Freyja reasoned, you had to bend the rules. Besides, until the little girl started talking properly, there was no way her mother could find out, since Fanney was about as likely to wander into a burger bar as she was to become a defender on Iceland's national team.

The place had zero charm. In one corner there was a play area, consisting of a large plastic slide and a ball-pit hardly any bigger than a bathtub. These offerings held no attraction for the scattering of children in there at this late hour. Instead, they sat with their adult companions, staring dully at the toys that came with the kids' meals.

Saga licked the ketchup off her finger and stuck it straight back in the bowl. 'Eat up.' Freyja picked up a small chunk of what purported to be chicken and held it to Saga's lips. The little girl wrenched her head away.

'Try dipping it in ketchup. That might work.'

Freyja raised her head, startled. Who should it be but Huldar, armed with a tray of the same kind of junk that was still sitting wrapped in front of her: burger, chips and Coke.

'Mind if I join you?'

She could hardly say no.

Huldar squeezed into the booth, sitting unnecessarily close, though there was plenty of room. Feeling his thigh against hers, she couldn't help enjoying the warmth he gave off. She was also grateful that he didn't seem in the least shocked to find her out so late with Saga. He was in a much better mood than he had been at the care home earlier, presumably because Didrik wasn't around. Being cheerful suited him.

'How's the search for Siggi's mother going?' Freyja tried dipping the chicken piece in ketchup as Huldar had suggested. Saga, taken in by this trick, bit off a chunk, chewed it and swallowed. 'Are you getting anywhere?'

'Oof.' Huldar unwrapped his burger. 'Can I trust you not to repeat any of this?'

'Of course. You know you can.' Freyja pushed her tray away. She'd lost what little appetite she'd had and was far more interested in hearing what Huldar had to say. 'Maybe I could help. Supply a bit of insight.' She smiled at him and he smiled back. For once, neither smile was artificial or forced. 'But first, how did you manage to find out his parents' names?'

Huldar took a bite of burger, polishing off half of it in one go, and washed it down with a swig of Coke before answering. He had ketchup in the corner of his mouth. 'Sorry, can't tell you that.'

'From A&E, I suppose?'

'I can't say.' He stuck a chip in his mouth. 'You're not the only one who knows how to be discreet. But I can tell you that it looks as if she was the victim of domestic abuse. And also that she's definitely pregnant.'

Freyja's gaze had returned to Saga but she looked round at that. 'I'd already heard about the abusive husband. How far along is she?'

'Eight months.'

'Oh God.' Freyja didn't know what to say. Having never been pregnant herself, she wouldn't be able to shed any light on the woman's probable mental state, if that's what Huldar was hoping.

But it seemed that wasn't what he wanted. 'Do you know anything about domestic abuse?'

'A little. Enough to know that it's extremely complicated. Are you wondering why women like her don't just leave their abusive partners?'

Huldar attacked his burger again, leaving nothing but a single mouthful. Not bad: a whole burger in three bites. 'Do you know any women in that situation?' he asked.

'Probably. But if I do, I'm not aware of it. Victims tend to cover up for their abuser, regardless of their sex. In fact, it's even more common when the victims are men.'

Huldar muttered something that Freyja took to be sympathy with this attitude. He didn't seem like the type who would report anything that happened to him, especially not if he came off worse in a fight with a woman. Not that this was likely for a big, strong guy like him. But the four walls of home weren't like a boxing ring in which the person who got knocked down was automatically the loser. Nor was it purely a question of bodily strength. Although physical blows came into it, the real damage could be caused by the mental injuries, which were decisive in determining who came out on top.

'It's messy, Huldar. I don't have much direct experience but we sometimes deal with the fallout from these cases at the Children's House. Even though we don't treat the adults, we do get an insight into the living hell it creates because of the impact it has on the kids.'

'I've had a bit of experience myself. Back when I was in the regular police I encountered a few cases and was bloody relieved to see the back of them, to be honest. They were a nightmare to deal with and our intervention never achieved much.' Huldar took another slug of Coke. 'I remember one woman who we persuaded to press charges after a series of brutal assaults left her with a broken nose and cheekbone, a fractured skull and two missing front teeth. But the day she was due to testify in court she withdrew her statement, claiming a bowl had fallen off the top shelf of a cupboard onto her head. She was sitting there in the courtroom, face permanently disfigured, lying to protect the bastard who did it. You almost never get that with other types of crime.'

Saga lobbed a chip at Freyja's head, annoyed at being ignored. Unfortunately she had dipped it in ketchup first, so it left a red streak in Freyja's blonde hair when she removed it.

'Want me to lick it off?' Huldar winked at Freyja. You had to hand it to him, he could turn anything into an attempt at flirtation.

Instead of allowing herself to be sidetracked, Freyja reached for a napkin and wiped away the sticky mess as well as she could. 'So you think Siggi's father could be behind their disappearance?' She hoped he would say no, but he nodded.

'Looks like it.'

'Do they think he killed her?' Although her instinct told her it was likely, Freyja prayed that he would say no.

'Well, we just don't know, of course, but it's a strong possibility, I'm afraid. It's difficult to come up with any other explanation. But we could be wrong. Not everything is consistent with that scenario.'

'Oh?' Freyja turned her attention back to Saga to avoid being pelted with any more food.

'Well, Forensics seached for blood-stains but couldn't find any signs of heavy blood loss. The place did light up like a Christmas tree, but it turned out to be small spatters of blood here and there, which almost certainly didn't all result from the same attack. We concluded that they were more likely to be evidence of a long period of sustained violence.'

Feeling slightly sick, Freyja offered Huldar her untouched burger and he accepted it gratefully, after asking twice if she was absolutely sure. Then she went on pumping him for information: 'Surely that increases the chances that she's still alive, then?'

'Death doesn't necessarily involve spraying blood all over the place, you know. She could have been strangled. Or drowned in the bathtub. Or received a blow that caused a fatal internal haemorrhage. Or a combination of the above.'

Freyja silently pushed her chips over to him as well.

'Bud.' Saga had got hold of a new word to add to her limited vocabulary. *Mummy, Daddy, Freyja, Molly, sweeties, no, bad, walkies* and now *blood*. What else did a person need? If her mother asked, Freyja would claim that she was trying to say 'brother'. Hastily, she dipped another nugget of chicken substitute in the tomato sauce and popped it in the little girl's mouth in the hope that she would forget the word.

'The big question now is what links the couple to the owner of the flat where Siggi was found. We've looked into every aspect of their lives but these people have literally nothing in common.'

'They weren't at school together or neighbours when they were kids?' As soon as she'd said it, Freyja realised how naive she was being. Of course the police would already have looked into these possibilities. But instead of rubbing her nose in it, Huldar merely said:

'No. They weren't the same age. Siggi's mother is two years younger than Helgi and his father is a year older. Neither of them was in the same class as him at school, or even at the same school. They didn't grow up in the same part of town, so they can't have been neighbours as kids or later. They've never worked at the same places, belonged to the same clubs, or even gone to the same gym. They seem to have moved in totally different worlds.' Huldar paused for a swig of Coke. 'But of course there's a connection somewhere. It could be through a third party but it's there. It's got to be. That's what we're looking into now. It's just a pity we're so bloody short-staffed thanks to the Chinese minister's visit. Still, he's going home tomorrow, thank God, and after that we'll have more manpower. I can just picture Erla showing up at the airport with balloons to give him a send-off.'

Freyja found it easier to picture her togged up in Rambo gear, chasing the minister onto the plane at gunpoint. 'So, why do you think Siggi was taken to the flat?'

'Our best theory so far is that Siggi's father must have left him there to make sure he was found. But it's unthinkable that the boy wouldn't have recognised his own father, even if he had covered his face, so the man must have got someone else to do it. Anyway, that theory's obviously based on the assumption that the father was responsible for bumping off both Helgi and Siggi's mother.'

'Where is he now, then?'

Huldar shrugged and started unwrapping the waxed paper from Freyja's burger. 'Your guess is as good as mine. He could have killed himself, fled abroad or done a runner here in Iceland. We'll find him sooner or later – I hope.'

Freyja held a paper cup of orange juice to Saga's lips and tilted it. The girl took one sip, then refused to drink any more. 'Bud,' she announced. So much for Freyja's hope that she would forget.

She turned back to Huldar. 'They haven't decided yet whether Siggi should stay in temporary care or go to his grandmother. The poor kid.'

'God, the system's callous.'

'It might look like that but it isn't really. The decision has to be based on careful consideration. His situation is extremely unusual and they would never normally hand over a child as young as him to anyone other than his parents.'

Huldar seemed to accept this. At least, he didn't argue with what she'd said. She went on to tell him about her conversation with the boy's grandmother. But Huldar, who seemed to have heard it all already, merely nodded and used the time to eat. The only detail that elicited the slightest interest from him was her account of Sigurlaug's abortive return to work. He stuffed three chips into his mouth and swallowed, before remarking that this hadn't come up when the police interviewed her. But after learning that it had happened three and a half years ago, he lost interest again.

Freyja had nothing more to tell. She had also run out of questions to ask about the case. No doubt they'd start pinging into her mind again the moment she was alone. 'Can I ask you something that has nothing to do with the investigation?'

'Sure, ask away. If you want to know if I'm free this weekend, the answer is yes.'

Freyja smiled. 'No, actually. What I wanted to ask is whether you know if anyone in Iceland keeps snakes as pets.'

Huldar burst out laughing. 'That's exactly why I want to ask you out. No one could accuse you of being boringly predictable, Freyja.' When she ignored this and merely waited for him to answer, he said: 'Sure they do. We come across all kinds of weird and wonderful creatures when conducting house searches, usually in connection with drugs. Tarantulas, lizards, amphibians, snakes, you name it. They all get humanely destroyed. Why do you ask?'

'Oh, it was just that someone mentioned it at work and I found it so unbelievable I thought I'd check with you.' She turned to Saga in case her face betrayed her. Seeing that the little girl had had enough, Freyja picked up a napkin and began to wipe her face, an operation that was greeted with indignation. 'Have there been any cases of people being injured – you know, like bitten? Or squeezed to death?'

'Is that what you've heard?'

When Freyja made a noncommittal noise, Huldar answered, 'As far as I know, nobody's ever been attacked by a snake in Iceland. But quite a few have had a nasty dose of salmonella. It's a common side effect of keeping reptiles.'

Freyja felt her interest in the flat rapidly cooling. 'I see. Thanks.'

'You're welcome.' Huldar finished the second burger, scrunched up the wrappers and then grinned at Saga. 'I'd like to invite you for a meal. Name the day.'

'That's a kind offer, but no thanks.' Freyja reached for Saga's hat and coat. It was time to go.

'I wasn't talking to you – I was talking to her.' Huldar pointed at Saga. 'We're good mates. And what's more, we have the same taste in restaurants.'

Freyja smiled. 'Yeah, right.'

'No, I'm serious. I'm inviting her out to dinner.'

'And I'm passing, on her behalf.'

'She's old enough to speak for herself, isn't she?' Huldar winked at Saga, who chose that moment to test whether the napkin was edible.

Freyja removed it from the child's grasp and peeled shreds of paper off her tongue, which Saga had stuck out when the napkin failed the taste test. 'Well, Saga, do you want to go out for a meal with Huldar?' she asked, confident that the answer would be no. Saga's answer to everything was 'no', even when she meant 'yes'.

Saga frowned and Freyja repeated the question. 'Do you want to go for supper with Huldar, Saga?'

'*Yeth.*' Would you know it? A new word for her vocabulary – with the worst possible timing.

'See!' Huldar gave Freyja a nudge. 'Shame you'll have to come along too. She's far too young to go out without a chaperone.' He slid out of the booth, took his tray and said goodbye, looking pleased with himself. 'I'll be in touch.'

Freyja sat there speechless beside her traitor of a niece. As she watched Huldar leave, snatches of their night together replayed in her mind. The memories were hazy, as they had both been drunk at the time, but she could still remember how amazing he had been in bed. Bloody Huldar Jónas.

She shook herself, firmly pushing the thought away. Clearly, it was too long since she'd seen any action.

Having dressed Saga in her outdoor clothes, Freyja perched her on her hip and headed for the exit. As they passed the counter, Freyja pointed to the illuminated photo of an ice-cream on the wall above the heads of the apathetic staff. An ideal opportunity to try out the new word in the little girl's arsenal as she was always in the mood for ice-cream. 'Would you like an ice-cream, Saga?'

Frowning longingly at the picture, Saga opened her down-turned mouth and enunciated firmly: 'No.'

Chapter 20

Tuesday

The interview room was already oppressively stuffy. The air conditioning must have broken down again, as there wasn't so much as a hiss from the grille. Instead, thick clumps of dust hung motionless in the vents. It didn't make much difference, though, since the atmosphere had been singularly flat even before they went in.

Huldar had turned up that morning freshly shaven, breakfasted and all set to watch more porn, only to discover that Erla had other plans for him. She was going to talk to one of Helgi's closest friends, the dentist Thormar, who had been with him the evening he died, and she wanted Huldar to join her. He chose to interpret his increased popularity with his boss as a sign of how short-staffed they were. Erla must see this interview as potentially significant because she had postponed the progress meeting in the hope that a solid lead would emerge.

Thormar had opted to come down to the station rather than receive a visit from the police at home or at work. This was a common reaction – it never looked good to have the authorities knocking on your door – which meant they shouldn't read too much into it. Instead, they would, as usual, have to rely on other clues during questioning, such as inconsistencies in his statement or signs that he was unnaturally stressed, or catching him out in a lie.

In this case, the subject proved hard to read. His distress seemed genuine: according to Erla he'd got quite a shock when she told him why they wanted to talk to him, and he didn't seem to have recovered yet. But he was eager to help when it came to describing the events of that last evening with Helgi and telling them stories about his friend, whether recent or from their shared past. And yet there was something about the man – Huldar couldn't put his finger on it. He was like one of those supermarket sushi trays: almost authentic, but not quite. There was a faint whiff of the dental clinic about him too, which made Huldar feel slightly nauseous.

'Of course I can't remember a hundred per cent of what happened. We were drinking, so my memory's a bit patchy. But I've tried to piece together the details and I've been through the transactions on my credit card for confirmation.' Thormar handed them a bank statement apparently printed out from his online account.

Erla took the sheet of paper with barely a glance. They could examine its contents later, while verifying that it was authentic. 'So the last place you remember seeing him was at 101 Bar?'

'Yes. He went to the gents. I passed him on my way back from there. But he didn't return to our table afterwards.'

'Didn't you and your friends find that a bit odd?'

'Yes, but, like I said, we'd been putting it away, Helgi especially. Time passes quickly when you're drinking. It took us a while to notice that he'd been gone an unusually long time, but we weren't worried when it finally dawned on us that he'd left. Like I said, he was wasted. You never know what people will do in that sort of state.'

'What did you all think had happened?'

Thormar expelled a breath. 'Well, I can't speak for the others, but I assumed he'd just had enough. Or that he hadn't been able to find us again because a large group had come in and were standing around our table. They were friends of one of our gang – members of Gunni's fly-fishing club, I think. They'd had their annual dinner but Gunni had chosen to meet up with us instead. Anyway, there was a whole crowd of them, so it's possible Helgi couldn't see us and got confused. He was pretty hammered, like I said.'

'What time was this?' Erla moved the pen to her notepad, ready to write it down.

'It must have been shortly after midnight. I bought a round just before Helgi disappeared and from my credit-card transactions that was at a quarter to twelve. I know he'd only drunk about half his glass, because once we realised he wasn't coming back, one of the boys decided it shouldn't go to waste and finished it.'

'Who was that?' Erla looked up from her pad.

Thormar appeared a little surprised at this question but he answered it anyway. 'It was Gunni. Gunnar, that is – Gunnar Bergsson.'

Huldar guessed why Erla had asked. If someone had spiked Helgi's drink, it would be possible either to eliminate that particular glass from their inquiry or to confirm that it was the one.

Erla's next question proved that Huldar had read her right. 'What sort of state was Gunnar in after drinking it?'

'State?' Thormar frowned, even more puzzled. 'Drunker.

Not much, just kind of what you'd expect when you drink booze on top of more booze.'

'Did he look like he was about to pass out or behave in any way oddly?'

Thormar smiled for the first time since he had entered the police station. 'Gunni's behaviour's always been a bit odd. But it wasn't out of character for him.' The smile vanished and Thormar's face grew serious again. 'Why do you ask? You don't think Helgi had put something in his own drink? I can assure you he wasn't on drugs.'

Although Huldar wasn't convinced that the man was right about his dead friend, this declaration at least proved to him that Thormar himself wasn't a user. Anyone familiar with drugs would know that you don't usually take them mixed with your drinks. 'Would you say that Helgi had a fairly healthy lifestyle, then?'

'Yes, definitely. He had a personal trainer, went to the gym regularly, only ate organic and so on. As far as I know he was in great shape.' Thormar shifted in his chair and adjusted his cuffs. 'Not that I've seen any medical reports or anything. But I was his dentist and can assure you that he really looked after his teeth.' Seeing that Erla and Huldar were unimpressed, he hastened to add: 'People who take care of their teeth usually take care of their general health.'

'I see.' Erla sounded underwhelmed by this logic.

Her reaction evidently provoked Thormar, since he leapt to the defence of his profession. 'We dentists can often spot the signs of various conditions by looking into people's mouths: diabetes, heart disease, osteoporosis, stress, cold sores—'

Erla cut him short before the conditions he listed could

become any more trivial. 'Your friend didn't die of anything like that.'

Huldar intervened before the man could give this the rude response it deserved. 'What were you wearing that evening?'

'My clothes, you mean?'

'Yes.'

'I was wearing a suit. Grey, I think, and a white shirt. Yes, and a coat. Which was blue. Dark blue. Why do you ask?'

'What about your friends?'

'Um . . .' Thormar seemed to have great trouble recalling this. Eventually he managed to describe more or less what each had been wearing. Mostly it came down to minor distinctions in the colour of their suit or shirt – apart from that they might have been in uniform. Certainly, neither of them had been dressed in jeans and trainers like the man accompanying Siggi in the CCTV footage.

'Did any of you have a bag with you? A change of clothes?'

'A change of clothes?' Thormar gave Huldar an uncomprehending look. Then, when he didn't explain, replied: 'No. Why would any of us have needed one? And what have our clothes got to do with what happened to Helgi?'

Huldar ignored the question and changed the subject, since it was in his and Erla's interests to disorientate the man, leave him unsure of where the conversation was leading. 'Moving on. Did Helgi mention any plans to meet up with someone else that evening?'

'No. He wouldn't have done, anyway. Our meetings always take priority. Like with Gunni, for example. He missed his fly-fishing do in order to spend the evening with us.'

'Couldn't Helgi's plans have changed, though? Did he use his phone at any point during the evening?' It was something of a redundant question. No one went anywhere these days without checking their phone. Not even funerals were exempt. 'Could he have got a text message asking him to meet someone else?'

'Well, naturally he had his phone out. But he didn't say anything about meeting anyone. I'm sure about that, although a lot of the evening is a bit of a blur. Like I said, when the old gang gets together, our meetings are sacred.'

'But he was single, wasn't he?'

'Yes. Him and Gunni.'

'Isn't it possible that he wanted to hook up with a woman, then? Maybe there was a girlfriend he was keen to meet?'

'No, definitely not.' Thormar looked thoughtful. 'I know that, because he was complaining about the women at the bar we were in.'

'Complaining about them?' Erla's interest quickened again. 'How do you mean?'

'He wasn't impressed with them.'

'Not fit enough for him or . . . ?' Due to the heat in the room, Erla had rolled up her sleeves. Huldar could have sworn he saw the hairs on her arms prickling as she asked this. She may not cut the other women on her team any slack, but she was quick to take offence at the slightest evidence of sexism in their cases. Which was, alas, all too common.

'No. Not so much that. They were just too old for him.' Before Erla could speak, Thormar continued: 'Which reminds me: he said maybe we should move on to another place where the talent was younger. So it's possible he went off on a bar crawl in search of some.'

Huldar reckoned they'd heard enough about Helgi's last evening. Thormar had told them all he knew and was now straying into speculation. But Erla's next question showed that she thought differently. 'Did any of you try to call Helgi after you realised he wasn't at the bar?'

'Yes. I rang him twice, I think. Tómas tried him as well. The first time his phone just went on ringing; the second time it was switched off.'

'What time was this?'

Thormar took his phone out of his pocket. 'Er, the first call was at quarter to one and the second at half past.' He looked up. 'That would fit with him having gone to the gents some time after midnight. It took us a while to notice he'd gone.'

'Can I see your phone?' Erla held out her hand, but Thormar hesitated and Huldar thought he seemed disconcerted. His mouth a little open, he stared at Erla's outstretched palm. There could be any number of reasons for this behaviour, none of which were necessarily linked to Helgi's murder. He could have private photos, emails or messages that he wouldn't want them to see. Come to think of it, Huldar wouldn't like the idea of showing Erla his phone either. But after a brief pause, Thormar apparently concluded that in the circumstances it would be best to hand it over. He watched uneasily as Erla examined his call log.

Huldar peered at the screen over her shoulder. She wasn't content simply to check the two calls Thormar had mentioned but scrolled down to see his more recent activity. This included his repeated attempts to get hold of Helgi, as well as a number of calls to the other two friends who had been with them on Saturday night.

Erla looked up and met the eye of the now agitated dentist. 'You seem to have been very anxious to get hold of Helgi ever since Sunday morning. Was there any particular reason for that?'

'I just wanted to make sure he'd got home safely. But his phone was off. I found that odd, so I kept trying his number. He'd said he was going to drop by my place at lunchtime with a present for my daughter, but he didn't show up, which was out of character.'

'Your daughter's called Hallbera, isn't she?' When Thormar nodded, Huldar told him that the parcel had been found at Helgi's flat and would be passed on to him in the next few days. He omitted to mention that it had been opened. It had been necessary to check the contents in case they had any bearing on Helgi's fate. But the shiny paper and curly ribbons had been concealing nothing more sinister than a doll. No ordinary doll, actually: according to the box, she could walk, talk, dance and count – everything you could wish for. Unfortunately, the police's attempts to rewrap this wonder of technology had been clumsy at best.

Erla continued to scroll through the call log. 'I assume these numbers listed as Tommi and Gunni belong to the friends who were there that night. Am I right?'

'Yes, that's right.' Thormar licked his lips.

'You seem to have called them quite a lot yesterday as well. Why's that?'

'I was worried because I couldn't get hold of Helgi. I rang them to ask if they'd heard from him. Nothing strange about that.'

If so, Huldar wondered why the man was looking so twitchy. Erla allowed a silence to develop before handing back the phone. Thormar looked visibly relieved to have it restored to him.

When Erla spoke again, it was on a different subject. 'Did you often fall out? You and Helgi?'

'No, never. We've been friends since we were at school and we've always got on well.'

'Really? That's not what we've heard. Didn't your friendship go through a bumpy patch about four or five years ago?'

Thormar pretended to be searching his memory but it was glaringly obvious that he knew exactly what they were referring to. 'Oh, yes. Now that you mention it, we did have a bit of a falling-out back then.'

'Do you remember why?'

'No, I don't, actually. But it can't have been anything important.' Thormar clasped his hands on the table in front of him as if in prayer.

'Could you repeat that?' Erla locked eyes with him. 'You've been friends for more than twenty years, you only fell out once and now you're telling me you can't remember why. I don't buy that for one minute.'

Thormar's knuckles whitened. 'I swear, I don't remember. Anyway, what does it matter? You can hardly think I killed Helgi over some trivial quarrel that happened five years ago?'

Neither Erla nor Huldar replied to this. They sat in silence for a few moments before Erla resumed. 'We're going through your friend's finances. It's proving tricky, but we'll get to the bottom of them eventually. He has assets in a number of different companies, most of them registered overseas. If you could help us on one point, that would assist our inquiry.'

'Of course, ask away.' Thormar sounded sincere. He was visibly relieved that they had moved on from the source of friction between him and his murdered friend. 'Although I should say that I know nothing about Helgi's finances. Except that he wasn't short of money.'

'We're not asking about the details. All we want to know is whether he owned any other properties apart from the flat he lived in.'

'Properties?' Thormar looked baffled, though of course he must have understood the question.

'Yes. Did he own any other flats or houses in Iceland or abroad that he could have registered under another name, for example one of his overseas companies?'

Thormar's face still wore the dopey look from when Erla had first asked about Helgi's property. But then he got his features under control and answered hesitantly: 'Er, yes. He had a summer house. And an apartment in New York, because he spent so much time there. But he may have rented it out. I don't remember the subject coming up and I never asked him about it.'

'Where is this summer house?' Erla held her pen poised. 'You must have been there?'

'Yes, sure. Several times. It's on a large estate in Sudurland that Helgi bought just before the crash. He had the old farmhouse knocked down and built a new place. This was while he was still based abroad, but when he came over he'd sometimes spend a few nights there if the weather was good.' Thormar did his best to give them directions to the location in south Iceland, though, according to him, Helgi had removed a couple of signposts that used to stand at the turn-off, in order to deter visitors. Erla conscientiously wrote all this down. While she was doing so, Thormar asked why they wanted to know, but neither of them answered.

'No other property here in Iceland, then?' Erla watched the man, her face unreadable.

Thormar paused and licked his lips before answering. 'No, none – that I'm aware of.'

Under the table Huldar felt Erla prod him in the thigh. He got the message and turned over the top page of the pile of papers in front of them. 'Do you recognise this boy? His name's Sigurdur Margeirsson and he's a year older than your daughter. He's known as Siggi.'

Thormar stared at the picture, nonplussed. After studying the little boy's face, he looked up and shook his head. 'No, I'm sure I don't know him.'

'Quite sure?' Huldar pushed the picture a little closer.

Thormar studied Siggi's face again. Then he exhaled sharply and shook his head again. 'Absolutely positive. I don't recognise him. I mean, of course it's possible I've seen him at my daughter's nursery school or somewhere like that and don't remember. But I don't think so.' He raised his eyes, looking searchingly at Huldar and Erla in turn. 'What's his connection to Helgi?'

Huldar didn't answer but turned to the next picture, of Siggi's father Margeir. The photo had been taken from the man's Facebook page. The only two photos of him on there were almost identical profile pictures, which made it hard to see why he had bothered sharing them. His posts were few and far between as well; he only really seemed to come to life when he was angry about the political situation or something else in the news. His comments were all negative, the subjects of his ire ranging from the traditional New Year's Eve comedy special to public-sector institutions, feminists, football managers and oil companies. In between these rants he sent birthday greetings to his handful of Facebook friends, which did not include Helgi or anyone else connected to him. 'Do you recognise this man? His name's Margeir Arnarson.'

'No, I don't know him. Who is he? The father of that little boy? Do you think he killed Helgi? Has he been arrested?' Thormar looked up angrily.

'We're not holding any suspects at present.' Huldar discreetly studied the man's hands, which were resting on the table. They were well manicured, unmarred by calluses or abrasions. 'Are you good with your hands?'

'Me?' When this question got no response, Thormar answered: 'Well, I got nine out of ten for the tooth I sculpted as part of my dentistry degree, so I suppose you could say I am.'

'I meant more like, are you the handyman type? Do you do the DIY at home, for example? Did you build decking in your back garden? That sort of thing.'

Thormar frowned. 'I don't know why I should have to answer that. It's hardly relevant to what happened to Helgi.' When Huldar and Erla merely stared at him in stony silence, he got down off his high horse: 'No. I haven't built any decking. When we bought the flat it already had a concrete patio out the back. As for DIY, I take care of the few bits of maintenance that come up but our flat was renovated shortly before we moved in.'

Huldar let it go and, moving swiftly on, held up a photo of Siggi's mother. Her Facebook page had contained far more pictures than her husband's, though most of them featured her son at the various milestones in a child's life, including a lot of photos of the boy in Majorca, just over a year earlier, looking ever more tanned as the holiday progressed. Recalling the red circle drawn around Majorca on the globe in the little boy's room, Huldar realised what it meant: either his mother or his father must have wanted to show him where they were going on holiday.

The mother's Facebook posts were far more positive than her husband's. Despite this, she had remarkably few friends on the site and none of them had any link to Helgi. 'What about this woman?' Huldar asked. 'Recognise her?' He pushed the picture towards Thormar, who ran his fingers through his hair as he pored over the young woman's smiling face.

'No.' He looked back at Huldar. 'Can I ask who she is?'

'Her name's Sigurlaug Lára Lárusdóttir.'

Thormar examined the picture again. She was facing the camera and her short dark hair was combed well back, so her features were clearly visible. Apart from the hair colour, mother and son were astonishingly alike, but Thormar didn't seem to notice. 'No, I've never met her. At least, if I have, I don't remember her.'

Obeying another poke in the thigh from Erla, Huldar turned over the last picture. 'Is this one of the beds in Helgi's summer house?' It was a still of the headboard that had featured in all Helgi's porn videos, with the couple on the bed carefully edited out. This had proved easier said than done: the naked figures grappling in front of it had taken up a lot of the shot.

Thormar stared at the picture, frozen into stillness. Without raising his head, he asked: 'What exactly is this?'

'A headboard.' Huldar pushed the picture closer to him as he repeated the question: 'Is this one of the beds in Helgi's summer house?'

'Er . . .' Thormar tilted his head from side to side, as if to get a better idea of what he was seeing. 'No.' Once again, he kept his head down as he answered, never taking his eyes off the photo.

'So you haven't seen this headboard at the summer house?'

'Not in my guest room, anyway. I can't answer for the other rooms because I always slept in the same bed. But no, I haven't seen one like that there.'

'What about somewhere else? At Helgi's flat here in Reykjavík or in photos of his pad in New York, for instance?'

Thormar cleared his throat. 'No.'

He seemed unable to tear his eyes from the picture. Erla and Huldar exchanged meaningful glances. The man had sure as hell seen it before. They took it in turns to repeat their questions, varying the wording slightly, but it was no good, Thormar stubbornly insisted that he'd never seen the bed before.

When Erla abandoned the subject, Huldar grabbed the chance to ask about the bodies that had washed up on the shore near the crime scene. 'So you don't recognise the bed or Margeir, Sigurlaug Lára or Sigurdur. What about a man by the name of Dagur Didriksson?'

Thormar was visibly relieved by this change of direction. 'No, never heard of him.'

'Olgeir Magnússon, then?'

'No, nor him either.'

'What about Maren Thórdardóttir?'

Thormar hesitated for a fraction of a second before giving the same answer: 'No.'

'Quite sure?'

'Yes, quite sure.'

Huldar and Erla contemplated the man silently for a while.

His discomfort was palpable as he struggled to sit still and to stop himself from repeatedly licking his lips.

Finally, Erla gave up and thanked Thormar for coming in. She told him he could expect to hear from them again and asked him not to discuss his interview with anyone, as they still had other people to talk to. Otherwise, he was free to go.

Thormar didn't wait to be told twice. He was in such a hurry that he was still pulling on his coat as he strode away down the corridor.

'Did you notice that he didn't ask how Helgi died?' Erla was standing at Huldar's side, her arms folded, eyes following the man's departing back.

Huldar nodded.

'The bastard's hiding something. He's seen that bed before, he remembers perfectly well why he and Helgi fell out, and I have a hunch he's heard Maren's name before as well.' Erla breathed out forcefully through her nose. 'But he's not our killer. He's way too much of a wuss.' Without another word, she uncrossed her arms and walked off.

A few minutes after the door had closed behind Thormar, Huldar tried ringing him on his mobile and wasn't remotely surprised to find it engaged. Erla's orders that he shouldn't discuss the interview with anyone had almost certainly been ignored.

Chapter 21

For once Fannar – the very last person Thormar wanted to see right now – was sitting downstairs in the living room. Not that *sitting* adequately conveyed the boy's attitude. He might have been made of melted wax as he lounged on the sofa in front of the TV, his long legs propped up on the coffee table. The china bowl that usually stood in the middle was now teetering precariously near the edge. Beside it was a plate with a half-finished slice of his sister's birthday cake, a chocolate sponge with screamingly pink icing. The magazine that Sigrún had put down by the bowl had fallen on the floor. Thormar doubted it had so much as crossed the boy's mind to pick it up again, but then he was young enough himself to remember what it had been like to be a teenager.

Like Fannar, he had regarded everything apart from his own trivial affairs as unbearably boring and lame. The only thing that had mattered were his friends Helgi, Tommi and Gunni. They had understood one another. The only music worth bothering about was the music they listened to. The same applied to films, computer games, cars, clothes and food. Their shared opinions were way more important than anyone else's: the rest of the world was populated by losers. But of course it hadn't really been that simple. There had been times when he'd had to pretend to hate something because his friends had dismissed it as uncool. No doubt they had all experienced the same thing, all sacrificed their individual thoughts, opinions and desires for the sake of fitting in.

Then there had been Anna Gudrún in Year 9. Small, with dark hair, brown eyes and delicate hands that he used to fantasise would feel so warm and soft to the touch. She was forever chewing gum, which gave her sweet minty breath, but always discreetly, never making the ugly smacking noises that some girls did. She was a good student too, always paid attention in class, and used to write her name with a heart instead of an accent over the 'u'. She wasn't a rebel, wasn't cool. And yet he'd had a desperate crush on her. So desperate that he found it hard to concentrate in class if she was sitting in his eyeline. Until one day, during break, Gunni had pulled a face and announced to the group that Anna Gudrún was such a total loser, destroying in one fell swoop Thormar's dream that she would ever be his. Especially when the others had sniggered in agreement. Being with a girl his friends despised was unthinkable, so he had played along with them, mooning over the school's most popular girls and exchanging comments about how hot they were. Knowing as well as his friends did that none of those girls would ever so much as glance in their direction.

The only member of their gang who had managed to pull before they started at sixth-form college was Gunni. He was cocky enough to go up to girls and pester them until they gave in. But none of these girls had come anywhere near the ones the boys fantasised about. And none of them, in Thormar's private opinion, were any prettier or nicer than Anna Gudrún. But Gunni's relationships never lasted long

– even now. He was fickle and easily bored; always kidding himself that he could do better. Since making a packet at the bank he'd had women coming out of his ears, but if anything this only made it harder for him to settle on one.

Anna Gudrún, meanwhile, had got together with a boy in the sixth form, who she later married. He'd been in the same year as Thormar throughout his dentistry degree, a constant painful reminder of what might have been – assuming she'd ever have wanted anything to do with Thormar, which was by no means guaranteed.

Instead of Anna Gudrún, Thormar had ended up with Sigrún. She was eight years older than him, which, contrary to his fears, had met with his friends' approval. No doubt because she was beautiful, intelligent and good company. Fannar had come as part of the package. At the time he'd been a little boy; a nice kid, just cute enough. Thormar had had no choice but to resign himself to the situation. If he wanted to be with Sigrún, he would have to put up with her son. But over time Thormar had actually become quite fond of him. Until he turned into a typical sulky, lazy, pain-in-the-arse teenager.

'What on earth are you watching?' The action on screen resembled a computer game, though the boy wasn't holding a controller. Perhaps Icelandic state TV had started showing them live in an attempt to appeal to a younger audience.

'YouTube.' Fannar didn't look up. He just stared, mesmer-ised, at the lurid nonsense on screen, though his face revealed no pleasure, let alone excitement, at the unfolding action.

'Where's your mum?'

The teenager shrugged. Clearly nothing, including his mother, mattered apart from what was happening on screen.

Thormar was in no mood to try and force a conversation. He had pictured himself coming home and flopping on the sofa – which Fannar had now commandeered – and lying there for a while to recover from his visit to the police station. 'Shouldn't you be at school?'

'Shouldn't you be at work?' Fannar shot back, his gaze still fixed on the screen.

Thormar could feel the rage boiling up inside him but controlled it. It would be extremely unwise to enter into a quarrel with the boy while he was in this mood. Like opening a bottle of Coke that had just been dropped on the floor. However careful you were, it always ended in disaster. So he acted as if he hadn't heard Fannar's insolent remark. 'What's wrong with the computer in your room?'

'It's broken.' Fannar didn't explain. Anyway, the cause of the problem was irrelevant as Thormar would inevitably have to cover the cost. Fannar's father, who could barely scrape together the cash for his maintenance, had none left over to pay for incidental costs related to his son. Incidental – ha! – the boy was a constant drain on Thormar's finances. Not a day passed when he didn't need money for something or other.

'I'd been looking forward to lying on the sofa myself, actually.' Thormar threw his coat over the back.

'What am I supposed to do, then? My computer's not working.'

'You could try doing your homework.' Thormar loosened his tie, pulled it over his head without undoing the knot and dropped it on top of his coat. 'You might actually surprise yourself by enjoying it.'

'I haven't got any homework.' Fannar finally tore his eyes

from the screen to look at Thormar. 'Can I borrow your computer?'

'Absolutely not. I need it myself and I don't want it getting a virus.'

'I won't infect it with a virus.' Fannar rolled his eyes as if the idea was totally absurd.

'Go and study or read a book. You're not having my computer. Or your mother's either.' Thormar had had enough. He hadn't postponed his day's appointments in order to stand here arguing with a stroppy teenager. 'We've been over this again and again.' When Fannar opened his mouth to protest, Thormar finally snapped. 'My friend has been murdered,' he said sharply, 'and I'm in no mood for an argument. Get up!'

Fannar heaved himself to his feet like an old man and slouched resentfully out of the sitting room, clearly unmoved by the talk of murder. A slam echoed from the bedroom corridor as Thormar collapsed on the sofa. But despite lying on one side, then the other, and re-arranging the cushions under his head, he couldn't relax, and the tight knot of fear burned like acid in his chest.

The cops were onto them. There could be no doubt. When he realised this, he had been a hair's breadth from opening up about his fears and showing them the video. Thank God, he'd managed to get a grip on himself, taken a deep breath and kept his mouth shut.

It would only give them a temporary breathing space. The police obviously knew too much already. It was only a matter of time before his world came crashing down around his ears. The thought that Tommi and Gunni would be crushed by the same rubble was no consolation. Even Gunni had seemed jittery when Thormar rang and told him about the interview and the photo he had been shown. The friends all had a huge amount at stake in ensuring that their secret never came out. Pretty much everything, in fact.

Chapter 22

The rubbish from Helgi's building had been deposited in a shed in the car park behind the police station. Erla had worn a malicious grin as she marched up to Huldar's desk, presented him with two pairs of yellow rubber gloves and announced to the entire office in ringing tones that he and Lína were to sift through it. She was in a foul mood following her disastrous phone call to Helgi's American employers, which Huldar had inadvertently overheard when he'd popped by her office shortly after the interview with Thormar. From what he had gathered, before beating a hasty retreat, the person at the other end couldn't make head or tail of what Erla was saying and seemed to think it was some kind of nuisance call. Erla was understandably annoyed that Huldar had witnessed her humiliation. The chore of grubbing around in refuse was her revenge.

Huldar had just sat down when Erla slapped the gloves on his desk, putting paid to his hopes of being sent to Helgi's summer house on a quest to find the bed from the sex videos. The weather was as beautiful as you could ask for on a winter's day: crackling frost, not a breath of wind, and everything covered in a fresh layer of snow. Ideal conditions for a drive through the south Icelandic countryside. He wanted to protest at the unfairness of it all, to bring up the videos, and plead with Erla to give the garbage-sifting job to someone else. But he bit back the impulse, knowing it would be a waste of time and achieve nothing apart from providing amusement for his colleagues. He got to his feet, silently beckoning Lína to follow. She'd been keeping her head down in the vain hope of being passed over. If she hadn't already started looking forward to getting back to her university studies, now was surely the time.

'Jesus Christ.' Huldar clapped a gloved hand over his nose and mouth as he opened the door to the shed and was hit by the pungent stench that poured out, rejoicing in its freedom. 'Maybe we should get ourselves some clothes pegs.'

'What are clothes pegs?' Lína asked in a muffled voice.

'Oh, forget it. They were obviously way before your time.' Counting up to three, Huldar dropped his hand and started breathing vigorously through his nose. The sooner you got used to the stink, the sooner you'd become inured to it. The job would take them forever if they had to work one-handed. 'Right. Ladies first.' He ushered her into the shed ahead of him.

Lína took a wary step inside as if half expecting the rubbish to burst from its plastic sacks and ambush her. 'What's the recommended method?'

'Well, it's a first for me, so I was kind of hoping you'd know. Didn't they teach you anything about sorting refuse on your course?'

'No.'

Seeing that Lína wasn't amused, Huldar abandoned the attempt to tease her. They'd better just roll up their sleeves and get cracking.

By his calculations, the shed contained twenty-one

bulging black bin bags and one that was only half full. As the weather was dry and, for once, perfectly still, he reckoned they should drag the sacks out in the open, empty them onto the tarmac one at a time and systematically go through the contents there. Although they risked being the butt of jokes from every passer-by, anything was better than putting up with the rotten odour in the enclosed space.

Once they had gone through six sacks, Huldar called a halt for a break. All they'd unearthed so far was leftover food, old newspapers, junk mail and other bits of post, milk cartons and a variety of packaging. These items were quickly disregarded apart from the post, which required closer scrutiny. Unfortunately, the occupants of the luxury flats weren't too conscientious about separating out their recycling. Nothing of relevance to Helgi or his murder had yet come to light, but the fact that all the bins in his flat had been empty meant that their contents must be lurking somewhere in these sacks. The prime objective was to find the scraps of paper from the envelope that Helgi had torn up and thrown in the rubbish chute just before leaving the building for the last time.

Huldar took off his gloves and dropped them on the tarmac. He had no particular desire to touch them after what they'd come into contact with, though God knew how he was to avoid contamination when it was time to pull them on again. He extracted a packet of cigarettes from his pocket, leant back against the wall and lit up. To his surprise, Lína came over and stood beside him.

'I'd never have believed I'd actually welcome the smell of cigarette smoke.' She inhaled appreciatively, leaning her head back against the wall. 'Do you realise we haven't even got through a third of them yet?'

'We'll have got used to it by the time we're halfway through,' Huldar reassured her, though he didn't believe it himself. Some things were impossible to get used to. 'Anyway, how are you enjoying the job generally? Apart from the present shitty assignment?'

Lína didn't answer immediately. Perhaps she thought Huldar might have to write her a reference at the end of her internship and didn't want to blurt out something she'd regret later. Eventually she said cautiously: 'It's different from what I was expecting.'

'Isn't that always the way? You have this picture in your head beforehand but the reality's never like you think.' Huldar took another drag. 'I remember when I started out. It was totally different from how I'd imagined.'

'In what way?'

'Well, for example, I thought the public would be pleased to see us. It was a bit of a comedown when I discovered that nobody wants us around. They have to be literally on the ground with a lunatic crouching over them with a knife before they're happy for us to be there. After all, nobody needs us when everything's peachy. So when we do turn up, we tend to be the bearers of bad news. It's not surprising, when you stop to think about it, so I should have been prepared.'

'Oh.' Evidently this thought hadn't occurred to Lína, but then Erla hadn't let her loose on the public yet, for obvious reasons. 'Do you enjoy your job?'

Huldar shouldn't have been taken aback by this question, but the realisation dawned on him now that he'd never actually stopped to consider it. There were lots of things that got on his nerves, that could in his opinion be done better, and plenty of colleagues who rubbed him up the wrong way or were simply pricks. Not to mention the internal power struggles that led to tensions and split the force into factions. But overall? Was he happy? Did he get a kick out of it on some level? Or, given the choice, would he rather go back to carpentry?

No one puked up on carpenters and there was rarely any reason to lie to them. But however satisfying it was to build a cabinet, say, or create a perfect joint, it couldn't compete with his present job. There was no buzz to beat the moment when he and his colleagues got their hands on one of the bastards who injured, stole from or otherwise mistreated their fellow citizens. If he set out the pros and cons in a table, the good parts would outweigh the bad.

Huldar sucked on his cigarette again, then slowly blew out a thick cloud of smoke. 'I think the answer to that has to be yes. OK, not every day's like Christmas, but overall I find it rewarding. Sometimes I actively enjoy it.'

'Hmm.' Lína appeared to be digesting this and Huldar regretted not having expressed himself more eloquently. But he wasn't really the articulate type. Even if he gave himself until tomorrow to rephrase his reply, it would sound exactly the same. If the girl was looking for an inspiring mentor, he was the wrong man.

'Right. Shall we tackle the next five?' He crushed the butt under his shoe, then picked it up and put it in one of the sacks they'd already been through. Lína trailed behind, showing no signs of being restored by her break. She seemed even less enthralled with the task than before.

The next five sacks yielded nothing of interest. It wasn't until they'd grubbed their way through all but the last two that they finally hit upon what they'd been searching for. Or at least they believed they had. An envelope and a letter, or rather a collection of scraps of paper that could be pieced together to make up an envelope and a letter that resembled what Helgi had thrown in the rubbish chute in the grainy CCTV footage.

'Ta-da!' Huldar straightened up, rubbing the small of his back. 'This has got to be it.' He handed Lína the torn pieces of an envelope on which part of Helgi's name could be read. It was printed in a standard font. Perhaps it would just turn out to be mail from some institution that had annoyed Helgi enough for him to rip it up. 'There may be something else there, but this is definitely what we're looking for.'

'Can we stop then?' Lína looked like a child who knows the answer's going to be 'no' but asks anyway.

Huldar shook his head. 'If we take this up to the office now they'll chase us back down again to finish the job. So let's get it over with.' He glanced at the two remaining bin bags. 'If our luck's in, there won't be any rotting food in them.' Giving Lína an encouraging smile, he added: 'Be grateful for small mercies: at least we haven't come across any dirty nappies.'

Lína didn't look remotely grateful. She didn't smile again until they had tossed aside the last piece of rubbish – a limp cucumber.

Erla wrinkled her nose for the tenth time since Huldar and Lína had reappeared, clutching the letter and accompanied by a rotten miasma. Huldar deliberately stood as close to Erla as he dared without it being positively indecent. She deserved it.

'I've had it up to here with this fucking case,' Erla growled. 'Isn't there anything that can get things moving?'

In front of her lay the scraps of paper, loosely pieced together to reconstruct the message to Helgi. The letter was short and perfectly legible, despite the gaps where the paper had been torn. 'What the hell's this supposed to mean?'

'It looks like a complaint from a neighbour. Maybe he held too many parties.' Lína picked up a biro from Erla's desk and pointed carefully at the scraps while her boss looked on in impatient disbelief. 'It's impossible to read it any other way.'

'Of course it's a bloody complaint. We don't need you to tell us that.' Erla reached across her desk and snatched the biro from Lína's hand. Huldar reminded himself to have a quiet word with Erla afterwards about treating Lína with more respect. With her innate air of authority, he wouldn't be surprised if the girl ended up as police commissioner one day.

Still, Erla could be forgiven for her impatience. Any idiot could see what the letter was about. It was an anonymous note addressed to Helgi, pointing out that he had done nothing about the noise coming from his flat at weekends. The writer referred specifically to the previous Saturday night, a week before Helgi died, saying that since Helgi obviously hadn't taken any notice of his previous complaints, the writer had no choice but to resort to more drastic methods. Helgi was reminded that this could have been avoided and his attention was drawn to the rules of the building, which required residents to maintain quiet by midnight at weekends and 10 p.m. on weekdays.

'This can hardly be linked to the murder.' Huldar edged after Erla as she recoiled step by step from the smell, until she was backed up against the wall. 'Disputes with neighbours can get nasty but I don't believe that they'd lead to a man being hanged in a lava-field. That's way over the top.'

'Tell me about it.' Erla scowled, either because the pieced-together letter hadn't lived up to expectations or because of the suffocating odour. Or both, maybe. 'It strikes me as a bit odd, though. Couldn't the writer have knocked on his door and asked him to keep it down? Why send a letter?'

'According to his immediate neighbours and the caretaker, he was a model resident. They didn't say a word about parties. It just doesn't make sense.'

'There's always one whinger who keeps their ear glued to the wall in the hope of finding something to moan about.' This sounded unusually heartfelt from Lína.

'I don't think that's the case here.' In Huldar's opinion, none of the neighbours he'd met from the adjoining flats had come across as the fussy type. 'Of course, we can talk to them again, but I very much doubt they'd admit to it. The letter's anonymous and now that the news of Helgi's death has been made public, no one's going to want to come forward and complain about him.' It wasn't done to speak ill of the dead, especially not of a murder victim. That was one of the few advantages of this form of death. It worked wonders for your reputation, acting like catharsis on most members of the public, if not on the police.

Erla seemed to agree, though she didn't admit it. Instead,

she pushed the scraps of paper into an evidence bag, using the biro she'd snatched from Lína, then sealed it. 'This is bullshit. It has bugger all to do with his murder.'

'Have I remembered wrong?' Lína was staring at the bag in Erla's hands. 'Wasn't Helgi abroad that weekend? Didn't he fly home the Thursday before he was killed?'

Erla and Huldar were both silent. Lína was absolutely right. Helgi had been in America the weekend of the alleged disturbance. 'Does anyone else have keys to the flat?' Erla asked by way of reply.

Lína was quick to answer, having memorised every detail of the investigation. Before the age of computers, this talent would have made her indispensible. 'No. Everyone agrees that no one else did. There was a spare bunch in his flat. But since the building has a key system, they can confirm that there are no other copies.'

'What about the master key?'

'The master key? What's that?' Lína asked, revealing her youth and inexperience.

Erla grinned for the first time since they'd entered her office. 'Go away and google it.'

As Huldar was about to leave with Lína, Erla stopped him. 'Talk to the caretaker again. If someone's been holding parties at Helgi's place, they must have either borrowed the key directly from him or got hold of the keys from the caretaker. They're the only alternatives – assuming the caretaker hasn't been holding parties there himself, which I find hard to believe from your description. I suppose you can never be sure, though. Go and have another word.' Meeting Huldar's eyes, Erla grinned nastily and added the stinger: 'When you've finished watching the porn.'

'One thing before I go. Did the bed turn out to be at Helgi's summer house?'

'Nope. It's not there. The guy supervising the search just called to say they're on their way back to town. They found nothing of interest. No bed like the one in the videos, no computers or cameras. No signs of a struggle, or drugs or anything else suspicious.'

'Is there any other evidence that Helgi owned further properties here in Reykjavík?'

'No, not yet. The estate agents claim not to have sold him any flat apart from the one he bought when he relocated from New York. Of course, it's possible he invested in property through one of his shell companies but it's proving tricky trying to unravel his business affairs and so far nothing's cropped up.' Belatedly, she cottoned on. 'You mean this letter might not be referring to the flat he was living in?'

'It crossed my mind. If he turns out to own another flat, he could have used it as a party pad, to avoid pissing off his neighbours at the luxury place. Or a shag pad, maybe. A flat where he could invite women back whenever he got lucky. Perhaps he didn't want to bring them home with him in case they were the type who are impossible to get rid of afterwards – you know, pestering him for a relationship. Either way – party flat or shag pad – there's every chance the noise disturbed his neighbours.' The moment he'd said it, Huldar could have eaten his words. The bit about women being impossible to get rid of was bound to hit a sore spot with Erla, given their history. But it was too late to take it back, so he went on quickly: 'Maybe the whingeing neighbour knew he lived somewhere else and sent the letter to his home address.'

Erla nodded slowly. 'Maybe. But that doesn't alter the fact that Helgi wasn't in the country on the weekend in question.' She waved at Huldar to leave. 'Anyway, the porn's waiting. Once you've finished that, go and see the caretaker. Take Gudlaugur with you. But for Christ's sake, change your clothes first. You stink to high heaven.'

Chapter 23

Huldar arched his back, running his hands through his hair. He badly needed a cigarette but it wasn't long since his last fag break so it would have to wait.

Watching sex videos hadn't sounded like much of an ordeal, so it had come as a surprise to him to discover that he hated every minute of it and found the footage anything but titillating. The experience just made him deeply uncomfortable. The naked women on screen had never intended these intimate moments to be shared with anyone and he was acutely aware that watching them was a violation. Even reminding himself that he was doing it in an official capacity didn't help much. He realised that part of his discomposure stemmed from the knowledge that he hadn't been exactly straight in his own dealings with women over the years. Of course, he hadn't secretly filmed anyone, but his behaviour had been underhand and frequently dishonest. And much like Helgi he had never had a lasting or meaningful relationship with a woman. Although he thought of himself as basically a good guy, maybe he and Helgi weren't really as different as he would have liked to believe.

Mercifully, Erla had provided him with a private office after he complained that he couldn't concentrate properly with his colleagues breathing down his neck all the time. This had been done, not out of consideration for him, but for the sake of the young women writhing around naked on screen, one minute underneath, the next on top of Helgi. Iceland was a small country and the fewer people who saw the videos, the better. You never knew when someone might spot a friend or relative.

Like now.

Thank God, the woman sending a lust-filled gaze in his direction wasn't one of his five sisters or the woman from the canteen or anyone else he regularly associated with. She couldn't even be called a friend. He'd spent a night with her once, two years ago. Ordinarily, he doubted he'd even have recognised her, but the circumstances had triggered a memory and then there was no mistaking her. The file name fitted too: she was called Ugla.

'Oh, fuck no.' He'd spoken aloud, the words sounding ridiculous in the empty room. He breathed out heavily. What now? Should he go and alert Erla? Or keep quiet and hope he'd recognise one of the girls in the two remaining videos from somewhere other than a one-night stand? The purpose of watching them was to find someone who could tell them about the circumstances in which the videos had been made. To that end, one of his tasks was to crop the frames to produce images of the women's faces that would help identify them. So far he had managed to create four usable headshots, though this had been easier said than done as their poses were not exactly what you'd get in a passport photo: wild hair, eyes shut, mouths open in a coital grimace. To make matters worse, they rarely faced the camera and when they did, their features were often obscured.

His mind cleared. Of course he couldn't pretend it hadn't happened. He would have to tell Erla that he'd managed to dig up the name of one of the women. He scrolled through the contacts list on his phone. Yes, there was her name and number. He'd meant to call her but never got round to it, if he remembered right. That wasn't the end of the world, as she'd taken his number too and never got in touch. Not wanting to pursue a closer acquaintance after a one-night stand was normal enough. So it shouldn't be embarrassing to talk to her – if the job fell to him. Perhaps it would be delegated to one of his colleagues, he thought hopefully.

Huldar selected the best screenshot he could get of the woman's face and printed it out. Laying it aside, he wondered how best to account to Erla for his acquaintance with Ugla without telling a bare-faced lie. After all, Ugla might ask how they'd traced her and in that case the story would have to be convincing. Best to say they'd met in a bar, had a long chat and exchanged phone numbers, which was true as far as it went. He couldn't face telling Erla that he'd gone to bed with the woman. If he did, he could guarantee that she would dispatch him immediately to interview her. She wouldn't be able to resist the temptation, aware from personal experience of his modus operandi when it came to one-night stands. She had every reason to want him to get his comeuppance.

Huldar stood up. Best get it over with. But Erla's office was empty and she was nowhere to be seen. Choosing to interpret this as fate telling him to postpone his announcement, he fetched his coat and went outside for a smoke. It would give him a chance to think.

With his lungs full of smoke and nicotine pulsing through his veins, everything seemed simpler. Of course, he would ring Ugla. That would be much less awkward than talking to her face to face or sitting there imagining the worst if his colleagues were sent round instead. Christ, the job might go to Jóel and it would be intolerable if that prick got wind of the fact that he was linked to one of the witnesses in this way. Huldar couldn't be sure the truth would emerge, but he didn't want to take the risk.

He got out his phone, found the number, took a drag, then pressed 'Call'.

Ugla answered after only one ring, causing Huldar to choke on the smoke that he had just inhaled. As a result, the conversation didn't begin as planned and things only went downhill from there.

It took the woman a while to work out who he was. 'Huldar. Remember me? We met in a bar about two years ago. During the Winter Lights Festival, I think.'

Ugla ummed and ahhed until finally she seemed to place him. 'Oh. You.'

Huldar could tell from her voice that she hadn't formed too high an opinion of him. 'I gave you my number,' he said in mock rueful tones, 'but you never called.'

There was a brief silence, then the woman answered coldly: 'You gave me a number that didn't exist.'

'What?' Huldar closed his eyes like the women in the videos, but from frustration rather than pleasure. How could he be so unlucky? He didn't often fob women off with a false number, so the odds had been on his side. He attempted to retrieve the situation. 'It wasn't deliberate. I must have been totally wasted.'

'You were driving.'

Again there was a heavy silence. Huldar couldn't think of

anything to retrieve the situation. The fact was he'd behaved like a shit and no words or excuses could make up for that. He closed his eyes, rubbing a hand over his forehead. Fate kept contriving to force him to confront the truth about himself and his past behaviour. He couldn't say he particularly enjoyed this flash of insight.

But when Ugla spoke again she sounded suddenly more cheerful. 'Never mind. You're calling now. Better late than never.'

'Yes, er, right. Actually, my call's work related.' When Ugla didn't say anything, Huldar ploughed on: 'Presumably you've seen the news about the murder inquiry. Well, I'm working on that and there's something I need to ask you.'

'What?' This time her tone was icy enough to freeze Huldar's ear off.

'The murder victim was called Helgi Fridriksson. You may not have twigged, since it's a common name, but I think you were acquainted with him. The man was an investor and I have reason to believe that your paths crossed a bit under a year ago.'

'I'd already worked that out.' Ugla fell silent again, apparently determined not to make Huldar's life easy. He couldn't blame her.

'I see. May I ask if you had a long relationship?'

'No.'

'Was it only the one night, maybe?'

'That's none of your business.'

The cigarette had almost burned down to his fingers. The woman's answers were so curt that he didn't have time to take a puff. 'Two nights? Longer?'

'Does it matter? Surely you don't think I killed him?'

'No, of course I don't think anything of the sort. And you're right that it doesn't matter how often you met him. What I'm trying to find out is where you went on the night or nights you spent with him.'

'Where we went?'

'Yes.' Huldar tried to think of a way of phrasing his question without having to say the word *bed*. 'I'm not talking about a restaurant or a bar or a cinema or anything like that. I'm talking about a flat or apartment block that you might be able to help us find.'

'Are you joking?'

'It must sound a bit odd but, the thing is, we're trying to find a property that we think Helgi had at his disposal. I have reason to believe that you visited him there and can help us locate it.'

'Why the hell would you think that? Because I made the mistake of going home with you that one time?'

Huldar dithered. Ugla had a right to hear the truth. It was a question of how to break it to her. It would be no joke to learn that you appeared in a sex video that was being used as evidence in a criminal inquiry. 'No. That's not the reason. Absolutely not. Look, we've got hold of some video files of Helgi's that seem to have been filmed in a bedroom.' He paused, hoping she would say something, but she didn't, so he was forced to go on. 'They're recordings. Let's just say that we suspect the women involved may not have been aware of the camera.'

'Recordings?' Ugla's mouth sounded as dry as if she'd just crossed the Sinai Desert without a water bottle.

'Yes. Recordings. Hopefully I don't have to spell it out.' Huldar guessed she understood from the fact that she didn't answer. 'Let me stress that we're very conscious of how extremely delicate this is. The videos will only be seen by a select few, when it's strictly necessary for the investigation.'

She didn't sound remotely reassured. 'And you just happened to see it by chance?'

'No, not by chance. I was given the job of going through the material. You're not the only woman to have been filmed like this. We recovered a number of other video files from Helgi's computer. The only coincidence is that I recognised you.'

There was silence at the other end and Huldar grabbed the chance to take a drag before his cigarette burned right down to the filter. 'I take it you had no knowledge of this.'

'How could it even cross your mind that I'd have consented to something like that?'

Huldar refrained from pointing out that he barely knew her, in spite of their intimate encounter. 'I had to ask. I guessed that was the case.'

'How dare he? What the hell's wrong with him?'

'What *was* wrong with him, you mean. He's dead.'

'Good. I'm glad. Jesus. What exactly did he do with the video? Did he share it?' Ugla's horror was all too understandable. 'Is it on the internet?'

'No, not as far as we know. We believe he made these films for his own private use.'

'Then I insist you delete it immediately. Jesus, what the hell are you lot thinking of? Don't you have anything more important to investigate?'

The answer was no, but he wasn't about to admit that. Helgi's life appeared, on the surface at least, to have been singularly respectable, with the exception of this sleazy habit.

'Do you remember the address of the property where the video was filmed?'

Ugla hung up on him. And didn't answer when Huldar immediately called her back.

Chapter 24

Erla glanced at the clock on the wall, then back at her computer screen. It was the second time she'd done this since Huldar dropped by her office and he guessed she was waiting to hear that the Chinese delegation had left. He had come to tell her about Ugla and to request her permission to speak to the woman face to face, as little as he relished the thought.

'Don't bother me now. I need to concentrate.' Sighing irritably, she added: 'I just got a call from upstairs to tell me I've got to give a press conference. I can't do it. They've given me no bloody warning.'

So this was the reason for today's short fuse. The investigation was making next to no progress and now that the media had got wind of the murder, the pressure from upstairs for results must be intolerable. Not to mention totally counterproductive. The police simply didn't have the resources to do everything necessary: interview witnesses, analyse the evidence they'd amassed so far, comb through Helgi's complicated financial affairs, find out what had happened to Siggi's parents, brief the rescue teams who were due to commence a major sweep for them, and examine the various computers they'd confiscated. The only tasks that could be ticked off the list so far were sorting through Helgi's rubbish and going through the CCTV from the city centre, which Gudlaugur had finished in time for the progress meeting, only for it to be postponed once more because of the press conference.

Since Huldar sat opposite Gudlaugur, he had already seen the fruits of his work and knew that, while they wouldn't solve the case, they did fill in a small but significant piece of the jigsaw. Gudlaugur had managed to track Helgi's progress up Laugavegur, where he kept stopping to talk to a succession of dolled-up young women, all of them slim and leggy, with long blonde hair. It was obvious that he was trying without success to persuade them to go home with him. If he'd got lucky, the girl in question would no doubt have appeared in a video on his computer. It was their good fortune that they'd all turned him down; but Helgi's failure had had lethal consequences for him.

Instead of bedding a blonde, he had fallen into the clutches of a sadistic killer.

From the CCTV footage, it seemed that Helgi's communication with the other revellers had been limited almost exclusively to women. Only once could he be glimpsed talking to a man. The individual in question was holding a cigarette and appeared to be asking for a light, which Helgi couldn't provide. If the smoker had been as drunk as he appeared to be in the recording, he could hardly have been the perpetrator, though of course there was always the possibility that he was acting. The plan was to put out a request for the man to come forward, in the hope of eliminating him from their inquiries.

Huldar didn't say a word when he noticed that the video clip in which Gudlaugur blundered into the frame after Helgi was noticeably shorter than the other clips he had edited together. There were two longer sequences. In one, Helgi turned off Laugavegur into Vitastígur. In the second, he appeared on Skúlagata, walking towards the bar at the Kex Hostel, now carrying a beer bottle. As there was no CCTV on Vitastígur, there was no telling where he had acquired the beer. It had taken him over a quarter of an hour to cover a distance that should have taken him around four minutes, five at the most. There were no bars or restaurants in the vicinity, so it was impossible that Helgi could have got hold of the bottle that way. He also turned up earlier on another recording, crossing Hverfisgata, with no sign of a bottle at that point. So he must have acquired the beer somewhere on the short walk between Hverfisgata and Skúlagata.

Logically, therefore, he must have met someone who had given it to him. Whether this was the killer or someone else entirely had yet to be established, but one thing was certain: the individual in question could not have been on foot, since no other pedestrian had been picked up by the cameras at either end of the street after Helgi had emerged onto Skúlagata.

There was, however, a car. It turned and followed Helgi, hanging back a little, then drove up to him as he stood outside the entrance to the Kex Hostel, draining the bottle before going inside. Helgi could be seen bending down to the open window on the passenger side, saying something to the driver, then getting in. After that, the car drove away. What appeared to be the same car was later picked up by several other cameras on the roads leading out to Álftanes. There was no doubt about it: this was the vehicle that had taken Helgi to his death, which meant that the driver was almost certainly the killer. But in none of the shots could his face be seen.

The vehicle was a grey or silver Land Cruiser. Gudlaugur and Erla disagreed about the colour and Huldar was in two minds. Even more frustratingly, its registration number couldn't be seen, making it almost impossible to identify the owner. The police had requested a list of all vehicles of this type in the country and were expecting it to run to several hundred, though if they could establish the exact model, they would be able to narrow it down a bit. Stills had been sent to the Land Cruiser dealership for this purpose.

The Rohypnol was now believed to have been in the beer Helgi had acquired on his way down Vitastígur. But since it would hardly have begun to take effect by the time Helgi climbed into the car, they deduced that he had either been acquainted with the driver or had been so drunk that his instincts had been blunted. Drunks tend to see a friend in every face. Other members of CID were now going through Saturday night's footage from cameras near Siggi's and Helgi's homes, hunting for the Land Cruiser and Siggi's parents' Yaris. The loan company had confirmed that they still had their car, although it was due to be repossessed shortly.

The theory was that one or both vehicles would turn up, either fetching Siggi or dropping him off, and that this would also shed light on his parents' movements. From what Gudlaugur had told Huldar, however, those entrusted with this task were getting nowhere. There was no camera in the residential streets near either address, and both neighbourhoods had numerous different access points, almost none of which were covered by CCTV.

This turned out not to be the only frustrating gap in the coverage. Huldar had been surprised, after watching the recordings from Helgi's building, to discover that there was no security camera outside the entrance or covering the nearby parking spaces. He had been meaning to ask the technician from the security company why this was, but the man still hadn't returned his call. He made a mental note to ask the caretaker when he dropped by to see him about the keys.

But before he did anything else, he needed to speak to Ugla. He opened his mouth to ask permission but Erla cut him off again: 'Unless you're about to give me tips for the press conference, you can shut up.' She looked up from the screen, even more stressed than before. The Chinese delegation was clearly still on Icelandic soil. 'As if I didn't have enough to do already. This is a complete fucking waste of time. Since when have the public ever helped to solve a crime?'

Huldar shrugged and didn't bother to point out that tip-offs from the public had frequently come in useful. She knew that as well as he did. It was just the stress talking. Still, she had his complete sympathy this time, as nothing in their training had prepared them to stand up in front of a crowd of journalists to outline the progress of the inquiry and respond to awkward questions. It would make more sense to send them on a PR course than to yet another session on how to develop outstanding team skills or how to set objectives. Like him, Erla wasn't particularly media friendly. He didn't suffer fools gladly and Erla was forever on the verge of losing it; qualities that did not come across well on the evening news.

Still, at least she'd look good. Her uniform, which was customary on these occasions, suited her, enhancing her slim, muscular build. For once, she had put on lipstick too, which made her look almost benign – to those who didn't know her. The effect was disturbingly sexy, as if she were wearing another woman's mouth. But he mustn't think like that. It was very, very unwise. Getting too close to Erla had already caused him more than enough grief and he had no intention of making that mistake again. Besides, he reckoned he finally had a foot in the door with Freyja, and he could be sure that door would slam in his face forever if she discovered he was messing around with Erla again.

But he was probably being presumptuous to think either of them would ever want anything more to do with him.

'You'll be fine, Erla. It'll be over before you know it.' This wasn't quite true. A minute up there in front of the press could feel like an hour. 'It'll be a doddle.' Yet another lie. But she needed a boost.

'Huh.' Erla wasn't buying it. 'I'm tempted to send Lína out there instead.' Her face cracked in a rare grin. 'She'd soon shut them up by droning on about the boring details.'

'I reckon she could handle it.' Huldar watched Lína through the glass wall. She was staring intently at her computer and intermittently making notes. 'She's good, Erla, and she's going to turn into a useful officer. Don't forget she's only young. We were no better when we started out – in fact, we weren't nearly as clued up.'

Erla scowled, her red lips turning down at the corners in an expression that reminded Huldar of Freyja's little niece. He hoped the child would break into a smile when he took her out. One thing was sure: he wouldn't be able to keep the grin off his own face once he was sitting next to Freyja.

Erla narrowed her gaze. 'I need someone to stand behind me. These conferences always have that kind of set-up.'

Suspecting what was coming next, Huldar tried feebly to deflect it but in vain.

'No buts. You're coming too. You're already in uniform.'

Huldar had changed to get rid of the stink of rubbish. It had been a choice between his uniform and the sports gear he'd been planning to wear to the gym after work.

Erla buttoned up her jacket. 'And drag Lína and Gudlaugur along too.'

The press conference had gone much as expected. While not exactly endearing herself to the press, Erla had at least managed to rein in her temper. And her request for information had resulted in a flood of calls and emails from the public. Lína, who had been ordered to join the team manning the phones, now marched over to Huldar looking very smug indeed and waving a rolled-up sheet of paper. 'At last!' She came to a halt by his desk, smiling broadly, and laid the paper on his desk with a flourish. 'The cigarette guy rang.'

'You mean the one who asked Helgi for a light?'

'Yes.' Judging by Lína's triumph over this minor result, she must have had to deal with more than one crank caller. 'He recognised himself from the still and remembers it, more or less. He said he was very drunk at the time. But he called in, which is a good sign.'

'Great.' Huldar tried to match her enthusiasm. 'Really great. Erla will be pleased.' Picking up the sheet of paper, he read the man's name and phone number. He wasn't anyone who'd come up in connection with the inquiry. 'Have there been many time-wasters?'

'Quite a few.' The excitement faded from Lína's face. 'Some of the calls were just stupid, some were based on a misunderstanding and others were plain nasty.'

'Nasty in what way?'

'One said he couldn't give a shit about Helgi. Another man

rang to say the same about Siggi's parents. Mind you, he was drunk.'

'What did the man have against him?'

'He said Helgi had ripped off the Icelandic people. And the other man said Siggi's parents were losers and scroungers. It was as if they thought a death sentence was a suitable punishment.'

'You always get a few morons.' She was so young that Huldar felt an urge to shield her from the knowledge of how large this group was. She'd find out for herself in due course. 'No calls about the Land Cruiser?'

'No. Not a single one.'

'What about the Yaris?'

'Two. But it turned out the cars they were talking about weren't white, so they were a waste of time.'

Huldar was surprised that she hadn't received more calls, given how common Yarises were in Iceland. The press conference had led on all the online news channels. It was the day's most read story, so virtually no one could have missed the fact that the police were hunting for it.

'Hadn't you better tell Erla about the cigarette guy?' Huldar handed back the sheet of paper.

Lína's smile faded. 'Yes. I just wanted to tell you first.' She blushed slightly.

Huldar groaned inwardly, hoping that it was only because Lína had wanted to share the news with someone who would react kindly. The last thing he needed was for her to develop a crush on him. In a way he was asking for it by being the only person in CID who was nice to her. But following the fiasco with Erla, he had forbidden himself any further entanglements with female colleagues.

'I didn't know you were such a dab hand at drawing, Huldar.' It was Jóel, Huldar's least favourite colleague, who had just come indoors, bringing the cold with him. He gestured at Siggi's drawing, still hanging on the wall above Huldar's desk. Jóel had been part of the security unit guarding the Chinese delegation, but the minister had been safely ushered onto his plane while the press conference was going on. And now he was back. Which was a bloody nuisance. Over the years he and Huldar had traded insults, had numerous run-ins and even come to blows.

'Or did the girl draw it?' Jóel never referred to Lína by name. He called her either 'the girl' or 'you there' or 'hey, embryo cop'.

'Oh, just fuck off.' Huldar couldn't be bothered to come up with anything more subtle. In Jóel's case, it paid to be direct.

'Now, now, don't take offence. Your drawing's very nice.' Jóel grinned sarcastically.

'Shut the fuck up and piss off.' Huldar gripped the arms of his chair, ready to stand up. If the man didn't go of his own accord, he would have to help him on his way.

'Whoa, take it easy. Mind you, I can understand why you're in such a hurry to have me back at my desk. Now I'm here, the investigation will finally start getting somewhere. You two might as well go home.'

The joke was that Jóel wasn't only the biggest arsehole at the station, he was also one of the worst detectives.

But Huldar let the prick have the last word. For Lína's sake. He didn't want to expose her to any more of this crap. As Jóel sauntered off, looking insufferably pleased with himself, Huldar rolled his eyes at Lína.

'Thanks. I can't stand him. He really gets up my nose.' Lína put her head on one side and smiled ruefully. Huldar smiled back. She wasn't only clever and hard-working, he reflected, she was also an excellent judge of character.

Chapter 25

This time the boys had put their foot down: there was no way they were meeting up at the Icelandic tourist trap again, so Thormar had had to come up with another venue in a hurry. All he'd been able to think of was the gym, but, as it turned out, he couldn't have made a worse choice. The place was heaving. Even the sauna was full. Everywhere you looked, people were toiling away in garish Lycra or spandex, to their own private soundtrack. Pumping iron, stretching, pulling or pushing on the equipment, flexing their muscles, scarlet with the strain. There was a queue for the treadmills where people were doing their best to burn off the Christmas calories. Others were posing in front of the mirror wall at the end of the room, drawing themselves up and grimacing as they scanned their bodies for any imperfections.

There was nowhere for three men to hold a private chat.

In the end, they had opted to perch in a row on the wooden bench at the back of the men's changing rooms, keeping their voices to a murmur. Few of the other members took any notice, but one or two looked at them askance, as if they might be about to comment. No one actually did, though. Changing rooms had a way of inhibiting people.

'I suggest we delete the site.' Thormar was gripping his phone in the pocket of his gym hoodie. Mobile phones were frowned on in the changing rooms. He had put on the hoodie in a feeble attempt to blend in with the crowd, and Tommi had changed into his sports kit too. Gunni, in contrast, stood out like a sore thumb in his suit and overcoat. In hindsight, though, they might as well not have bothered to change. Their behaviour – skulking at the back of the room, conferring in low voices – already marked them out. Thormar added: 'I don't know why we didn't think of it straight away.'

'Delete it?' Gunni reared back as if Thormar had suggested mass suicide as a way of solving their problems. 'But I don't have any copies. Do you?'

Tommi shook his head, but Thormar was fairly sure, seeing his shiftily lowered eyes, that he was lying. 'If you've got any copies,' he said, 'I'd delete them. Maybe even throw out the computer they're saved on, just to be on the safe side.'

'What the hell are you talking about?' Gunni nudged Tommi for back-up. 'There's no need to freak out like this. The cops don't know anything. If they did, they'd have hauled us all in by now. The only one they seem interested in is you, Thormar. After all, you and Helgi were best mates. It's hardly strange if they want to talk to you. Jesus, man. Don't be such a pussy.'

Thormar took a deep breath. 'How often do I have to repeat it? They're onto us. Just because they don't know the whole story yet, that doesn't mean they won't find out.' He didn't add that he had no intention of shouldering the blame alone.

'Gunni's got a point.' Tommi avoided Thormar's eye as he said this, bending down to fiddle with the laces of his trainers. 'They didn't say a word about it at the press conference and I've read all the news reports. They don't seem to know a thing.'

'Oh, get real. They never disclose everything they know at press conferences. How naive can you be?' Thormar was fed up with constantly having to bring home to them how serious the situation was. Not having been summoned to the police station like him, they found the whole thing easier to shrug off. 'We've got to delete the site,' he repeated. 'Before they find it.'

'They won't find it. How are they going to do that? It's a hundred per cent invisible and access is controlled as well.' Gunni broke off as a man wearing a towel round his waist came in and went over to one of the lockers. He gave the three of them a sideways glance but seemed resigned to having to get dressed with them there. They turned away tactfully and began a random conversation about football but were too distracted to concentrate on what they were saying. When the man finally slammed his locker and headed for the exit, they picked up where they had left off.

Thormar got in first: 'Hasn't it dawned on you yet that the police have Helgi's computers?' Neither of them said anything. 'They've got an IT department. They must have. How long do you think it'll take them to find the site once they start digging through his files?'

Gunni sighed irritably. 'How the hell should we know? We're not computer experts. Anyway, isn't the site meant to be secure? The fact they've got his computer probably won't make any difference.' He put his hands on his thighs as if about to stand up. If he left, Tommi would follow suit.

'Guys.' This time Thormar made an effort to keep the stress and exasperation out of his voice, since that approach obviously wasn't getting him anywhere. 'We've just got to accept that the site has to go. It's been fun but personally I have to say the whole thing has lost its appeal. Is it really worth the risk, now that the police are onto it?' He'd begun to lose interest in the site some time ago, a fact he'd never have dared admit were it not for their present predicament. In some respects their group dynamic hadn't changed since they were boys. 'You can't seriously think so?'

Tommi started to shake his head but quickly stopped, afraid that Gunni might disagree. He glanced at Gunni, waiting to take his lead from him, and, as usual, Gunni obliged. It was a pity Thormar couldn't get him onside. If he could, Tómas would immediately fall in behind him.

'Let's just hold our horses,' Gunni said. 'We can always delete it if it looks like the inquiry is directly linked to the site. If it is, then – zap! – we wipe the content.' The phone rang in his hands and he checked the screen. 'Work. Shit. I told them—' They never did find out what lie Gunni had told in order to slip out to this meeting. While he was talking, the others kept quiet.

By the end of the phone call, Gunni had undergone a dramatic change of heart. 'Delete the site.' He thrust his phone back into the pocket of his short overcoat. 'The police called my office and spoke to my assistant. Are they even allowed to do that?' He searched his friends' faces and, when neither of them answered, continued: 'They want to talk to me.'

Thormar hid his relief. He was no longer the only one in the police's sights. Now that Gunni was in the firing line, his attitude had undergone a complete U-turn.

Sounding extremely twitchy now, Gunni asked: 'What if the murder's connected to the website and the police manage to access it? They'll go looking for the flat too, won't they?'

Thormar hadn't thought that far. 'Yeah, they're bound to. They asked me if Helgi owned any other properties.'

'How come? Do they already know about it?' Gunni's foot started drumming nervously. He cut a faintly incongruous figure in his slick, stockbroker suit and socks.

'No. I got the impression they didn't know anything concrete, just suspected its existence.'

Tommi's eyes widened and suddenly he looked like he used to when they were boys. 'Hadn't we better clean it? Destroy any fingerprints and that sort of thing?'

The question was directed at Thormar. Since he had got them worried, apparently the problem was his responsibility. 'I don't know. None of us have police records, so they won't have our prints. And I think they need a warrant before they can take them. Don't they?'

Nobody knew. Tommi searched on his phone and read out the laws relating to the taking of fingerprints, which did nothing to allay their concern. The police, it seemed, were permitted to fingerprint those who'd had access to a scene in order to eliminate them from their inquiries. If a person refused, he or she could be compelled to comply, on condition that a warrant was issued by a judge. Tommi added gloomily that the police's requests for warrants were always granted, no matter what. Neither of them contradicted him or asked where he'd got this information from.

'Delete it.' Gunni waved at Thormar. 'The prints won't matter if the website no longer exists.'

Instead of protesting and pointing out that Gunni had a phone and could do it himself, Thormar went online. 'How do you delete the site, anyway? Do either of you know? You don't have to delete every post, do you?'

It turned out his friends hadn't a clue either. The site had originally been set up by Helgi, who was the only one of them with any computer know-how. Thormar tried this and that but couldn't find any way of deleting it. Then he started trying to destroy the individual posts one by one, envisaging having to postpone even more appointments, given that they'd been posting stuff on the forum for over a decade. At this rate, he might have to fake illness all day tomorrow as well. 'If each post needs to be removed individually, we'll have to divide up the task. I haven't got time to do it all on my own.'

Neither of the others volunteered to help. But it turned out not to matter since the posts refused to vanish. When he tried with the first, a small window popped up announcing that he wasn't authorised to delete any material. Only the administrator could do that. 'What the fuck's this?'

The others then tried and got the same message. Gunni was the first to think of checking the admin page and let out a loud groan. They'd all been deprived of their administrator status. Only two users now had that title: Helgi, and the person going by the username *administrator*.

Gunni stood up. 'I suggest you clean out the flat.'

'Us?' Again it fell to Thormar to voice what Tommi must be thinking. 'Excuse me but why not you?'

'Because the cops are onto me. For all I know, they might even be watching me. We don't want to lead them straight to the address, do we?'

Thormar checked an impulse to tell Gunni that he was almost certainly exaggerating his importance to the investigation. The fact was, it was better to have Gunni anxious than his usual reckless self. So he said nothing and he and Tommi stayed behind after Gunni had left, wordlessly changing back into their clothes before heading their separate ways. They still hadn't come to any decision about who should clean the flat. The only thing they had agreed on was that it would have to wait until next day as neither of them had time that evening.

Once Thormar was behind the wheel of his car, it occurred to him that maybe they could hire contract cleaners to do the job. Pay them in cash; keep their own names out of it. Spirits rising a little, he decided to run the idea past Tommi. But when he picked up his phone and saw the screen, all such thoughts were instantly dispelled. There was a message waiting on the website. His first reaction was to ignore it, but curiosity got the better of him.

Well, boys. Which one of you wants a lift with me next?

This was accompanied by a photo in which Thormar thought he could make out Helgi, lying on the back seat of a car, eyes shut, mouth open; asleep, probably. Wearing the same clothes he'd worn on Saturday night – and in the video of the hanging.

Hands trembling, Thormar closed the message. When he scanned the car park, he could see no sign of Tommi or his car. Gunni had left well before them, of course. Instead of calling, Thormar put his phone back on the passenger seat and gripped the wheel, his knuckles whitening. The timing of the message had been uncanny. Was that a coincidence? Or should he face the fact that the new user might not be a stranger? Was it possible that it could be one of them?

Chapter 26

Huldar had called ahead and Doddi the caretaker had said he was happy to meet him and Gudlaugur whenever they liked. Although he had finished work for the day, he lived on the premises, so it was no problem for him to answer their questions or show them around. When he let them into the building, he had crumbs on his chin, suggesting they'd interrupted his supper. He invited them to his flat but Huldar declined. There was no need to inconvenience the man for long, and conversations tended to become unnecessarily drawn out when people were sitting too comfortably.

Doddi was still sucking food out of his teeth as he showed them the lock on his office in the basement. 'As you can see for yourselves, no one's broken in.'

Huldar bent down to examine the keyhole and door frame. If the lock had been picked, it must have been done by a professional. 'Any chance that you forgot to lock it?'

The caretaker gave a short laugh. 'None whatsoever.' Seeing that the two detectives were unconvinced, he added: 'I always lock the door behind me. There are keys in there to flats whose contents are worth a fortune. And to cars that cost a bomb too. Believe me – I make sure that this door is locked at all times. Are you still wondering how the little boy got into Helgi's flat? Haven't you found out yet?'

'We've received information that there was a loud disturbance at Helgi's flat the weekend before last. As he was abroad
at the time, we wondered if someone else could have got in.
Of course, that doesn't necessarily mean they used a stolen
key. Helgi could have lent his flat out. Assuming our information is correct.'

'There was no one in his flat while he was away; not to my
knowledge, anyway. And I think he'd have told me if he was
going to lend it to friends or family. Though I can't be sure,
of course.'

'You weren't aware of any strange comings and goings or
any noise?'

The caretaker shook his head. 'No, nothing like that.'

'Do you do a security patrol of the building in the evenings?'

'No. That's not part of the job. I work normal hours. After
I knock off for the day, I'm free. It's a quiet building. There's
no need to patrol it like a bank or something. Though I do
occasionally deal with emergency incidents out of hours if I
happen to be home. Like now.'

Gudlaugur took over the questioning. 'Which floor is your
flat on?'

'The ground floor. Why do you ask?'

'Helgi's flat is eleven floors above yours. Surely there could
have been a party or people staying there that weekend
without your knowing about it?'

The caretaker had to concede that this was possible. 'Well,
you're welcome to ask the neighbours,' he said. 'But I'd be
surprised if you didn't get the same answers as last time.'

Huldar considered this for a moment. On their previous
visit they had asked general questions about Helgi and
whether people had heard any odd noises on the night of the

murder. But they hadn't asked specifically about the previous weekend, and they had nothing to lose by interviewing the neighbours again, seeing as they were here anyway. 'I think we'd better.'

Nobody was home in the flat below Helgi's. Presumably the occupants still hadn't returned from abroad. There was no answer either at the flat of the couple who lived by the lift. But the woman who'd been there when the police had found Siggi opened the door at their knock.

When she saw who it was, she raised a bony hand to her heart. 'Oh, God.' This was rather an unusual greeting, but then they were used to all kinds of reactions.

'Hello. We're from the police.' A redundant comment, given that he was in uniform. 'My name's Huldar. You saw me here on Sunday. This is Gudlaugur.'

'Oh, God.' The woman said again, her face petrified. 'Are you here about the murder? Is the murderer in the building?'

Huldar smiled. 'No, no, nothing like that. Don't worry: we're not here to warn you or anything.'

The woman relaxed a little and lowered her hand. 'You should have told me what had happened when you were here on Sunday. I had to learn about it from the news like everyone else. Surely witnesses are entitled to more information than the general public? And I was a witness, wasn't I?'

'Not as such, no. You saw us doing our job. I'm afraid that doesn't count.' Huldar's reassuring smile was met by a stony look.

The woman wrapped her arms around herself and shivered. 'Was he murdered in his flat? I'm alone here. My husband's abroad. Should I go and stay somewhere else?'

'No. As the news said, the murder happened out on

Álftanes. You have nothing to be afraid of.' Huldar was losing patience. It wasn't the first time he'd encountered this egocentric desire by members of the public to plant themselves in the middle of an unfolding crisis or tragedy. As if the whole thing revolved around them. 'We're here to ask you about the previous weekend, before it all happened. Were you at home then, by any chance?'

'Yes, I was. I was in bed with flu.'

Huldar allowed himself the uncharitable thought that her 'flu' had probably been no more than a cough and sniffle. 'So you would have heard if there had been a noise coming from Helgi's flat on the Saturday evening?'

'Yes, if it had been loud. But I didn't hear anything. And I was under the impression that he was abroad. I'd bumped into him in the corridor with a suitcase on the Friday.'

'So, as far as you know the flat was empty?'

'Yes. But now you're worrying me again. What's going on?'

'It's really nothing for you to be alarmed about.' Huldar put on his fake smile again. 'We just have to follow up various possible leads as part of the inquiry. As there's nothing else, I'll just say good day and thanks for your help.'

The woman wasn't about to let them go so easily. 'But . . .'

Huldar waited. When she didn't go on, he prompted: 'Have you remembered something?'

'Nothing recent, no. Helgi seemed like the perfect neighbour. But what do we really know about the people we only run into in passing? When he first moved in, I was very concerned.'

'Oh?' Gudlaugur cut in. 'Why was that?'

'Because not long after he moved in, a madman got into

the building and started banging on Helgi's door. He made such a racket I thought he was going to break it down. I peered outside to see what was going on.'

'What did he want?'

'I haven't a clue. I closed my door immediately and rang the caretaker, who came and removed him. Helgi wasn't there: he was abroad as usual. I thought maybe the man had been looking for the previous occupants as they were much less respectable. Afterwards, I learnt from the caretaker that the man had got the wrong address. That seemed the most likely explanation to me.'

Once it was clear that she had nothing to add, they were able to escape from her and return downstairs, where they tracked down the caretaker. The sound of a television was coming from his flat. After declining another invitation to come in, Huldar asked him straight out about the incident described by Helgi's neighbour. It was the first clue linking the victim to any sort of trouble and, however vague, it was worth following up.

'Oh, that nutter,' Doddi said. 'I threw him out. He got into the building by leaning on the bells until someone buzzed him in. After that, we sent round a reminder to the residents to be more careful about who they let in, and I'm happy to say we haven't had any further incidents.'

But Huldar wasn't interested in the house rules: 'Do you know what the man wanted to see Helgi about?'

'Nothing, as far as I could tell. He was just a nutter. You couldn't reason with him. All I could get out of him was that he wanted to beat Helgi up. Why, I've no idea. I don't think he really knew himself. He was literally foaming at the mouth with rage. Couldn't get the words out. I managed to drag him to the lift and escort him out of the building. He cooperated in the end because I lied that I'd called the police. Just as well – I'd have been no match for him if he'd decided to resist.'

'Did you ask Helgi about it?'

'Of course I did. As soon as he got back. Helgi was a new resident and, frankly, I was a bit worried about what kind of person they'd allowed into the building. I didn't like the idea that this sort of thing might start happening regularly. All I could think of was that the man must have been a debt collector, but of course that didn't make sense. You don't make a down payment on one of these flats if you're too broke to pay off your dealer. Anyway, I'm sure Helgi wasn't the type to do drugs. When I told him what had happened, he was bewildered. I'm a good judge of character and there was no way he was faking it. He obviously hadn't a clue who it could have been. In the end, we agreed that it must have been a case of mistaken identity. That the man had got the wrong Helgi. And since that was the last we saw of him, I assumed we were right and thought no more about it.'

Huldar pulled some folded photocopies from his coat pocket. 'This is the man who let the boy into the flat.' He handed the caretaker a printout of the best still they'd managed to capture from the security recordings. All it showed was part of the man's profile, with the scarf obscuring everything below the eyes, and his forehead partly hidden by a hood and the baseball cap he was wearing underneath it. 'Is that him? By our calculations, the man in the picture must be between five foot ten and six foot tall.'

The caretaker examined the picture, then handed it back. 'That's not really very helpful. It could be anyone. But his height sounds about right. He was my kind of height but much more heavily built. Much bigger than the man in that photo.'

'So the picture doesn't ring any bells? You don't recognise this man from somewhere else?'

'No. Sorry. Judging by his clothes you can be pretty sure he doesn't live in this building.'

Huldar held out the next photo. 'How about this man, then?'

The caretaker took the printout and studied the picture, then looked up wonderingly. 'Yes. Would you believe it? That's him. Who is he?'

Huldar didn't answer but, catching Gudlaugur's eye, raised his eyebrows meaningfully. *At last*. They thanked Doddi and asked him to drop by the station the following day to give a formal statement. Before leaving, Huldar asked him if there were any CCTV cameras monitoring the nearby parking spaces. The caretaker, still rather dazed, explained that no one had been willing to install cameras outside the building as they all kept their cars in the underground garage. In other words, the residents hadn't wanted to shell out for the surveillance of other people's vehicles. Then he offered a rather lame apology for not having brought up the incident of the madman himself, claiming that he'd acted out of a desire to protect the dead man's reputation and hadn't wanted to cast a shadow on it by referring to a one-off event that had almost certainly had nothing to do with him. Neither Huldar nor Gudlaugur made any attempt to relieve the man's conscience. The fact was that if only he'd come clean about it straight away, they would have spotted the link between Helgi and Siggi's father much earlier. Now they just had to find out what had driven Margeir to try to batter the murder victim's door down. Finally, finally, they were getting somewhere.

Chapter 27

Huldar reclined in his chair, watching over his colleagues' heads as Erla briefed them on the latest developments. The decision to skulk at the back was a hangover from his school days, an attempt to avoid being dragged up to the front. At least there was no danger of that here: Erla was unlikely to summon any of them to the board, hand them a piece of chalk and order them to solve the equation. Or recite a poem by heart.

She had reviewed the current state of the inquiry, bringing them up to date with the areas where progress of sorts had been made. When she played the edited CCTV footage from Laugavegur, Huldar noticed Gudlaugur slumping down in his chair like a doomed man, unable to relax until she pressed 'Stop'. Huldar knew that everyone present would have reacted in the same way as Gudlaugur in the circumstances: no one wanted their work colleagues to see them out on the town, the worse for wear. It made no difference whether they were attracted to their own or the opposite sex. It was a shame he didn't dare raise the subject with Gudlaugur.

Erla still hadn't reported yesterday evening's breakthrough. Huldar, who was beginning to think she wasn't going to, couldn't understand why not. The link between Siggi's father

Margeir and the murder victim was a major milestone in the investigation, however obscure the details.

'Any of you lot got something to add?' Erla looked searchingly around their faces. Huldar got the feeling that her gaze lingered longest on him but that was probably just his guilty conscience. This would be the perfect moment to report that he had recognised one of the women in the sex videos. But he kept his mouth shut, excusing his behaviour to himself on the grounds that he was respecting Ugla's privacy. It would be better to tell Erla one-to-one. So far, his feeble attempts to do so had been frustrated. Yesterday evening she hadn't been interested in discussing anything but the caretaker's statement, and by the time Huldar had turned up to work this morning, she had been shut away in an interview room with that bastard Jóel, questioning Gunnar Bergsson, another of Helgi's friends. As Huldar hadn't been invited to partner her on this occasion, he'd had to wait until the progress meeting to hear what had emerged.

Little of interest, it seemed. According to Erla, Gunnar had told essentially the same story as Thormar. His account of the fatal evening had been broadly consistent with his friend's, though there were more holes in his version, since he had obviously been considerably drunker. He didn't recognise the bed in the videos and wasn't aware that Helgi had owned any property in Iceland apart from the luxury flat and the summer house. He claimed not to know Siggi or his parents either.

Nevertheless, Erla reported that Gunnar had betrayed signs of being unnaturally agitated during questioning, despite making a visible effort to come across as relaxed. Jóel agreed, but had little else to contribute. He also seconded Erla's opinion that Gunnar had probably known in advance what they were going to ask him, despite his claim that he hadn't spoken to Thormar.

Erla added that there were no plans to take an official statement from Tómas, the other friend who had been with Helgi on the night he was killed. It would be a waste of time listening to him trotting out the story they already had in duplicate. A phone call would have to suffice for now, though that might change as the picture became clearer. Erla briefly summarised the results of the other interviews that had been conducted, including one with Siggi's uncle, who had done little but express the same suspicions as others who knew the couple – that Margeir was a nasty piece of work who had subjected Sigurlaug to mental and physical abuse. But the uncle hadn't been able to shed any light on the couple's disappearance, let alone provide any clues to their where-abouts. He hadn't known Helgi and, as far as he knew, neither had his sister or brother-in-law.

The connection between them remained tantalisingly obscure, though the caretaker's statement removed all doubt that it existed.

When Erla resumed her update, it was to break this piece of news. Huldar smiled approvingly. The human relations side of the job wasn't usually her forte: on past performance she was more likely to tear a strip off her team about slacking than provide encouragement. But she proved cannier than he'd given her credit for: closing the meeting with their small piece of progress was a brilliantly effective boost to morale.

Huldar watched his colleagues sit up straighter as Erla filled them in on Margeir's visit to Helgi's flat. At last the investigation had turned up something of interest. Erla finished by announcing that Margeir Arnarson was now their number one suspect for Helgi's murder.

This time when Erla invited questions there was no shortage of raised hands, the most eager of which was Lína's porcelain-white one. Erla ignored her, but it wasn't personal as she ignored the others as well. It seemed her question had been purely rhetorical. 'I expect you want to know if this conclusion is based entirely on the evidence I've just described. The answer is no. There's more.'

Now it was Huldar's turn to prick up his ears along with the rest.

'Just before this meeting I was informed that IT have gone through a computer believed to have belonged to Margeir. It turns out he's been searching for information that seems to link him pretty conclusively to Helgi's murder. According to IT, he doesn't appear to have made any attempt to hide his search history, which suggests either that he wasn't afraid of falling under suspicion or that he didn't intend to live long enough to be arrested.' Erla paused to allow comments from the floor, but even Lína kept quiet. No one wanted to hold up proceedings by butting in now. 'Anyway, among the material Margeir looked up online was information about Rohypnol and its effects.'

When no one said a word, Erla continued: 'So, at this stage it looks as if Margeir's our man. But we're still in the dark about his motive for killing Helgi. Maybe he lost money as a result of Helgi's financial wheeling and dealing. Or Helgi made a move on his wife. Either scenario would be consistent with Margeir's violent reaction. According to the descriptions we've been given of him, he may have been in a mentally unbalanced state. That should become clear in due course.'

Lína stuck up her hand, and Erla had no choice but to nod curtly and allow her question. 'What about Sigurlaug's computer? What did it show?'

Erla looked as if she was going to brush this off, but seeing that the rest of the team were eager to hear the answer, she relented. 'His wife's search history didn't reveal any connection to Helgi. Or to Rohypnol. Just recipes for lasagne, information about pregnancy and foetal development, knitting patterns for baby's mittens, and other equally nail-biting stuff. Nothing useful for our inquiry. The only interesting fact is that she looked up the number of the Women's Refuge the day after she'd been to A&E with the head injury.'

'Do we know if she called them?' It was Gudlaugur who asked, and Huldar suspected him of competing with Lína. He didn't want her to get ahead, even if it was only in speaking up during a progress meeting.

'No, she didn't. I rang them and they assured me they'd never had a call from her, either then or later.'

Lína raised her hand again and, without waiting for a nod from Erla, commented: 'I have to say, I find it a bit strange that a woman stuck at home like that wouldn't have searched for a broader range of stuff than what you describe. Is it possible that something's missing, like, maybe she's deleted her search history?'

Once again, Erla was obliged to answer, since it had been a perceptive comment. It hadn't occurred to Huldar, but Lína was right: it was unusual for people to restrict their browsing to recipes and knitting patterns. 'Remember who the woman was living with,' Erla said. 'Presumably she was afraid her husband would check up on her. Even if she tried to hide her browsing history, there are ways and means of recovering it, as he could easily have found out by googling the subject. So IT reckon she restricted herself to safe topics – things that were guaranteed not to set him off.'

No doubt Erla was right. Thinking about it, Huldar guessed that Sigurlaug wouldn't have dared to search for anything related to men, for fear her husband would accuse her of being attracted to them. And as men dominated news and culture – perhaps giving even cats a run for their money in the popularity stakes – there wouldn't be much left if you wanted to exclude them. She may not even have dared to look at shopping sites in case he flipped his lid, interpreting it as a sign that she despised him for not being able to buy her things.

Huldar decided to raise his hand. Erla seemed taken aback as he didn't usually have much to say at these meetings. 'Are we assuming then that it was Margeir who took his son to Helgi's flat? His height would fit.'

'Yes. Until we learn otherwise.'

Erla showed signs of wanting to wrap things up but Huldar wasn't finished. 'Isn't it a bit far-fetched to think Siggi wouldn't have recognised his own father, even if Margeir had his hood up and a scarf over his face?'

Erla looked suddenly weary. 'I don't know. Maybe his father made him promise not to tell. Maybe the boy was taken in. It's one of a number of details that need looking into. Then there's the question of where the hell Margeir got hold of the Land Cruiser and where it is now. But we'll be here all day if I start listing all the jobs that are outstanding.' Erla pointedly switched off the projector – an unmistakeable message that the meeting was over. 'Right, you lot, back to work. Those of you who have nothing to do, come by my office. We need to get cracking if we're going to find this couple. Dead or alive.'

Huldar made yet another abortive attempt to speak to Erla following the meeting. There were three colleagues already in her office, waiting to be assigned new jobs, one of whom was Jóel, and there was no way he was telling Erla about Ugla in front of that bastard. So he went back to his desk and wondered what to do. Now the investigation had acquired a new focus, it would be absurd to delay sharing such vital information any longer. As a last resort, he decided to send her an email.

Since they'd hardly ever communicated that way, even when their relationship had hit its lowest point, he began with the excuse that she was always busy. No doubt she'd raise her eyebrows at that, but it was true, so she might just buy it. After this rather clumsy beginning, he got straight to the point: he thought he recognised one of the women in the videos. After sending the message, he had a bad taste in his mouth.

'How are you getting on?' He peered round his monitor at Gudlaugur.

'I'm not.' For once the young man seemed pleased to be interrupted. 'I'm going over a list of retailers that sell nail guns in the hope of finding out whether Margeir recently bought one.'

'Are you asking them about his wife as well?' Huldar guessed the guy might have sent her instead so the purchase was less likely to be traced to him.

'Yes. But no one recognises her either.' Gudlaugur sighed. 'I've gone through pretty much all the shops in the Greater

Reykjavík area that sell tools. After that, I've got the rest of the country. Oh, and Customs, in case he ordered it from abroad. But I have the feeling I'm not going to get anywhere. I expect he already had it lying around in the basement.'

Huldar stood up and went to get a coffee. Then, remembering how much better it had been in Sexual Offences, he decided to stick his head round the door there. To give himself a pretext for his visit, he looked in on the man he had talked to before and asked if there was any news.

'Good question.' The man picked up his phone and put a call through to the colleague he'd asked to check if Helgi's videos had cropped up on their radar. Huldar was encouraged when the man met his eye and nodded, looking pleased, as if he'd received good news. He scribbled a note, then said goodbye and hung up.

'So, this may not solve the case – but you never know.'

'What?'

'The videos haven't turned up. Not yet. But one of the guys who's been monitoring the file-sharing sites I told you about says they look familiar. He's fairly sure he's seen something similar. Not necessarily involving the same women, but the same room, same bed.' Huldar waited in suspense for the man to go on. 'He hasn't managed to track it down yet but he's going to carry on searching the main sites featuring Icelandic content. It's anybody's guess when or if he'll have any luck, though.'

'Do you think there's any chance it could be today?' Huldar caught himself sounding like the kind of difficult customer who thinks he can speed up a delivery by asking impossible questions.

'Your guess is as good as mine. He's reluctant to report it

until he's got his hands on the evidence, but that could take a while.'

'What happens if he does find it? Can he tell who posted it?' Huldar couldn't decide whether this constituted progress or not. How would the unearthing of yet another video further their inquiry?

'Well, if nothing else, you'd get the name of the woman in the video. You may remember me telling you that almost all the content on these sites includes the woman's identity.'

Huldar smiled thinly. The fact was, he already had a name.

The man handed him the note he'd jotted down. 'These are the web addresses of the forums where my colleague thinks he might have come across the video. If you have nothing better to do, you can help by taking a look yourself.'

Huldar took the note, thanked the man and left his office. After helping himself to a cup of the superior coffee, he went outside where he leant against the wall and lit a cigarette. Thus fortified, he made yet another unsuccessful attempt to get hold of Ugla. When she didn't pick up, he sent her a text message that was so long he had to break it up into two parts. In it, he explained why it was so vital that she help them find the address where the video had been made: a pregnant woman's life was at stake. After that, he smoked his cigarette and waited.

Not until he had stubbed it out and was on his way upstairs again did his phone bleep. Unlike his, her text was brief and to the point. The flat was in the big tower block on Sudurhlíd in Fossvogur. She couldn't remember the number.

It was better than nothing. Huldar bounded up the rest of the stairs, two at a time.

Chapter 28

Tommi put down the window-cleaner spray and looked around. A drip fell from the cloth he was holding. He bent down to wipe the floor but only succeeded in spreading the wet patch. Looking up, he sighed. 'What do you reckon? Are we done?'

Thormar surveyed the flat critically. He'd lost sight of what they had and hadn't cleaned. They'd gone over some of the surfaces several times, others only once, and may well have missed something but it was impossible at this stage to tell what they'd left out. They weren't exactly the most experienced cleaning team in the country. It hadn't helped matters that they had arrived to find the place trashed. Empty bottles, dirty glasses, an overflowing ashtray, a half-finished pizza, used towels. In contravention of all Helgi's house rules, whoever had used the flat last hadn't bothered to tidy up after themselves. Going by the cigars in the ashtray, the culprit must be Gunni. He and Helgi were the only ones who smoked. But Helgi had been a neat freak, and it was typical of Gunni to leave the place looking like a bomb site. If they had a go at him about the mess, he would no doubt be quick to respond that he had been meaning to clean it later. He was always ready with an excuse.

'Did you clean the sink?' It was all Thormar could think of. They would either have to go over the whole place again systematically or take a risk and just hope that they'd obliterated all signs of their presence. He really didn't have time for this. The sooner he got home, the less likely he was to face an interrogation. Sigrún mustn't suspect that he'd borrowed her rubber gloves and cloths or she would demand to know why. The full bottle of window cleaner that he'd pinched from the utility room was now completely empty. He would have to go to the shops on the way home and buy a replacement.

'I think so.' Clearly, Tommi was as muddled now as Thormar. Perhaps they were high on all the fumes from the cleaning products: the reek of chemicals was certainly powerful enough. 'Yes, I cleaned it. The handle of the fridge too.' Tommi pulled off his rubber gloves. 'And inside the fridge and the oven. Though I don't think I've ever touched it. Have you?'

'No. Of course not. I didn't come here to cook, any more than you did.'

Tommi stuffed the gloves into a plastic sack he'd brought along. The spray bottle he was holding still had a bit of liquid in the bottom, which suggested he hadn't been as thorough as Thormar. Or else he'd just wasted less of the stuff. Thormar had to admit he'd been splashing it around pretty liberally. 'Are you sure window cleaner gets rid of fingerprints?' Tommi met Thormar's eye anxiously. 'Might it leave a trace behind, like when people try to clean up blood?'

'It cleans up everything. I'm positive.' There was nothing positive about it. The fact was, Thormar hadn't a clue. The spray had been all he could think of when he told Tommi what to bring. He chucked his empty bottle at the bin bag and missed by a wide margin. Blaming the gloves, Thormar peeled them off. 'That bastard Gunni. We'd have finished ages ago and be home by now if it wasn't for him.'

Tommi mumbled something noncommittal. He didn't like to bitch about the other members of their gang. Or admit to having any opinion of his own. He just went along with whatever everyone else thought and did. Since he was standing closer to the bag, he bent down, picked up the bottle and put it in. While he was doing so, he spoke, but not about Gunni. 'I'm going to tell Silla.'

'Tell her what?' Thormar genuinely wanted to know. He couldn't immediately think what Tommi meant.

'About this. About everything.' Tommi waved towards the bedroom.

They had closed the door behind them after scrubbing the room from top to bottom. It had been vital to make sure all the fingerprints had been obliterated in there. They had even discussed removing the headboard and throwing it in the sea. If it was missing, the police couldn't be sure this was the flat they were looking for as it was the only piece of evidence they had. But there was a risk that the two of them might be spotted carrying it out of the flat. There were so many other apartments in the building and the last thing they wanted was to attract attention. As a precaution, they'd both arrived wearing anoraks with the hoods up, kept their eyes lowered and strode briskly along the landing to the flat. They wouldn't be able to make an inconspicuous getaway if they were trying to manoeuvre the headboard between them.

Thormar was staring at Tommi as if he'd lost his mind. The fumes must have got to him, he decided. 'Are you crazy?'

'I've been thinking about it for a while.'

Thormar groaned under his breath. On the rare occasions when Tommi thought for himself, the results were invariably disastrous. No doubt that was why he usually went along with the others' opinions. Especially Gunni's. 'You can't do that. Are you mad?' Thormar was so shocked that he raised his voice, though up to now they'd been careful to talk in murmurs so as not to be overheard by the neighbours.

Tommi avoided his friend's furious glare. 'I know it sounds bad, but it'll be much better if she hears it from me. Than from the police, I mean. She'd never forgive me if she learnt about it that way. I've got a chance if I come clean to her first.'

Thormar laughed sarcastically. 'Don't kid yourself. She wouldn't forgive you if you hired a plane and wrote "Sorry" across the sky. Besides, you've no right to do it. It's not your secret.'

Tommi looked hurt. 'It is if it affects my relationship with Silla.'

'How stupid can you get?' Thormar whispered angrily. 'As soon as you tell her, Silla will be on the phone to Sigrún. It wouldn't only be your marriage you'd be wrecking but mine as well, and you've no right to do that.' Thormar broke off and took several deep breaths to calm himself down. 'We've destroyed all the evidence that we were here. The police won't be able to prove anything. If you go and tell Silla, all our hard work will have been wasted.'

Seeing that Tommi didn't look convinced, Thormar tried again: 'You just need to hold your nerve for a few more days. We both know that it wasn't one of us who killed Helgi. The police will find the killer soon and once they've done that, they'll lose interest in us and in this flat. In a few days' time this whole thing will have blown over and everything will go back to normal.' What bullshit. Nothing would ever go back to normal. But, oddly, Thormar felt nothing but relief at the thought. They weren't twenty any more. It was high time they started behaving like responsible adults. 'Just a few more days, Tommi. You have to hold out. You owe it to us.'

'Hmmm.' Tommi met Thormar's eye. 'You don't think the pregnant woman they mentioned on the news – Sigurlaug, was it? – could have been murdered as well?'

'No. Of course not. Definitely not.' It was amazing how persuasive Thormar managed to sound, considering he had zero evidence for what he was saying. If the bottom fell out of the dental business, perhaps he should go into PR.

But for once Tommi wasn't buying it. 'Oh, come on. Where is she, then? She must have been killed. Do you reckon it could have been her husband? The one the police are appealing for information about?'

'Bound to be.' Thormar forced himself to sound confident. The truth was, he didn't know what to think. Neither of his friends had mentioned the message from the *administrator* or the photo of Helgi lying in the back seat of the unidenti-fied car. But they must have seen it, unless they were avoiding the site in case it was being monitored by the police. Of course, it was also conceivable that they were all waiting for one of the others to take the initiative. It wouldn't be the first time. He'd lost count of all the gigs and matches they'd missed because none of them ever wanted to be the first to suggest anything or stick their necks out, for fear of being ridiculed. And while they were all hanging back, the tickets invariably sold out. Such a stupid waste.

But of one thing he was sure: in the unlikely event that one of his friends turned out to be behind the username *administrator*, he'd bet his life it wasn't Tommi.

'Look, it's obviously some kind of marital problem. The man must have killed her and Helgi as well. That's the only possible explanation.' Thormar said this not only to allay his friend's fears but his own as well.

'Why Helgi, though? I just don't understand.'

Thormar didn't either. 'Maybe he caught Helgi in bed with his wife. Helgi could have picked her up in town after he left us and gone home with her.'

'But isn't she supposed to be heavily pregnant? I really can't picture it.'

'No, neither can I, actually.' Thormar blew out a breath while casting around for another explanation. 'Or Helgi could have accidentally come across the guy murdering his wife. Anything could have happened.'

'You don't think it's connected to . . . you know?' Tommi couldn't bring himself to put it into words. But then none of them could. They'd all done their best to try and wipe the incident from their memories.

'No. Out of the question.' Thormar managed to control his face, though of course the same thought had crossed his mind. Together with all the other things they'd done. 'Look, you can't tell Silla. You've got to promise me you won't.'

Tommi sighed heavily. 'OK, OK. I'll wait a few days. But if the police are still on our backs then, I'm going to have to think again. I don't want to lose Silla.'

Thormar couldn't think why, since in his opinion Silla was a boring, pushy, stuck-up bitch. She would just love the chance to break the news to Sigrún. 'There's no risk of that.' He glanced around the flat again. 'Shall we get going then?' As he said this, his gaze fell on the floor-length curtains that were drawn across the living-room windows. 'Shit. What about the balcony? Hadn't we better wipe down the furniture? I've sat out there a few times.'

'Me too.'

Thormar checked the time. 'Oh, fuck.'

'It'll only take us a minute.' Tommi retrieved the window spray from the sack and started to force his hands back into the bright-yellow gloves. Thormar didn't envy him. They must be as damp and revolting inside as his own had been after all their efforts. He was quite content to leave this job to Tommi.

Thormar watched as Tommi drew back the curtains, infuriatingly slowly. They'd been in this flat far too long already. He doubted he would ever set foot in here again once they'd shut the door behind them.

Distracted by this thought, he was caught unprepared when Tommi suddenly let out a shrill scream, a noise Thormar hadn't heard him make since they were teenagers. Then Thormar froze with shock and only just stopped himself from yelling too.

A chair had been drawn up to the balcony door and a man was sitting there outside in the dark.

Chapter 29

Erla wasn't in her office. The man at the nearby desk told Huldar she'd been called to a meeting with the top brass and had left looking anything but happy. Huldar doubted her mood would have improved by the time she returned. However important the news he had, he knew he wouldn't be well received if he barged in on her meeting with her bosses. Instead, he sat down at his desk, tilting his monitor so he could see her office out of the corner of his eye.

Since this prevented him from doing anything that required much concentration, he decided to go on scrolling through the file-sharing platform where there was a chance the same sort of video as they'd found on Helgi's computer might show up. Following his conversation with his colleague in Sexual Offences, he had started checking the posts on there whenever he got a minute. They'd divided up the task between them, Huldar beginning with the oldest uploads and the other man working backwards from the most recent ones. The content Huldar was watching now had been posted four years ago. He hadn't been combing through the site very methodically or for long at a time, and his colleague was also doing it whenever he got a moment between other jobs. Since he hadn't heard from him yet, presumably nothing had cropped up on his radar either.

Post after post turned out to be repetitions of what he'd

already seen: pictures of naked or semi-naked teenage girls and young women. Some were obviously selfies that hadn't been intended for a wider audience. Most had no doubt been sent to boyfriends who had then betrayed the girls' trust. There were also pictures of fully clad girls that the site users had digitally manipulated to make it appear they were nude. Huldar didn't know whether to laugh or cry when he saw the results.

The most unpleasant of the lot, though they were all pretty sickening, were the photos of girls who had passed out drunk and had their clothes pulled up to expose them. Huldar scrolled quickly past these.

He came across the occasional video of couples having sex but these were very few and far between. Presumably the creeps who used the platform didn't enjoy much success with women and rarely got the opportunity to make a video. He guessed they had to make do with these pathetic photos and a tub of their mother's hand-cream.

None of the videos he did come across were anything like the ones from Helgi's computer.

It wasn't until he had scrolled through several months' worth of posts that he hit the jackpot. The post in question was from three and a half years ago.

'Gudlaugur. Come and see this.' Huldar stood up to catch Gudlaugur's eye. He wanted to get hold of him before he made yet another call to one of Margeir's former employers, for whom, on the evidence of his bank statements, he had worked in a freelance capacity. From what Huldar had over-heard, the employers were often reluctant to admit to having hired him, since the majority of the jobs had been cash in hand, however trivial that seemed in relation to the crime under investigation. 'I reckon I've found a video of Helgi on this Icelandic porn-sharing site.'

Gudlaugur didn't exactly leap out of his chair and Huldar couldn't blame him for his lack of enthusiasm. But he did come round to stand beside Huldar and bent down to peer at the screen. 'Is that the headboard we've been looking out for?'

'Yes. I should recognise it by now.' Huldar was the only member of the team who had watched all the videos from Helgi's computer. The others had only been shown stills, carefully edited to omit the women's faces. Apart from that, only a few, who'd been at work when IT first discovered the recordings, had seen a couple of videos all the way through, though none of them were prepared to admit it. Gudlaugur hadn't been among those who had given in to the temptation.

Huldar pressed 'Play' and they watched as a blonde woman approached the bed with her back to them, sat down and slid the straps of her dress off her shoulders. It was hard to get a glimpse of her face while she was taking her clothes off, but when a fully dressed man appeared, also with his back to the camera, she looked up at him and smiled, giving them a clear view of her features.

'I recognise her.' Gudlaugur said. 'Pause it a sec.' He bent closer to the screen and peered at the woman, frowning. 'What's her name?'

'I haven't got that far. The user who posted it didn't give a name. He just said: *You'll never believe this, guys!* Then followed it up with some crap about what a pro he was.'

They both stared at the woman until Gudlaugur shook his head and shrugged. Huldar was also beginning to think he recognised the woman after concentrating hard on her face for a while. He pressed 'Play' again and they watched the back view of the man taking off his clothes, then sitting down beside the woman and starting to fondle her. It was unquestionably Helgi. At one point they briefly saw his face but, even without that, the white patch on his back was a dead giveaway.

'He didn't post it himself, did he?' Gudlaugur asked.

'Given that he didn't post the other videos online, it seems unlikely. Though this one's a bit older than the rest. Perhaps he used to share them, then stopped. Maybe he didn't like the comments he got. There aren't many videos on this site that show the bloke. The camera angle normally cuts out the man. And they tend to look as though they've been filmed on a phone, usually when the woman's being taken from behind. I get the feeling that the guys who hang out on this site are mostly kids, though there may be a few adults among them. It seems implausible that Helgi would have been one of them.'

Huldar stopped the video and the original post reappeared, along with the comments. An unusual number of users seemed to have felt compelled to express an opinion about it. The top comments didn't give away anything about the woman's identity. Instead, they were all in the form of questions: *Who is that? Name? WTF?* And so on.

'Can't we find out which user uploaded the video?' Gudlaugur asked.

'No. The site's on the Deep Web, which means that anyone who follows the URL can see the content, but to post something you have to use a Tor browser, which covers the user's tracks. The names of the users on this platform give nothing away either. They're just numbers. The whole thing's designed to preserve their anonymity.'

Huldar clicked to see more comments. Many of them were full of praise for the man who'd posted the video. His own claim to be a 'pro' was modest compared to the enthusiasm expressed by the other users. Huldar had never seen so many positive responses on the site. Nor as many comments. He noticed that the usernames often appeared in numerical order, which suggested that many of them had signed up to the site at around the same time. And his attention was particularly drawn to a comment towards the bottom of the screen, in which the person who'd posted the video finally supplied the woman's name.

Sigurlaug Lára.

Though her patronymic was missing, it could only be Lárusdóttir.

Huldar jabbed his finger at the screen. 'Christ! It's Siggi's mother. No wonder her face looked familiar.'

The pictures he'd seen on her Facebook page had confused him. In those she'd had short, dark hair and worn little make-up. She'd appeared very ordinary – unusually ordinary, in fact. In the video she could have come straight from the Miss Iceland contest, with her long blonde mane and heavy make-up. Her image had certainly undergone a dramatic transformation over the last three and a half years. Huldar guessed that Margeir had been the reason for that. Abusive partners were often pathologically jealous and the poor woman had probably been trying to make herself less attractive to the opposite sex. If so, she'd done a good job.

Huldar leant back. 'So now we know why Margeir had it in for Helgi.'

'Because she slept with him, you mean?'

'Because she cheated on him with Helgi. This was posted three and a half years ago. They were already married by then.'

'The video could be older.'

'True. But Margeir may have believed the affair was still going on. And it can be hard to reason with nutters like him.'

Huldar was still keeping half an eye on Erla's office. Now he not only had information about where the bed was located, he'd also uncovered the link between the two cases. It was almost enough to make it worthwhile knocking on the door of the meeting room upstairs. All they needed now was to track down that bastard Margeir. And Sigurlaug, of course. For that, Erla's meeting would have to be curtailed and the team would have to get their arses into gear. He sent her a text.

'What's with all the messages? Emails, texts . . . what the fuck next? A telegram, a smoke signal? That should be no problem for you.' Erla's temper came as no surprise to Huldar, considering that she'd just emerged from the lion's den. He needn't have bothered to turn his monitor towards her office because she came storming straight over to his desk a few minutes after he'd sent the text. Gudlaugur had scuttled back to his seat, snatched up his phone and dialled the next number on his list. No one wanted to be in Erla's firing line. No one except Huldar, who had become inured to it.

'Come on, admit it – I threw you a lifeline.' He grinned at Erla. She didn't return it but neither did she contradict him, which proved he was right. She'd used it as an excuse to escape, but he would wait forever and a day before she thanked him. 'What do you say to a quick trip over to Sudurhlíd?' he asked. 'You never know what we'll find there.'

Erla took a deep breath, thinking it over. Then she breathed out and nodded. 'OK.' Her gaze travelled to Gudlaugur, who was doing his best to avoid her eye. 'Gudlaugur!'

He was forced to look up. 'Yes?'

'How are you getting on with the phone calls?'

'All right. As far as it goes.' He picked up a page of notes he'd made. 'Margeir's old company sacked him about six months ago. Apparently his temper was always getting him into trouble – he kept being rude to customers. The people who are prepared to admit to employing him on a casual basis after that give him a mixed report. Some say he did the work without any problems, others that he was bad-tempered and offhand for no reason.'

'Who are these people?'

'Individuals and small companies. A beauty parlour, a bakery and most recently a garage. He advertised his services online and electricians are in such short supply at the moment that he seems to have had enough to do.'

'How far down the list are you?'

Gudlaugur seemed to have something in his throat. 'Um, I've finished actually. That was my last call. Unless you want me to try again with the people who won't admit to having hired him?'

Erla shook her head. 'Nope. Get your coat. You're both coming with me.' Her eye fell on Siggi's drawing hanging on the wall above Huldar's desk. 'And take that crap down. This isn't a kindergarten.' Spinning on her heel, she strode off to her office to fetch her coat.

Huldar thought it wiser not to answer back, but defiantly

left the picture where it was. Obeying her would come across as too submissive. Instead, he got to his feet and pulled on his outdoor clothes.

As they were on their way out, Jóel came running over to ask where they were off to. Lousy detective though he was, he had a talent for sniffing out breakthroughs in other people's investigations. When Erla barked at him to get back to his desk and wait for the progress update like everyone else, he shot Huldar a look of pure hatred. Huldar drew his lips back in a grin and winked at the prick, which did nothing to mollify him. On second thoughts it would have been more sensible to ignore him, but Huldar could never resist the chance to wind him up.

'This has to be it.' Erla pointed at the only unmarked bell in the lobby. 'All the rest have names by them.' She tried ringing the bell and they waited in silence for a while but nothing happened.

'What now?' Huldar was itching to get inside the building. From his misspent youth he knew that if they rang all the bells at once, someone was bound to open the door, but these tactics were unlikely to meet with Erla's approval.

'We wait.' She peered in the window to the stairwell, then took out her phone and without a word to them made a call. Huldar and Gudlaugur stood listening impatiently as she talked to the Land Registry in the hope of finding out whether the flat belonged to Helgi.

Erla was still on hold when one of the residents, a middle-aged woman, came up behind them carrying two heavy shopping bags. She looked startled to see them standing in the lobby.

Huldar gave her a friendly smile. 'Hello. We're from the police.'

The woman raised her eyebrows. 'Oh? Has something happened?'

'No, not as far as we're aware. But maybe you can help us. We need to speak to the occupant of this flat. You don't happen to know who lives there, do you?' He indicated the unmarked bell.

'Oh, I see.' The woman relaxed a little. 'Did Einar ring you?'

'Einar?' Huldar thought Erla was going to hang up, now they seemed to be getting somewhere, but she didn't, so he asked: 'Who's Einar?'

'He lives in the flat next door to the one you're asking about. He's a bit peculiar, poor man. Takes up half our residents' meetings complaining about the noise he claims he hears from that flat. The people living on the other side say they haven't noticed anything, except on a couple of occasions. They think Einar's making a fuss about nothing and they're probably right. It didn't occur to me he'd go as far as to call the police – let alone that you'd actually turn up.' Her wondering gaze took them all in. 'Or that they'd send three of you.'

'We're not actually here on a callout.' Huldar watched as Erla switched her attention back to the phone, then half turned away from them to carry on talking. 'So you don't know who lives there?'

'No. I live on the ground floor and I've never seen the owner. He doesn't come to residents' meetings and I gather he's very rarely here. According to Einar, he rents it out through Airbnb, but I don't know if that's true. It would be against the building rules, if it is. But that's hardly a police matter, is it?'

Before the woman could advise them any further on their duties, Huldar thanked her and made it clear that the conversation was over. Realising she'd been dismissed, she squeezed past and went inside. There was no point grabbing this opportunity to follow her through the door as they still wouldn't be able to enter the flat. Huldar and Gudlaugur waited instead for Erla to finish her conversation.

'It's definitely the right flat,' she told them. 'It's been registered to an American company for the last nine years. Something tells me that Helgi either has a share in that company or owns it outright. Anything else would be too much of a coincidence.' She shoved the phone back in her pocket. 'What was that bloke called? Einar?' Huldar nodded and Erla turned to the panel, found his name and pressed the bell. After a brief interval a man's voice crackled over the intercom. Erla introduced herself and he eagerly invited them to come up. They waited for the lock to buzz, then hurried in and climbed up to the third floor. The flats turned out to be accessed from an outdoor walkway, and they waited there, shivering in the icy wind, for Einar to open up. Beside them was the door to what must be Helgi's flat. While they were waiting, Gudlaugur pressed his ear to it. When Einar opened his door, the young man moved away, reporting that the flat must be empty as all was quiet inside.

'Are you Einar?' The man, who must have been about seventy, looked rather frail. He'd lost most of his hair and his face was set in deep lines of discontent that appeared to be habitual.

Erla came straight to the point as it was freezing hanging around on the concrete walkway. 'Is it possible that the flat next door to you belongs to a man called Helgi Fridriksson?'

The man's scowl deepened. He tightened his grip on the door as a gust threatened to tear it out of his hands, but didn't invite them in. 'It depends how you look at it. Officially, the flat belongs to a foreign company, but he owns it through the company. I heard on the news that he's dead – murdered. Are you investigating?'

Erla said they were. 'Did you send him a letter recently, complaining about the noise from this flat?'

'Yes. I've sent him several. The man's hardly ever here, so I had to do something. The racket they make is totally unacceptable. I can't be expected to put up with it.'

Erla ignored this: disputes between neighbours weren't her department. 'How would you describe the disturbance?'

The man snorted. 'I don't know. All kinds of things. Booming music, people having noisy sex and just general loud voices and crashing about. If you ask me, the flat's rented out for parties. At least, you never hear anything midweek. It's not only the city that's plagued with this bloody Airbnb menace.'

'Did you have a word with Helgi about it?'

'No. I never saw him. The people responsible sneak out at night after everything's gone quiet. When I knock during the worst of it, no one answers the door. Maybe he left instructions to ignore the neighbours' complaints.'

'Has anyone else complained?' Huldar asked, although he already knew the answer after talking to the woman in the lobby. It could be useful to put interviewees on the spot when they were exaggerating.

The man looked annoyed. 'I wouldn't know. But I assume they must have done. The noise was so bad that I can't have been the only one who got woken up at weekends.'

'Every weekend?' Erla took over the questioning again.

'No. Not every one. But it's still been intolerable. I'd never have moved in if I'd known. I've only lived here for two years and I can't believe the problem only started then.'

Erla huddled into her anorak. 'How did you find out that the flat belonged to Helgi?'

'I lay in wait for one of his tenants or whatever I should call him. He was a bit of a wimp. Stammered out all Helgi's details when I cornered him.'

'Did you get his name?'

'Tómas. I can't remember his patronymic. But I've got it written down somewhere, if you want it.'

'Was this recently?'

'No. About a year ago. I tried ringing Helgi, but he slammed the phone down on me and wouldn't answer my calls after that. So I resorted to writing him letters. Not that that worked either. I heard a scream from the flat earlier.'

'A scream?' Erla snapped to attention. 'What kind of scream?'

'You know, the kind someone makes when they get a shock.'

'What time was this?'

The man grimaced as he looked at his watch. 'A bit over an hour ago. Something like that.'

'Could it have been someone in distress?'

The man shrugged, and shrugged again when Erla asked about the sex of the person who'd screamed.

'All right, thanks.' Erla turned to Huldar and Gudlaugur, but when she didn't hear the door shutting behind her, she turned back to Einar, thanked him again and asked him to go inside and close his door: they had nothing more to discuss with him for the moment. He obeyed and went back inside, looking even more disgruntled.

'Call a locksmith.' Erla nodded at Gudlaugur who immediately whipped out his phone. After that, she sent him downstairs to let the man in while she and Huldar kept watch outside the flat. Although there was no sound from inside, it was possible that someone was waiting for the chance to sneak out unobserved. If so, it was almost certainly Margeir, Huldar thought.

But when the locksmith opened the door for them, Huldar's guess turned out to have been wide of the mark. Inside they found two men, the dentist Thormar and another man who identified himself in a shaky voice as Tómas, Helgi's friend. They were both in a state of shock, having been interrupted in the middle of a job that they seemed to be struggling with. Both wore yellow rubber gloves and they were holding open a large black bin bag. When the door opened, they made frantic attempts to kick it under the sofa.

But it wasn't until Huldar, Gudlaugur and Erla looked out onto the balcony that they realised what the bag was for.

There was a chair just outside the window, propped against the concrete partition that separated the balcony from the neighbour's. In it sat a dead man with a nail gun on his lap. They recognised him at once: it was Siggi's father, Margeir Arnarson.

Chapter 30

Thursday

Helgi's friend Tómas, an economist at the Central Bank, took the tissue from Erla and blew his nose. He probably hadn't cried this much since the banking system collapsed. Erla and Huldar watched impassively as he wiped his nose and tear-streaked face. The man's blubbering was getting on their nerves so much that Huldar longed to pick him up and shake some backbone into him. His sobbing and hiccupping were interrupting the flow of information that up to now had been pouring out of him. He'd struck them as a pathetic specimen when they arrested him yesterday, and, as often happened, a night in the cells had stripped him of any last vestige of courage. According to the officers guarding the cells, Thormar had shown more guts, though perhaps his toughness was only a veneer. They'd soon find out as he was next on the list to be interviewed.

Erla's decision to lock the men in the cells and let them stew until morning seemed to have paid off, in Tómas's case, at least. But she hadn't only done it to get them shaking in their shoes. The discovery of the body had had to take precedence and the crime-scene investigation hadn't been completed until nearly midnight. By then it had been too late to question the men. The interviews were too important to be entrusted to exhausted officers, and besides the team didn't yet have a clear picture of the events that had led up to the killing. There was still no sign of a murder weapon and the two men's cleaning frenzy hadn't exactly made life easy for Forensics. It was the most pristine crime scene they'd ever had the misfortune to examine; almost every single fingerprint had been erased.

Huldar had tossed and turned for much of the night, trying in vain to figure out the sequence of events following this latest bombshell. If anything, he was even more perplexed by the time he finally fell asleep than he had been before their visit to the flat on Sudurhlíd.

The preliminary report on the cause of death had forced them to revise their initial theories. When Huldar, Erla and Gudlaugur spotted Margeir sitting out there on the balcony, they had naturally concluded that he had murdered Helgi and probably his wife as well, before taking his own life. But the moment they walked round behind the chair, it became evident that they were not looking at a suicide. Nor had the coatless man frozen to death out there. The big, ugly wound on the back of his head couldn't possibly have been self-inflicted. Between the clumps of dried blood in his hair Huldar had glimpsed splinters of bone and what appeared to be brains, before beating a hasty retreat inside the flat.

Although Margeir's post-mortem was not yet complete, the preliminary examination at the scene indicated that he had died on Sunday. A more precise time frame was not yet available. They'd been working on the assumption that he was Helgi's killer, regardless of who had subsequently murdered him. They still had a long way to go in clarifying

Tómas's role in events too. He flatly denied having had anything to do with Margeir's death, and the name of the dead man had apparently come as a complete surprise to him. If his story was to be believed, he and Thormar hadn't had a clue who the man in the chair was. They claimed not to know anything about him apart from what they'd heard on the news. The dead man had looked very different from the picture the police had used in their appeal for information. Tómas was adamant that he didn't know Sigurlaug Lára or their son Sigurdur either, and stuck to his statement, despite repeated questioning. He was equally insistent with regard to Helgi's death. He hadn't killed him – it would never have crossed his mind to murder one of his closest friends. What possible motive could he have had for wanting Helgi dead, let alone a complete stranger? According to Tómas, he and Thormar had stumbled on Margeir's body by chance. They had come to the flat to clean it from top to bottom in order to remove all the evidence of their own presence there. It was only after they'd finished that they'd spotted the corpse on the balcony and completely lost their heads.

When they realised the man hadn't died of natural causes, they'd panicked about whether they'd scoured the place thoroughly enough. Deciding to go over it again, they had dashed out to the shops to buy some more heavy-duty cleaning products. Tómas admitted that they'd discussed removing the body, but swore they'd immediately abandoned the idea. Instead, they'd rolled up their sleeves but had only just got started again when they heard a commotion outside the flat and froze. They had been discussing in whispers whether they should let themselves down from the balcony on sheets or climb over onto the neighbouring one, when the door suddenly opened.

The veil of secrecy surrounding the ownership of the flat had mostly been lifted, assuming that Tómas was telling the truth. According to him, Helgi owned it through a Luxembourg-based shell company. He had acquired it more than eight years ago when it was repossessed. At first he had rented it out, but when the tenant left, Helgi had used it himself on his short visits to Iceland, before deciding it was too small for his needs and buying another, larger place that was more to his taste. He'd been intending to sell it but this had turned out to be disadvantageous for tax reasons, so in the end he had held on to it. Because he'd never got round to finding a new tenant, the flat had ended up as a party pad for him and his friends. Each of them had a key and could use it as a bolthole to throw parties and mess around without the risk of causing friction with their own neighbours. By the time Helgi moved back to Iceland and bought the luxury apartment he'd been living in at the time of his death, he was so satisfied with the arrangement that he had decided to keep on the weekend flat. As soon as the interview was over, Erla was going to get the man who was trying to unravel Helgi's financial affairs to verify this story. Huldar thought it would probably prove accurate. It was hard to see what Tómas had to gain from making it up. Suspects usually saved their lies for the things that really mattered.

'You've got to let me call my wife.' Tómas put down the tissue on top of a heap of used ones on the table in front of him. 'Please.'

'No.' Erla pushed a keyboard towards him. 'Concentrate on what we're doing. Show us your website.'

Tómas turned pleading red eyes on her. 'Why won't you believe me? You won't learn anything of interest from the website. I don't think it's even legal for you to see it. There's a lot of stuff on there that's not intended for public consumption.'

'We're not the public. We're the police. Type in the address, your username and the password. Now.' Erla folded her arms uncompromisingly across her chest. Huldar suspected she did this to prevent herself from reaching across the table and wringing the man's neck. He was on the verge of doing it himself. They were both dying of curiosity to see the site.

From what they had managed to extract from the snivelling wreck in front of them, the case hinged on an internet forum that the four friends had been maintaining for the last ten years. But Tómas obstinately refused to explain what it contained that was so private. With any luck, they were about to find out. Huldar suspected the content would include Helgi's sex videos. That would explain the man's scarlet cheeks and flustered reaction every time the subject of the forum came up. In the end Erla had paused the interview and dispatched Huldar to fetch a projector and a computer with a Tor browser.

'Get on with it.' Huldar stood up to watch as Tómas reluctantly started to type in the address. He prodded the man when he hesitated, and tried to jot down the address but could barely keep up with Tómas's fingers once they started flying over the keyboard. Afterwards, he showed what he'd written to Tómas, who corrected a few letters. Once this had been done, Tómas sat with his head drooping. Huldar shoved the keyboard back to Erla, then turned to the wall on which the site now flashed up.

Not much effort seemed to have gone into the interface. The colour scheme and font were enough to turn a graphic designer queasy, so the main attraction must be the content.

Huldar moved over to stand beside Erla, who chose a page at random from the bottom of the screen. Up popped several posts dating from a year before, with the friends' reactions underneath. Three were football related, but one came with a video that Erla clicked on. The familiar headboard appeared, this time providing a backdrop for a young woman who was different from the others Huldar had seen. She had close-cropped dark hair and appeared shorter than the blonde stunners in the other videos, her lean body muscled like a CrossFit pro. The man wasn't Helgi either. He was more careless about concealing his identity from the camera and they frequently got a clear view of his face as the action hotted up.

'Who's that?' Huldar asked Tómas, who was keeping his eyes lowered. 'Answer me. Look up and tell us the name of the man on screen.'

Tómas obeyed, his face like a frightened child's, his voice hoarse as he whispered the name. 'Gunni. Gunnar Bergsson. You should recognise him – you've already had him in for questioning.'

Erla shifted her gaze from the wall to Tómas and commented dryly: 'He had all his clothes on then and he wasn't wearing his orgasm face.'

She selected another page, located a video and pressed 'Play'. This time the man involved was Helgi and it turned out to be a film Huldar had already seen. Erla stopped it and went on searching until she found another video featuring Gunnar. Her third attempt resulted in a video of Thormar, the dentist currently sitting in the cells. Leaving the film running, Erla turned down the volume of the groans emanating from the tinny laptop speakers. She fixed her eyes on Tómas again. 'I don't get it. Were you sharing videos of each other having sex?'

Tómas cleared his throat and answered in a strangled voice: 'Something like that.'

'Where can I find a video of you?'

The man looked as if he was going to faint. 'I don't know. I'm not on there . . .'

'Oh come on. Which is it? You're not on there or you don't know which videos you're in?'

'I want a lawyer.'

'Of course, no problem.' Erla smiled maliciously. 'In a bit. First, though, I'm going to browse through a few more videos.' She put her fingers on the keyboard.

Tómas raised his voice. 'I want a lawyer. It's my right. You've got to provide one when I ask. You're not allowed to ask me any more questions until he gets here.'

'Who said anything about questioning you? We're just going to watch some movies.' Erla caught Huldar's eye. 'Have we got any popcorn?'

Huldar grinned and watched as she scrolled through the video clips until finally she found one with Tómas. 'Now what have we got here?' She turned up the volume again, then lifted her hands from the keyboard and reclined comfortably in her chair. 'Is that your wife? No need to answer. We can wait until your lawyer arrives. I expect he'll enjoy the show as much as us.' She met Huldar's eye again. 'What do you reckon? Should we call in the IT department as well? The more people who watch it, the more chance someone will recognise the woman. You know, she reminds me a bit of Jói's sister.' She prodded Huldar under the table.

'Jói who?' Huldar had become quite adept at interpreting her prods.

'You know. Jói who was kicked out of special forces on account of his anger issues.'

Tómas flicked a glance at the wall, the whites of his eyes showing. Huldar guessed there were probably more videos of him on the site, featuring several different women. Presumably he wanted to check which one it was. He buried his face in his hands. 'That's not my wife. The girl's name's on there somewhere.'

'You needn't say anything until you have a lawyer present, remember?'

'I don't care,' Tómas muttered through his fingers. 'I'll speak if I want to. If you turn that off, I'll try to explain. It's not what it looks like.'

Erla paused the film on a frame that showed Tómas lying with his eyes shut and his mouth open wide, while a woman knelt astride him. Judging from his expression, the action was nearing its climax. 'OK. Fill us in on the facts, then.'

Tómas raised his eyes and caught sight of his stark-naked image, blown up on the wall. Letting out an anguished groan, he begged Erla: 'Turn that off first. Please.'

For the first time since he'd been brought in for questioning, Erla granted his wish. He was visibly relieved and sat up in his chair, though his gaze still skittered away from theirs. 'It's a site we set up for organising get-togethers, games of golf, trips to matches – both here at home and abroad.'

'Is that right?' Huldar grinned. 'So the woman in the video is a travel agent, is she? I trust you got a good deal?'

'I'm telling the truth. That's what the site was for. But we used it for other things too. Like that . . .' He pointed at the blank wall as if he could still see the image of himself in flagrante with the woman.

Erla leant forwards over the table in an attempt to capture Tómas's gaze. 'How the hell did that happen? I can understand the bit about the trips, but what sort of kick did you get out of watching each other shagging? I just don't get it.' She leant back again and turned to Huldar. 'What about you? Do you understand? Is it a bloke thing?'

Huldar shook his head. 'It's beyond me.'

Tómas started talking fast, desperate to explain their abnormal behaviour. This was par for the course. Suspects often discovered an urgent need to excuse their actions during interviews. Having convinced themselves that what they had done was understandable, they failed to realise that their rationalisation wouldn't wash with other people.

'It didn't start out like that. At first it was just sharing photos of girls we fancied. Helgi was living abroad and it was a way of keeping up our friendship. That sort of thing – and the other stuff we posted on the site.'

Huldar pulled over the laptop, unplugged the projector and started calling up the oldest posts while Erla continued the questioning. He wanted to check if Tómas was telling the truth.

'Which of you set up the site originally and what was it intended for? You went to a hell of a lot of trouble to conceal it, if the purpose was as innocent as you claim. Why couldn't you use email or Facebook like normal people?'

'Helgi set it up. With the help of an IT guy he knew in the US. He worked for a bank and his emails were monitored.

He thought it was better than setting up a separate account to keep in touch with us. It's more secure too. The site's on the Dark Web so it can't be traced.' Tómas briefly met Erla's eye. 'So we weren't breaking the law. We weren't sharing porn. Quite the opposite – we were taking care that it wouldn't fall into the wrong hands.'

Huldar chuckled inwardly at this lame excuse as he studied the laptop. The oldest posts confirmed Tómas's story, consisting mostly of pictures of fully dressed girls and the friends' comments about them.

'If, as you claim, you were so ultra-careful, perhaps you'd like to explain how one of the videos ended up on a porn-sharing site?' Erla asked, simultaneously glancing at the screen that Huldar had turned towards her to show that Tómas's story was true. 'Were you showing off by sharing the material on other forums? Individually, perhaps, without letting on to the others?'

'No!' Tómas exclaimed vehemently. 'It wasn't like that. None of us would have dreamt of sharing those videos. I mean, we were in the films ourselves. We'd have to be perverts to want to circulate any of them.'

'I don't think there's any doubt you're perverts.' Giving him no time to object, Erla persisted: 'The video posted on the file-sharing site tells a different story. It's there for all to see and it can't have wound up there by itself. Who else had access to the site apart from the four of you?'

Tómas shifted nervously in his chair. 'There are five users. Us four and someone whose identity we don't know.' He shifted again, thrusting his hands under the table, then bringing them back into view a moment later. 'But we do know he's got something to do with what happened to Helgi.'

'With what happened to Helgi?' Erla lunged forward over the table, grabbed the man's chin and roughly forced him to meet her eye. 'Helgi was murdered. He's dead. We're not investigating broken fairy lights on the fucking town hall Christmas tree. It doesn't get any more serious. If you're as innocent as you claim, stop dodging our questions and give us a straight answer. Who's the fifth user you're referring to?'

'I don't know. I swear it. He just appeared on the platform and took control. None of us know how.'

'Stick to answering for yourself. Your friends will get a chance to give us their version later. You can be sure of that.'

Huldar skipped forward a few years on the site to see how things had developed. Again there were pictures of girls, but this time a handful of videos too. He carried on scrolling closer to the present while listening to Erla grilling Tómas, only to stop short when he came across a video posted five years previously. Unlike the others, the information bar showed that it lasted almost two hours. That was far longer than any of the others he'd seen. The first comment was also interesting and atypical. *What do you reckon? Keep or bin? Could prove bloody risky if Miss Pissed-out-of-her-skull remembers anything.* Huldar pressed 'Play' while Erla was tightening the thumbscrews on Tómas to force him to reveal the name of the fifth user.

At first, the events on screen appeared little different from the other videos. A young woman removed her clothes and flopped down on the bed. She attempted to take a selfie but was too drunk to hold her phone steady. In fact, she seemed much drunker than the other girls, though she didn't appear to be under the influence of Rohypnol. At this point a man came into the room. He was holding a wine glass that he handed to the girl and she drank some while he was getting undressed. The man, whom Huldar recognised as Gunni, took back the glass, placed it on the bedside table, then got onto the bed beside her. Huldar fast-forwarded through the subsequent action and was surprised to see the man stand up, hand the glass back to the girl, and leave the room. She emptied it and lay back again, giving the impression, from her movements and expression, that she was by now extremely drunk.

She appeared to fall asleep.

The strange thing was that the video had only been running for twenty minutes. Huldar fast-forwarded again, expecting to see nothing but the woman sleeping it off, and assuming that the explanation for the length was that Gunni had forgotten to switch off the camera. But not a bit of it. The woman carried on sleeping, having presumably passed out cold. But that wasn't all that happened.

Huldar focused on the unfolding events, deaf to what Erla and Tómas were saying. He fast-forwarded again, until he'd come to the end of the film. His heart was pounding in his chest and he had that iron taste in his mouth that went with violent rage. Yet he managed not to betray himself, merely reached for the projector cable and plugged it back in, even taking time to make sure it was screwed in tight. He was hoping this delay would help him get his anger under control. Then he started the playback from the beginning.

When the image flashed up on the wall, Erla jerked her head round so fast that Huldar thought she'd crick her neck. The look she gave him was one of the blackest he had ever encountered, which was unsurprising as he had broken the one condition that Tómas had set for answering their questions without a lawyer present.

But it was worth it.

When Tómas saw the footage, he leapt to his feet and ran for the door, only to find it locked.

'I want a lawyer. I'm not saying another word.' He broke down in tears again, his howls even louder and more pathetic than before.

Chapter 31

After the recording had finished, there was a deathly silence in the small interview room. Watching the video with Huldar and Erla this time were a police lawyer in his early fifties and a representative from the Sexual Offences Unit, the man Huldar had consulted when the videos turned up on Helgi's computer. He seemed the least affected by what he had just witnessed.

All four of them stared at the white projector screen until Erla broke the silence, addressing the lawyer: 'Well, what do you reckon? Does it constitute a clear case of rape?'

'Yes and no. That's the problem.' The lawyer laid down his pen on the blank sheet of paper in front of him. He had been intending to take notes during the video but in the event he hadn't written anything. This was understandable, since the contents could be summed up in a few words. A young woman sits on a bed and tries to take a selfie. A man enters, they undress and have sex, which appears to be consensual on her part. She then passes out and the man's friends take advantage of her unresisting body, one after the other. From time to time she regains consciousness and seems unhappy about what's happening but is held down until she passes out again. After the men have finished, one of them goes in, shakes her awake, and orders her to get dressed and leave. The dazed woman struggles into her clothes and disappears from view, looking dishevelled and moving as if her body hurts. The video ends.

When Erla didn't respond, Huldar couldn't hold back: 'What other evidence do you need to prove that this is rape? A declaration from every man in the video of their intention to rape the woman? Just before they jump on top of her?'

'That would help, of course.' The lawyer did not appear to be joking.

At this point the representative from Sexual Offences intervened. 'We had a case involving a film that showed what we judged to be a gang rape. That case was lost in the District Court and again in the Supreme Court.'

'Yes, despite the fact that the plaintiff was available in that case.' The lawyer grimaced. 'Unfortunately it's not that cut and dried, regardless of how it looks to us. At no point did I hear the woman clearly say *no* or that she didn't want it.'

Erla wasn't about to give up so easily. 'All the woman's attempts to sit up or push them off her were thwarted. It should be blindingly obvious to anyone that her participation wasn't voluntary. That ought to be enough to charge them.'

When the lawyer replied, they could hear the weariness in his voice: 'It's possible. But I wouldn't like to bet on the chances of getting a conviction. The defendants could make any claims they like since they know there's no statement from the alleged victim. They could say the whole thing had been pre-arranged and that she'd agreed to it before they entered the bedroom. I'm afraid it would be difficult to disprove if they claimed that her feeble attempts to sit up had been part of the game: that she'd wanted a turn on top, for example, but they'd preferred to stay on top themselves. Something like that. How are we supposed to disprove that?'

The man sighed heavily. 'But, on the bright side, at least we've got a fairly watertight case against them for sharing the video. It's illegal to distribute or exchange pornographic material, and there's no question that they did that. It's like the other videos on the private site; if any of the women involved press charges we might have a case there too. But the content of this recording means it's our best chance of a successful prosecution. The only hitch is that the man who posted it is dead. If I've understood correctly?'

Erla confirmed this. 'We've only Tómas's word for it that Helgi was responsible, but I assume the others will back him up. The username matches the one on material posted from the US during his time there. So the odds are that it *was* Helgi who uploaded the video.'

'Ahh.' The lawyer sounded disappointed. 'Well, that's that, then. But all's not lost. The law contains a whole section on damage to reputation and offences against an individual's right to privacy. The clauses relating to violation of modesty are often used when bringing a charge of non-consensual porn. Perhaps this could be used against the surviving members of the group. They were all aware that the incident was being filmed and yet none of them posted an objection in the comments section to the fact that the video was shared. So we could argue that they took an active part in violating her modesty. When was the video posted on the site, by the way?'

Erla checked in the notes that had been compiled on the video and on Maren, the young woman who featured in it. 'It was uploaded the day after it was filmed.'

'Oh dear.' The lawyer sighed again. 'The woman was dead by then, wasn't she?' When Erla nodded, he explained: 'To my knowledge there are no precedents involving deceased individuals. Can you commit an offence against the modesty of someone who's dead? I'd have thought so. After all, the right to privacy is extended to the dead, but I would need to re-read the clause pertaining to modesty. Unfortunately, it's possible that the law wasn't designed with that in mind and only applies to the living.'

Erla wasn't about to be drawn into a discussion of legal niceties. 'What kind of sentence is handed out in cases of non-consensual porn?'

'If a prosecutor brings a case based on the clause I mentioned, you can expect short or suspended sentences. The framework for penalties is limited and in this instance all the individuals involved are of good character and have no previous convictions.'

Huldar felt his shoulders sagging. It wasn't going to be easy to get justice for the poor woman in the video, though he didn't suppose it would matter to her now. Her name had turned up in the comments, and although her patronymic had been omitted, they had identified her immediately. Plenty of Icelandic women had been named Maren and, of these, there were around 150 still living, according to the National Register. But only one woman by the name of Maren had been washed ashore close to the foot of the Gallows Rock: Maren Thórdardóttir, the twenty-four-year-old who had drowned after walking into the sea the night the video had been made.

At this point the man from the Sexual Offences Unit spoke up again. Aware from bitter experience how hard it was to get a conviction in cases like this, he wondered aloud about another possible approach. 'What about her death? Is it conceivable that they raped her and bumped her off afterwards? They can't have wanted to run the risk of her going straight to the police? Although they all used condoms, the chances are it would have been possible to obtain significant biological traces. They could have ended up in big trouble. Perhaps they took the precaution of drowning her in the sea. It's not that far down to the shore from the flat on Sudurhlíd. What is it – a hundred metres? Two hundred?'

No one commented on his conjectures; they all knew how short the distance was. But Huldar answered his question anyway. Once the interview with Tómas was over and they'd found out the woman's name, Erla had asked Huldar to call up the files on Maren while she herself was preparing the next steps. Her fury with him for playing the video during the interview had evaporated the instant Maren's name came up.

'I've been reading the reports on Maren's death,' Huldar said. 'They contain no indications of anything suspicious. The post-mortem concluded that there was no evidence to contradict the idea that she entered the sea of her own volition. There was no head injury or signs of strangulation or any other evidence to suggest that her hands had been tied or that she had been held under water. There were signs of rough intercourse, but as the search for her didn't start immediately, her body had been in the sea for three days before it was found. By then it was impossible to tell whether the intercourse had been consensual or not. Or when it had taken place.'

'Didn't they try to find the man who'd had sex with her?' The representative from Sexual Offences was obviously reluctant to let it go.

'No. There was no point. She was receiving treatment for depression. Her coat was found folded up beside her shoes and bag near Fossvogur Cemetery and a verdict of suicide seemed uncontroversial. She'd gone out clubbing with a girl-friend, she'd been drinking heavily and they got separated during the evening. Alcohol and depression are a toxic combination. That explanation was regarded as sufficient. But now we'll have to contact her next of kin again. They may turn out to be sitting on information that didn't emerge in the files. I can't imagine what, though.'

Silence fell again. No one could think of anything to say. If the young woman's parents had any evidence that could prove their daughter had been murdered, they were unlikely to have withheld it at the time.

Huldar made a vain attempt to pursue the murder angle: 'The woman is apparently gang-raped and drowns the same night. Regardless of whether the men actively took part in drowning her, anyone in their right mind can see that it's a case of cause and effect. At the very least, it must have tipped her over the edge, given that she was already in an emotion-ally fragile state. Isn't there any chance they could be charged with manslaughter?'

The lawyer pondered for a moment. 'It's a criminal offence to encourage or cause suicide. But it's never been tested in Iceland and the punishment in circumstances like this would be no more than a year's imprisonment. I doubt we could find a prosecutor to take on the case. It would be almost impossible to prove that the alleged rape had been the decisive factor. It's not as if she left behind a letter stating that that was the final straw.' The lawyer picked up his pen and started to gather his things together. 'Anyway. Keep me posted, Erla.

If none of these suggestions work, there are plenty of other women out there who might be prepared to press charges. Are there plans to go through the videos on the site and trace the women in them?'

Huldar kept his head down at this point. Erla had completely swallowed his lie about how he knew Ugla. But once the murder inquiry was over and attention was focused on the friends' internet forum, she was bound to find out the truth: that they hadn't merely swapped phone numbers in a bar.

'I've got two men who can take care of it alongside their other jobs.' The officer from the Sexual Offences Unit got to his feet. 'It would make sense to start with the video that turned up on the file-sharing site. That's probably the most serious example of distributing pornography.' He looked at Huldar and Erla. 'Was Tómas able to tell you who posted it?"

Erla shook her head. 'He claimed not to know. He blames the fifth user but swears he has no idea who it is. IT are looking into it but they say it's pretty much a lost cause because the site's on the Dark Web. Though they did spot one detail straight away: the new user only popped up *after* the video was posted on the file-sharing platform. So he or she can't have had any connection to that. Which means it must have been one of the four men who shared it.'

'Then all we have to do is find out which one. He'll be charged, at least, even if it's only a token gesture in the circumstances.' The lawyer paused by the door. 'But to be honest with you, I doubt you'll be granted custody for those two on the basis of the video alone. Though there's nothing to stop you trying.' He flicked a glance at the clock. 'The twenty-four hours you're allowed to hold them for is nearly up. But you can get an extension for another twenty-four if you bring them before a judge and demand they be kept in custody – assuming the judge requires that amount of time to come to a decision. Let me know as soon as possible. It'll take me an hour to put a case together.'

Erla nodded dully. She knew the clock was ticking. Everyone working on the case was aware of that.

'But let me give you one piece of advice.' The lawyer's face remained grave. 'Find the woman. That should be your absolute priority.'

'The woman?' The man from Sexual Offences was confused, his thoughts clearly still on the video and the website. 'Which woman?'

'Sigurlaug. The wife of the latest victim, Margeir.' Erla got to her feet as well. 'She's top of our list. It's just that the search has drawn a blank. The rescue teams have been combing the entire Greater Reykjavík area without any results and the search from the air hasn't achieved anything either. It's not exactly encouraging that her husband has turned up dead. I need to make a decision about the next step.'

No one envied Erla. It was extremely unlikely that the woman was still alive after this length of time and a corpse would be much harder to find than a living person. Although no one said as much out loud, they were all afraid that Sigurlaug was dead. Anything else was almost impossible at this stage.

Thormar was a very different proposition from his friend Tómas. He sat bolt upright, his face set in uncompromising lines, clearly determined to tough out his sojourn at the police station. Huldar welcomed the change. At least Thormar was unlikely to beg for tissues like that wimp of an economist, though of course the downside was that he was proving much harder to crack.

'Think about it for a moment.' Huldar pushed his nicotine gum into his cheek with his tongue. It was hours since he'd last been able to step out for a smoke. 'You and your friends gang-rape a woman who's found shortly afterwards washed up on the shore by the Gallows Rock. Five years later, Helgi's found hanging in the same spot. Does that sound like a coincidence to you?'

Thormar shrugged. 'That's for you to work out. I'm not a policeman. I'll say it again: it wasn't rape. I didn't kill that man Margeir. I didn't kill Helgi. And I don't distribute porn.'

'So you claim.' Huldar glanced at Erla, who seemed content to let him take care of the questioning at this stage. 'They're doing a fingerprint check on the video camera you chucked in the bin bag. I wouldn't be surprised if all of you had handled it.'

'We'll just have to wait and see. But I don't know what difference that's supposed to make. Surely you're not saying the man on the balcony was killed with a camera? And Helgi certainly wasn't. Isn't that what this is all about? Murder?'

Huldar had no intention of letting the man take over the interview. He carried on talking as if he hadn't heard Thormar's comment. 'The camera will be handed over to our IT department, who say it should be easy to establish whether it was used to make the recent recordings on your site. We've found where it was set up and connected to a switch on the wall. As the camera was well hidden inside a speaker and trained on the bed, it's blindingly obvious that the purpose was to film without the knowledge of the women involved.

You can deny it until you're blue in the face but you're wasting your time because we've got incriminating videos of you with several women, taken using the same camera.'

'Bullshit.' Thormar ground his teeth in a manner hardly appropriate for a dentist, though the circumstances were of course exceptional. 'When can I leave?'

'When we decide to release you. You're under arrest, remember?' Huldar wondered yet again why Thormar hadn't requested a lawyer. Unless it had something to do with the fact that his wife was a solicitor. If he asked for anyone else to represent him, she would smell a rat. 'Now that your friend Tómas has shown us how to access the website, you'd be better off telling us the whole story. We can see all the content, and the next task on our agenda is to call in the other member of your charming little gang. The last person to come clean will be left holding the baby. I don't believe you want to be that person.'

'I don't know anything about the murders. Or about a rape, because it wasn't rape. This is a waste of time.'

'You said it.' Huldar stared at the uncooperative man, his face expressionless. Then said: 'Let's turn to a couple of questions you should be able to help us with – minor details that shouldn't concern you.' When Thormar didn't react, Huldar went ahead and asked anyway: 'One is about the fifth user. I can't see what possible reason you'd have for protecting him. The question is this: who posted the video of Helgi and Sigurlaug Lára on the file-sharing site? I recommend that you give us a straight answer. If you choose to remain silent, I'll interpret it as meaning that you're protecting yourself.'

'I don't know who the new user is. I didn't share the video

myself and I can't tell you who was responsible – for the simple reason that I have no idea.'

There was a light tap on the door. Erla glanced at Huldar, her eyebrows raised, then got up, opened the door and went outside, closing it behind her. Huldar caught a glimpse of Gudlaugur in the gap. He had been tasked with going through all the content on the platform, so he must have come across something significant or he would never have interrupted.

Huldar turned back to Thormar. The interruption had momentarily broken his concentration, and he hoped it didn't show. Groping around for some line to take, he decided to return to the subject of Thormar's presence in the flat. It would give him breathing space to contemplate his next move while the dentist was repeating his earlier excuse. 'What were you doing in the flat if you weren't destroying the evidence of your presence there? Let me remind you yet again that your friend has already told us the whole story.' Huldar omitted to add that the moment Tómas's lawyer arrived, he had dried up, like a tap being switched off. He hadn't answered a single question after the video of the gang rape had been played back to him, so it was a bit of an exaggeration to claim that he had told them the whole story.

'Like I said before, we were cleaning. Gunni borrowed the flat for a party the weekend before Helgi died and left it in a disgusting state. We didn't want Helgi's parents to find it like that.'

'Did they know about the flat?'

'No, as I've already told you, they weren't aware of it. But they're bound to learn about it when his will is read. That's why we were tidying up. Of course, I can't speak for Tómas but that was why I was there.'

'So you were cleaning the place purely out of the goodness of your heart when you happened to spot the body on the balcony. But instead of ringing the police, you and Tómas rush out to the shops to buy more household cleaner and then go over the whole flat again. Bit of a strange reaction, don't you think?'

'Tómas is getting muddled. We'd only just found the corpse when you burst in. Our trip to buy more cleaning products had nothing to do with that. We'd just run out in the middle of the job.'

Thormar was no fool. His story sounded plausible. But Tómas's account was more believable and would hold more sway with a judge if the case ever made it to court.

Erla came back in, radiating satisfaction. Huldar watched as she sat down and pulled over the keyboard with an air of schadenfreude. He thought he saw a hairline crack appear in Thormar's smooth façade as he also picked up on this.

The projector whirred into life again. They had switched it off after showing Thormar the forum at the beginning of the interview to shake his composure. The shock hadn't worked for long, however.

The website's primitive interface reappeared on the wall. Erla's fingers rattled the keyboard and a video Huldar hadn't seen before started playing. Unlike the others he'd watched, it showed a different bed in a different room. The man wasn't visible either. It looked more like one of the videos on the file-sharing site where it was obvious that the man was filming the action with his phone. Huldar stole a glance at Thormar and saw that he was licking his lips nervously.

'Who's the woman, Thormar?' Erla paused the recording on a frame in which the woman's face was revealed.

'I don't recognise her.' For the first time since the interview began, they could detect a faint tremor in his voice.

'Really?' Erla pressed 'Play' again. After a brief interval, the couple changed position and the phone was briefly directed at the man. It was unmistakeably Thormar. 'Who's the woman? You should be able to remember. The recording's only two years old.' Erla turned from him to look up at the wall. The image shook as if during an earthquake as the man pounded away on top of the woman. As the rhythm slowed, Erla paused the recording on another frame showing the woman's face. 'Are you sure you don't recognise her?' Thormar merely shook his head. His face was grey, a fact that seemed to tickle Erla. 'That's strange. The officer who found this checked your Facebook page and reckons she looks uncannily like your wife. He actually thought it was her. Is that possible?'

'No.' Thormar's eyes dropped to his clenched fists, which he quickly slid under the table.

'I see. Well, not to worry. I'm going to call her in and ask her to identify the woman. Just to be on the safe side.' She stared at the man without an ounce of sympathy: he didn't deserve any. 'She may be surprised to discover that you've posted the video on your friends' internet forum. It looks to me as if she knows she's being filmed, but somehow I doubt she intended anyone else to see it. Still, never mind.'

It worked. Thormar finally agreed to talk in return for their promise to leave his wife out of it. Unfortunately, however, it soon became apparent that he didn't know anything that could help solve the murders or trace Sigurlaug. His old quarrel with Helgi turned out to have resulted from a disagreement about what to do with the video of Maren. Thormar had wanted to delete it; Helgi to keep it on the website.

Thormar didn't seem to derive any satisfaction from having been right, though he and his friends would have been in a much better situation now if he had won that particular argument.

Thormar revealed that the anonymous *administrator* had shared a video of Helgi's hanging and another of him lying unconscious in a car. When the police searched for these, however, they couldn't be found. If the videos had ever existed, then logically the user must be Helgi's killer or at least connected to him. But they couldn't rely on Thormar telling the truth. Erla had rung down to IT from the interview room and, according to them, no one could access the site uninvited, let alone strip the others of their admin privileges. Whoever it was must have accessed the site with the help of one of the four friends.

The only significant piece of information they managed to prise out of Thormar was how the video of Sigurlaug might have ended up on the porn-sharing site, with serious repercussions for her. How serious remained to be seen.

Erla had Thormar taken back to his cell.

The two of them sat there for a while without speaking. Huldar guessed that Erla hadn't immediately charged off because she wanted to postpone having to decide about whether to apply for a custody order. If the judge refused her request, it would look bad for her at the office. On the other hand, if she didn't apply for it and the men turned out to be guilty of murder, she would look bad in the eyes of the public.

Lína put her head round the door. She was wearing her red hair loose today and it stood out around her head in a haze of static electricity. For once, Erla was polite to her, which Huldar took as a sign of her distraction.

'I've spoken to Maren Thórdardóttir's mother,' Lína announced. 'She says her daughter had tried to kill herself before and that no one in the family had thought there was anything suspicious about her death. She didn't try to find out whom Maren had spent the night with before she drowned herself, because it would only have made her grief more unbearable. She couldn't see what it would achieve. She and her husband were living in Norway at the time but came home as soon as they heard the news. They also have two sons, one older than Maren, one younger. The boys took her death very hard, especially the older brother who was living in Iceland when it happened. The younger boy had moved to Norway with his parents.' Lína looked at Erla for approval. 'I didn't tell her about Helgi and his friends, as you instructed. I just said I was looking into old cases linked to the Gallows Rock in order to eliminate them from our inquiry.'

'Should we talk to her brothers?' Huldar asked Erla, but before she could answer, Lína pre-empted her:

'One's abroad studying – the younger brother. The other's on a trawler and has been away at sea for three weeks. So they're unlikely to have anything to do with the murders.'

'Did the mother know Margeir or Sigurlaug?' For once, Erla didn't react to Lína's interruption with irritation but sounded as if she genuinely wanted to know.

'No. I asked her that and she said she didn't.'

'What about the father, Thórdur? Did he recognise the names?' Huldar asked, though he thought he already knew the answer to this. If he had, Lína would have told them so immediately.

'I haven't been able to get hold of him. They're divorced and Maren's mother said they aren't in touch any more. He's registered as based in Akranes but she said she's heard he's actually living in town. He's only got a mobile number registered in his name but isn't picking up his calls. Shall I carry on trying to get hold of him?'

'No. You take over, Huldar. It's better if a man talks to him.'

Huldar noticed that Lína seemed hurt by this. 'What's Thórdur's number, Lína?' Of course, she knew it by heart and reeled it off for him. Huldar keyed it into his phone. As he entered the last digit, his phone informed him that the number was already assigned to a contact. Under the name of Doddi.

The phone number belonged to the caretaker in Helgi's building.

Chapter 32

Although the police had made careful preparations for the arrest of Maren's father Thórdur, aka Doddi, they had overlooked one thing: the timing. They turned up at 5 p.m., just as the residents of the building were coming home from work, with the result that there was a steady stream of cars into the basement garage and of people wandering into the lobby to fetch their post. The lift was constantly on its way up or down. None of this was ideal for the arrest of a potentially violent suspect. If, as they feared, he had already committed two, possibly three, murders, the risk was that he wouldn't hesitate to kill again.

The sun was setting in a cloudless sky and the tower block cast a cold shadow over the car park, making Huldar shiver. With no breeze to blow the fumes away, the air was tainted with pollution from the commuter traffic on Sæbraut. He was almost looking forward to entering the building.

The plan was that Huldar and Gudlaugur should go in and speak to the man, since they had handled all previous communication with him. Erla was hoping they would be able to get him to admit enough to justify an arrest. The moment this happened, they were to cuff him. Not a minute before. The fact that he was Maren's father didn't constitute sufficient grounds for arrest, not even when combined with the fact that he worked as the caretaker in Helgi's building. The top brass would come down like a ton of bricks on Erla if it emerged that this was just one of those Icelandic coincidences; the inevitable consequence of living in a small society, and that the police had, for no good reason, arrested the grieving father of a girl who'd taken her own life.

Huldar and Gudlaugur had been ordered to don bulletproof vests over their uniforms and conceal them with oversized jumpers. As a result, their bulky top halves and spindly legs made them look like body-builders who'd neglected to work on their thighs and calves.

Their uniforms were intended to unnerve Thórdur by bringing home the gravity of the situation. But no one explained why the vests were necessary, and Huldar suspected that they were mainly for reassurance rather than protection. The caretaker had never applied for or been granted a firearms licence, making it unlikely that he would pull a gun on them. Huldar couldn't help wondering how much protection the body armour would provide against other weapons, especially since these vests didn't last forever and the ones the department owned were looking a bit battered. After all, this guy had proved resourceful – he'd already used a nail gun against somebody. But he avoided sharing these concerns with Gudlaugur as the young man was stressed enough. It was the first high-risk arrest he had been involved in, apart from handcuffing drunk and disorderlies on weekend shifts when he was in the regular police. Although that kind of arrest could be hazardous, it was usually carried out on the spot, not preceded by a nerve-racking wait.

'You OK?' Huldar laid a hand on Gudlaugur's shoulder and studied his face. His objective assessment was that the younger man would get through it all right. His main fear was that Gudlaugur would let the cat out of the bag prematurely, before they'd finished interviewing Thórdur. They were hoping they'd be able to arrest him without the use of force, and that all their precautions would prove unnecessary.

'I'm good.' Gudlaugur squared his shoulders. 'Is it time?'

Huldar nodded. He was wearing an earpiece and had just heard Erla give the order to go in. Gudlaugur was wearing one too, but the plan was that she would only communicate directly with him if Huldar was unable to respond for some reason. He sincerely hoped it wouldn't come to that. They were both miked up as well, so that those in charge of the operation could listen in. If Erla deemed it necessary, she would give the word to the back-up team waiting in the wings. Everyone was hoping this wouldn't be needed. There was always a chance that Thórdur would prove as cooperative as he had hitherto, but they weren't betting on it. People were highly unpredictable when cornered.

'We're going in,' Huldar said aloud for Erla's benefit. The vehicles where she and the back-up team were waiting had been parked out of sight in case the suspect happened to pass through the lobby.

'Are you sure we'll be able to hear each other down in the basement?' Gudlaugur had meant this for Huldar's ears only but Erla answered immediately, saying that it should work. Huldar thought he heard a hint of doubt in her voice. But perhaps that was just the poor sound quality.

Huldar rang the bell marked *Caretaker*. While they were waiting, he wondered if he would have cottoned on sooner if it had said *Thórdur* instead, but to be honest he doubted it. So many names had cropped up in the course of the inquiry.

The first time Lína had mentioned Maren Thórdardóttir, he hadn't really taken in her patronymic.

Gudlaugur shifted from foot to foot beside Huldar, then raised his hand as if to ring the bell again but Huldar put out an arm to stop him. They'd only rung it once on their last visit and they didn't want to give the impression of being on edge. After a few moments, the caretaker's voice was heard over the intercom. He asked who it was and Huldar told him. This was followed by a silence that didn't bode well, but then the lock buzzed and they opened the door.

Huldar headed straight for the caretaker's flat, with Gudlaugur close on his heels, but before they could reach it, the lift doors opened behind them and the caretaker called out to attract their attention. Huldar and Gudlaugur turned, trying to act normally. They exchanged brief greetings and shook the man's hand – a hand that had in all likelihood fired a nail into a man's chest before cold-bloodedly pushing him to his death.

'I was down in my office,' the caretaker explained. 'What can I do for you? Is there any news?'

'Yes, there is actually, but obviously we can't talk about it.'

Thórdur nodded. At that moment a man came barging in from the entrance hall, carrying two shopping bags and a briefcase. Registering Huldar and Gudlaugur's presence with surprise, he asked the caretaker if there had been a break-in. When Thórdur assured him there hadn't, the man's curiosity was roused and he demanded to know what was going on. Huldar informed him it was connected to an inquiry that he needn't worry about, after which the man disappeared into the lift. When another resident breezed in immediately afterwards, it was difficult to decline the caretaker's invitation to continue their conversation in his office in the basement. As Huldar accepted, he heard Erla groan in his ear.

They descended the stairs without speaking.

The instant they entered the office, Huldar realised it was a bad move. The space was far too cramped for them to react effectively if the caretaker tried anything. It wasn't his own or Gudlaugur's safety he was concerned about; it was Thórdur's. If they were forced to restrain him, the man was bound to collide with the furniture. This was an unwelcome prospect, not because he gave a damn if Thórdur got hurt but because of the inevitable inquiry it would trigger. The incident would have to be investigated, involving endless meetings, reports and sessions in which he and Gudlaugur would be interrogated about their actions. And to make matters worse, they were on their own: Huldar hadn't been able to hear Erla breathing in his ear since they reached the bottom of the stairs, so it was unlikely that a recording would be available to support their statements.

'I'm afraid I don't have any coffee. Would you like me to go and fetch some?' The caretaker leant on the back of his office chair. Now he came to think of it, Huldar reckoned Thórdur was about the height of the man who had been with Siggi in the CCTV recording. His build and movements were similar too, and Huldar could have sworn his eyes were the same. But he dismissed the thought; there would be plenty of time to review the footage later.

'No, thanks.' Sensing that the muscles of his face were clenched unnaturally tight with anger, Huldar took out a piece of nicotine gum and stuck it in his mouth. It was difficult to wear any particular expression when you were chewing.

'You didn't come down to the station yesterday. I asked you to drop by so we could take your statement, remember?'

'Oh, yes. I'm sorry.' The man seemed relieved that this was the reason for their visit. 'I've been so busy that I haven't had a minute. It didn't occur to me that it was that urgent. I'll definitely drop by tomorrow, though. Or did you want me to come this evening?'

Huldar would have liked a moment's breathing space to consider this offer. Would it be better to get Thórdur down to the station, then put pressure on him once he was confined in the interview room? The decision was entirely up to him since no help could be expected from his earpiece. He chewed his gum, thinking furiously, before finally having to give an answer: 'We need to confirm your statement as soon as possible. But our urgent priority right now is to track down the pregnant woman.'

'I understand. Unfortunately I can't help you with that.' The caretaker's eyes slid away from Huldar's. 'Are you any closer to finding her?'

'Yes.' Huldar launched into the story he had rehearsed with Erla. 'It may come as a surprise to you to hear this, but it appears Helgi wasn't the nice guy you took him for.'

'Oh?' Unlike Huldar, the caretaker had had no opportunity to rehearse, so his attempt at surprise rang hollow. 'In what way?'

'Don't spread it about, but it appears he was in the habit of videoing himself having sex – without the knowledge of the women involved. That's why we're here. We need to enter his flat to make sure Forensics didn't miss any hidden cameras in his bedroom.'

The caretaker slapped his thigh in a pretence of astonishment so hammy that if it had been up to Huldar – and if the actions of the police weren't so closely scrutinised – he would have arrested the man on the spot. But bad acting wouldn't count as sufficiently compelling evidence of guilt. 'You're joking!' Thórdur said. 'Of course I'll let you in. Do you want to go up there now?'

'In a minute. Tell me first, have you been aware of young women visiting Helgi's flat? We thought you might have forgotten to mention the fact.'

'No, absolutely not. I'd have told you if I had.'

'Quite sure? They were all blonde. Slim, long hair, all real stunners.'

'No – like I said, I'd have told you.'

Huldar nodded, still chomping away on his gum. 'He treated those women appallingly. The way he abused their trust was despicable.' When the man didn't react, Huldar added: 'Have you got a daughter yourself?'

The caretaker drew a sharp breath. 'No.'

'Never had one?' There was silence in the enclosed space. Huldar decided to crank up the pressure, deviating from the script he had been given. Sometimes you had to play it by ear and, besides, it was unlikely Erla could hear him. 'I don't have any kids myself but I can imagine what a terrible shock it would be if someone mistreated my daughter. Especially if it was the kind of man who thinks he only has to snap his fingers to get everything he wants. We're inclining to the view that Helgi's murder is linked to this little quirk of his. That he was made to pay for what he'd done to one of those young women. I can't say that I regard it as a justification for killing him, but, like I said, I'm not a father, so I can't put myself in a parent's shoes. I do have five sisters, though, and I wouldn't react too well if I heard that their trust had been violated like that.' Huldar paused, at a loss how to continue, but eventually decided to chance it: 'Does the name Maren mean anything to you?'

The man was silent, his eyes lowered. Then he said, without looking up: '*The hole*. That was what they called Maren. To Helgi and his mates she was nothing but a hole for them to poke.'

Huldar felt the adrenalin begin to surge through his veins. But he was disconcerted; he hadn't been expecting this reaction. It was unusual for suspects to confess so willingly. Instinct warned him that something was wrong and his hands moved to his belt, unobtrusively closing on his truncheon and canister of pepper spray. But Thórdur showed no signs of trying anything on. Instead, he started speaking again, his voice level:

'I was hoping I'd get one more day. To tie up a few loose ends. But it sounds as if there's no chance of that.' He raised his head. 'I've got something to show you.'

Their orders had been to keep the man sweet at all costs, so they agreed to go with him and he led them to the back of the underground garage, well away from all the parked cars. There he stopped in front of a door next to the one marked *Rubbish Store*. A nauseating stench reached their noses while Thórdur was fumbling for the right key on his bunch. Huldar, who had become a bit of a connoisseur after sifting through all that trash with Lína, registered that the smell seeping out from under the door was different in quality.

When the caretaker finally opened the door, Huldar's instinct proved right. The stench from what turned out to be the boiler room was not caused by rotting food or other rubbish.

Erla would have done better to forget the back-up team and request an ambulance instead.

To Huldar's intense frustration there was no gum left in the packet he was fiddling with under the table. The fact shouldn't have come as a surprise to him as he'd had few opportunities to grab a smoke that day. He tried to calm his agitated nerves by promising himself that he would smoke three cigarettes in a row as soon as the interview with Thórdur was over. It wouldn't be long now.

He shouldn't even be here. Erla had been intending to conduct the interview with another officer, believing correctly that Huldar was too tired and strung out after the events of the day. But he had been fed up when she picked Jóel instead of him, feeling that however tired he was, he was still a far better detective than that idiot. In the event, though, their relative merits weren't put to the test because Thórdur refused to say a word unless Huldar was present. Jóel had been forced to leave the interview room with his tail between his legs. As they passed each other in the doorway, Huldar was filled with schadenfreude, which lent him a temporary burst of energy. Jóel rammed him in the ribs with his elbow as he passed, hissing, 'Just you wait.' Usually his threats were empty but this time Huldar had the uneasy feeling that there was some-thing more behind it. Perhaps that was just the effects of exhaustion and nicotine deprivation.

Thórdur's lawyer looked at his watch. 'Are we done here? My client has answered all your questions clearly and without prevarication, and I can't see what purpose sitting here any longer will serve. Do you actually need to ask him anything else?'

Erla, acting as if she hadn't heard, asked Thórdur to run through the sequence of events again in chronological order.

Thórdur coughed and sighed heavily. At first he had seemed glad of the chance to unburden himself, but the endless repetitions had robbed his voice and manner of any last vestige of relief. 'Five years ago my daughter was found dead,' he began again tonelessly. 'They thought it was suicide. She'd been suffering from depression since her teens and had made one previous, rather half-hearted attempt to take her own life. She'd been doing better, though. The last time we saw her she was looking really well and seemed to have got a grip on her life, so what happened came as a complete shock. But we just had to accept that we must have misinterpreted the signs. We were living in Norway then, so we thought maybe she'd managed to trick us, pretending to be in a better state than she really was. Anyway, we flew straight home and tried to cope with our grief as best we could. Shortly after the funeral, I came to the police station to fetch her things, because she'd left her bag, coat and shoes behind on the shore where they reckoned she'd walked into the sea. I went through her phone searching for any clues about what had happened that night but couldn't find anything. Nothing except a picture she'd taken after becoming separated from her friend. All it showed was the headboard of a very ordinary-looking bed. Nothing else.'

Huldar recalled the video and Maren's drunken attempt to take a selfie. Having seen how out of it she was, he wasn't surprised to hear that she'd missed herself completely and only managed to snap the headboard.

Her father continued: 'Since the post-mortem revealed that she'd had sex the night she died, I assumed the bed had something to do with that. But no one came forward to admit that they'd been with her that night. It wasn't exactly surprising, but I was a bit disappointed that the police weren't prepared to check the CCTV footage to identify the man Maren went home with.'

Neither Erla nor Huldar said anything, though Thórdur paused here to give them a chance to respond. Perhaps he wanted an apology, or an explanation. In the end he looked down again and continued his story, his eyes on his hands.

'I was haunted by the picture of that bed. For years. All through the dark times my wife and I went through after Maren's death and during our divorce. We didn't go back to Norway and neither of us was capable of working for some time afterwards. We started fighting a lot too. But whatever happened, I couldn't get the image of that head-board out of my mind. As time went by, I began to forget about it and would probably have stopped thinking about it altogether if fate hadn't thrown it my way just over a year ago.'

Thórdur broke off for a sip of water. It must have been lukewarm by now but he gave no sign of minding.

'I was called up to a flat on the top floor of the building because some nutter was trying to break down the door of a resident who'd recently moved in – Helgi, in other words. I managed to get the man into the lift and take him down to the lobby, although he was beside himself with rage. He kept ranting about his wife and the bastard she'd cheated on him with. I tried to calm him down and finally got it out of him that he believed Helgi was the man. The bastard hadn't just slept with his wife, he'd actually put up a video of it online. The man showed me a printout of a still from a video showing a couple having sex. He claimed the woman with Helgi was his wife. I couldn't stop staring at the picture – not at the naked couple but at the headboard. I was convinced it was the same bed and the same room as in the photo on Maren's phone.'

Huldar glanced sideways at Erla but she was silent and plainly had no intention of explaining to Thórdur how the video had ended up on a file-sharing site. She was in no hurry to correct his misapprehension that Helgi had been respon- sible. He would find out in due course that it hadn't been him. Ironically, the entire disastrous chain of events that had claimed the lives of Helgi and Margeir had been sparked by Thormar's then thirteen-year-old stepson Fannar. Though, of course, you could argue that it was ultimately Thormar's fault for his carelessness in leaving the forum open on his computer where the teenager could find it. You could just imagine the boy's glee, especially when he came across a video featuring his new teacher, Sigurlaug Lára.

Instead of being satisfied with watching it, the kid had copied the video and posted it to a file-sharing site, presum- ably so his classmates could enjoy his incredible find too. His motivation would become clearer once they had spoken to him, though this wouldn't be happening any time soon: the police had more than enough on their plates right now. As the boy was still a minor, he would presumably get off lightly, apart from having to admit to what he'd done in front of his mother. It was possible that children's services would be alerted, and that he would be sent for therapy for juveniles with impulse-control disorders. Huldar certainly hoped so.

The boy's action had had such devastating consequences that he couldn't be allowed to get away with it.

'Go on,' Erla prompted Thórdur, whose mind, like Huldar's, had momentarily wandered. The room was so stuffy and the atmosphere so subdued that it was hard to stay focused.

Thórdur picked up where he'd left off. He had invited Margeir into his flat in the hope of learning more about the bed in the video and there he had heard the tale that Margeir had, in his own words, 'beaten out of his slut of a wife', after she had tried to wriggle out of explaining why she'd given up work. He had forced her to show him the video that had made it impossible for her to continue as a teacher. It had appeared on the site fairly recently. Thórdur had managed to calm Margeir down enough to get him to show him the website in question, though first he'd had to listen to an incoherent rant about how Helgi probably ran it himself. Thórdur hadn't believed this, since most of the posts were transparently from much younger men or boys.

After this, Thórdur had sent Margeir home. But his curiosity had been roused and after lying awake for much of the night, he had decided to enter Helgi's flat using his master key to see if he could find any evidence linking his daughter to the new tenant. And he was lucky. It turned out that Thormar wasn't the only one who was careless about security. Helgi had left his desktop computer on and unlocked, with the forum open. Acting fast, Thórdur had created a special access for himself, then made a quick exit. From then on he had been able to see the posts on the forum whenever he wanted. Helgi's fate was sealed when Thórdur finally came across the video showing the gang rape of his daughter. After that, he became obsessed with thoughts of revenge.

Thórdur was growing hoarse. He paused to drink the last few drops of water in his glass, swallowed, then resumed, looking increasingly haggard: 'It took me several months to come up with a plan. But once it was fully formed, I realised I couldn't do it alone. I found Margeir's number and invited him to meet me for coffee, since he'd seemed crazy enough to be willing to help. I didn't know how to introduce the subject at first but when I did, he jumped at the idea.'

The lawyer coughed, leant over to his client and whispered in his ear. But Thórdur merely pulled a face and went on with his story: 'Two weeks ago we got together to take the plank out to the Gallows Rock, with the noose tied around it ready to go. Not many people visit in winter, so I didn't think anyone would notice it and wonder what it was doing there. And I was right. We had to leave it a while before putting the rest of the plan into action, in case we'd been spotted. Then all we had to do was wait. Margeir said he knew of a car we could use that couldn't be traced to him, and said he could supply the Rohypnol too. Everything was in place. Helgi came home from abroad and when I overheard him in the corridor talking on the phone and making plans to go out on Saturday night, I reckoned the moment had come. Margeir delivered the drug and the car, a beaten-up Land Cruiser, to me in the morning and I trailed Helgi into town that evening. I waited near the restaurant, then followed him up to 101 Bar. After about an hour I sent him a suggestive message from a withheld number, pretending to be a woman and asking him to meet me at Kex. He left the pub soon afterwards and I parked on Vitastígur, where I could watch the entrance to Kex. Then I waited. Eventually he turned up and I got out, said hello and offered him a beer that I'd spiked with Rohypnol. But I couldn't persuade him to get in the car with me, so I had to let him go. The moment he left, I sent him another text, supposedly from the same woman, saying I'd got bored of waiting and moved on. When I drove up to him outside Kex he was reading the message, and after that he accepted a lift.'

Thórdur kept talking, although his voice was so husky by now that it sounded as if his vocal cords would give out any minute. Huldar forced himself to listen, fighting off an over-powering drowsiness that made him long to close his eyes, switch off and go to sleep. In spite of his best efforts, he nearly did nod off as Thórdur repeated yet again, almost word for word, his description of the drive out to Álftanes and the walk through the lava-field. It was easier to stay awake during the account of how Margeir had come to die.

'We'd agreed to meet at Sudurhlíd after I'd . . . you know . . .'

Neither Erla, Huldar nor the lawyer made it any easier for the man by acknowledging that they knew what he was refer-ring to. After a moment, Thórdur continued: 'I'd taken a bunch of keys out of Helgi's pocket and the ones to the flat turned out to be on it. Margeir was desperate to get a look at the place. But when we met there, what do I find but the idiot has brought along his wife and kid. The guy was completely off his trolley. The woman was sitting in the front seat and the little boy was asleep in the back. Of course, I got a terrible shock when I saw them because that wasn't what we'd agreed to at all. For one thing, his wife had nothing to lose by going to the police, whereas he and I were both equally guilty, so neither of us was likely to talk. If you ask me, Margeir had a screw loose. We had a row in the car park but it was no good, the damage was done. He said he'd brought her along to teach her a lesson, and he'd been forced to bring his son too because he couldn't leave him alone at home. The boy had been asleep and hardly stirred when he was moved, so there was nothing to worry about. He said he'd make sure his wife didn't say a word either. From what I could understand, he was planning to drag her upstairs and rape her in the bed where she'd cheated on him. I was sickened by the idea and things only got worse when the woman got out of the car and I saw that she was heavily pregnant. Margeir chased her back in again, telling her not to interrupt when two men were talking.'

Thórdur's shoulders, which had been sagging ever lower during his account, now straightened up again and his voice gained strength, as if he were describing an act of heroism: 'I was there to avenge the rape that had led my daughter to her death. No way was I going to stand back and do nothing while another equally innocent woman suffered the same fate. So I did the only honourable thing in the circumstances. I tricked Margeir into going upstairs with me and I killed him. Hit him on the back of the head with a heavy toolbox that happened to be lying on the floor.'

'What happened to it?' Erla got in before Huldar, who had been wondering the same thing. Forensics hadn't found any toolbox in the flat. In fact, Huldar was rather surprised that Helgi should have owned such a thing since he'd automatically pigeonholed him, together with his friends, as the kind of man who didn't own so much as a drill.

'I put it in the car and later I threw it in the sea, off Sæbraut, near the *Sólfar* sculpture.' Seeming irritated by this interruption, Thórdur quickly resumed his story, as if to prevent Erla and Huldar from throwing him off his stride with any more questions: 'Anyway, before I killed Margeir, I got a kick out of telling him that I'd deviated from our plan. Instead of putting the suicide note I'd made Helgi sign in his pocket, I'd stapled it to his chest with a nail gun. Margeir totally lost it at that point, which meant he was off his guard. The fact he couldn't control his temper was what brought him down in the end. There's a kind of poetic justice to that, don't you think?'

When none of them reacted, Thórdur shrugged. 'What did you think of his suicide note, by the way? I don't suppose you were taken in by the idea that a suicidal man would nail a note to his own chest?'

'The letter blew away so we never saw it.' Erla didn't ask what it had contained – it didn't matter. 'Do you really expect us to believe that you'd made up your mind in advance to nail the suicide note to his chest? That you didn't lose control once you'd got the man you hated in your power? It must have been hard having to act as if you liked him for all those months. Having to fix a sycophantic smile on your face whenever he asked you to help him. Accepting the tips and pretending to be oh-so-grateful.'

'I didn't lose control. I knew precisely what I was doing.'

Thórdur's lawyer groaned in despair at this declaration.

Ignoring him, Thórdur persisted: 'Unlike Margeir, I never expected to get away with it. He insisted on the suicide note, but I didn't care if it was obvious that it was murder. I did it deliberately. I wanted to shake up Helgi's mates, those fucking creeps who took part in humiliating my daughter. The only reason I didn't give myself up immediately was because I was toying with the idea of bumping them off as well. I prised their names out of Helgi once the drug had taken effect. But that plan came to nothing when Margeir turned up with his wife. That's partly why I was so shocked to see her there. And why I took her with me when I left Sudurhlíd. If I'd let her go, it would have put paid to my dream of getting revenge on the others. In the end all I managed to do was frighten the sick bastards. Still, it can wait. How long will I have to be in jail?'

The lawyer banged the table. 'That's enough. My client is tired and doesn't know what he's saying. I insist we take a break.'

Erla agreed. They already knew the rest.

Huldar grabbed the chance to step outside and smoke the three cigarettes he'd promised himself. But in the event one was enough. It didn't live up to expectations, perhaps because of the acid taste in his mouth.

Chapter 33

Freyja hadn't contributed much to the conversation. She'd had difficulty following Siggi's mother's story and didn't really know what the police expected of her. Erla, on the other hand, seemed to have no problem understanding the pregnant woman's account, but then she knew more about the background. They were standing by the bed where Sigurlaug Lára was lying looking worryingly fragile, her face white apart from the grazed red skin around her mouth and the ugly scar on her temple. The latter looked older, and must have been from the wound that had taken her to A&E just after Christmas. Freyja asked no questions, either about the abrasions around her mouth or the scar. The poor woman had more than enough on her mind.

She was hooked up to a drip and a number of other machines monitoring everything that could be monitored. Her pregnancy bump rose in a high mound under the blanket. At one point, Freyja had noticed a slow but definite stirring in the mound and hurriedly looked away so as not to be caught staring. She also averted her gaze from the grimy toy rabbit that was tucked under the woman's arm. Neither Sigurlaug nor Erla had referred to it, but Freyja guessed it was the cuddly toy Siggi had mentioned at the Children's House.

When Sigurlaug closed her eyes, the dark circles around

them were less obvious and she looked a little better; not well, but at least no longer at death's door. The police had told Freyja confidentially that the woman had been held prisoner for four days in the boiler room in the basement of the block of flats where Siggi had been found. She'd been there since the early hours of Sunday morning, initially knocked out by Rohypnol. When the effects of the drug wore off, the perpetrator had resorted to taping her mouth shut and had threatened to harm her child if she made the slightest sound. Sigurlaug was still very muddled, unsure when she had woken from her drugged stupor, though she thought it must have been at least a couple of days ago. Since the boiler room where she had been lying chained to the wall was windowless, she'd had no way of knowing how much time had passed. She said she'd slept most of the time, dipping in and out of consciousness once the drug had worn off. The boiler room was hot and there had been a horrible smell from the bucket she had been forced to use as a toilet, so in the circumstances it had been best to try and sleep.

'It would really help us if you could stay awake just a bit longer. We need to piece together what happened before we apply to take your kidnapper into custody. If we get it over with now, you can see Siggi for a little while afterwards. He's longing to see you.'

At her son's name, the woman opened her eyes and pulled herself up a little higher against the pillows, wincing from the needle in her arm. 'When can I see my son? Can't I see him now?' She looked from Erla to Freyja and back again, her gaze no longer drowsy but suddenly wide awake, her face a mask of terror. 'Is there something wrong? Has something happened to him?'

Erla was quick to reassure her. 'No, he's OK. The moment we're finished you can see him for yourself. I promise you he's absolutely fine.'

Sigurlaug calmed down a little on hearing this but didn't seem convinced. It was as if she didn't entirely trust Freyja and Erla, which was only natural given what she'd endured over the last four days. She was in such a fragile state that Freyja wondered if she should discreetly nudge Erla and suggest they come back tomorrow morning. But it wasn't her decision and if the doctors and nurses judged that Sigurlaug was up to being interviewed, presumably they must know. Her own role seemed to be that of an onlooker, no more. It wasn't as if she was working for the police or officially involved in the investigation.

It was an hour since the Child Protection Agency had called and asked Freyja to go up to the National Hospital as their representative, to assess whether it was safe to let Siggi see his mother now that she had been found. In particular, she needed to make sure the woman was fully conscious and in her right mind. Since the boy's father had apparently been found dead, they needed to ensure that this shocking news was broken to the child in an appropriate manner.

Freyja had explained that the timing was awkward as she was babysitting and about to put Saga to bed. But she couldn't really refuse their request since no one else who knew the boy was available. They told her she could take Saga with her to the hospital and that the police would look after her.

Strictly speaking, Freyja no longer needed to do these extra shifts since she had taken the plunge and signed the rental contract with Baldur's friend Tobbi. In the end, the prospect of having a place to live had outweighed her horror of the snake. But she cared about Siggi and would hate to think that her refusal might delay the reunion between mother and son. The Child Protection Agency also wanted her to establish whether Siggi's mother was willing for him to go to his grandmother, which would mean one less night in temporary care for him. As his legal guardian, his mother was free to decide who should look after him.

In the event, it had all taken far longer than expected. Huldar and Erla had met Freyja at the hospital, though not equally warmly. Huldar had taken Saga while Freyja spoke briefly to Sigurlaug. It hadn't taken her long to conclude that it was perfectly safe for Siggi to come and visit his mother at the hospital, and to confirm that she did indeed want him to go to his grandmother. But when Erla and Huldar came to take over, they encountered a hitch.

Sigurlaug refused point blank to allow a man in her room.

Since Erla needed a witness in order to take the woman's statement, she had no choice but to ask Freyja to stand in, however much it pained her. Huldar promised to look after Saga in the meantime and the little girl seemed perfectly happy with this arrangement, even holding out her arms to him when he came to take her back from Freyja. Throughout the interview, Freyja's ears were strained for the slightest complaint from outside the room but all she'd heard was Saga chuckling. She couldn't begin to imagine what had triggered this rare phenomenon. Perhaps a patient had fallen flat on their face in front of her.

Sigurlaug resumed her story in a husky voice. 'Sibbi . . . Margeir, I mean, was a sick man. It was as if something had broken inside him. I believe he did love me in his own way – he kept insisting he did – but he treated me as if he hated me. It was a bit like being pregnant. I know I'm going to have a baby, but I don't know exactly when. I can see the bump growing, just like I used to see the storm clouds gathering. I would do everything in my power to postpone the inevitable. I kept the flat spotless. Avoided doing anything I knew would get on his nerves. But the list of things that set him off just kept getting longer, and it got harder and harder to keep him happy.' She bowed her head, staring unseeingly at the hospital blanket. 'I know it's not very nice of me, but now he's dead I have to cling to the memory of how badly he treated me. I want to push away all the good times. It makes the grief easier to bear.' Sigurlaug broke off for a moment, then went on: 'But I didn't love him any more. By then, the only emotion I felt was fear. We went to Majorca on holiday and he attacked me so viciously that I was scared he'd kill me. But shortly after we got home, his mood suddenly improved and he seemed happy. He stopped worrying about our finances, which were in a complete mess, and his behaviour completely changed. It was as though he was looking forward to some-thing – a side of him I hadn't seen for a long time. Before that he'd always been so pessimistic about the future.'

Sigurlaug winced and tried to find a more comfortable position so the drip wouldn't pull at her arm. Then she sighed and continued her story: 'In some bizarre way, I still cared about him, you know. In spite of everything. I convinced myself he'd change. If only I did this and not that. But deep down I knew it was hopeless.'

Freyja reached out and took her hand, squeezing it gently, then let it go.

'That night Sibbi woke me and ordered me to get up. He said he had something to show me and I could tell it was bad news. Although I usually gave in to him, this time I put my foot down and refused to leave Siggi alone. He was sleeping so I pulled on his clothes and carried him out to the car. I don't think he was aware of anything; he was just fast asleep. Sibbi drove us over to Sudurhlíd. When he pulled into the parking area, I realised I was in trouble. You see, I recognised the building and I knew Sibbi hadn't brought me there by chance. What had happened there five years earlier had had such shattering consequences that I'd never forgotten it . . .' Her voice trailed off.

Erla prompted her: 'Could you tell us about that? We need to hear your side of things, because all we've heard so far is your husband's version, which is hard to prove now.'

A hint of colour rose in the woman's pale cheeks. 'I didn't cheat on Sibbi, though he refused to believe me. I went home with a man called Helgi, Helgi Fridriksson.' She lifted the hand that wasn't hooked up to the drip and stroked back her matted hair. 'I looked better in those days. Much better. But Sibbi couldn't stand it when other men looked at me, so I stopped making an effort. That's how he wanted it.' She gave a faint, rueful smile. 'That's one thing I'm looking forward to when all this is over – being able to dress up and wear make-up again when I'm in the mood.'

Freyja smiled at her but said nothing. Erla remained as coldly detached as before. Perhaps the need for a witness had been a pretext; perhaps Erla actually needed someone who was capable of showing a bit of humanity.

'Anyway, Sibbi and I weren't together at the time. Our relationship had been on and off for a while, though we ended up moving in together. So I went home with the man and that's all there was to it. He didn't call me afterwards and I didn't call him. I had no reason to think that night would cause me problems any more than any other night I've spent with a man.' She turned her head quickly to look at them. 'You mustn't think I'm the type who goes home with just anybody. It was just one of those things.'

'You were an adult and free to conduct your sex life as you pleased. You have no need to make excuses for anything.' Finally Erla had said something Freyja approved of.

Sigurlaug looked relieved. 'Anyway, not long after I went back to work after maternity leave, the boys in my class started behaving oddly. They kept sniggering and whispering in lessons. Then it spread to the rest of the school and before long most of the older pupils had started copying them whenever I walked down the corridors. They wolf-whistled and made moaning noises and called out stuff that I'd rather not repeat. In the end I got the story out of the only girl in my class I could trust to tell me what was going on. She not only told me, she showed me where to find the video as well. After that I pretended I was ill and went home. I kept that up for a few days but in the end I realised I couldn't face going back to work. I couldn't handle it on top of the stress of coping with Sibbi's temper at home. It was too much. When I told Sibbi I wanted to quit teaching, he sensed that something was up. He wouldn't leave me alone, just kept on and on at me. I held out, but in the end he beat the truth out of me. I was so frightened that I told him where to find the video, and Helgi's name and address as well. Of course Sibbi went charging straight over there but there was nobody home. He kept trying but the man was never there. In the end he asked one of the neighbours, who said he thought Helgi lived abroad.'

Sigurlaug fell silent and closed her eyes. Erla and Freyja waited patiently for her to recover. This wasn't an easy thing to rake up, especially when the woman was already in a weakened state. Before opening her eyes again, she heaved a deep breath, which seemed to give her new strength.

'A couple of years passed. Sibbi brought up the incident less and less often, but that didn't mean he'd forgotten about it. Then one day he found out that Helgi had moved back to Iceland and was living at a new address. After a fit of rage that left me covered in bruises, he stormed out, saying he was going to beat the man to a pulp. When he came home he had calmed down but I didn't dare ask what had happened.' The woman paused and bit her lip. Then she took another deep breath. 'I don't know what went on after that. Sibbi was calmer for a while but when he did lose it with me he was far more violent than before. During our holiday in Majorca, he went for me out of the blue – he almost killed me – and started going on obsessively again about how I'd cheated on him. Then, just after Christmas, he attacked me so badly that I ended up in A&E. A doctor spoke to me while I was there and although it might sound a bit feeble, I had started to think about leaving him. I just hadn't summoned up the courage. You see, he was always threatening to kill me if I ever left, and swearing that he loved me.'

The story continued in fits and starts. Sigurlaug described how Margeir had parked in front of the block of flats on Sudurhlíd and sat there in silence instead of getting out. Then a scruffy old SUV had driven up and Margeir had got out and spoken to the driver, a man Sigurlaug didn't recognise. They started arguing and from what she could hear it was about her. After that they went inside and she waited in fear, sure that the night was going to end with a beating. She knew the signs.

But nothing happened. The other man came back alone and at first she mistook him for Margeir because he was wearing his anorak and a baseball cap. When he came over to the car she saw that his face had blood on it and there were blood-stains on his clothes as well. He ordered her to get out and get into his car instead, which she did, while he carried Siggi over. The boy stirred but then went back to sleep. The man drove off in their Yaris, and a minute or two later returned on foot. At this point Sigurlaug interrupted to ask if her car had been found and Erla told her that it had been parked by a hotel just round the corner from Sudurhlíd. Since there were lots of cars parked there, no one had noticed that a Yaris had been there for several days.

Sigurlaug seemed relieved and returned to her story. She said she'd suspected that the man had done something to Margeir but had been too terrified to ask what. She had just sat there, staring dazed at the road ahead, while he silently drove them over to Sæbraut and parked on Lindargata. At this point, he ordered her to keep quiet and threatened to hurt her son if she wasn't in the car when he got back. As proof that he meant business, he showed her a recording on his phone of a man being hanged and told her that it was Helgi. Then he lifted Siggi out of the back seat and disappeared with him, having first taken off Siggi's scarf and wrapped it round the lower half of his own face.

When he came back, he got in the car and ordered her to keep her mouth shut. They sat there until it was nearly morning. Then the man drove to a nearby kiosk and ordered her to put her hood up before he pulled up to the window and bought a bottle of soda water. He put some sort of powder in the water and ordered her to drink it. Sigurlaug had tried to refuse but he insisted, promising that it wouldn't do her any harm. After that her memory became hazy.

She did recall having fallen asleep in the car, then later getting out once it was daylight. The man had led her inside a building and taken her down to the basement where he had locked her in a hot, dark room. After that she could remember only snatches, like being given a drink and a sandwich to eat, and also him saying that if she called for help, Siggi would pay the price. Despite that, she'd found it almost impossible to stay awake. At some point she'd been given an air mattress and a blanket that she didn't need because it was so hot in there. After the drug had worn off and she regained conscious-ness, the man had taped her mouth shut, drilled a hole in the wall for a large hook, tied her hands behind her back with wire and fixed it to the hook. He made sure it was long enough for her to be able to lie down, though. She had slipped in and out of sleep after that, right up until the moment when the door had opened and the police were outside.

'But I have to say that he didn't treat me badly, in spite of everything. He seemed concerned about my wellbeing and kept insisting that he was going to let me go. I just had to be patient. He assured me that the drug I'd been given wouldn't harm my baby. And the doctors have confirmed that he was right.'

Freyja and Erla didn't say anything to this. It sounded as if the woman was suffering from Stockholm syndrome, although this usually took longer to develop. Perhaps her years with a violent husband had taken their toll.

Now that Sigurlaug had finished, she seemed utterly

exhausted. 'I want to see my son,' she said fretfully. 'When's he getting here?'

Freyja told her they were expecting him any minute. She'd passed on the message that it was safe to bring him to the hospital. Sigurlaug closed her eyes at that and asked to be left alone.

By the time they left the room she appeared to have fallen asleep.

Huldar was sitting outside with Saga on his lap. The little girl showed no desire to leave him when Freyja reappeared. She had to go over and almost drag her away. Then she stood there with Saga on her hip while Erla brought Huldar up to date on what they'd learnt, adding various details that filled in some of the gaps in the woman's account.

Sigurlaug's abductor had been forced to wait before smuggling her into the building because of the security cameras. He had reasoned that if he allowed a long enough time to elapse after Siggi's arrival, the police were less likely to notice that the camera covering the garage entrance had been switched off briefly later that day. Freyja also learnt that after locking the unconscious woman in the boiler room, the man had driven the Land Cruiser back to the garage Margeir had taken it from. Margeir had been working on the electrics there and managed to steal the car keys. Thórdur hadn't known exactly where the Land Cruiser had been parked but had hit on the right place purely by chance. As a result, no one noticed that the car had been moved or that the keys were missing. The garage owner was now demanding compensation from the police for a new set of keys and for cleaning the vomit from the back seat. Huldar and Erla had laughed at the absurdity of this.

They went on discussing the case. Freyja stood by, temporarily forgotten, so she learnt that some questions remained unanswered, like how Margeir had got his hands on the Rohypnol. The most plausible theory was that he'd bought it from a Facebook page that dealt in the drug. The following morning, a search was to be launched for the phones belonging to Margeir, Sigurlaug and Helgi, which Thórdur claimed to have chucked into the sea off Sæbraut, the coast road near Helgi's flat. A number of other names also came up that meant nothing to Freyja: apparently the police were not going to apply for custody of two men called Thormar and Tómas. The men's relief at this was tempered by the fact that Erla and Huldar were united in their determination to charge them and two others with distributing pornography.

By the time they finally wrapped up their conversation, Saga was growing restless. Erla announced that she had to head off but asked Huldar to hang around for Siggi's arrival to make sure that everything went smoothly. After that, he was to get his arse back down to the station. Then she marched off without a word to Freyja.

'She's unbelievable.' Freyja shook her head in disgust over Erla's rudeness.

'She's not having an easy time. It's no joke being head of department, especially for a woman in a man's workplace.' Huldar grinned at Saga.

Freyja was about to object that this didn't excuse Erla's lack of common courtesy when the door at the end of the corridor opened and Didrik appeared, accompanied by Sigurlaug's mother Margrét, holding Siggi by the hand. The boy was all eyes as he took in these strange new surroundings.

Instead of stopping at the reception desk halfway down the ward, they made a beeline for Freyja and Huldar.

As soon as they started talking, the little boy turned shy. Although he recognised Freyja and Huldar, he wasn't used to seeing them in this new environment. His grandmother, on the other hand, couldn't stop talking, one minute bubbling over with joy that her daughter had been found alive, the next frantic with worry about her condition and the wellbeing of the unborn child.

Huldar, dazed by the woman's excitable chatter, sent her off to talk to the nursing staff who would be better able to answer her questions.

'Any chance you could take it from here?' Didrik turned an imploring gaze on Freyja. 'They couldn't find anyone else to bring the boy and his grandmother over but it's my wife's birthday today and she'll never forgive me if I don't go straight home.'

To her chagrin, Freyja noticed a smile twitching at Huldar's mouth.

'You can leave too, the moment the visit's over,' Didrik continued. 'The boy'll be going home with his grandmother.'

Freyja was about to draw his attention to Saga, who was still sitting on her hip, now frowning curiously at Siggi, but he could hardly have failed to notice her. 'OK, you go,' she said. 'I'll wait here.'

Didrik didn't wait to be told twice but almost ran off down the corridor. Freyja watched him go, a little disappointed that he'd turned out to be taken. But Huldar's attitude had undergone a complete transformation. 'He's a good guy, isn't he? I don't know why, but for some reason I thought he was single.'

Ignoring him, Freyja crouched down carefully to talk to Siggi. Saga immediately reached out a hand for his hair and Freyja moved back out of harm's way before she could grab a fistful. 'Well, Siggi. Would you like to see your mummy?'

The boy, who had been staring at Saga, now smiled warily. 'Yes please. Is she hurt?'

'No, sweetheart. Don't worry. She just needs to stay here for a bit so the doctors can check that the baby's all right. I'm sure she'll be allowed to go home soon.' Freyja stood up again. 'Come on.' She led the little boy to the door of his mother's room where she let go of his hand and watched him break into a run and fling himself into his mother's arms.

They exchanged a long, wordless hug until eventually the questions started tumbling out of Siggi's mouth. 'Were you lost? Where have you been? Is your mouth hurting? Why have you got a plaster on your hand? What's this tube? Where's Daddy?'

The last question was the hardest. Sigurlaug hugged the boy to her again and handed him the rabbit, which he immediately tucked under his arm. Then he repeated: 'Where's Daddy? Is he dead?'

Freyja thought Sigurlaug's eyes were wet, but apart from that she seemed to have herself well under control and was obviously perfectly capable of breaking the news to her son in private. Deciding to leave them in peace, Freyja tiptoed out, pulling the door to behind her. The last thing she heard was Sigurlaug saying to Siggi that there was something she had to tell him . . .

Huldar was hovering in the corridor of the ward, looking impatient. 'I've just had a text and I need to get down to the station immediately.'

'Has there been another development?'

'No, this is personal. Remember Gudlaugur?' Of course she did. 'One of the biggest pricks on our team has found out something he can use against him. The message was from him. It's clear he wants to get as much mileage out of the situation as he can and he's trying to wind me up. Unfortunately for him, he's succeeded. I've got to go and beat some sense into him before he sends the video round the whole department.'

'I see.' She didn't actually, but didn't want to pry. If Huldar wanted to beat someone up, it was none of her concern. Besides, the guy presumably deserved it if he was persecuting that nice young Gudlaugur. Then again, remembering the black eye Huldar had been sporting when he'd escorted her to her class reunion in December, she thought the result might not be a foregone conclusion. 'Maybe you should try and solve it some other way,' she suggested mildly.

'No chance.' Huldar grinned. 'By the way, Saga and I have made plans to go out for dinner tomorrow night. You don't happen to be free then, do you?'

Freyja couldn't suppress an answering smile. 'Sure, why not?' She hoped he wouldn't be black and blue this time, but suspected this was a vain hope.

Chapter 34

Sigurlaug buried her face in her son's hair and breathed in his scent. He smelt strange, alien.

'Is Daddy dead, Mummy?' His voice sounded just the same, though. It hadn't changed just because he was being looked after by strangers. When Sigurlaug didn't immediately answer, he repeated the question.

Sigurlaug cupped his head in her hands and turned his little face up to look at her. The needle tugged at the back of her hand but she ignored the pain. Meeting his blue eyes, she said: 'Yes, I'm afraid so, my darling, darling boy.'

'Because you made a hole in his head? Why? *You* didn't die.'

Sigurlaug licked her lips, which were flaking and sore from the tape. 'I didn't make a hole in his head, Siggi. You were dreaming, remember? The man killed him. But you needn't be afraid because the police have arrested the man.'

'Oh.' The boy looked confused.

'Have you been a good boy and done everything I said?' Her son nodded gravely. 'Did you tell the police you only remembered a car and the man who took you to the flat?' Again, he nodded. 'You're the best – the best boy in the whole world.'

Sigurlaug bent his head so she could kiss it and hide the tears that were pouring down her cheeks into his fair hair.

She wept soundlessly until she had no more tears left. She wept over the past and over what was to come. Over what awaited her and her son and her unborn baby. Siggi kept perfectly still. At last, Sigurlaug sniffed and rewarded him by dropping another kiss on the top of his head.

What would become of them? Would life without Sibbi be as good, as wonderfully peaceful for herself and her children as she had dreamt? Or would everything come crashing down around her ears? Would she be taken away and her children sent for adoption? There were long waiting lists for children and some people would do anything to get hold of a newborn as they were rare these days, that much she knew.

Sigurlaug closed her eyes and tried to work out her situation. She had answered the police's questions clearly, without any problems or lies – except at the end. They hadn't seemed remotely suspicious, but then it hadn't exactly been a proper interview. They were bound to want to talk to her again. They hadn't asked the most important question of all, so she assumed they must be keeping it back until later. That was the question that would demand the most from her. Unless they meant to spare her on account of her condition. Surely the police would go easy on a woman who was about to give birth?

She would have to keep the child inside her as long as possible.

She allowed herself a glimmer of relief over what she'd achieved so far. They'd believed her when she said she hadn't got out of the car in front of the block of flats on Sudurhlíd. Which meant Thórdur must have kept his side of the bargain and assumed the responsibility for Sibbi's murder. Not told the real story of how he had been standing arguing with Sibbi when she had crept up behind her husband and struck him on the back of the head with the heavy toolbox she'd found in the Yaris. It had weighed a ton and normally she wouldn't have been capable of lifting it but rage had lent her an astonishing strength. The anger had flared up inside her when she heard Sibbi pouring out the usual unspeakable filth, not only about her but about Siggi too. It was one thing for him to take out his hatred on her but she wasn't going to let him turn on her son as well. With a sudden surge of strength she had swung the toolbox up in the air and – whack! – hit him right on the back of his head. Sibbi had crumpled as if he didn't have a bone in his body and lain there jerking convulsively on the cold tarmac at her feet. When she looked up, the stranger was gaping at her in shock.

'He deserved it.' That had been all she could say at the time. Then she had looked round and to her horror seen that Siggi was awake and watching her through the car window, his eyes huge. The toolbox had fallen from her hand and she had opened her mouth to scream when the stranger clamped a hand over it, marched her back to the car and made her get in. She sat there, stunned at what she'd done, and watched him drag Sibbi's body inside the building. When Siggi asked if his daddy had got a hole in his head, she sat staring blankly and told him, in a voice not her own, that he had been dreaming and should go back to sleep. Eventually he did, after she had kept repeating over and over again: *'It was just a dream. Nothing's happened to Daddy. Go back to sleep.'*

Although she had been driven to violence for her son's sake, he should never have had to witness it. She had acted in the heat of the moment, though the desire to do it must have

364

been unconsciously growing for a long time. Never, when she'd been racking her brains for a way of escaping unharmed from her marriage with her son, had anything like this occurred to her. If any such thoughts had been stirring, her subconscious must have whispered them too quietly for her to hear. But when she'd bashed her toe on the heavy metal toolbox in the car, the idea had lanced into her mind as if from nowhere and before she knew what she was doing, she'd grabbed the handle, climbed out of the car and was striding towards her husband. The last thing she heard him say was: *'The little bastard won't say anything and neither will my cunt of a wife.'* She could still hear the sickening wet crunch the sharp edge of the toolbox had made as it sliced through his scalp and cracked open his skull.

He deserved it. She had to keep reminding herself of that. He had been plotting to kill a man who had done nothing to him except sleep with her – a long time ago. It had bothered him less that the man had posted a video online of them having sex. To Sibbi, she was his possession and no one else was allowed to touch her.

There had been one thing missing from the policewoman's questions. Sigurlaug didn't know if this was good or bad. She smiled weakly at her son, then, her face solemn again, asked him: 'What did you do with the piece of paper, Siggi?'

'What paper?'

'The paper the man put on the bedside table when he left you behind in the big bed. What happened to it?'

'Oh. I don't know.'

Sigurlaug breathed through her nose. 'Try to remember, Siggi. What happened to the piece of paper?'

The boy frowned, thinking hard. Then suddenly he beamed.

'I put it in my pocket. I drew a picture on it at the police station. But not on the side with the writing on it. Only on the back.'

'You drew a picture on it?' Sigurlaug repeated, at a loss for anything else to say.

'Yes. Of you, me and Daddy. I had some crayons in my pocket. Only two, though, because I forgot the others. I left them in the room, by the bed.'

'What happened to the drawing?'

'The police took it.'

Sigurlaug's heart gave a sickening lurch. Something had gone badly wrong. If the police had seen what the paper said, they would have asked her about it. Unquestionably. This couldn't be a good sign.

'The man stuck the picture on the wall. At the police station.'

The relief was so great that Sigurlaug thought she was going to faint, but the dizziness soon wore off. What if they never took the picture down? What if they never saw it? How was she to let them know?

'I want to go to Disneyland.' When Sigurlaug didn't immediately answer, Siggi added: 'Or to Majorca again, if we're poor.'

She almost burst out laughing. If they'd never gone to Majorca, she wouldn't be lying here now. Sibbi would still be alive and nothing would have changed. Everything would have been just as awful – but at least she wouldn't have been in uncharted waters.

The holiday had started well. Siggi had played in the sun and splashed around in the swimming pool. All three of them had relaxed in the heat, all their worries left behind at the departure gate. It was when their skin started to turn brown in the sun that the axe fell. Sibbi had noticed a large, colourless patch on Siggi's back that hadn't been obvious before but now couldn't be missed. Although Sigurlaug had taken care of bathing and dressing him since he was born, the penny had never dropped. After all, she had only been persuaded to watch that disgusting video once and then only a brief clip. But Sibbi had pored over it until he knew every detail by heart, like the similar patch on Helgi's back. And then it had dawned on him: Siggi wasn't his son but Helgi's.

Sigurlaug had been lucky to escape with her life from the ensuing explosion. She was a whore who had cheated on him and only got back together with him so her child could have a father. Helgi hadn't wanted anything more to do with her, had seen through her, had seen what a disgusting bitch she was. It was useless for her to point out that Siggi had been conceived at a time when she and Sibbi had kept breaking up, then getting together again. It didn't help either when she told him that lots of people had birthmarks and patches of colourless skin. Perhaps it was just a coincidence.

It wasn't, though. In the lull between their fights she had done the maths. Siggi had in all likelihood been conceived during that night with Helgi, but instead of giving birth at the right time she had been overdue, like many first-time mothers. That would also explain why Siggi had been such a big baby.

She didn't tell Sibbi this: it would be better if some doubt remained in his mind. But his behaviour afterwards suggested that he was sure. He stopped having anything to do with Siggi and began treating her even worse than before, right up to the moment when it occurred to him that he might be able to squeeze some money out of Helgi for his son. His mood worsened again when he found out that the child-support payments would be so low that they would change nothing.

Then he had received a phone call. Later he told her that it was from a man who wanted to kill Helgi. If he helped him, Siggi would stand to inherit, since Helgi was unmarried and childless, as far as Sibbi could discover.

The story was so ludicrous that she hadn't taken it seriously, not until Sibbi woke her up in the middle of the night and forced her and Siggi to get in the car. Apparently the intention was to incriminate her as well, so she wouldn't go to the police, but then Sibbi had never been troubled by common sense.

'Hopefully we'll be able to go to Majorca *and* Disneyland, Siggi,' she said now. 'But not right away. Not until the baby has arrived. We need to wait for it to be born and to get a bit bigger first.'

The boy seemed to accept this. She hoped she'd be able to keep her promise. It would do them so much good to go away, just the three of them, with no man to order them about and insist that everything was done his way.

She mustn't fall into the trap of believing that all men were like Sibbi. Thórdur, for example, couldn't have done more for her.

She hadn't lied to the police about that journey to Sæbraut. They had driven in silence, with Siggi asleep in the back. Thórdur had parked the car and sat there thinking for a while, before handing her the piece of paper that was now hanging on a wall in the police station. As she was reading what it said, he told her he was supposed to leave it in Helgi's flat

for the police to find after he was dead. It was a brief declaration that Helgi believed he had a son and that he wanted to
do a DNA test to make sure. Siggi was named as this possible
son. The page had been signed. According to Thórdur, it had
been Sibbi's idea to make it look as if Helgi had killed himself,
in order to make sure that his heir would get what was owing
to him. The note was meant to convince the police that it
was suicide, and the declaration would explain the motive.
But Thórdur said he had doubted anyone would believe it
was suicide.

As they sat there in the car, he had offered to shoulder the
blame for Sibbi's death in return for a share of Siggi's inher-
itance. He didn't need much, he said, and didn't name a sum;
he just wanted to be sure of a comfortable income while he
was serving his sentence. After all, he was going to prison
anyway. It would mean her having to put up with difficult
conditions for a few days, a week at most, as Thórdur needed
time to tie up a few loose ends. But he would see to it that
Siggi was taken to safety.

She had thought about his offer for a long time. In the end,
though, the choice had been simple. So simple that there was
no real choice. If Sibbi had been right about the size of Helgi's
fortune, no one would be able to spend it all. There would
be enough money there to enable dozens of people to live the
high life. Of course, strictly speaking the money belonged to
Siggi, but she persuaded herself that the boy would want to
sacrifice some of it in order to be with his mother. She could
cope with being shut up in a boiler room for a few days; with
taking the drug and letting herself be treated badly to make
the whole thing seem more plausible.

So she had nodded and said she would do it, on condition

that Siggi was put into safe hands as soon as possible. Thórdur had promised, saying he would tell Siggi to wait for a while to give him time to hide her, but that he would make an anonymous phone call if the police didn't turn up by early afternoon. He had added that there was no chance of that since the Chinese delegation was due to visit Bessastadir at midday. One of the numerous guests at the reception was bound to look out of the window and spot Helgi's body dangling from its gallows.

Before Thórdur took Siggi upstairs to the flat, she had got a chance to talk to her son. She'd done her best to rehearse with him what he should and shouldn't say. He had seemed to take it in and left obediently with Thórdur, having given her his rabbit in parting. At that she had nearly broken down. When Thórdur came back, he said he had frightened Siggi into staying quiet by showing him the video of Helgi and threatening to do the same to his mother if he didn't stick to the script. This had almost been enough to make her change her mind about the whole thing. What kind of monster had she got involved with? What sort of person would dream of showing a small child the video of a man being hanged? But it had been too late to turn back. All she could do was keep quiet and dismiss her doubts. The only alternative was prison, which would mean losing custody of both Siggi and her unborn baby. So she had gone on listening while Thórdur told her that he had left the letter containing Helgi's declar-ation that he was Siggi's father on the bedside table and ordered Siggi not to touch it.

They had made their plans while waiting in the car until it was safe to enter the building. Once everything was decided, Thórdur had gone to his office, reappearing after a while to take her down to the boiler room. And after that she genuinely remembered very little.

There was a tap on the door of the hospital room and her mother put her head round it. 'Can I come in? I really can't wait any longer.'

Sigurlaug beckoned her over. Her mother kissed her gingerly, then sat on a chair by the bed and started talking about the future and how lucky she and Siggi had been. But all Sigurlaug could think of as her mother chattered away was the letter at the police station.

How could she ensure the police read it? What would happen if Thórdur had second thoughts when it became clear no one knew about the paternity issue? Would he give the game away if he suspected he wasn't going to get any money? On no account must that happen.

She could feel how rapidly and unevenly she was breathing. Soon one of those machines would start beeping. Calm down, calm down.

She inhaled deeply through her nose and exhaled again several times. After that she was relaxed enough to see a way of solving the problem. The moment she was discharged, she would go to the police station with a box of chocolates to thank them for rescuing her. Spotting the picture, she would ask if she could have it for Siggi as a reminder of what their family had been like before Sibbi's murder. She could rehearse her amazed reaction when she discovered what was written on the back.

She felt better immediately. Until it occurred to her that the picture might have been thrown away. Calm down, calm down. If that had happened, she would just have to find another way.

She had nothing else to do while she was lying in hospital but make her plans. Sigurlaug smiled at her mother and hugged Siggi to her again, dropping another kiss on the crown of his head. They had got through the worst. From now on, things could only get better.